Brenda,

the **ART** of

SPIES

A NOVEL

At least we have rowing

Robert E. O'Connell III

OiA

PRAISE FOR
THE ART OF SPIES

"Featuring an art detective with a haunted past and shocking family secrets intertwined with America's deepest conspiracies, The Art of Spies is an international thriller that will keep you turning pages until the final revelations, The Thomas Crown Affair meets Day of the Jackal and The Manchurian Candidate."

- **Travis Heermann, author of *The Hammer Falls* and the *Shinjuku Shadows Trilogy*.**

Robert E. O'Connell has been one of the fixtures in the art insurance world for over 25 years. Sure, this novel is fiction, but you can't tell me that it's not based on the experiences, case studies, characters, and wild antics that comes from being on the front lines in the battle against art theft and art crime. I thoroughly enjoyed The Art of Spies.

- **Christopher A. Marinello, Esq. CEO Art Recovery International**

"Supercharged and engrossing... From Caravaggio to Rufino Tamayo and RFK to James Bond, The Art of Spies is chock-full of art, crime and espionage. The author's clear expertise shines through in rich detail and glamorous settings. You won't be able to put it down!"

- **Richard P. Townsend, career art museum director and President, Townsend Art Advisory LLC**

The Art of Spies/OIA Productions, Inc.
Printed in the United States of America

Front Cover:
Marilyn Crying
Suicide Pink
by Russell Young
(c) Bankrobber LLC

This is a work of fiction. Names, characters, places, and incidents are a product of the author's imagination. Locales and public names are sometimes used for atmospheric purposes. Any resemblance to actual people, living or dead, or to businesses, companies, events, institutions, or locales is completely coincidental.

The Art of Spies/ Robert E. O'Connell III. -- 1st ed.

ISBN 978-1-7357858-0-6 Print Edition
ISBN 978-1-7357858-2-0 Ebook Edition

To Okie and Honey, Thanks for the memories...

ACKNOWLEDGEMENT

In 1988, Joseph Campbell told me to "follow my bliss." Thank you for charting the hero's journey.

Heather Smith Callahan's memoir, A Drop of Rain, about her journey to post-traumatic growth following a violent attack, inspired me to write my post-traumatic growth story. Heather introduce me to her editor, Mark Graham.

Mark became my editor and mentor. Our journey of exploration and adventure was enhanced by the phenomenally talented Travis Heermann. Thank you, Mark and Travis, for your constant encouragement and riding shotgun with me on this adventure.

My friends and colleagues are my sounding board. You listen to my conspiracy theories and tolerate my wit. You have volunteered for this journey and your praise and encouragement have become my light at the end of the tunnel, especially when I assumed it was an on-coming train. There are so many people to thank, and I fear that I may forget someone. You know who you are and thank you for your support.

Thank you, Tom Trinley, for teaching me the creative process and partnering with me on several documentaries and films to our credit. I must not forget to thank Jeff Ward for teaching me the art of insurance adjusting and fraud investigations. A special nod to Paul Hering for being a positive role model who has, through his philanthropy, encouraged me to serve and to give back unconditionally.

John Mason Griswold has been my friend for decades. He is a gentleman, a scientist, an artist, a scholar, a father and my authoritative colleague. You will always be my Dr. Watson. Our journeys have only just begun.

I am eternally indebted to Mark Fedota for his keen sense of nuance and his precision for the written word. A mentor without compare. You had me at Roma. Hail Lake Zurich!!

Thank you, Russell Young, for the use of your beautiful painting of Marilyn Monroe. You are a wonderful friend and an extraordinary godfather to our Finnian.

For My Brothers in the USD Boat. Our life-long friendships have bonded us together and continue to shape our post-collegiate lives. Thank you, Dr. Steve Estes, Dr. Betty Block and Brian Hamilton, for reading my manuscript and providing essential remarks for consideration.

Thank you to Mike Jeske, Dave Tosch and Mark Hanschmidt. Friends since grade school and high school. Partners in life. William Conrad Tosch, you are a wonderful father and grandfather. Thank you for being present and involved.

My endless appreciation to Sandra Dijkstra for her consideration.

My siblings are survivors and I applaud their many accomplishments. May we break the silence and live our truths. Our children and grandchildren deserve our collective love and support. Our mutual creativity is a gift we must perpetuate without hesitation.

Thank you to my brother, Jim, for reading my manuscript and encouraging my love for writing. I look forward to reading your brilliance. Thank you to my sister, Kate, for being a great listener and for providing honest, artistic critiques of my work. You are a wonderful artist and constant inspiration. I must also thank my brother, Michael, for enduring my constant conspiracy theories and interviewing our father that proved to be revealing and confirming. For my sister, Felicia, thank you for your love and support.

My world would not be complete without the constant love and encouragement from my wife, my partner, and my best friend, Darci Marie Tosch O'Connell. She has loved me in spite of my obvious baggage that my therapists have helped me to own and process. There has always been forgiveness and never blame. I love you without hesitation. My love and wisdom to our children, Billy, Matt and Finnian.

My story is my Truth and my journey for the Truth motivated me to write my first novel and hopefully not my last novel.

"For when the One Great Scorer comes
To write against your name,
He marks-not that you won or lost-
But how you played the game."
- Grantland Rice

INVICTUS

Out of the night that covers me,
Black as the pit from pole to pole,
I thank whatever gods may be
For my unconquerable soul.

In the fell clutch of circumstance
I have not winced nor cried aloud.
Under the bludgeonings of chance
My head is bloody, but unbowed.

Beyond this place of wrath and tears
Looms but the Horror of the shade,
And yet the menace of the years
Finds and shall find me unafraid.

It matters not how strait the gate,
How charged with punishments the scroll,
I am the master of my fate,
I am the captain of my soul.

William Ernest Henley (1875)

PROLOGUE
1968

"Even in our sleep, pain which cannot forget falls drop by drop upon the heart until, in our own despair, against our will, comes wisdom through the awful grace of God..."
- **Aeschylus (523 BCE - 456 BCE)**

THE WOLFHOUND WAITED quietly in the shadows of the grand political theater. He was still, unnoticed, a nondescript presence among hundreds of others who craved the spotlight. In the crowd were professional athletes, the Hollywood glitterati, and Democratic sycophants. He was a predator waiting for his moment.

The lavish ballroom of the Ambassador Hotel had been the hot spot for the Hollywood elite for over thirty years. Even during Prohibition, it was a gilded dreamland of Art Deco splendor, complete with Arabian doorways, papier-mâché coconut palm trees from the set of Valentino's film *The Sheik*. Some of the trees even had mechanical monkeys with glowing eyes. It was known as the place where careers were made and shattered.

The hotel was located on twenty-three acres of a former dairy farm three miles west of downtown Los Angeles. It was seven stories tall with Mediterranean Revival and Art Deco styling, Myron Hunt's grand vision of a thousand rooms and bungalows creating a mini-city that included thirty-seven shops, a private school, golf course, bowling alley, theater and the city's very first nightclub, the Cocoanut Grove.

The Wolfhound took note as Kennedy and his entourage swaggered into Room 511, across the hallway from his room, which overlooked Wilshire Boulevard.

The night before, Kennedy was nowhere to be seen amongst his followers. Kennedy had stayed in Malibu at the private residence of film director John Frankenheimer. His masterwork, the adaptation of Richard Condon's novel *The Manchurian Candidate*, had quietly been restricted from public viewing after the Kennedy assassination in 1963. Those who knew how close Condon's novel was to the CIA's dirtiest laundry would not fill the smallest conference room at the Ambassador. But the Wolfhound was one of those who knew from experience.

The Wolfhound scanned the room again. And with practiced ease, he picked out the overt and undercover agents on the stage around Kennedy and scattered about the ballroom.

Finally, Kennedy was able to address the crowd. "I want to first express my high regard to Don Drysdale, who pitched his sixth straight shut-out tonight and I hope that we have as good fortune in our campaign..."

Kennedy went on to thank an endless parade of people for the next several minutes. "Ladies and gentlemen, if I can just take a moment more of your time because everybody must be dying from the heat. But what I think all of the primaries have indicated—if I can just take a minute..."

Then the Wolfhound spotted the Patsy edging his way toward the narrowing hallway behind the stage. He was a gaunt, swarthy man wearing a pale-blue sweatshirt and blue jeans. How much of tonight would that drug-laced young man remember?

The Wolfhound faded into the same hallway, pausing as an innocuous, nondescript man, in the shadow of an ice machine.

Withdrawing a pack of Pall Malls from his jacket, his fingers brushed his Iver-Johnson .22 revolver sequestered there. The gun was a superior weapon for head shots because its bullet bounced around inside the skull, scrambling the brain. Larger calibers such as .38s and .45s often pass through the tissue. He flipped, tapped then lit a cigarette and took a long drag while leaning on the old rusty ice machine, watching the kitchen staff coming and going.

His earlier assessment was correct. This narrowing hallway was a perfect place to create a bottleneck and chaos.

Sam Yorty, the Mayor of Los Angeles, was an avowed Nixonite and detested Kennedy. He had publicly refused to provide the campaign with any police protection and seemed intent on having his officers put traffic tickets on the Kennedy campaign vehicles.

Kennedy's voice echoed down the hallway. "Mayor Yorty just sent a message that we have been here too long already. My thanks to all of you; and now it's on to Chicago, and let's win there!" A chorus of euphoric cheers rose. "Kennedy! Kennedy! Kennedy! RFK! RFK! RFK!"

It was three minutes to midnight.

The Wolfhound watched through the windows of the swinging doors leading into the hallway as Kennedy shook hands and waved to the crowd, attempting to make his way towards the kitchen exit.

Then the doors swung wide and Kennedy's entourage shouldered a crush of reporters and cameramen led by the hotel maître d'.

Kennedy came immediately behind but ahead of the athletes and sycophants, including LA Rams defensive tackle Rosey Grier, Olympic decathlete Rafer Johnson, and sports journalist George Plimpton. Grier hung close to Kennedy's wife Ethel in a bodyguard capacity.

And right behind, edging forward through the scrum with surprising efficacy for an untrained radical, came the Patsy. The scrum entered the bottleneck, which slowed then controlled its movement. The Patsy took the opportunity to shoulder past the maître d'.

During chaotic heartbeats, pistol shots from another Iver-Johnson .22, this one in the Patsy's hand, reverberated in the compressed space. Kennedy sagged and then stumbled virtually into the Wolfhound's arms. Hidden by the tangle of body parts, the Wolfhound slid his weapon out and fired directly behind Kennedy's left ear.

Three men tackled the only shooter they saw and buried him under bodies as his pistol discharged twice more into the crowd. Grier wrestled that gun away. And the Wolfhound slid his piece in with his cigarettes.

A cacophony of screams grated over his ears. Busboys fled toward the kitchen, ducking away from the gunshots. The Wolfhound fled with them.

In the enormous kitchen, chefs and busboys were scattering like roaches under a sudden light, as if they'd forgotten where the exits were.

The Wolfhound had not.

Neither had his accomplice. She had been covering the other most likely kill zone the Wolfhound had identified days before.

Honey-blonde and beautiful as ever, wearing a black polka dot dress, she matched strides beside him, raising an eyebrow expectantly. He nodded to her, took her hand, and they continued to pace for the exit.

When they emerged into the parking lot, he slowed to light another cigarette. He checked his wristwatch. Twelve after midnight.

She grinned in appreciation and snaked an arm around his waist.

Terrified people, bleating like sheep, darted past them.

They strolled across the parking lot toward the getaway car, a red Cadillac DeVille with the motor running.

He caught the red cherry of the driver's cigarette behind the wheel, recognizing El Gordo's silhouette in the darkness. Pausing to open the door for her, he scanned the parking lot for potential witnesses. There were none. He slid into the back seat with her.

"Did you get the little bastard?" said the driver.

"The job is finally done," said the Wolfhound. Dealey Plaza had been only the beginning.

David "El Gordo" Sanchez Morales slapped the dashboard in exultation, releasing much of his accumulated tension from his shoulders. The Wolfhound knew how personal this had been for him. El Gordo had lost friends when the Kennedys had refused to send air cover into the Bay of Pigs and turned it into a fiasco. "What happened with the Arab?"

"The little shit did pretty well. He got a couple good shots in before they tackled him." The drugs and conditioning had worked, just as they had for so many of the Cuban exiles Project MK Ultra had conditioned to run sabotage raids on Castro.

"Is he still alive?"

"Yes."

"Well, we can't have everything, I suppose."

The Cadillac eased into the sparse late-night traffic, headed for the airport. They had a plane to catch.

She snuggled up into the crook of the Wolfhound's arm and looked up at him. She smelled wonderful, like lavender and mandarin orange over flowers and sandalwood. "You think he'll be upset we missed his birthday?"

He said, "Are you wearing the new perfume I bought you?" Norell, it was called, and coupled with the thrill of the kill, it set his blood on fire, making him wish they were going somewhere besides the airport. His hand slid up the inside of her thigh.

From the front seat, El Gordo said, "Tell him happy birthday from me. How old is he now?"

"Eight," she said.

El Gordo whistled. "Time does fly. Pretty soon he'll be old enough to join the family business."

The Wolfhound said, "Dick is moving us to Denver to lay low for a while."

"You don't sound any too happy about it."

"Why would I be?" the Wolfhound grunted.

El Gordo said, "Not many bluebirds and artichokes out there, eh?" He chuckled at his reference to the code names for MK Ultra's predecessor projects.

She patted his leg in consolation. "I'm sure it'll only be for a while. The mountains will be lovely."

PART I

CHAPTER 1

"*MY FATHER WAS BRUTAL, I mean, he physically beat me, he would banish me to my basement bedroom and tell me to write a thousand times, 'Honor thy mother and father.' He would say, 'You can't come out of your room, you can't eat, you can't go to the bathroom, you can't go to sleep, you can't do anything until you write the Fourth Commandment a thousand times.'*"

"*A thousand times?*"

"*Yeah, and he'd be lurking upstairs waiting for me until I was finished. I could hear him parading around. And he knew exactly how many pages of notebook paper it took. I tried to mis-number the pages to save me some incarceration time just once.*"

"*What happened?*"

"*He bent me over the foot of his bed and whipped me with his belt until I stopped crying and made me start over with the regurgitation of his favorite fucking Commandment.*"

"*I'm so sorry. That must have had terrible effects on you.*"

"*It sure as hell made me hate lies.*"

***

Trey's silver Mercedes-Benz SLK55 AMG roadster convertible flowed like mercury down the streets of Lido Isle, Newport Beach, California. Top down, engine purring, its feel of power and class invigorated him after the flight from Chicago. Resting half-finished in the console beside him, a medium, wet quad-cappuccino with one raw sugar and a dash of cinnamon did the rest of the job.

It was a quintessential southern California afternoon, sun and sea breezes so pleasant, so ubiquitous, so commonplace, it was easy for people to forget that "beautiful" people did bad things here.

Trey tooled the roadster down streets of affluence. Lido Isle was a manmade island in the harbor of Newport Beach, accessible from land only by a single two-lane bridge. Every house on the water had European cars in the garage and a yacht on the pier. Those on the island's interior streets were the hangers-on, those who loved the water, loved the idea of living on an island, but could not afford the extra zero in the purchase price of the houses on the water. This was not Beverly Hills' long, sweeping driveways and walled enclosures. The houses here were crammed in close, on real estate priced by the square foot, but that did not mean they lacked panache. He rolled past some truly stunning architecture and designs, interspersed with meticulously manicured palm trees that reminded him of Bithiah's bathing pavilion from the Cecil B. DeMille film *The Ten Commandments*.

The flashing lights of the Lido Isle private security cars signaled the house's location from three blocks away. They had blocked the two-lane street with barricades and were routing cars around the block. As Trey rolled closer, he spotted what was likely an unmarked police car also parked outside the house.

He parked near a barricade and texted Mason: ARRIVING AT THE HOUSE NOW. VIA LIDO SOUD PAST VIA ZURICH. ETA?

Then he grabbed his Florentine leather briefcase, compulsively tucked his phone into his right sport-coat breast pocket, and got out. He let the California sun warm his face in a sensual moment, transporting him to his happiest place, then took a deep breath and girded himself. Game time.

He circled one of the barricades and approached the yellow police tape. Two rent-a-cops charged forward to intercept him, puffing themselves up with each oncoming step.

The nearest one was six inches shorter than Trey but weighed about the same. His name tag read Jeske. "Sir, you can't be here."

Trey handed Jeske his die-cut business card printed on extra-heavy stock paper. "My name is Emmett Hansen III. I'm with Lloyd's of London, here to investigate the reported theft."

"If you're not LAPD, you can turn right around and—"

"I assure you gentlemen I have every right to be here." Trey pulled a manila folder from his briefcase and opened it. "The owner has a fine art insurance policy with Lloyd's of London that appears to cover the reported missing paintings. Here's the policy number, the claim number, and information about the paintings on his fine art Schedule."

Jeske peered at the business card. "Your business card says THIS, not Lloyd's of London."

"Trey Hansen International Solutions, LLC. I'm an art expert, an investigative consultant, an 'art dick' engaged by Lloyd's and sent here specifically to investigate this claim. With one hundred and twenty million dollars at stake, you can either let me in to do my job or bring me somebody above your pay grade who will."

"Is that like some sort of private investigator?" Jeske said.

"Yes," said Trey patiently.

The two guards chewed on this, trading annoyed but uncertain glances.

Trey's phone buzzed with Mason's incoming reply: STUCK IN TRAFFIC. TEN MINUTES.

Trey pointed at the unmarked police car. "There is an LAPD police detective here, isn't there?"

"Uh, yeah."

"Go get him, please."

The other rent-a-cop, Hanschmidt, departed and went into the house.

Jeske shuffled his feet. "So you're some kinda investigator, huh? A real Columbo or Monk or something?"

"I'm an art historian trapped in the insurance industry."

"The police aren't good enough?"

"Not with this kind of money and works of art at stake, no."

Moments later, Hanschmidt returned with a detective who looked about two weeks from retirement. His badge and ID hung from a lanyard around his neck. The sight of the distinctive LAPD shield brought the musical theme from *Dragnet* immediately to mind, and Jack Webb's voice *This...is the city...* Trey noted the detective's acceptable choice of shoes—gleaming black leather, Robert Clergerie Oxfords—and a well-tailored but well-worn suit, all of which stretched a cop's budget, but this was southern California. Image was everything.

Trey introduced himself and offered his hand.

The man shook it firmly. "Detective Conrad Tosch, LAPD Art Theft Detail."

The staggering amount of wealth accreted to the greater Los Angeles area brought with it billions of dollars in fine art and collectibles. For many of the filthy rich, art was a repository for wealth, for ego—and one of the most common routes for money laundering. The higher the dollar values, the more the police paid attention. Such stories seldom made a media splash, but because theft and fraud were more rampant than most people realized, the LAPD maintained a dedicated art theft detail.

"Then I'm talking to the right person," Trey said. He showed Detective Tosch his bona fides.

Trey sensed the detective's sharp but subtle scrutiny as only one with similar skills could. The man's eyes, behind his designer glasses, were relentless, never looking away, never giving an inch. This was dangerous ground. Police did not like interlopers. Trey said, "I'm not here to step on your toes, Detective. But I am here at the request of the fine art and specie underwriters on the London market insurance policy regarding the reported missing works of art. My job is to conduct an independent investigation of the claim, starting with the reported loss location."

"You think there's fraud here?" Tosch said with a certainty that bespoke long experience on the criminal art beat.

"I have to assume fraud in every single case until the facts prove me wrong. If the facts do prove me wrong, so be it, but ninety percent of all insurance claims for fine art and collectibles prove to be fraud of some sort." The perpetrators of art fraud always thought they were being so clever and inventive, when in fact they were nearly always breathtakingly unoriginal. "Just to be clear, Detective, I'm more than willing to share with you whatever my associate and I discover."

"Associate?"

"My associate Mason *Getty* is en route." Trey let Mason's surname hang there for a moment. "He is an expert in art conservation, and he has a keen scientific eye for forensics."

Detective Tosch frowned. "You're not going to interfere with our own forensics, no way."

"With all due respect, Detective, LAPD's forensics unit is of world-class quality in fields like vice and homicide, but they do not have the training to tackle the art world. Is there a forensics team coming?" Trey looked around pointedly for a van.

Detective Tosch chewed his lip. "They already left. You said your associate's name is Getty?"

"Of *the* Getty family, yes." The Getty family loomed enormously in the global art world, their name practically synonymous with patronage, like the Medici family of Florence centuries before, a family so wealthy they could not even spend the interest on their investments every year. Trey felt it beyond the realm of Tosch's need-to-know that Mason's family was a less well-heeled branch. Nevertheless, the name alone added some weight to Mason's credibility.

The sound of an approaching engine whining up the street gave them pause. It was the distinctive sound of a Porsche, Mason Getty's 1966 Golf Blue 911. After parking beside Trey's exotic rental, Mason got out, straightened his immaculately pressed Armani suit and bow tie, and circled to the trunk in front to retrieve his vintage leather Prada messenger bag, filled with tools of his trade.

"That him?" Detective Tosch said.

Trey nodded. "It is."

Mason Getty habitually looked like he stepped out of the pages of *GQ* magazine. Salt-and-pepper hair jauntily waved, a dapper silk bow tie, round-rimmed tortoiseshell spectacles, stylish 1937 Rolex Chronograph, and a pair of Donald J. Pliner antique crocodile loafers. It had been Mason Getty who molded Trey from the baseball cap, sweatshirt-and-jeans type into a fellow aficionado of men's fashion, in particular cultivating in Trey the appreciation of fine Italian footwear.

Spotting Trey, Mason smiled broadly. "Trey, my brother from another mother, it's been too long." He circled the barricade, and they shook hands and hugged. Mason said with mock affront, "How dare you come to a crime scene without a proper haircut! Did I not tell you to go to my barber in Abbot Kinney?"

Trey grinned. "And this is—"

Mason stepped forward and extended a hand. "Detective Conrad Tosch. I've read about your work recovering the Stradivarius cello. Well done, sir. A pleasure."

Tosch warmed visibly at that. "Likewise."

Trey said, "Mason, you're just in time. I believe Detective Tosch was just about to let us into the crime scene."

Tosch nodded. "Come on."

Tosch led them past the sheepish-looking rent-a-cops, through a seven-foot, Art Deco wrought-iron gate toward the front door, a massive oaken portal that looked like it could withstand marauding

Huns. The house was a two-story, ultra-modern edifice of angles and floor-to-ceiling glass. Tosch opened the door.

Trey had memorized his file on the plane. "So where's the owner, Dr. Francis Xavier Cahill?"

Tosch said, "On his way back from Italy. Vacation with his wife."

"Any kids?"

"Empty-nesters."

"What can you tell me about the owners?" Trey said.

Tosch said, "Doctor Francis X. Cahill, plastic surgeon to the stars. Got himself a practice in Beverly Hills. Gets invited to a lot of exclusive parties."

"And the break-in?" Trey asked.

"No sign of forced entry."

"Who reported the theft?"

"The maid, about nine o'clock this morning."

They stepped into the foyer, a grand amalgam of traditional values and modern design, with a stunning Dale Chihuly Murano chandelier reminiscent of Chihuly's *End of the Day* sculpture, which permanently hung in the Tacoma Union Station. A grand staircase led to the second floor. Tastefully arranged paintings and sculptures populated the entry, the staircase, and the hallway leading deeper into the house.

Mason set down his Prada bag and pulled out a pair of XL TNT blue nitrile, powder-free disposable gloves. Each went on with a clap of his hands. He offered a pair to Trey, who knew better than to argue.

Trey didn't need to check his file. As he put on the gloves, he said, "So, the missing paintings. *Nativity with San Lorenzo and San*

16

Francesco, by Caravaggio, circa 1609, and *Annunciation* by Piero di Cosimo, circa 1489."

Tosch checked his notepad. "Those are the ones."

Caravaggio was an Italian Baroque painter with a gift for painting from models only matched by his tumultuous lifestyle. His career of humanizing the divine followed the Italian Renaissance Period of artists like Leonardo and Michelangelo. The other artist, Piero, was recently discovered as a magnificent example of early Renaissance painting, most famous for his mythological and allegorical subject matters. His contemporaries were Raphael, Titian, and Bramante. Bramante was also known for designing St. Peter's Basilica in Rome. Raphael and Titian paintings had sold for as high as seventy million dollars while Caravaggio had sold for a hundred million dollars.

Tosch said, "We dusted for prints and found a few, but we need to check them against the Cahills and the staff."

"Where were the paintings kept?"

"Master bedroom."

"Really?" Trey said.

"Is that a big deal?"

"In my professional experience, Detective, art lovers put the art that is most meaningful to them in their master bedroom, most often on the wall above the bed. It's what they see every day, what they most *wish* to see every night before they go to bed." Trey's investigative brain was already churning on this. Why religious art? Was Dr. Cahill a devoutly religious man? Most of the artworks in the foyer were secular in nature, such as Mexican artist Rufino Tamayo's oil on canvas *Watermelon Slices*. The exception was

Henry Moore's *Madonna and Child* bronze maquette. "If nothing else he certainly has eclectic taste. What about the alarm system?"

"Alarm system was never turned on last night." Tosch's expression bespoke the same suspicion Trey immediately felt.

"An inside job," Trey said.

"Maybe. But look, the theft is insured, right?" Dr. Cahill would be compensated for his loss via the insurance settlement on which he had paid premiums. It was why the police seldom sustained investigative effort on cases like this, even for one hundred and twenty million dollars. "I mean, who's really losing here? Where is the victim?"

"First of all, the world, Detective. The two paintings that were reportedly stolen represent some of the most important art commissioned for the Catholic Church in existence. If someone threw that Stradivarius cello into a bonfire, even if it were insured, the cultural heritage of this planet would have suffered a grave blow. I care about two things: the art, and the truth. Everything else is negotiable."

Tosch nodded in appreciation. "Very well, Mr. Hansen."

"Call me Trey, Detective. I'm the third of my name, as they say."

"Don't tell me they called your father Deuce." Tosch chuckled.

"No, they most certainly did not," Trey said and left it at that, moving on quickly up the grand staircase. "The master bedroom is this way?"

Tosch and Mason followed.

"End of the hallway," Tosch said, pointing down a long hallway. More sculptures and paintings, as if a private museum.

Mason and Trey traded glances of appreciation. There was a pink silkscreen and diamond dust portrait of Jackie Kennedy, which he recognized to be by British artist Russell Young, but it was one Trey had never seen before. There was a Degas maquette of a galloping horse under Optium acrylic on a pedestal. There was a John Steuart Curry oil on board from 1939, *The Abolitionist John Brown as Moses*, wherein the nineteenth-century Kansas abolitionist was under siege by a tornado. Dr. Francis X. Cahill, plastic surgeon to the stars, had exquisite taste in fine art.

The bedroom was a grand affair, with a high vaulted ceiling. The room would have been ablaze with California sunlight coming through the wall of windows opening to a balcony that overlooked multimillion-dollar yachts on the slip. The glass, however, was sun-activated, self-tinting, UV-protecting, no doubt to shield the artworks within.

The high ceiling allowed for the appropriate display of a painting as expansive as Caravaggio's *Nativity with San Lorenzo and San Francesco*, also known as *The Adoration*, a framed oil on canvas more than seven feet high and five feet wide, depicting St. Francis and St. Lawrence in attendance at the birth of Jesus. Di Cosimo's *The Annunciation*, much smaller at only two and a half feet, roughly square, had been hung nearby.

Their former locations were clearly visible. Both hung across the room from the king-size bed, dominating the view of anyone lying there.

Mason put on an Optivisor magnifier and began to examine the wall, the mountings, and the carpet below the missing paintings.

Mounting a seven-foot painting required some serious hardware. Trey saw no alarm apparatus on either of the paintings' locations. Both looked as if they were hung from open hooks and two "D" rings attached to the back of the wooden frames.

Mason confirmed Trey's cursory observation. "Neither of these paintings were set with alarms. No hard wires, no magnetic contact points. No locking hardware."

Trey pointed to two small boxes in opposite corners of the ceiling. "But there are motion sensors."

Tosch said, "Like I told you, the alarm system was never turned on last night."

"Whose job was it to turn it on with Dr. Cahill away on vacation?" Trey said.

"We don't know yet," Tosch said. "We'll ask Cahill tomorrow morning when he arrives back from Rome."

"Then we need to find that out." That was their chief lead at this point. "Is there anything else missing?"

"Only these two were reported to us."

"Mason will look for ghosts while I do a walk-through of the house."

"Ghosts?" Tosch said.

Mason's Optivisor magnifier made his eyes enormous. "If an art object has been in one place for a while, it will leave a shadow on the wall or on the pedestal showing it was there."

"My people would have noticed that," Tosch said.

Trey said, "But sometimes, when the theft is an inside job, another piece will replace the stolen item, but the ghosts won't match."

Tosch raised an eyebrow and nodded.

Trey suppressed a smile of satisfaction. No one would ever tell him he didn't know what he was doing. This was Trey's métier.

Without further preamble, Trey began to walk through the house, taking it all in. The Cahill home was a testament to modern taste and affluence. Elegant lines, immaculate placement, gleaming surfaces and custom museum-quality lighting for displaying their collection. The place looked more like a designer showroom than a place where real people might kick off their shoes and watch the Bulls and Lakers. The ultra-hi-def screen in the living room was the size of a small billboard. The electronics, worth more than many people's houses, were chosen and placed to complement the room.

Whoever did the interior design was a genius. With this much wealth at one's disposal, crossing the fine line between tasteful and gauche would be all too easy. During his walk-through Trey took copious photos with his iPhone, some of which he would send to his wife Marie later. As a renowned architect and designer herself, she would appreciate the qualities of the place.

He studied every room closely, checked every closet, every cupboard, building a picture of the Cahills' lives as he went. There was very little feminine influence here.

Detective Tosch followed him every step of the way, apparently still unwilling to let anyone tromp unescorted around his crime scene. After an hour of this, Tosch started checking his watch.

Trey surveyed the house, taking copious notes.

Tosch asked him, "What are you looking for?"

Trey responded, "Anything out of place. Anything that tells me who this doctor is. Plastic surgeons to the stars no doubt make good money, but do they make *this* kind of money? Those Genesis speakers over there retail for over two hundred thousand dollars."

"Jesus H. Christ," Tosch said. "Are they made of platinum?"

"I believe the wiring is mostly silver. When do the Cahills return?"

"They're supposed to be on a 1:40 p.m. flight to LAX."

"You mean Alitalia flight number 620 from Rome Fiumicino? I'll need to speak to them as soon as possible."

"You can have them after we're done with them."

"Of course. What do you make of the fact the alarm was left off and there was no sign of forced entry? In a house like this, that can be no accident."

"Like we were saying. Inside job. But who?"

Trey's course through the house ended back in the master bedroom. Mason was kneeling on the floor with some scientific tweezers.

"What's he doing?" Tosch said, hands on his hips, tapping a foot.

Mason gave him the bug-eyed look again. "I'm picking up gold-leaf flakes and oil paint chips, either from the painting itself, or from the frame. Difficult to say at this point."

"Detective," Trey said, "I believe we're almost done here. Mason?"

The sun was heading toward its green flash. Trey and Mason had been here almost two hours.

"Just wrapping up," Mason said, dropping something from his tweezers into a clear, plastic re-sealable bag.

"As a professional courtesy," Trey said, "I have some serious concerns I want to share with you."

The detective crossed his arms. "Shoot."

"A random burglary is all but out of the question at this point. The thief took these two specific paintings. Why? One of them is more than seven feet high. Extremely difficult to transport without significant damage. The Henry Moore maquette in the foyer is easily worth a few million dollars, and it fits in a duffel bag. The Rufino Tamayo is one-fourth the size and easily worth ten million, and both of them are right at the front door, not upstairs at the end of the house. No, these two religious pieces were the target. A theft for hire. Are you following me so far?"

Tosch nodded, fixing Trey with that relentless stare.

"As far as I'm concerned, everybody is a suspect, including Cahill himself. I hope you'll keep that in mind when you interview Dr. Cahill tomorrow." Trey gave the detective his card; Tosch offered his own.

"I appreciate your openness in sharing all this with me," Tosch said.

"Mason and I need to discuss things and review our collective findings. It's been a pleasure, Detective. I'll be in touch. Have a good evening."

CHAPTER 2

"WE GREW UP PLAYING basketball and tennis. My father used my mother's inheritance to construct a custom basketball half-court and a tennis court in the back yard. This was when we lived in Colorado, when I was in grade school, junior high, and high school.

"My parents had Catholicism. I had basketball and tennis. They were my religion. My brother's, too. We were huge John McEnroe fans.

"I remember it as if it was yesterday, we were playing three-on-three hoops on the court he built, me, my father and brother, Patrick, and Uncle Don and my two best friends since fourth grade. Don's not my real uncle, but that's what we called him. My father routinely physically abused us around the court. He was bigger and stronger than us, of course, and he used that, pushed us around. Trying to make us tough, I guess. I probably hold the world record for instances of road rash on my arms and legs, but anyway... I remember, during that game—Uncle Don was on my team—Patrick went in for a lay-up, and I knocked the ball out of his hands. It was a clean steal, but my father called it a foul. I protested for half a second. Then he called me a liar, and I remember it felt like my whole body turned to Jell-O and splatted onto the pavement.

"*He made me grab onto the stanchion that held the hoop, pulled my pants down in broad daylight, neighbors watching, cars driving by,* my friends *watching, and whipped me with his belt.*"

"*No wonder you still have nightmares about him.*"

"*It's been twenty-five years since I've seen the son of a bitch. But, yes. Still. Occasionally.*"

"*On your next visit, I'll have some specific therapeutic tools pre-pared. There are some things we could try to get at the deep-seated shame, guilt, and paranoia.*"

"*There was a girl, Chrissie was her name, lived next door, her dad was an officer in the Air Force, a colonel, I think. I never had the guts to talk to her, but she was just achingly pretty, big, brown eyes. I saw her watching this through the window. She saw the whole thing. I still remember the heartbreak on her face. At least somebody gave a shit... Wow, I haven't thought of her in thirty-five years.*"

"*What about your Uncle Don? What did he do?*"

"*He and my father went way back. They talked about Berlin sometimes, stories from the '50s and '60s when they were in the Army. I think it was some sort of off-hand comment from Don that distracted my father long enough to let the moment die. I don't re-member if I saw my friends again after that. And since Chrissie had seen my bare ass getting striped by a belt, that was the end of that little crush.*"

***

The sun was reaching for the ocean as Trey finally left Lido Isle. His mind clattered as the moving parts of the investigation struggled to mesh. Still too many missing gears. Plugging in his Bluetooth headset, he used this time in the car to call all the major fine art auction houses—Sotheby's, Christie's, and several others—to inform them these paintings had been reported stolen, and to be on the lookout for them. No institution that relied so profoundly on reputation would willingly risk theirs by knowingly selling stolen works of art. Stolen goods were worthless without someone willing to buy them. The list of potential buyers for such paintings as these was fairly short. Oligarchs, museums, the Vatican…

After that, heavy traffic was still going to keep him for another hour on the 405 before he reached Mason's place, and there was something he needed.

He called home.

Marie answered the phone, "Hello, Boooo."

The sound of her voice brought a smile to his face. He was going to miss her when he got to his hotel room and its empty bed. Between his job, her job, and the kids, they hadn't had a grown-up night together in weeks. "I wanted to call before it got too late. Kids in bed?"

"Annie is still rumping around up there, but Lauren is out like a light. Annie had a rough day at school."

"Do tell."

"Well, she called her teacher a liar."

"What?" Trey laughed, half with alarm and half at yet another instance of Annie's brazen forthrightness and intolerance for deception. The little apple had not fallen far from the tree. "Let me guess. The teacher is, in fact, a liar."

"It's complicated, but yeah, Annie called bullshit on the teacher.

You can hear the whole story when you get here." She tried to restrain it, but he could hear the annoyance in her voice. This elementary school drama was an extra plot twist she did not need today.

"I'm so sorry, BD." Short for Baby Doll. "I was hoping to be home tonight. I was practically on the plane home when I got a call from Nicklaus to do this job. I'll be in LA for a few days now." His sudden change in travel plans had doubtless necessitated a burgeoning spiral of last-minute plan changes in her day and the rest of the week. Fortunately, she was not the kind to hold a grudge. Nevertheless, he *would* make it up to her.

"Is it big?" she said.

"The biggest yet. Two Italian paintings, a Caravaggio and a di Cosimo, insured for one hundred and twenty million, missing from a wealthy doctor's home."

She whistled. "And the prognosis?"

"Something is definitely rotten in the state of Denmark. Too early to say how rotten, though."

A moment passed, in which she sighed and said, "I miss your feet."

He smiled. Every night in bed, she warmed her arctic-frigid icicle feet on his. "I'm sure Daisy would be happy to oblige."

"Maybe Daisy snuggling will lull me to sleep in my tragically empty bed as I weep disconsolately for the absence of my globe-trotting, rock-star husband."

"A tragic image indeed. Someone should make a movie about that." The moment of missing her stretched long and filled with sighs.

Marie was the best wife he'd ever had, as he liked to say—when she was out of earshot. She was his intellectual equal, an oasis where he could retreat and recharge and be his most authentic self, complete with emotional scars and excessive baggage.

Wife Number One had been an artist he met in college. Her boyfriend had just died in a motorcycle accident, and Trey had swooped in to "rescue" her from her grief and support her *joie d'art*. He loved the fact she was an artist, a painter and sculptor, wildly passionate and exuberant, and in bed, a young man's dream. But her bottomless troughs of despair and depression, fueled by alcohol, had dragged Trey into the blackness with her, a blackness he fought against even as he enabled it. Clawing his way out of that abyss had taken him a couple of years.

Wife Part Deux, whom he met while on the upward crawl, had been a fellow shattered train-wreck. He could rescue her, too, he thought, but when they emerged from the blackness together, her own sleeping demons roared back to life. Based on her behavior, Trey was pretty sure she had borderline personality disorder. She had been reenacting her own shattered childhood with verbal and emotional abuse, manipulation, and control. She used his insecurities as a weapon against him, tearing at him when the mood struck. His skill at walking on eggshells became world-class. Walking through the world with blinders on became a way of life, lest an attractive woman cross his field of vision, as she constantly accused him of cheating. At the supermarket, she once spotted a beautiful woman before Trey did, and she leaped into his face with a snarl. *So you want to fuck her?* In a flash of defensive rage, Trey took one long, appreciative look, and said, *Yes, actually. Care to arrange it?* Her speechless jaw-drop was one of his most cherished memories.

His therapist had things to say about those previous relationships. Some of it he believed. Some of it he still wrestled with.

Marie sighed at last. "Seriously, though, honey, you're the best at what you do. You love a good fraud, and you love dropping the hammer on the culprits. Take as much time as you need. We're okay here."

His voice caught for a second. Yes, he was definitely going to make this trip up to her. "I'll see you soon," he said, and they hung up.

***

By the time Trey exited the 405 into Brentwood, the sun was nearly gone. Mason's house was only a few minutes away now, but first Trey had to make a small pilgrimage.

He pulled off San Vicente Avenue onto South Carmelina Avenue and then found Helena Drive, an unassuming cul-de-sac. At the end of Helena Drive lay a chest-high wooden gate wide enough to admit a car. It was only a small space, the end of the cul-de-sac, but beyond that gate lay the hacienda-style former home of one of the celebrity icons of the twentieth century, a figure who epitomized beauty, glamour—and the tragic truncation of life.

He keyed the song into his iPhone, which interfaced to the car's Bluetooth entertainment system. Moments later, Elton John's "Candle in the Wind" began to emanate from the speakers.

Marie and Marilyn shared a similarity in the nose and eyes,

but Marie had the mind of Eero Saarinen. The ache of missing her throbbed in his chest.

Marilyn's death was neither accident nor suicide. The "barbiturate overdose" that killed her had been administered, of that Trey had no doubt. She'd had affairs with both Kennedy boys, John and Bobby, and she'd been killed as a message to them, or perhaps as retribution for John winning the election. Politics in the late '50s and early '60s had looked decorously civil on the surface, but behind closed doors it had been a knife fight, and the CIA and FBI were the weapons. J. Edgar Hoover and Richard Nixon were bosom buddies for years, even while Nixon was not in office. From 1952 until his humiliation and resignation in 1974, Richard Nixon was the Kingmaker of American politics, and Marilyn Monroe had been one of the many casualties left in his wake.

All the papers had to say was that Marilyn was found in the nude.

Trey mourned the beautiful soul extinguished in her prime, a pawn in a chess game played by evil men who hungered for power.

Your candle burned out long before
Your legend ever did.

When the final piano chords of "Candle in the Wind" faded, he sniffed once, got back in the roadster, and drove back up the dead-end street.

***

Trey and Mason stood on Mason's spacious veranda overlooking the glittering tapestry of Los Angeles, the second of the US's cultural centers. The theater was concentrated in New York; in LA, the film and television industries, and much of the music industry. Hundreds of years hence, its history would go into the annals of cultural influence up there with Florence and Paris, even if its star had faded.

Mason's house was not nearly the showpiece Cahill's was, but it bore the same stamp of elegance and culture as Mason's wardrobe, from the kitchen fixtures to the furniture and the art on the walls. His wife Julie was out this evening at a society function, and both of their children were away at university. Trey had been glad to find that Julie was out for the evening. Her half-concealed disdain for her husband put Trey's teeth on edge. She was one of the few people he had met who could suck the life out of a room simply by walking into it, and she lacked the self-awareness to recognize it. Trey suspected Mason would have divorced her years ago, if not for the fact the divorce would have impoverished him. He could apparently withstand the lovelessness of their marriage if it meant he still got to enjoy other aspects of life.

As soon as Mason uncorked the bottle of 2009 Clos des Papes, Châteauneuf-du-Pape, the majestic, fruity bouquet reached Trey's nose and made his mouth water. This ruby-red wine was a mutual favorite, an explosion of intense aromas of red fruit preserves, anise, lavender and exotic spice nuances on the front end, tannins coming on later, building with exposure to air. It was a cultured and elegant wine, but still affordable. They would let it breathe for a while, then pour. Meanwhile, the two men, longtime friends and colleagues, caught up on family and professional news.

Mason was busy on a conservation project for the Los Angeles County Museum of Art, LACMA. René Magritte's *La Trahison des images (Ceci n'est pas une pipe)* from 1929 was in desperate need of cleaning and examination, as visitors loved to pose for surreal selfies pretending to smoke the pipe on the canvas.

Before coming to LA, Trey had been busy establishing the chain of provenance for some questionable Hittite artifacts said to be circa 1400 BCE.

As Mason set a tray of exotic cheese, fruit, honey, and Dijon mustard on the table between them, the time came to get down to brass tacks. Mason said, "I suppose I should tell you right away, I found a fingerprint the police seem to have missed. It was on the wall near the Caravaggio, in a place no one likely would touch by accident. Then again, it could be just the maid."

"It could be just the maid who stole them."

Mason chuckled and poured the red nectar of everlasting life into stylish heirloom stemware, but did not yet take a drink. "You really do suspect everyone, don't you?"

"It solidifies the odds I'm right. Every case is *Murder on the Orient Express.*"

"Even if there's no forensic evidence to back you up."

"You just said you found a fingerprint."

"But I don't know if it's relevant. How irritated do you suppose Detective Tosch would be if I ask him to run it?"

Trey said, "We'll have to ask him."

Mason swirled his wine glass to inject additional oxygen. "So, what do you think, fraud or legitimate theft?"

"My instincts are telling me fraud." Trey's instincts were nearly always right.

"Even if there's no forensic evidence to back up that assertion?"

Mason peered deep into the wine, deep red in the deepening twilight.

"But there is. There's no sign of forced entry. The alarm was not activated, on a night when the owner just happens to be away."

"It could be one of the employees whose job it was to activate the alarm system."

"That would narrow the list of suspects to what, two or three people? Anybody who's going to steal one hundred and twenty million in fine art would have to know the police would be breathing down their necks instantaneously."

"Alas," Mason sighed, "the abundance of that kind of stupidity makes me fear for the future of the human race." He sank his nose into the bowl holding the French wine and offered his glass for a clink. "To stimulating new cases."

Trey clinked with him.

They drank. The expansive array of flavors burst across Trey's palate, filling his nostrils with a richness he had found in few other wines. A lovely wafting note of Lapsang souchong tea stayed with him.

Comfortable silence lay between them, the kind only found by people at ease in each other's company.

Mason said, "What's new in therapy?"

"Seems to be going well. Fewer flashbacks and nightmares. I haven't had a panic attack in a couple of years."

"Any contact with your parents?"

"Nope." Trey sipped his wine; it was opening well. "And I'm keeping it that way." If his father were on fire in front of him right now, would Trey piss on him or add napalm? Interesting question.

"A few memories have emerged since we started digging. Hypnotic regression, PTSD and such. Some of that stuff was like a forgotten splinter, buried so deep I didn't even know it was there. That part has been...difficult."

"I can imagine."

Trey considered asking about Julie, but that subject would sour the mood.

Mason said, "I've long wondered something about you, if you don't mind me asking."

"Shoot."

"Why all this conspiracy stuff? Why Marilyn and JFK and Martin Luther King Jr.? You stopped at Marilyn's house again, didn't you?"

Trey smiled a little. "Yeah, I did." What was it about those historical personages, and the conspiracy theories swirling about their deaths, that fascinated him? He had an entire bookcase at home devoted to the subject. Many of those books were utter nonsense, but even in the nonsense were hidden kernels of truth, nuggets that pointed to mysteries within mysteries, dots waiting to be connected by someone who knew what to look for. "I don't know, to be quite honest. Could be that I feel a kind of closeness to those events, even though I was only two years old when Marilyn and JFK died. It's like they help define me somehow, in ways I can't untangle."

"That's what the therapy is for, right?" Mason smiled. "To find those connections."

"Maybe it's as simple as this: I *love* a good mystery. I love to dig. The truth will out."

"Just as long as you keep the conspiracy theory stuff to yourself. It makes you look like a loony." Mason said it with good-natured tongue-in-cheek, but he was right. It was a facet of Trey's life only Mason and Marie knew, a guilty pleasure, a satisfying release of energy, cathartic for a mind that would not stop looking for new angles, new clues.

The night deepened. The lights of Hollywood twinkled. And someone with nefarious intent had possession of paintings that were collectively a thousand years old. The only way to ensure those paintings never came to light again was to destroy them. Even worse would be for someone to cut the large paintings into smaller pieces, re-frame them as 'new, undiscovered masterpieces by the artist,' as if they were a triptych, and sell off the paintings one by one. Each would have the legitimate DNA from the original monumental painting. The police would be looking for a large painting and never suspect three smaller paintings excised from the original. They would be untraceable.

These great paintings might be used to launder money in the criminal underground. Sold into slavery. The sex trade of the art world.

Tomorrow, he would talk to Dr. Francis X. Cahill, and then he would know. And fraud or not, there were two precious paintings somewhere in need of rescue.

CHAPTER 3

"MY PARENTS DRANK A LOT. My dad could kill a case or two of Falstaff beer every weekend. He had his own advertising business, but we never thought he was an alcoholic because he could always get to work, I guess.

"When he would slam my head repeatedly against the walls, I could see my mother down the hallway sitting in one of these green swivel chairs, drinking chardonnay and not responding to my screams for help.

"My dad used to take myself and my brother, Patrick, he would call us to his bedroom and he would shut the door and say, 'Your mother told me you lied,' or 'You've done this,' or 'You've done that.' So, he would ask me, 'Did you do it?' And I would say no. Then he says, 'You're lying to me.'

"The whole thing would escalate. So it was bend over, pull your pants down, bend over the foot of their bed, take the punishment. He'd whip us with a belt. If we cried, he kept hitting us. Over the years, I started laughing. He couldn't take it when I started laughing. He tried hitting me harder, but that just made me laugh harder."

"Did the drinking make things worse?"

"No, most of the times he beat us, he was stone sober. It was all about control for him."

***

Darkness hung like a living thing, shrouding the ceiling, the corners, the door. The only light filtered through thick curtains into the baby boy's bedroom. Silver starlight pooled at the foot of his crib.

Mommy and Daddy's room was through the door, which lay open just a crack. The crack was dark. They were asleep. Big sister was asleep, too.

But he was awake now, and so, so alone.

He gave a plaintive bleat, but no one came.

He unleashed a piercing wail, but no one came.

He screamed until his throat was raw, cheeks soaked with tears, arms and legs waving in desperation, but the room remained dark and silent.

The pool of moonlight crept like a ghost across the floor.

He cried as if there was no one left in the world.

Except he was not alone now.

Someone was standing over him, a looming featureless shadow.

Across the room, the door clicked shut.

His throat cinched off his cries, and his soft, pliable muscles froze. He lay there as if he were already dead.

The shadow leaned over the crib.

He could not scream, could only stare goggle-eyed and try to hide in plain sight.

The shadow regarded him for a while. Then it lowered a pillow onto his face and *pressed*.

Warmth filled his diaper.

His pudgy fists flailed. He screamed into the pillow, but no one could hear. And when the scream was done, there was no air to draw breath. There was only the pillow pressing harder, harder.

Then the darkness behind the pillow burst with sparks and flashes and...

***

Trey burst awake with a sharp cry, sucking great gasps of air, clutching his chest, his cheeks wet with tears.

He flung himself out of bed and stood in the middle of a dark room. Where was he? His legs were cold jelly, and his hands trembled. A sheen of frigid sweat soaked his neck and pate. Slivers of light crawled around the edges of the curtains and from under the door.

His heart was a trip hammer thudding against his breastbone.

He sat down on the edge of the bed, trying to catch his breath, wiping at the sweat.

The air conditioning system hummed cool, lifeless air into the room.

A sound in the corner caught his attention, a shuffled footstep.

The instinct to freeze like that baby seized him. But he didn't dare.

Someone was in his room.

Slowly, fearfully, he turned to look, and ice water sluiced through him. A human form, black and all but silent, leaned over his suitcase, going through it, digging through socks and underwear, running black leather fingers over the lining.

His mouth was a desert, devoid of the saliva needed to talk. "Who are you? What are you doing?" he croaked.

The figure ignored him and unzipped a suitcase pocket, rifling.

"I said, who are you?" Trey said, louder this time, but it still sounded hollow and distant.

The figure turned away from Trey's suitcase and moved to the armoire, where Trey's suits and shirts had been hung.

Trey cranked his courage into a tight iron ball, but could he walk? His neck was a wooden post. "Hey! What are you doing?"

The figure rifled through Trey's suit pockets for long moments. Did the intruder have a weapon? If Trey tried to stop him, would the response be a garrote? A knife between the ribs? Why did the intruder seem oblivious to Trey's presence?

Trey could discern no details, just a figure so black its outlines were indistinct.

Suddenly anger flared. The brazen audacity! To come into his room, toss his stuff, and then *ignore* him!

The anger released his muscles, and he lunged toward the figure.

His hand stretched out, his fingers reaching.

***

The infinitesimal moment before his hand seized the figure's shoulder, his eyes snapped open, and his fingers closed on the empty air above his bed.

Sheened with sweat. Heart pounding.

But teeth clenched in anger.

He was lying in bed, twisted like a pretzel into his tortured sheets, arm reaching into the air.

He rolled out of bed, then lurched toward the window and flung the curtains wide. The brilliance of LA night flooded his room. He was alone.

The locks on the door were still in place. His room was on the nineteenth floor. The windows did not even open.

Nevertheless, he checked the armoire. He checked the closet. He checked under the bed. He checked the bathroom.

Alone.

With trembling hands, he turned on the water, cupped his hands and washed it over his face and neck.

He hadn't had a dream like that in a long time. The therapy sessions had helped him dredge up the old traumas and begin to deal with them. Over time, that had meant fewer flashbacks, fewer panic attacks, fewer bouts of crushing insomnia.

The clock on the night stand said 3:13. He sank into the chair beside the bed, afraid for a moment it might swallow him like a living predator, and he would go down into that killer whale's gullet and...

No, take a deep breath. Just breathe. You're in a hotel room. You're in LA. No one is going to get you.

Deep breaths. Deep breaths.

Until the morning, four hours later.

***

Daybreak was a long, long time coming; when it finally did, Trey's eyelids were strips of sandpaper dragging across his corneas with every blink. A few eye-drops helped but did nothing for his diminished mental acuity. He had really needed a good night's sleep before launching himself wholly into the investigation, but apparently that was not to be. A quadruple espresso would have to suffice instead of rest.

Step One was his meeting with Francis X. Cahill, who by now had returned from Rome. The address he received from Lloyd's indicating the meeting place was not the Cahill home on Lido Isle; it was a high-rise on Wilshire Boulevard.

In the lobby, Trey discovered the suite number corresponded to the law firm of Ward, Anderson & Dunwood. He had thought the meeting place would be perhaps Cahill's office, but no. Lawyers were already involved, and the investigation had barely begun. This development did nothing but heighten Trey's suspicion of Cahill's guilt. One did not immediately lawyer up if one was innocent.

During an ongoing investigation, his habitual wardrobe—his shtick as he liked to call it—was blazer, vintage T-shirt, jeans, and Donald J. Pliner shoes. On the elevator up to the twenty-ninth floor, Trey brushed lint from his blazer and straightened his Bill Reid Haida T-shirt, as if this might sharpen the dullness of mind that still plagued him.

The elevator doors opened into the lobby of Ward, Anderson & Dunwood, as chrome and stylish as one might imagine from a high-powered Los Angeles law firm. The receptionist could have been an actress in her spare time, dripping with the kind of beauty, charisma, and aspirations that even waitresses had in this town.

Trey introduced himself, the receptionist made a quick phone call, and then she told him, "They're waiting for you in the conference room. I'll take you back."

"Thank you," he said.

She came out from around the desk like a star on the rise and led him through glass doors, down a glass hallway, to a floor-to-ceiling glass conference room.

Inside the conference room, two men sat a table the size of a basketball court. The brash blue sky and bustling landscape of an LA afternoon filled the glass wall beyond them.

Trey entered and approached the end of the table. The two men stood, one of them nervously. Francis X. Cahill looked in his mid-fifties, trim, toned, chiseled, and bronzed in the quintessential SoCal tan, clad in Polo Ralph Lauren chinos, Gucci sandals, and a Dolce & Gabbana polo shirt. It was the other man, however, who seized Trey's attention. He was maybe 6'5", about 40 years old, a silverback gorilla in an ill-fitting, off-the-rack suit that exaggerated his obesity. With hulking shoulders and hands the size of hams, he was at least four hundred pounds, a sedentary lifestyle padded onto a nose tackle's frame.

Trey did not offer his hand but set his briefcase on the table. "Gentlemen, thank you for meeting me. My name is Emmett Hansen III. I represent Lloyd's of London in this investigation."

The huge man interposed himself in front of Cahill. "Richard R. Dunwood. Dr. Cahill has retained me as counsel in this matter."

Trey pulled the file from his briefcase. "Let us get down to the specifics." In the immensity of the conference room, across six feet of table, the focus of Dunwood's adversarial glare, Trey had the sudden sense that dicks were measured across this table, in this fishbowl, and there would never be a moment where he was not in such a contest.

"So, Dr. Cahill," Trey said, "I've requested the policy and endorsements from Lloyd's to ascertain what's covered under your policy—"

"That's bullshit," Dunwood growled. "You know damn well what's covered. You'd better have a check in that briefcase."

Cahill squirmed a little at Dunwood's sudden bluster.

Trey cleared his throat and maintained his composure. "It has been reported to the police that there was a theft of two works of art from your home in Newport Beach, *Nativity with San Lorenzo and San Francesco*, by Caravaggio, oil on canvas, framed, circa 1609, and *Annunciation* by Piero, oil on board, framed, circa 1489. Is this correct?"

Dunwood leaned forward, obscuring Cahill with his bulk. "Let me do the talking, Frank. My client just came from talking to the police. Everything you need to know is in the police report."

Dunwood's menace of physical intimidation rolled across the table and made Trey's muscles tense, his teeth clench. It had taken thirty seconds for the gloves to come off. But Trey was ready to go fifteen rounds, and he'd pick his opponent apart with precision and patience. "I have not yet seen the police report. Can you please confirm these are the paintings in question?"

"Of course they are!" Dunwood snarled.

"So, do you own the paintings?" Trey said.

"What the hell kind of question is that?" Dunwood said.

"Your client may have borrowed them on approval or temporary loan from a third party. We need to confirm he has an insurable interest under the policy. Are they yours, sir?"

"They're in the policy, aren't they?" Dunwood said.

"As I said, I have not yet seen the policy—"

"Look, I can't believe Lloyd's sends you down here to waste my client's time. You're telling me you don't have a check."

Trey leaned forward and put steel in his voice. "Mr. Dunwood, a check will be forthcoming when it has been determined to *my* satisfaction that this is a covered loss. Now, Mr. Cahill, when did you purchase these paintings and from whom?"

"How the fuck is that relevant?" Dunwood said. "What's the point? The paintings were stolen. They're on the insurance policy. Maybe you don't have the policy, but I sure as hell do." He shoved a paper-clipped sheaf of papers across the table. "There they are. Agreed value, one hundred and twenty million dollars."

Trey took the sheaf of papers and flipped through pages of dense legalese and tables, sublimits and deductibles, transit coverage, the kind of stuff that would make anyone else comatose in ten seconds or less. This was a sum insured policy, a spreadsheet containing works that totaled several hundred million dollars.

He fixed his gaze on Cahill, only barely able to see him past Dunwood. Cahill shrank into Dunwood's shadow, his gaze on the expanse of empty tabletop. "What did you pay for the paintings, sir?"

"Again, not relevant," Dunwood said. "This is an agreed value. Lloyd's signed off on that."

Then something from the papers jumped out at Trey. "Is it true these two paintings were previously on loan to the Los Angeles County Museum of Art? What was the period of that loan?"

Dunwood sighed with exasperation. "Agreed value. Eighty-five five for the big one, thirty-five point-five for the little one. The paintings are gone. A police report has been filed. Present check."

"I have more questions."

"There is no question. This is a covered peril." The disdain in Dunwood's voice, as if he were talking to a naughty three-year-old, made Trey's teeth clench. "So, are we to conclude that you did not, in fact, bring a check?"

When he was nine years old, Trey broke the record for fifty-yard breaststroke at the swim club in Littleton, Colorado. That record stood for twenty-five years. He could hold his breath underwater for incredible periods, without fear. He could outlast anyone trying to hold his head underwater. He would be damned if a bully like Richard Dunwood was going to push him around, much less break him.

He kept his voice steady, professional. "When my investigation is complete, I will forward my recommendation to Lloyd's. Any settlement is contingent upon my satisfaction."

Dunwood stood. "Then we're done here. Frank."

Cahill sheepishly stood.

Dunwood then withdrew a document from his briefcase and slid it across the table to Trey. It was signed, notarized, and labeled at the top: SWORN STATEMENT IN PROOF OF LOSS. It was a printed statement by Cahill outlining the particulars of the case. Near the bottom of the document of legalese was the figure $120,000,000. It stunned Trey for a moment because it meant Cahill and Dunwood would never accept anything less than the full declared value. According to California law, Lloyd's now had thirty days to settle the claim, or they could find themselves in the crosshairs of a lawsuit.

They had had this document already prepared before Trey even showed up.

"You can see yourself out." Dunwood gestured to Cahill to follow him out. He headed for the door like a rodeo bull.

CHAPTER 4

"*I THINK YOU NEED* to confront him. You're a mature man now, with a lucrative career, with agency, with a lot of wonderful things going for you."

"I tried this in my twenties, when I was right out of college. College was this shattering period of cascading enlightenments, like tactical nukes that destroyed so many of my preconceived notions, my Catholic indoctrination. I came home with a head full of fresh ideas and something resembling a distant relative of courage, and I didn't know how else to do it, so I sprang it on him one Sunday dinner. My older sister Mary was there, and my younger brother Patrick was still in high school. Mary was having one of her good days. I remember her giving me a little hug that day, which was odd because she never let anyone touch her. We hadn't seen each other in a while.

"Anyway, I just dropped the bomb. I said, 'Dad, why did you beat me my entire life?'

"And it was just like the vacuum after a nuke. Mary and Patrick looked like they wanted to crawl under the table. Patrick had never gotten the brunt of the abuse like I did, but watching it had made him terrified of rocking the boat. Mary's good day ended the second I asked the question. The light just went out in her eyes. That might have been the last time I saw it."

49

"So what happened?"

"My dad wiped his mouth with a napkin and just looked at me with that stony gaze. He could intimidate you with his silence. For half a second, I felt like my life was in jeopardy, but I chalked it up to PTSD. The moment passed.

"My mother leaned forward, glass of white wine in one hand, and said, 'Oh, honey, your father never beat you. I don't know where you'd get such an idea.'"

***

Trey had two phone calls to make now.

In the lobby of the law firm's high-rise, he pulled out Detective Tosch's business card and called the number.

The detective answered on the second ring. "Tosch."

"Detective, this is Trey Hansen."

"What can I do for you?"

"I just met with Francis Cahill and his attorney, Richard Dunwood. Am I to understand you met with them earlier today?"

"About an hour and a half ago. Just Cahill, though. No lawyer."

"Cahill came alone?"

"Yeah."

Trey chewed on this for a moment. Lying to the police was a felony. Lying to an insurance company didn't mean shit. "I'm sure Mr. Cahill was as innocent as the day is long during your interview."

"Seemed straightforward enough. Look, do you think he's involved?"

"Why would he meet with you without his lawyer present and then meet with me *with* his attorney present? Dunwood tells me the police report is complete. Is that true?"

"Uh, no. It'll be Friday at the earliest."

"Dunwood spent the entire proceeding trying to bully me into paying up. I'm not telling you this to complain about it. I can handle bullies. I'm telling you this because now I'm sure Cahill's involved. No one comes to a meeting like that, lawyered up, unless they have something to hide."

"Go on, I'm listening."

"Detective, would you please provide me with an advanced courtesy copy of the police report?"

"Sure, I can do that—"

"But I need it before Friday. Today if possible."

"Well, now—"

"The clock is now ticking on a larger matter. California is a 'bad faith' litigation state. At the meeting, Cahill's lawyer presented me with an executed Sworn Statement in Proof of Loss, basically an affidavit asserting the paintings were stolen and what they are worth. This started the clock ticking. I now have thirty days from when he files it, presumably today, to prove this is a case of fraud, or else Dunwood is probably going to file a bad faith lawsuit trying to force us to cough up a one-hundred-and-twenty-million-dollar check to a man who stole his own paintings."

The urgency of it must have translated through the phone line, just like the intensity of Tosch's gaze. The detective's interest had been piqued. "I'll see what I can do."

"Thank you. I owe you one."

As soon as Trey hung up, he checked his watch. It was 9:00 p.m. in London. Nicklaus Palmer might still answer a phone call. Trey was an independent art expert, a hired gun. Nicklaus Palmer was the man at Lloyd's who hired the guns. They had worked a number of smaller cases together. Trey's investigations had already saved the London Market millions of pounds in fraudulent claims, enough that the previous year Nicklaus had invited Trey and his family to the UK and treated them to a couple of days at his family's country estate. Nicklaus came from old gentry, the picture of an English gentleman, firmly rooted in both tradition and modernity.

First, Trey tried Palmer's Box at Lloyd's. Palmer worked hard, rail to rail, and then on the rare occasion he chose to play, he played even harder. Trey's call went to voicemail, so he left a detailed message describing the situation. But he had one more option. He called Palmer's mobile phone.

Palmer's smooth British voice came through clearly. "Hello, Trey."

"Hello, Nicklaus. Thanks for taking my call so late."

Palmer said, "Is all well in Los Angeles?" One of Chopin's nocturnes played in the background, along with hints of conversation.

"Unfortunately, no, or I'd have waited until tomorrow. Are you at Lord's? Apologies for intruding on your evening at the club."

"Intrude away. That is why you have my mobile number."

Trey told him about the investigation at the house, about the meeting with Cahill and Dunwood, about the forthcoming police report. After all that, he said, "This is pretty clearly a case of fraud, and my gut tells me Cahill is behind the whole thing. But here's the catch. At the meeting, Dunwood presented me with an executed Sworn Statement in Proof of Loss. According to California statutes, I only have thirty days to prove this is fraud, or we're going to be slapped with a bad faith lawsuit. One hundred and twenty million plus punitive damages."

Nicklaus paused as that sank in. Every heartbeat cranked Trey's nerves tighter. Finally, Nicklaus said, "Understood. The policy documents are waiting for you to download from the secure server."

"Thanks."

"Please give my best to Marie and the children."

***

Back in his hotel room, Trey pulled out his laptop to download the policy documents from the secure server.

Within a few minutes of poring through them, he uncovered another bit of incriminating evidence against Cahill. Two months ago, Cahill instructed his broker to endorse the insurance policy to move the paintings from the Blanket Coverage under which they would be included with other items in his house, up to the agreed Sum Insured value, to the Agreed Value schedule, for which he paid an additional, minimum premium for the privilege.

Only these two paintings.

With this change, the paintings were now insured for an agreed one hundred and twenty million dollars. Before that, their current market value was unspecified, but he suspected their purchase prices were significantly less. The policy had no information about the purchase price or the seller from whom Cahill had acquired them. So, what was the origin of the one-hundred-and-twenty-million-dollar value?

This discovery represented more smoke, but still no gun. This certainly looked damning, but it *proved* nothing.

He checked his watch and felt a little thrill. There was still time to follow a lead before the end of the business day, and oh, did he love the chase.

CHAPTER 5

"I WAS TEN YEARS OLD. I remember going to school and my sister Mary was sick that day. My dad went to work, my mother went to run some errands, and Patrick and I got on the school bus. We got bussed to St. Mary's.

"We came home, and Mary was a different person. She was locked in her bedroom, crying hysterically. There was no sign of forced entry. She had no injuries we could see. But that was the day she all but stopped talking."

"What do you think happened?"

"We thought somebody came into the house while she was there and scared the shit out of her. She's over fifty years old now, and she's never spoken about what happened that day. Something in her was broken, irreparably."

"Do you suspect she was raped?"

"That's what I think. My parents would never say that, though. When she was awake, she wouldn't look anyone in the eye. I felt terrible about that. She was my sister. But I was just a kid. I hadn't the first clue what to do. She'd wake up every night screaming like someone had stabbed her. So, they institutionalized her. She was gone for months. When she came back, she said she didn't remember what had happened. I don't know if they did shock therapy or what.

Lobotomizing her would have been a mercy, like the Kennedys did with their oldest daughter."

"The Kennedys?"

"Yeah, John and Bobby had an older sister, Rose Marie. Joe Kennedy had her lobotomized at twenty-three, lots of behavioral problems."

"I didn't know that."

"The Kennedy family is a hobby of mine, you might say."

***

Surrounded by majestic Queen palm trees, swimming in California sun, the campus of the Los Angeles County Museum of Art, LACMA as it was often called, was a wonder of architecture and design. Near the entrance was a breathtaking art installation called *Urban Light*, a densely packed grid of cast-iron street lamps.

For Trey, chasing down leads was like candy to a kid. Excitement thrummed through him as he approached the museum entrance on Wilshire Boulevard. LACMA's exterior skin of creamy yellowish stone, a recent renovation, wrapped around the original concrete structure from the 1960s. The wide concrete steps felt like the tongue of a great whale, and Trey was Jonah. But inside was not a prison; it was a paradise. Inside was Art with a capital A, visual, aural, even tactile. Inside its walls, human hearts were opened, plumbed, and filled.

He passed signs pointing to the Japanese Pavilion and the La Brea Tar Pits. Two massive doors of polished brass and glass dwarfed him as he opened them to enter the foyer, where two uniformed security guards stood. He passed them with the indifference of a bloodhound on a scent.

Beyond them, the interior space was immense, then shrank into galleries with lowered ceilings, acoustic tiles, and pools of brilliant light, artificial spaces created by the architect to customize this colossal, concrete box of a building.

Trey's footsteps echoed as if in a silent cavern. He knew the place well, although he had never had the opportunity to meet with any of the administrative staff. Would they cooperate? Did they have anything to hide? Regardless, he would leave this place with new information.

He checked in at the security desk and offered his credentials. He had called ahead and requested a meeting with the museum registrar, Julia Gutierrez, who handled matters pertaining to insurance.

While he waited, he took the time to admire the infamous 1981 photograph by Annie Leibovitz of Steve Martin wearing a white tuxedo covered with black paint, standing before the Franz Kline oil painting *Rue*, which Martin owned, trying to "blend in."

A pair of sharp heels, coming nearer, caught Trey's attention. A woman in a stylish business suit and gleaming black pumps approached him and extended her hand. "Dr. Julia Gutierrez. Mr. Hansen, I presume?"

Her grip was firm—all professional, all the time. They sized each other up. "Call me Trey." He offered her his business card.

"I'm the registrar at LACMA. You say you want to talk about Dr. Francis Cahill?"

"Yes, you had two of his paintings on loan recently, I believe."

"Right. A Caravaggio and a di Cosimo."

"If I may, I'd like to discuss the particulars of the arrangement the museum had with Dr. Cahill."

"Of course." She led him around a corner into the museum's administrative offices. The worry on her face and tension in her shoulders increased with each step. She passed her own office and approached the door at the end of the hall, labeled Director. Her knock brought no response. She opened the door, gestured Trey inside, and offered him a seat at a guest table in the center of the room, near a fine, art deco-style sofa.

"Coffee? Tea? I made it about half an hour ago." She clasped her hands tightly before her.

"Black would be lovely. Thank you." He gave her his best smile.

She poured from an old-style percolator across the room and offered him the beverage in an Andy Warhol Blue Campbell's Soup mug featured in the gift shop. He had profiled Julia Gutierrez before he arrived, as he did before all such meetings. Her credentials, including a doctorate in art history from Stanford, had impressed him.

He expected little resistance from anyone at LACMA. They had a cordial relationship to maintain with the London Market, one of the handful of international companies that insured fine art. Nevertheless, he remained watchful. "Dr. Gutierrez, may I please see the Cahill loan documents?"

"Just a moment, they're in my office." She left and returned less than a minute later with a manila folder, which she laid on the table before him. While she was gone, he had prepared his notebook.

He perused the file. "So the curator, Georgiana Walker, requested the loan of the paintings from Dr. Cahill. And he happily accepted, correct?"

She nodded.

"How many paintings in the exhibition?"

"Fifty. All Italian Renaissance and Baroque works of religious
iconography. 'From Giotto to Caravaggio' was the exhibition title."

In the loan documents were the dates of possession, and the
agreed-upon value—one hundred and twenty million for both
of Cahill's paintings. The paintings had been returned about two
months ago.

Trey said, "May I have a copy of this file?"

"I think we can arrange that. If I may ask, Mr. Hansen, what is
this about? Has something happened?"

He smiled at her again. "Call me Trey. This file says the two
paintings are valued at one hundred and twenty million dollars.
Do you think that's accurate?"

She smiled ruefully. "This is the art world."

"So, you don't think it's accurate."

"It's what we agreed upon."

"Did Cahill request this specific figure?"

She nodded, squirming a little in her chair. "It took some doing."

"Did he tell you how much he paid for them?"

"About forty point-eight million for the pair as I recall."

"Did you discuss the date of purchase and the seller?"

"Not that I recall."

"When you say, 'it took some doing,' what do you mean? What
happened?"

At that moment entered a man in suspenders and two pieces of a three-piece suit. The jacket hung on a peg near the door. He was bald, a little mussed and harried looking, with thick glasses, modest jowls, and a pencil-thin mustache.

Trey stood to introduce himself.

The man said, "Archibald Torvaldsen. I'm the Museum Director." An imposing name and a long way from his Viking ancestry. "Sorry I'm late. Julia told me you were coming. What can we do for you, Mr. Hansen?"

The museum director seated himself across the table while Trey gave him a quick rundown of what he and Dr. Gutierrez had discussed. Torvaldsen crossed his legs and folded his hands carefully in his lap, listening intently. When they arrived at the valuation of the paintings, he said, "When Cahill requested that figure, I flatly refused. Julia agreed with me, didn't you?"

Dr. Gutierrez said, "One hundred and twenty million sounded pretty inflated to me." She wrung her hands on the tabletop. Trey had not answered her question about whether something was wrong.

Trey said, "So what convinced you?"

The museum director sighed. "Georgiana. When a museum is planning an exhibition of fifty paintings, you must find fifty paintings. We can't have empty spaces on the walls, and we don't want to fill them with inferior works. She practically begged me to approve the valuation."

Such major exhibitions routinely borrowed from collectors, even other museums. For the legitimate collector, loans to museum exhibitions enhanced the artworks' provenance and increased the value. LACMA was one of the major museums in the United States. Loaning one's paintings to LACMA carried a significant weight of prestige and pedigree.

Dr. Gutierrez said, "The art world is often just a big game. A painting is worth whatever someone is willing to pay for it. For us to put these works on display, stroking the collector's ego is part of the game." She slipped into an exaggerated, high-pitched voice. "'Oh, *yes*, sir, we'd *love* to show your paintings to the public! Of *course*, they're worth quadruple what you paid for them!'" She cleared her throat, slipped back into her cultured contralto. "So, yeah, we agreed to it, because what are the chances the art will be stolen while it's here? It was all about not offending the collector."

Trey nodded. There had been a handful of notable museum heists, but modern museums were incredibly secure, especially those hosting works of art totaling hundreds of millions of dollars. Museum heists were far less common than theft from homes or disappearances during transit.

"For the sake of culture," the director sighed again, "we must occasionally pander."

"Is everything okay with the paintings?" Dr. Gutierrez asked.

Trey said, "Well, unfortunately, no. Two days ago, they were reported stolen from Dr. Cahill's home in Newport Beach."

Gutierrez and Torvaldsen glanced at each other in the mutual realization that their deal with Cahill had suddenly become much more important.

The director said, "That's terrible. I'm so sorry to hear that." Trey could see he meant it. Both Torvaldsen and Gutierrez paled slightly. They knew as well as Trey the paintings were now in jeopardy.

The potential for damage or destruction was a real threat. There was also the realization that their acceptance of the inflated valuation had opened the door for Cahill to make a tremendous profit if the paintings were "stolen."

"Part of my job is recovering them," Trey said. "That's why I'm here, to find out what happened and where the paintings went."

"Do you have leads or suspects?" the director asked.

"I'm not at liberty to discuss that during an active investigation. I do very much appreciate you both being so willing to sit down and talk frankly about this with me. The game is afoot, as they say."

They smiled at that.

"If anything comes up or you remember anything helpful, please do give me a call. The police have all but abandoned the case."

Dr. Gutierrez said, "There's something, I have no idea if it's important. But I recall during the negotiations Dr. Cahill often used the word 'we.' At the time, I thought he was referring to his wife, but then, she was not present. I got the impression he was referring to a male partner. I wish I could remember his exact words, or what led me to that impression. Forgive me, that was over six months ago."

Cahill had a wife, but that didn't mean he wasn't also secretly gay or bisexual. He was of the generation who might still abhor homosexuality. Or perhaps he had an accomplice. It was time for more sleuthing.

CHAPTER 6

"HOW'S YOUR SISTER NOW? Are you close?"

"She was in and out of institutions for years. My grandmother discovered Mary slept every night with a hammer under her pillow. She recovered well enough to get married so she could get out of the house, get away from the family. She got divorced, then got married again. They had a son, he's twenty-eight now, but he lives at home to take care of her. Her second husband would probably divorce her, but she'd end up living in a dumpster."

"Do you have any contact with her now?"

"I visit her sometimes, but it's just heartbreaking. The elevator doesn't go to every floor, you know? What's interesting as I look back on it is that I don't know if they did shock therapy or what, but nobody talks about it. Nobody talks about it. It's a dark, dark, dark secret in our family. I don't know if my dad did it. I don't know who it was, but something happened to her that just fucked her up."

"Why do you think your dad might have done something?"

"Before I cut off contact with my parents, my mom told me he was going to therapy. The biggest regret of his life, he says, is what happened to Mary."

"Does that mean he was involved?"

"You tell me."

***

After the meeting concluded, Trey strolled the galleries of the museum until closing time. He always made time to visit Mark Rothko at LACMA. Rothko was one of his heroes. The six-foot by seven-foot oil on canvas entitled *White Center* plucked something deep inside and tightened his throat. Tears glazed his vision. He stared at the painting for a while and sighed.

Rothko was born in Latvia and created this abstract expressionist color field in 1957. The painting reflected the artist's fascination with the color red, suggesting ritual and elemental associations (blood and fire, life and death), while the center white panel of color produced an alluring, mesmerizing white light effect.

Trey's mind fell into the colors, into the juxtapositions, the contrasts, while some child deep within him ached and grieved and feared. It almost felt as if Rothko knew a little boy named Trey would need comfort, or maybe a message, on this particular day, in this particular place, when shadows lurked in dreams.

The next thing Trey knew, an announcement came over the PA system that the museum would be closing.

In the background, on his way to the exit, behind his admiration of the art around him, the wheels of deduction and speculation were quietly turning. This was his biggest case ever, and the culprit was right there in plain sight, but how did he prove it? Everything was still circumstantial. He *must* find the smoking gun.

With daylight fading, he returned to his hotel, ordered room service, and settled in with his laptop.

An email from Detective Tosch containing the police report sat at the top of his inbox. After responding with a note of thanks, Trey downloaded and opened the document. In less than a minute, his worry was confirmed. There was absolutely nothing earth-shattering in the police report. It was all dry and perfunctory.

At 0900 we were notified by the Lido Isle security service that a theft had been reported at the home of Dr. Francis Xavier Cahill... No sign of forced entry... Two paintings were reported missing from the master bedroom...

Tosch had made it clear in the report that the investigation would be ongoing, but without any clear leads, little further work would be done.

The gardener, Miguel Gomez, admitted it was his responsibility while the Cahills were away to set the alarm system every morning and every evening. He claims to have forgotten to do so. Gomez is an LA native, no criminal history. He has been doing contract work for the Cahills for about two years.

Trey found Gomez in about thirty seconds of internet searching. Gomez Gardening and Landscaping. Family man. Family business. Looked aboveboard, with a few dozen positive reviews on small business websites.

Was it coincidence the gardener forgot to activate the alarm system on the very night the paintings were stolen?

As Nicklaus Palmer would say, *Not bloody likely.*

Judging by his smiling, ingratiating photo, Gomez didn't look like the kind of man who would pull off an art heist, but he might have associates who would. But if they weren't present at the scene, how would they know he had forgotten to activate the alarm? Was the gardener the real culprit? Or was he going to be the patsy?

Trey would contact him tomorrow hoping to uncover a smoking gun. His immediate suspicion was that Cahill, or some unknown third party, had arranged the "forgotten" alarm activation with Gomez. Gomez might be an accomplice, or he might be the victim of blackmail, or the subject of bribery. If this were true, *and* if he could get Gomez to admit it, that could lead to the smoking gun.

In the meantime, Trey switched his background check to Cahill himself. Trey emailed a few of his SIU friends, ex-cops and special agents who assist insurance companies. These Special Investigations Units use their professional resources to conduct extensive and thorough background checks at the highest level. Trey would be able to scrutinize every financial detail, every traffic violation, every lawsuit and business transaction associated with Dr. Cahill. His contacts would shine a very bright light on his suspect. Unfortunately, all of it would be off the books and inadmissible in court; but if necessary, he would legally acquire the evidence later, with the assistance of an anticipated appointed Lloyd's attorney.

An hour later, he had generated a significant surface picture of Francis Xavier Cahill. Graduated from Mater Dei High School, attended the College of the Holy Cross in Worcester, Massachusetts, then Georgetown Medical School. Plastic surgery residency at Johns Hopkins. Cahill's professional pedigree was long and illustrious. He had been groomed from childhood to be the cream of the crop, with Catholicism the soil from which the crop grew.

Such devout soil was familiar to Trey, the same kind as his upbringing. His own parents had pushed him—hard—to go to Holy Cross. His paternal grandfather, the original Emmett Hansen, had been captain of the Holy Cross football team as a freshman. Trey's father had dropped out of Holy Cross after three semesters, for reasons he would never discuss, and joined the Army.

But if Cahill was such a good Catholic, why only one child? The stereotype of unbridled procreation was alive and well, particularly among the previous generation, despite recognition of the necessity of birth control among the Church's more modern, liberal-minded members. Cahill's wife Barbara also came up through parochial school and Smith College. Their daughter, Alexis, was attending Georgetown Law School. Together they formed the picture of the good, privileged, Catholic family. They were members of Our Lady of Mount Carmel Church in Newport Beach, but there was no way to tell how active they were.

One interesting tidbit was that Cahill's name had appeared in several recent newspaper and magazine articles calling him a "prominent art collector and philanthropist." Because of the LACMA exhibition, the art world had taken notice of Francis X. Cahill. How that must have stroked his ego.

Cahill's practice had been well established over the last twenty years. As soon as Trey's contacts got back to him, he would know Cahill's bank accounts and balances—personal, business, investments, everything. Credit reports. Personal or corporate lawsuits, past and present, including their nature and the verdicts. Arrests and criminal cases going all the way back to childhood. Car accidents. DUIs. If Cahill had shoplifted a candy bar at 13, the background checks would reveal it. The modern digital age made collecting this information shockingly fast and easy. Within a couple of days, every curtain shrouding Cahill's life would be peeled back.

Then it would become a matter of collecting evidence that was admissible.

As his focus began to dissipate with fatigue, Trey wrote an email to Nicklaus Palmer.

Nicklaus:

As expected, the police report returned nothing earth-shattering, except that there was a gardener who apparently "forgot" to activate the alarm system on the night in question. Will follow up with him soonest. Meanwhile, Cahill is not cooperating with the investigation. Clearly has something to hide. What's surprising to me is how clear a picture the circumstantial evidence paints.

My fear is that a bad faith lawsuit is coming, unless we produce an offer or an advance. There's no way I would recommend the issuance of any payment whatsoever. What I would recommend is that we retain legal counsel soonest.

Trey closed with salutations and hit SEND.

His eyes hurt, and he wished Marie was here to rub the tension from his shoulders. He missed his wife. He missed his girls. He missed his own bed.

He was surprised to see a reply from Nicklaus arrive in his inbox less than two minutes later. What on earth was Nicklaus doing awake at 4:00 a.m.?

You have a meeting tomorrow morning at 10:00 with Buck Travis of the law firm Travis & Associates. We will conference call at that time. Stay sharp. All my best.

Nicklaus was always one step ahead of him. It felt good, though, that they were on the same page. Things were moving quickly, and there was no time to waste on time zone differences. It would also never be said that Nicklaus spared the firepower. Travis & Associates was one of LA's top three most powerful law firms, and the other two didn't count. They were the kind of law firm that worked billion-dollar cases for companies like Warner Brothers and Google. When a bully like Dunwood found out who he would be facing, his sphincter-pucker factor would reach toward infinity.

If Trey could find the smoking gun, however, there might be no need of a lawsuit, only an arrest and a recovery of the paintings.

CHAPTER 7

*"**I REMEMBER MY** thirteenth birthday as if it were yesterday. It's my earliest complete memory. Everything before that is just snippets, things I might have pieced together from things people said or old photographs. We were living in that house where the assault happened on my sister, so she would have been fifteen.*

"Normally we opened our birthday presents at night, but I begged my mom to let me open one in the morning.

"She said, 'Sure,' and gave me a box. I opened it up and it was this amazing shirt. It was a short-sleeved shirt, purple and yellow, with stripes, and it had a button-down collar. It was so amazing, I can still see it.

"I said, 'Can I please wear it to school?'

"She says, 'Well we need to wash it.'

"I said, 'Please, please, I'll wear an undershirt.'

"So, she let me wear the shirt to school. I remember running to the bus stop like I was running through a field of golden wheat. I was the happiest kid in the whole world at that moment. I had this shirt. It was so cool.

"Before then, it's mostly just pictures. My siblings would send me photos over the years of us kids together, but I didn't remember those times or those photos."

"That's probably related to the trauma you endured."

"No doubt, but it also destroyed the memories I want."

"With your permission, I'd like to suggest using a technique called Eye Movement Desensitization Reprocessing. We may be able to recover some of the memories you want."

***

The next morning, a recorded video clip on his phone of his three beautiful ladies, big and small, waving to him and blowing kisses on their way to school, choked him up for a long moment. He gave a wistful sigh and blew them some kisses in return.

Then he turned to business. Knowing gardeners and landscapers were early risers to avoid working as much during the heat of the day, Trey called Gomez Gardening and Landscaping.

The call went immediately to voicemail, but he received the automated message, *"This mailbox is full. Please try again later."*

This disturbed him. What might have happened to Gomez Gardening, a venture that just days ago appeared to be a long-standing, legitimate business? Nobody keeping up on business allows a full voicemail box. Trey's instincts tingled. A key witness falling off the planet on the eve of a major investigation felt too convenient, nefarious?

The address was in an industrial park in Compton. He would check it out directly after his meeting with Buck Travis and Nicklaus.

***

Compared to the over-exaggerated glass and chrome of Ward, Anderson & Dunwood's legal offices, the design in the halls of Travis & Associates was like stepping into another world.

When Trey exited the elevator, he proceeded across the marble floor, stepping across an inlaid, metal star with the word "TEXAS" encircling the bottom half of the circle. The main lobby felt like a library from another century, elegant and cultured. The circular lobby was surrounded by floor-to-ceiling, dark cherry-stained bookcases, with a domed ceiling reminiscent of the interior of the Texas State Capitol building. This was Texas BIG in the heart of Wilshire Boulevard.

The receptionist, beautiful and charismatic as only an aspiring starlet could be, ushered him into the office of William Barret "Buck" Travis IV. The fourth-generation scion of a famous lawyer family from San Antonio, Texas, Buck Travis traced his lineage all the way back to Lieutenant Colonel William B. Travis, defender of the Alamo. In an interview with Travis in the *San Antonio Express-News* a few years ago, wherein Travis was asked why he was pulling up stakes and leaving Texas for Los Angeles, he replied it was time to step out of his family's shadow and make his own mark.

When Travis stood up behind his expanse of mahogany and leather, Trey wondered if the man was standing in a hole. He came around the desk to shake Trey's hand, and Trey towered over him. His hand, bearing a large signet ring on his forefinger, was small but firm as he shook Trey's. The man stood perhaps 5'3", his hair an unruly, Beatles-like mop. Nevertheless, his presence filled the room. He wore a well-tailored, Western-cut suit, silver bolo tie, and chocolate-brown, alligator skin Lucchese cowboy boots. Travis's office was decorated in historical Alamo memorabilia—a tattered Texas battle flag, a Bowie knife mounted under glass in a custom shadow box, a Mexican cavalry saber, a flintlock pistol. Travis's gaze was as sharp and penetrating as the Bowie knife on the wall. Playing poker against this guy would be extremely ill-advised.

Also on the wall was an original oil on canvas painting by Robert Jenkins Onderdonk, *The Fall of the Alamo*, also known as *Davy Crockett's Last Stand*, executed around 1903 and depicting the hand-to-hand combat at dawn on March 6, 1836. A copy of this painting, anonymously donated by the Travis Family, resided in the Texas governor's mansion in Austin.

Travis spoke in a light Texas drawl. "Here you just showed up and I've already got news for you."

Trey raised an eyebrow.

"Dunwood and Cahill filed their lawsuit first thing this morning. Hell, they must have been waiting outside for the courthouse doors to open. Dunwood's gonna shit when he sees you've already lawyered up."

The receptionist brought a Mexican silver coffee service and poured for them into what looked like nineteenth-century porcelain cups. Trey appreciated good coffee almost as much as good wine, and this was *good* coffee.

Trey said, "A Maciel, Mexican sterling silver coffee service. Nineteenth century."

It was Travis's turn to raise an eyebrow. "Good eye."

Trey also noticed a four-foot by three-foot oval painting, set in a gold-leaf frame, of an elderly, stoic gentleman. "Is that Sam Houston?"

"It is."

74

"And the painter is Lucretia Nash?" In the painting, Houston was holding a wooden cane presented to him by Texan John D. Nash, the artist's father. Nash and Houston had fought side by side against Mexican General Santa Ana. "I thought this portrait was lost." In the art world, it was one of the greatest "mysterious disappearances" of the twentieth century.

Travis smiled, "Well, there it is. You found it."

Trey was speechless.

"We've been working with Lloyd's for years," Travis said, his gaze sharp and probing, "but your name has never come up."

"So have I, and neither has yours."

Travis chuckled at the riposte.

Trey smiled. "Actually, the name of Travis & Associates does come up quite often in this town."

Travis leaned back in his leather chair—his size made it look enormous. "So how does an art historian become a fraud investigator for Lloyd's of London?"

Trey shrugged and leaned back in his chair as well. He didn't need to justify his expertise to this guy, who was supposed to be on the same side.

"You've certainly pissed someone off," Travis said with a smirk.

"Why do you say that?"

Travis cleared his throat. "Because you're named personally as a defendant in the lawsuit. You may need to notify your Errors and Omissions Insurance carrier."

Trey's gut slammed into his spine, and his mouth dried up. This kind of thing, naming the investigator directly, was new. Usually only the insurance company was named as a defendant.

"They're trying to intimidate you." Travis folded his fingers. "They know who gives the go-ahead for any settlement. Plus, Dunwood is a vindictive bastard. You stood up to him, didn't you?"

"Yes."

Travis's drawl deepened. "He might coulda taken that personal."

The desk phone rang. Trey checked his watch. Ten o'clock sharp. Travis picked up the receiver and poked the speakerphone switch.

Nicklaus Palmer's voice came through the speaker. "Good day, gentlemen."

They all exchanged a few words of greeting, but then Nicklaus jumped straight into it. "So now we are embroiled."

"Before we get down to brass tacks," Travis said, "I would be remiss, Nicklaus, if I did not give you my recommendation we hire a real investigator for this case, a private eye. We have a couple whose work is—"

"Mr. Travis," Nicklaus said, "Trey has my complete confidence. You will not find anyone more tenacious who actually cares about recovering the paintings."

Trey fixed his gaze on Travis. "Thank you for the vote of confidence, Nicklaus."

Travis said, "Now, hear me out for a just a second. No offense intended to Mr. Hansen, but as a party to this lawsuit, he is now personally involved with this case. He may be the greatest thing since Hercule Poirot, but going forward now, his judgment might be in question. Might be better to get someone impartial. Especially now that Dunwood just put a gun to our head."

"Trey," Nicklaus said, "do you have any question about the soundness of your judgment?"

"None whatsoever," Trey said. "I'll be damned before I let these bastards beat me. And I'm the only investigator you'll find who really gives a damn about recovering the paintings."

Travis's gaze sank into Trey, then he raised his hands. "Fair enough. I just know I'd be shitting lava rocks if I was personally on the hook for one hundred and twenty million dollars."

Nicklaus said, "Trey, first I'd like you to summarize the quantum of your investigation for Mr. Travis."

Trey related everything in as fine a detail as he could manage, including his intention to track down the gardener, while Travis listened intently. When he finally finished the details, he said, "There's no question this is fraud. All that remains is proving it."

"And they are in one all-fired hurry to see the lawsuit goes forward before you can. You have twenty-nine days," Travis said, "or a judge is going to hang us up by our heels."

On one hand, that sounded like plenty of time, but days were often eaten up more quickly than expected during an investigation. Trey's only lead, the gardener, was nowhere to be found.

"So what happens next?" he said.

"What happens next," Travis said, "is you'll be deposed."

Trey's teeth clenched at the injustice of it all, his pulse racing.

"Anything can happen in a deposition," Travis said. "At the very least, Dunwood will probably try to stomp all over you."

"Better men have tried," Trey growled. "Dunwood and Cahill can go fuck themselves."

Travis leaned forward with a devilish grin. "That's the spirit."

CHAPTER 8

"WE HAD A TWO-CAR garage and a concrete driveway. They put ex-pansion cracks in the concrete, which basically created four major squares.

"My brother and I had toilet-papered the guy's house next door. He was a real dick. We had a sleep-out in the back yard that night, my brother and I, so we T.P.-ed our own tennis court to make it look like somebody got both the neighbor and us.

"But then my younger brother Patrick fucking squealed. I was like, 'We didn't do it. Look, somebody T.P.-ed our tennis court, too.'

"But we got busted. So Dad gave both of us a brick and put us in one of those driveway squares.

"Then he made us spell out 'LIAR' on the driveway in great big, thick letters. Broad daylight, our friends going by on their bicycles, laughing at us and stuff. We had to get down on the concrete and re-ally grind that red brick."

"You were drawing the letters with the brick?"

"Yeah, and when we were done, he said, 'Now, go in the house and get your toothbrush.' So we got our toothbrushes, and he made us get on our hands and knees and scrub the brick off the driveway. He wanted it slick and clean using only toothbrush and water.

"We were out there until almost midnight. No supper. Then we had to brush our teeth with those toothbrushes. It was just bullshit."

***

Trey took an afternoon drive to Compton, the address of Gomez Gardening and Landscaping. Ever since leaving Travis's office, he could not shake the pressure of a one-hundred-twenty-million-dollar anvil hanging over his head, waiting to drop. Such a lawsuit judgment would shatter his business, his reputation, and the future of his family. Fury tightened his jaw, tightened his fingers on the steering wheel, lent heaviness to his gas pedal. It was vindictive. It was controlling. It was unjust. It was his childhood replaying in his head. And it was all so glaringly obvious this was fraud.

But he had to *prove* it.

The police had talked to Gomez the day after the theft, but had something happened to him in the meantime?

The contrast between the unbridled, raging affluence of Wilshire Boulevard and the strip-mall-and-crack-house chic of Compton jarred him, even though he was expecting it. He could not help driving through these streets of poverty and abject despair without feeling some guilt for his success and relative wealth, mixed with caution for his own well-being.

There but for the grace of God go I.

Could this lawsuit land him on skid row?

At least this roadster was fully insured. A desperate carjacker wouldn't care that Trey was sympathetic to his plight and circumstances.

Gomez Gardening and Landscaping was a nondescript bay in a nondescript industrial building, a simple glass office entrance and large, windowless garage door in the beige building's face, situated between a screen-printing shop and an electronics recycling business.

Trey parked before the office, got out, and tried the door. Locked. No lights inside. Shadowing his eyes, he peered through the glass. Secondhand office desk with a computer, telephone. A few invoices on the desk. A file cabinet. Family photos on the desk. Decorating the walls were retro movie posters featuring the Mexican luchador El Santo. *Santo vs. Las Mujeres Vampiro: Santo vs. the Vampire Women.*

It certainly looked like a place where people actively worked. It looked a little too personal to be a front.

He tried the phone number again.

"This voicemail box is full..."

"Hey, man," a voice called. "You looking for Mike?"

A scruffy man in cargo shorts and a worn Star Wars T-shirt stood in the open door of the electronics recycling place. His ankles were as thick as his calves. The aroma of marijuana smoke drifted out.

"I am, actually," Trey said. "He comes highly recommended. I've been trying to reach him but haven't had any luck. You know him?"

"Well, you know, we're kinda neighbors."

Trey approached him. The smell of Chinese takeout emerged from under the weed smoke. Behind the man lay a chaotic maze of stacked CRT monitors, computer towers, stereo equipment, wires, cables. "Know him long?"

"I been working here about six months. He's a decent dude." The man's bushy red beard concealed a triple chin.

"Does he do a lot of business?"

"Sure seems to. I see his rig coming back in the evening most every day."

"He got many people working for him?"

"Maybe three or four, but I think they're all cousins or nephews or something. Say, are you a cop or something?" He edged back into the garage, looking over his shoulder.

Trey chuckled to put him at ease. "Would a cop drive *that*?"

The man cracked a hesitant grin. "I guess not."

Trey extended a hand. "I'm Trey. And you are?"

"Jed. My friends call me Jabba the Jed."

Trey felt a moment of pity at the kindness of Jed's friends. "Look, I've been trying to reach him for a couple of days, but no luck. Any idea why? I mean, it's a weekday after all. Did he go on vacation or something?"

Jed shrugged. "Maybe? It's not like we're best bros or anything."

"When did you see him last?"

"Monday maybe? Maybe. What day is it?"

"Thursday."

"Yeah, Monday. Probably. He came back early. Said he was going fishing. I said, 'Hey cool!' I always thought it sounded fun myself but couldn't find anyone to teach me."

"He say where?"

"No, but probably on the ocean somewhere. He's got a boat. Stored it here for a while."

"And you haven't seen him since?"

"Nope."

"What kind of boat? How big?"

"Uh, hmm, you know that boat in *Jaws* they were hunting the shark with?"

Trey nodded.

"Not that big."

"Inboard or outboard?"

"Dude, I don't even know what that means."

"Could you see the engine? Was there a cabin? What color was it?"

Jed's beady eyes squinted. "Dude, are you sure you're not a cop?"

Trey offered him a business card. "No, I'm an art dick."

Jed peered at the card with beady eyes. "You sound like a cop."

"The boat...?"

"Well, it had kind of a small roof over the steering wheel. It was mostly white with some green."

It sounded like a small fishing or leisure boat, meant for day trips, not sea voyages. "Was there a name on it?"

"Never saw it that close."

Trey pulled out a twenty-dollar bill and handed it to him. "Thanks for your time. Gotta roll. The *Falcon* awaits."

Jed's eyes widened, and he laughed. "Geez, thanks, dude!"

"Would you be willing to call me if Mike comes back? I'll make it worth your time."

Jed grinned. "Sure thing."

***

Back at the hotel, Trey looked up Miguel Gomez and M. Gomez in the White Pages and found ten possible hits. Four of them didn't pick up and the rest were not the right recipients.

He called Detective Tosch. When Tosch answered, Trey first thanked him profusely for the police report, knowing he had only about thirty seconds before the detective's annoyance at being hounded by a civilian reached its inevitable limit.

Tosch said, "Do you have any information for me?"

"I have a couple of big questions for you. The police report says the gardener admitted to forgetting to activate the alarm system. Convenient, yes?"

"Much too."

"Then we're agreed. I tried to track down Miguel Gomez and ask him some questions, but his voicemail is full. His business is locked. Neighbors haven't seen him since Monday."

Trey could almost hear Tosch lean into the phone. "Go on."

"He's the only witness we have right now who could prove the theft was an inside job."

"Or maybe he's the chief suspect," Tosch said.

"Or maybe he took his cut of one hundred and twenty million dollars and headed for Mexico."

"Or maybe someone shut him up for half a percent of that kinda money. I've heard of hits for much less. Has it occurred to you that you need to watch your ass?"

"It has now. Thanks for the warning, Detective. Does this mean the case now has a stronger police interest?"

"If I hear anything on Gomez, I'll extend a courtesy."

"Likewise."

Trey hung up, wondering what would have to happen for the LAPD to step in. Miguel Gomez washing up on the beach?

***

The phone call with Tosch stoked enough worry that Trey couldn't get it out of his mind. The feeling of being lost and unmoored grew stronger, so he did the only thing he could do: he called Marie.

The instant she answered, the ache of missing her sharpened. "It's good to hear your voice," he said.

"You, too, babe. Is something wrong?"

"I need to tell you what's going on. There are...developments. Pretty serious ones."

"Let's hear it."

He told her everything about the investigation, about his suspicions, and about the lawsuit, to which he was named a defendant. "This is so huge." He did *not* tell her about Tosch's warning to watch his back.

"But it's so obvious, right?"

"It's clear and obvious to anybody with a brain, but it's all about what I can *prove*."

Silence hung between them.

Finally, she said, "Are you trying to ask me something?"

"If I can't prove it, if we lose the lawsuit, it could destroy us."

Marie was the sharpest woman he had ever met. She knew immediately how big this financial hammer was. He was willing to risk it, but was she?

"I feel like it's my father breathing down my neck again," he said, trying to laugh it off, but it came out more as a cracked voice. This was the kind of primal terror he could only control on the best of days. "I've done a lot of investigations like this, but..." The stakes had never been so high.

Marie took a deep breath, let it out. "You have to do this. You have to do what's right."

"But what if I can't?"

"You're the only person on this continent with the *cojones* to pull this off. Lower the mighty boom of justice upon them with extreme comeuppance. Or something. Babe, I have faith in you. So does Nicklaus. You'll figure it out."

"I had a nightmare a couple of days ago."

"It's been a while."

"A few months, yeah."

"Oh, babe, I'm so sorry." The yearning to comfort him came through clearly in her voice. How many times had she comforted him in the middle of the night, using her voice, her kiss, her flesh, as he thrashed awake sweating and screaming?

But then her voice came through loud and clear, "You go get 'em, my stallion."

***

The Staples Center crowd exploded in exultant cheers as the Lakers' small forward, Metta World Peace, broke loose and made a spectacular dunk, putting them five points ahead of the Chicago Bulls.

"Was that a touchdown?" Mason said.

He and Trey were the only two in their section still sitting in their seats. "No, that was a slam dunk." Trey was the only one wearing a Bulls "Rodman" jersey. The score was still close, but it was early in the game.

"How many points is that?" Mason said.

"Only two."

"Something like that should be more points I think, like ten or something. Seems only fair," Mason said, sipping his red wine from a plastic cup. He wrinkled his nose at $6.99 boxed vintage, but he could not bring himself to drink anything as "parochial and boring" as American beer.

Trey chuckled. "We'll take it up with the NBA."

Mason's willfully uninformed disdain for sports was something Trey enjoyed flouting, especially when the Bulls happened to be playing anywhere within driving distance.

Moments later, the Lakers stole the ball—a brilliant move, Trey had to admit with a sigh—and scored an uncontested la-yup. To disrupt the Lakers' growing momentum, Chicago called a timeout.

As the crowd settled back into its seats, Mason said, "Really, these boys should wear some sort of protective gear, what with all the elbows and such. I would recommend the same for you, hence-forth, now that I mention it."

"I have you to watch my back, right?"

"Don't be flip. Detective Tosch is right. You're a wonderful friend and all, but I don't think I would take a bullet for you," Mason said. "Do you really think this is that big?"

Trey sipped his own wine. "It's just so blatant, so brazen. It's like giving both the police *and* me the finger, daring us to stop them. To do anything at all."

"Because they are absolutely certain they can get away with it."

"That kind of arrogance..."

"Like our current crop of politicians. That kind of arrogance has real power behind it. Money. Just look at my family for Chrissake. Political power. Secret influence. Dark dollars."

"There could be a lot of heat coming down," Trey said.

"What if Lloyd's gets cold feet and hangs you out to dry?"

"Nicklaus wouldn't do that." Nicklaus had had Trey's back on several occasions, but Trey had never stopped to consider where the limits of that loyalty might lie. Did it go all the way to one hundred twenty million dollars? Even if Nicklaus had Trey's back, Nicklaus was not the only one calling the shots at Lloyd's. He had to answer to the following market syndicates. What was the dollar figure beyond which they would hang Trey out to dry?

Mason shrugged, apparently tabling that uncomfortable subject. "So why *these* paintings?"

"You want me to speculate?"

"Let us indulge in a bit of whimsical conjecture, yes."

"If we assume Cahill is, in fact, the perpetrator, then we must assume he has a fence in mind, someone happy to hide them for a while in a private collection. Someone interested in Italian religious art. Someone beyond the reach of law enforcement. Or someone who thinks they are. The CIA maybe."

Mason choked on his wine. "What?"

"Back in the fifties, the CIA used American artists as psychological warfare against the Soviets. Jackson Pollock, Mark Rothko, and a few others, mostly modern artists, the Abstract Expressionists. The weirdest part is that they were mostly ex-communists, and they didn't even know. No way would their work be acceptable in the McCarthy era. Americans mostly hated it."

"Enlightened souls, our countrymen," Mason said.

"The CIA trotted it out onto the global stage as proof of American cultural superiority, the kind of intellectual freedom that Soviet artists were not permitted. Russian art was straight-jacketed by Communist ideology. Stalin's Russia viciously attacked any sort of noncomformity. So the CIA patronized these artists, promoted their careers—at several degrees of separation, of course. In 1950, the Congress for Cultural Freedom was set up, run by CIA funds. It was this huge extravaganza of writers, poets, artists, intellectuals. The ostensible purpose of it was to defend 'Western Values,' from the Big Bad Reds. It published magazines in something like thirty countries, promoted Western art and thought, especially the new wave of American Abstract Expressionism. It was also the perfect CIA front. They wanted to show the world that the United States was devoted to freedom of expression and intellectual achievement—and give Stalin the intellectual finger."

Mason said, "Where do you read this...fascinating stuff?"

Trey smugly waggled his eyebrows at Mason.

"You know what your trouble is, Trey? This constant diet of clandestine skullduggery has blinded you to simpler truths."

"This is the kind of stuff I always imagined my dad doing, back when he was in the CIA."

Mason choked again, this time slopping some wine over the brim of his plastic cup. "You told me your father had an advertising business. He was a graphic designer."

"It's not like I could prove it, or that he'd ever talk about it. He would often tell me, 'It's never like you think it is.'"

Eyes narrowed, Mason looked at Trey for a long time.

Finally, Trey said, "What?"

"I'm trying to decide if you're trying to bullshit me."

"Dead serious."

"You have evidence to back up this assertion, then?"

"All anecdotal."

"Care to share?"

"If I did, someone might have to kill you."

"That explains a lot."

"I suppose it does. It also makes me a good investigator."

"But there's also such a thing as Occam's Razor."

CHAPTER 9

"I THINK I TOLD you my dad was a gifted painter."

"Yes."

"It was the one thing he did that I actually respected. He had what we'll call his 'studio' in the basement. He loved to do oil on canvas. That's one of the most difficult media. I think he liked the challenge. There's one in particular I remember. It fascinated me.

"It was of a naked woman lying on a bed of white sheets, on her stomach, face turned away, one arm tucked under her, blonde hair mussed. Her head missed the pillow. There was almost no color in the painting, stark, like graphite grayscale, but it wasn't. I remember staring at her curves for hours, her ass, the way the sheets lay across the backs of her thighs. Hey, I was hitting puberty, and here was a naked woman. My dad was a total perv, painting a naked woman. I spent hours staring at that painting when he wasn't working on it, imagining how beautiful she must be.

"But as he kept working on it, it got weird. A shadow fell across her, a human shape. It was so ominous. So sexy and so...scary at the same time. I can still see it, clear as day."

***

The morning was gray and dismal, as Trey sipped his coffee and read the *Los Angeles Times*. The hotel restaurant served a passably fine Norwegian salmon and eggs Benedict. His phone rang, proclaiming an incoming call from Nicklaus Palmer.

"Good morning, Nicklaus," Trey said. "To what do I owe this pleasure?"

"Have you any more leads? How are things shaping up?"

"I'm still trying to chase down the gardener, but no luck yet. Right now, he's our best shot at breaking this open."

"Do what you must. In the meantime, you have an appointment at Dunwood's office at two o'clock today. Travis will meet you there. You're to be deposed."

"So soon? I wasn't expecting that for at least a week."

"The fire they've lit must be a hot one."

"Are we going to depose Cahill as well?"

"Travis is working on scheduling an Examination Under Oath. This might happen today." An unspoken impetus hung behind Nicklaus's voice. "Listen, Trey. I've put other resources on this case as well."

"Other resources?"

"You're our man in LA, but this is a huge case. While Cahill is being deposed, certain assets will be looking for information more directly."

Nicklaus had spoken that last sentence without missing a beat, as if he were talking about a shopping list, not having someone search Cahill's house. Trey took a moment to absorb it.

Trey said, "Are you sure that's a good idea?"

"These assets are very precise and meticulous. He'll never know anyone was there."

Trey's hesitation tightened, and Nicklaus seemed to sense it.

"As I said, Trey, we're casting a much wider net for anywhere those paintings might have gone. Fences, dealers, Interpol, the Vatican—"

"The Vatican!" The same thought had brushed Trey's conjectures, but he wanted to hear Nicklaus's reasoning.

"No entity on this planet possesses more religious art than the Vatican. It's too early to rule anything out. Let us not forget that Cahill was in Italy, on vacation with his family, when the paintings were reported stolen. His entire history is devout Catholicism. He's clearly someone with connections. And these two paintings are among the most important examples of Italian Renaissance and Baroque religious art in existence in private hands."

"Surely the Vatican wouldn't steal them."

"Unlikely, but they might be willing to buy them or hide them. Given Cahill's wealth and connections, this could be some sort of global money laundering scheme. I'll be in touch."

"So will I," Trey said, and thumbed off.

With his eggs Benedict safely stowed in his gastrointestinal tract, he pulled out his Macbook.

A quick search at the California Secretary of State website for the business registration of Gomez Gardening and Landscaping yielded a home address for Miguel Gomez.

Trey's email inbox was also filling with the results of his background checks on Cahill, but he would have to read those later. The first priority was finding Miguel Gomez.

***

Miguel Gomez's neighborhood comprised tracts of close-packed, single-story homes, cheek by jowl with crumbling storefronts and rusty, chain-link fences. Due to the presence of so many barred windows, doors, and even dumpsters, much of the city of Compton had the feel of a prison. No doubt it was, for many.

The driveway of Gomez's house was occupied by a beaten-down Ford pickup that looked as old as Trey. A waist-high, chain-link fence surrounded the front yard, a patch of earth beaten bare and dusty by some unseen pack of dogs. A sign hung on the front gate, beside the mailbox: BEWARE OF DOG. First, he checked the mailbox. It contained what looked like a few days' worth of mail. Then he whistled tentatively to see if some pit bull or German shepherd might explode out of nowhere. With no such assault forthcoming, he opened the gate and approached the front door.

Neither doorbell nor knock provoked a response from inside. Only empty silence. He peered through the glass but could see little of the dark interior through the gauzy curtain. He looked for signs of violence—blood, anything broken or out of place—but found none.

Circling the house, he found the back door. Also in the back yard, amid half-chewed bones and children's toys, was an open-walled shed of corrugated tin, just the right size for a boat on a trailer. Tire tracks made a well-beaten trail to a chain-link gate and then to the back alley. The gate was padlocked.

In the back yard next door, a dog that sounded the size of a chipmunk started barking frantically.

He tried the back door, but it was locked.

Then he tried the next-door neighbors, hoping someone might

know where the Gomezes had gone, but his knocks went unanswered, even when he heard some television game show playing inside. As he walked back to his car, he felt eyes on him from several directions.

Before departing, he tore a page from his notebook and wrote a note asking Gomez to call him immediately. He stuffed the note in the mailbox and departed.

***

Trey walked into the Los Angeles offices of the FBI and approached the receptionist's booth. She was ensconced in a booth of bulletproof glass with a small, pass-through slot atop the counter. Trey said, "I'm here to see Special Agent Jerry Alderman."

"You have an appointment?" Coming through the speaker, her voice sounded tinny and sterile. Her thin lips glowed raspberry red behind the glass.

"No, but I'm an art detective, working a huge case for Lloyd's of London, and I need to talk to him about a theft involving two paintings valued at one hundred and twenty million dollars. I believe they have been transported across state lines, putting the case squarely in the jurisdiction of the FBI."

"And you are...?"

Trey slid his business card into the pass-through slot.

"ID as well, please."

He slid his driver's license through to her as well. She busied herself with running both through a scanner, then made a phone call. Without the microphone, her voice was inaudible through the thick glass. Then she hung up and said, "If you don't mind waiting, Special Agent Alderman will be out to talk to you in a few minutes."

Trey thanked her and waited. The lobby of the building was empty, austere—and a veritable bunker, complete with a guard post, scanning equipment, a CCTV camera in each corner, and a man-trap entrance capable of locking intruders in a bulletproof glass cage. He felt like he'd stepped into an East German embassy, not an outpost of the bastion of Western democratic law enforcement.

"Mr. Hansen," a voice said from behind him.

Trey turned to greet an unassuming man in a dapper, pinstriped suit. He looked a G-man from the days of Eliot Ness, but shorter than Trey expected. "Jerry Alderman," the man said. They shook hands. Special Agent Alderman stood only about 5'7", but his grip was callused and bore the kind of inherent strength that didn't need the overt aggression of a hard squeeze. "What can I do for you?"

Trey said, "I'm investigating a case of art theft and probable fraud that falls under the jurisdiction of the FBI. One Italian Renaissance painting and one Italian Baroque painting valued at one hundred and twenty million dollars were reported stolen from a private home in Newport Beach." Special Agent Alderman's eyebrows rose at that. "I believe they've been transported across state lines, maybe even out of the country." He then went on to encapsulate the case's most important elements, including the disappearance of Miguel Gomez, the chief witness. He was hoping that, with the FBI's resources, Gomez's whereabouts might be ascertained, and better still, the paintings might be recovered.

Alderman listened with interest. Trey could see Alderman's was the kind of mind that latched onto and retained pertinent details. When Trey was finished, Alderman said, "It's an interesting case, but I'm not sure we have the resources to help you in a timely manner."

"Let's just say I'm afraid my primary witness has been silenced. I could really use your help tracking him down."

"What about LAPD?"

"Also overstretched and unwilling to commit resources."

Alderman sighed and rubbed his chin. "No guarantees, but I'll see what I can do. I've got a significant backlog."

Trey bit down on his disappointment and frustration. He thought the FBI would jump over art fraud with this kind of figure attached. "Whatever help you could offer, sir."

"Here's my card." Alderman offered a business card. "If anything comes up that's more time sensitive, call me. I'll see about putting it on the front burner."

Trey held his expression steady. The possible murder of a major witness wasn't time sensitive? But he couldn't say that and risk alienating his contact. Trey offered his own card.

They concluded pleasantries, and Trey left the building. On his way out the door, he could not help but wonder what would have to happen for law enforcement to take notice and actually help him. The more he thought about what could happen to those centuries-old treasures, the more the queasiness in his stomach grew.

CHAPTER 10

*"**THERE'S LOTS OF SHAMING** in the Catholic religion. That was one of my father's favorite weapons. When I made the baseball team for Buck's Hardware, I was so excited because my best friend Mike was on the team. I loved that uniform. I felt like one of the Yankees whenever I suited up.*

"One morning my father made me get my uniform and get in the car, and he wouldn't tell me where we were going. Shame and violence and silence, those were his favorite weapons. He wouldn't talk to me, and I'm crying and terrified. 'Where are we going? What's going on?' But he wouldn't say anything. It's like he became somebody else, somebody I didn't know. He was in a hypnotic trance. And he was taking me somewhere, I didn't know where."

"You must have been scared to death."

"Oh yeah. I'm sitting there in my mind going, 'What do I do? Is he going to hurt me? Is he going to throw me in a hole and lock me up? Is anybody ever going to see me again?'

"Then he pulls up to this house, I don't know whose fucking house it is. He goes, 'Get out of the car.' It's not, 'Please.' It's not, 'I'd like you to get out of the car.' He says, 'Get out of the car.'

"I said, 'Well, what am I supposed to do?'

"'Take your uniform, your cleats, your glove, take everything. Go up and ring the doorbell and tell your coach you quit.'

"I just sat there stunned..."

"What was that punishment for?"

"I think that was probably the summer before ninth grade, going into high school. He always had a rule we had to be home at nine o'clock on Fridays and Saturdays. All my other friends, their parents were so liberal they were like, 'We trust you, come home, just let us know where you're at.' So I had called home and said I was going to be a little late. Because that's what they told me to do. 'If you know you're going to be late, please call.'

"So, I was out with some buddies, one of them was Marie's brother, who was old enough to drive, my friend Mike and a couple others. My parents knew them all. They were all good guys. Fellow altar boys. We weren't getting in trouble. We were at the drive-in where my sister worked. I think it must have been a Bond film, maybe The Spy Who Loved Me.

"When it came nine o'clock, I told them I had to get to a pay phone to call my parents. It was always Mom, because he never answered the phone. I told her where I was, that I'd be home about ten thirty.

"So here I was the next morning, my baseball uniform and cleats sitting my lap. 'You were told to be home by nine,' he says.

"'But I called! You said I need to call if I'm going to be late.'

"He said, 'That doesn't mean you can be late.'

"So I never played baseball again. I rarely watch baseball."

***

Buck Travis met Trey in the lobby of the office building of Ward, Anderson & Dunwood and took him aside, out of earshot of the security guards. Travis looked like one of the Beatles shrunk into a five-foot Western suit, but his gaze was no less fierce than a gunfighter preparing for a showdown. He might as well have been wearing a six-gun thrust in his belt.

"You ever been deposed before?" Travis asked.

"A few times," Trey said. "This ain't my first rodeo."

"Good. Dunwood demanded this be on his turf. Home-field advantage and all that. They can control *all* the conditions. God knows what they're going to throw at us. Thing is, because there's no judge present, there will be no civility. Given Dunwood's behavior at your last meeting, you can expect it to get worse. Think you can handle that?"

Trey nodded, feeling the tension rising in his shoulders with the knowledge that a real fight was coming, everything short of fisticuffs.

"He'll try to destroy you as a witness, confuse you, make you crack under pressure."

"You sound like a boxing trainer."

Travis smirked. "Can you go twelve rounds, Sugar Trey?"

Trey punched his fists together and limbered his shoulders. "Fuck, yes."

Upstairs, the starlet-cum-receptionist ushered them into the same expansive conference room as before, but today the lighting was much brighter, glaring in fact.

They exchanged greetings with the court reporter, who already sat waiting behind her stenotype machine. A video camera was trained upon a nearby chair.

Trey checked his watch. Two o'clock sharp. He and Travis sat at the table, away from the witness chair. Travis leaned back and put his alligator boots on the table, filling the space, owning it, despite his diminutive stature.

At 2:15, there was still no sign of Dunwood. Trey was sweating inside his suit jacket. The air in the room was stale and considerably warmer than the hallway. The air-conditioning vents were silent, closed. The LA sun pouring through the windows would soon turn the room into a sauna. Dunwood was literally sweating his hostile witness. Trey controlled his burgeoning annoyance by exercising his tactical breathing for inner strength and relaxing his shoulders.

At 2:30, Trey's anger strained against the leash, tightening his throat. Knowing exactly what Dunwood was doing did not make the anger easier to control. Trey exchanged the twenty-sixth pregnant gaze with Travis, fuming at Dunwood's audacity. Travis merely shrugged coolly, but the steady ferocity of his expression neither grew nor diminished.

Across the table, the court reporter sighed often and dabbed sweat from her face, but sat placidly, as if she had accumulated numerous similar experiences.

At 2:42, Dunwood lumbered into view in the hallway, strolling toward the glass door as if walking on the beach.

Trey took another deep breath to tamp the anger down, control his racing heartbeat. He wiped sweat from the back of his neck with his monogrammed Egyptian-cotton handkerchief.

Dunwood bulled into the room. His voice was ridiculously sweet. "Sorry, everyone. Had a bit of an emergency." He circled the table and turned on the video camera. "Let's get down to business, gentlemen, shall we? Hansen, sit here." He gestured at the chair across from the video camera.

Trey bristled at the order, but he and Travis changed seats. Dunwood sat at the head of the table, his bulk forcing a groan of surrender from the leather chair.

The court reporter stood and said, "Will the witness please stand?"

Trey did.

"Please raise your right hand. Is this testimony you are about to give the truth, the whole truth, and nothing but the truth, so help you God?"

Trey raised his right hand. "Yes, it is."

She said, "Counsel may proceed with questioning."

Dunwood jumped in immediately with rapid-fire questions.

"Would you please state your name for the record?"

"Trey Emmett Hansen III."

"Are you employed, Mr. Hansen?"

"Yes."

"As what?"

"I own my own business."

"What's it called?"

"Trey Hansen International Solutions."

"The acronym is 'THIS'?" Dunwood smirked as if it was stupid-est thing he had ever heard.

Trey kept his voice even as he jousted in return. "It is that, yes."

Dunwood snorted. "How long have you owned that business?"

"Approximately thirty years."

"What does the business do?"

"Expert loss adjusting, loss control for museums, galleries, and private collections primarily."

"Have you ever testified as an expert before?"

Another jab meant to insult and demean. "Yes."

"On how many occasions?"

"Including depos?"

"Let's break it down. Have you ever been designated as an expert before?"

"Yes."

"You personally, correct?"

"Correct."

"How many times?"

Trey let the disdain for the question seep into his voice. "Thirty-five."

"Is that an exact number?"

"It's a rough number."

"Why a rough number? Is your memory questionable?"

"It is not. How many cases have *you* been involved in?"

"You're not the one asking questions here. Can you remember one single case off the top of your head sitting here today where you've testified at trial?"

Trey glared at him, and his voice deepened. "Of course, I can."

"What was it?"

"Proprietary and irrelevant to these proceedings."

"Can you give me a ratio of your testimony as plaintiff as opposed to defendant?"

Travis leaned forward and said, "Now hold on. That's ambiguous.

The insurance company could be a plaintiff as well. You may want to rephrase it."

Dunwood stared bullets at Travis. "Have you ever represented an insurance company being sued for bad faith—"

Travis opened his mouth to launch a protest.

Dunwood didn't miss a beat. "Withdrawn. Have you ever been designated as an expert in a piece of litigation where an insurance company was being sued for bad faith other than this one?"

Travis said, "He's not representing the insurance company. So the question is—"

Dunwood cut him off. "I think I just changed it. You obviously weren't listening. Have you ever been designated as an expert on behalf of an insurance company in a case where an insurance company's been sued for bad faith?"

Trey answered, "Of the cases I recall that I have worked for insurance companies, I would say, in at least half of those instances, a claim of bad faith was part of the litigation."

Dunwood plowed ahead. "Are you aware of the difference between the standards and disclosure that an insured must make for a Commercial Inland Marine Insurance policy as opposed to a policy that's not Commercial Inland Marine?"

Travis said, "Objection. Foundation."

What the hell was Dunwood talking about? As Lloyd's of London was a foreign corporation doing business in the State of California, they were bound by state and federal laws. In the US, most fine art policies were classified as either Inland Marine or Marine and written as a commercial coverage, hence the moniker, Commercial Inland Marine. Dunwood was trying to spin Trey in circles by using domestic terminology for a Lloyd's All-Risk Worldwide Nail-to-Nail insurance policy. "In thirty years of being in this business, I've never heard of that."

"Are you familiar with California Insurance Code 1900?"

"No."

"Have you ever read California Insurance Code 1902?"

"No."

"Have you ever read California Insurance Code 1904?"

"No," Trey sighed.

"Have you ever read the California Insurance Code at all?"

A chuckle welled out of Trey's gut, and he let it go, just like he used to when his father had him bent over the foot of the bed, whipping him with a belt. Laughing made the blows come harder and faster, which made Trey laugh even harder. Trey's laughter had the same effect on Dunwood.

Dunwood's face reddened. "Why are you laughing?"

"Do you want me to answer that question or the previous one?"

Slapping the table with his meaty palm, Dunwood snapped, "The previous one."

Trey let his chuckle trail off for a moment longer than he knew Dunwood could tolerate. Then he finally answered, "I've read 790.03, Subsection H."

"Is that the *only* provision of the California Insurance Code you've ever read?" Dunwood's snide tone made Trey's teeth clench.

"I'm sure I've read more of it, but that's the one I'm the most familiar with. It comes up a lot."

"Are you familiar with the term *uberrima fides*?" Again, Dunwood was trying to ramp up the speed of the questioning.

"No."

"Are you telling me you're trying to pawn yourself off as an 'expert' without knowing the meaning of this term?"

After sitting on his hands all this time, absorbing the proceedings, Travis finally jumped in. "Objection. Argumentative."

Dunwood said, "Are you aware that in California there's a heightened duty of disclosure for those obtaining Marine Insurance as opposed to any other type of insurance?"

"Objection," Travis said. "Calls for a legal conclusion. It's beyond the scope of this witness's designation. He's not going to answer questions on that subject. I've let you establish your foundation as to his knowledge, not that I think it's relevant or germane to this case and this witness's designation with respect to the Insurance Code sections you have cited, but beyond that, this witness's designation is limited to the adjustment of Francis Cahill's claim and his opinion with respect to the claims handling."

Trey breathed a sigh of relief, relaxing into Travis's torrent of legal jargon. He wanted to look at Travis and say *It's about goddamn time you waded in.*

Across the table, Dunwood fumed and blustered. All Trey saw was a bully, an abuser, someone who deserved only the most extreme comeuppance. But Dunwood was a practiced abuser, an accomplished bully. He had his technique honed to automaticity. The most frightening part for Trey was that even though he understood what was happening, he could not control his instinctive mental and physical responses. His chest hurt. Every sound seemed amplified. His clothes felt scratchy, his skin raw. His jaw ached from clenching. It was as if he were a terrified child again, looking out through the eyes of a man.

Dunwood plowed ahead. "Let me ask you this question: Your counsel has just spoken. Is your opinion in this case limited to the adjustment of Francis Cahill's claim and—what else? What was the last thing you said? You can read it back."

The court reporter read, "And his opinion with respect to the claims handling."

Travis said, "And subsumed within that would be loss control and the things he's already attested to that are within his qualifications."

Dunwood's snideness returned. "I just want to make sure I'm not barking up the wrong tree here when I ask him about his opinions. Please read what he said again, I want to make sure I have Mr. Travis's terminology down perfectly."

The court reporter read it again. "Adjustment of Francis Cahill's claim and his opinion with respect to the claims handling."

This was a bunch of nonsense. Dunwood was playing at gobbledygook to see if he could shake Trey into destroying his own credibility.

Dunwood puffed up and went on, "Let's make sure we're crystal clear here. Are your opinions in this case limited to the topics of the adjustment of Francis Cahill's claim and your opinion with respect to the claims handling in this matter?"

Trey restrained the urge to growl. "No."

"In rendering an opinion with respect to your investigation—actually, let's just ask you what your opinions are going to be. I want to know every opinion you plan on giving with respect to risk assessment as it pertains to underwriting. My question is this: You're here for a deposition, and as part of the deposition process, I'm entitled to know each and every detail of your investigation of my client. If you're not ready to give every detail and conclusion here today, then I'm entitled to depose you before you ever testify in this case. I'm entitled to depose you again and again and again. So, sitting here today, I am entitled to every opinion or hypothetical which you have formed."

Now, Trey resisted the urge to smirk. "Yes, I have formulated some opinions."

Dunwood's face went from red to purple. "If you don't answer my questions, I'll force you to testify in front of a judge. You will be held in contempt and sit in jail until you answer my questions about your investigation and conclusions. You are party to this bad faith lawsuit. You are the primary reason for us sitting here discussing bad faith." His voice turned to a sneer. "Maybe you should go back to your hotel tonight and write a thousand times, *I will not commit bad faith during my investigations.*"

Trey's hackles rose at the same moment a lead weight settled behind his breastbone. *Oh, it's on, motherfucker.* Perhaps sensing Trey was about to slam Dunwood through the plate glass window to the street below, Travis laid a firm hand on Trey's forearm.

Dunwood's voice rose with bluster. "I'm entitled to know what knowledge he has. If this is going to be your position, let's stipulate that none of the opinions he's given are based upon relevant law of this state. That they're all just based upon 'facts' which he has acquired over the course of his career." His air quotes dripped with contempt. As he spoke, he stood and circled the table to stand over Trey, like a pro wrestler preparing to hit someone with a chair.

Travis said, "I'm not going to stipulate to anything. I *am* going to assert certain positions, as I have, on the record, and that's as far as we're going to go here."

Dunwood scoffed with contempt. "I'm not going to finish his deposition today. I'm telling you that. I will be making a motion to compel him to answer my questions to the fullest."

Travis said, "We will produce Mr. Hansen again if your motion is granted. I don't believe it will be."

Dunwood sniffed and turned his back. "I think it will."

Travis shook his head. "Objection. Objection. Incomplete hypo-thetical. Lacks foundation. Assumes facts not in evidence that you will not be able to establish at trial." He turned to Trey to explain. "You still can respond to hypotheticals. He can compel a federal judge in Los Angeles to ask you, for example, to assume the earth is flat and you're going to walk five hundred feet, and five hundred feet is the length of the earth, and if you walk five hundred feet, what's going to happen, are you going to fall off? The answer would be, under that hypothetical, yeah, I'm going to fall. Counsel is free to conjure up whatever hypotheticals he wants, and you can re-spond appropriately as it pertains to that hypothetical. 'Flat earth, five hundred feet, are you going to fall?' And you would respond, 'Yeah, I guess I will.'" Travis turned back to Dunwood. "We know the earth is round, Counselor, but go ahead. Keep playing verbal games, and when you're done, you can banish Mr. Hansen to his hotel room for the night."

Dunwood snorted like a frustrated bull. To the court reporter, he said, "Read back my last question."

In a monotone voice, the court reporter read, "'My question is this: You're here for a deposition, and as part of the deposition process, I'm entitled to know each and every detail of your investigation of my client. If you're not ready to give every detail and conclusion here today, then I'm entitled to depose you before you ever testify in this case. I'm entitled to depose you again and again and again. So, sitting here today, I am entitled to every opinion or hypothetical which you have formed.'"

Trey looked Dunwood squarely in the eye while silently counting to ten. "Asked and answered."

An artery formed a scarlet bas-relief across Dunwood's temple. "If you refuse to answer my questions, then I'll drag you in front of a judge. You'll be held in contempt and sit in jail until you answer my questions about your investigation and conclusions. Do you understand?"

Trey turned to the court reporter. "Read back my last answer."

The court reporter quoted, "'Asked and answered.'"

Trey shrugged. "I have nothing else to say."

Suddenly Dunwood pulled off one of his gleaming black dress shoes and slammed the heel on the table. "You *will* answer my questions, or I'll drag you in front of a judge—!"

"Who the fuck do you think you are, Nikita Khrushchev?" Trey snarled. In 1960, Soviet Premier Nikita Khrushchev had banged his shoe on the podium at the United Nations while calling the Philippine delegate *a jerk, a stooge, a lackey, a toady of American imperialism.*

Travis stood up. "I think we're done here. Mr. Hansen can wait outside."

Trey's act of standing flung his chair backward against the glass wall. He fumed all the way out into the hallway, where he watched Travis arguing sanguinely with a blustering Dunwood. The glass was too thick for him to make out what was being said. The hallway must have been twenty degrees cooler than the conference room, chilling his sweat instantly. He willed himself to breathe, his fists to unclench and flex.

While the tumult raged in the conference room, Trey paced, trying to calm himself, chiding himself for letting Dunwood get to him.

The Cold War rose unbidden into Trey's mind, all the history he'd devoured in college and the years since, all the strange experiences he'd had as a child, all the weirdness surrounding his father. The Kennedys, Khrushchev, Nixon, Cuba, the Iron Curtain, all of it a swirl of chess games with the fate of the human race as the stakes. If people knew how close the US and USSR had come to launching full-scale nuclear strikes and obliterating all life on the surface of Planet Earth—within two or three minutes, at least twice—they might never sleep again. For decades, history had balanced on the edge of a knife.

Trey's composure had mostly returned by the time Travis left the conference room and approached him.

Travis said, "You did fine, kept your cool, didn't give him an inch."

Trey certainly didn't feel like he'd kept his cool. He still wanted to break a chair over Dunwood's head. "Let's get out of here."

In the elevator, Travis told him, "We're taking Cahill's Examination Under Oath tomorrow. At *my* office."

"How'd you manage that?"

Travis smirked and turned on the Texas drawl. "It's all a chess game, son."

CHAPTER 11

"**THERE WERE TIMES BEFORE** that basketball moment, that day I bowled him over, where I wanted to just walk away. He could be just castigating me, and I would just walk away from him. That was the fantasy. Maybe I tried, I don't remember.

"But then he would come behind me, grab my shoulders, and slam me against the hallway wall face-first. Then I'd be on the ground, and he'd start kicking me and screaming, 'Get up, you ungrateful bastard. All our problems are your fault! The world does not revolve around you!' I would get up and try to defend myself. As I got more vertical, he would start hitting me. If I tried to crawl away, he'd grab the back of my shirt and drag me back or stomp on my back with his foot."

"Where was your mother when all this was happening?"

"I could see down the hallway into the living room. She would be in this velvet, green, swivel armchair with a low back. I'm screaming for help. My brother and sister are hiding in their rooms. They knew if they didn't, they'd be next. My mother would be in this chair, and she would just...swivel away from me, grab her glass of chardonnay, and take a drink."

***

Trey tried to work out some of his frustration that evening with an extra-long workout in the hotel gym, but even when he was finished, Dunwood's snide tone and sneer still throbbed in his memory. There was nothing for Trey to do but to destroy Dunwood's client tomorrow, so he dug into the background check information he'd received. He was going to savor this.

Francis X. Cahill's first red flag, a big one, was his credit score, hovering just below 600, extremely low for someone with a multimillion-dollar art collection. He had a slew of bank accounts: a personal one, a joint account with his wife, a money market account, a debit card, a credit card, plus corporate accounts for his plastic surgery practice. The first mortgage on his Newport Beach home was for $10 million, plus a second mortgage for $8.5 million. Several payments had been late over the last couple of years. His investment accounts: a 401k, an IRA, plus a stock portfolio that looked meager compared to his debts.

He owned a penthouse in Beverly Hills, also burdened by two mortgages totaling almost $10 million. The corporate lines of credit on his medical practice totaled just over $18 million in debt.

Trey would have wagered Cahill's entire debt that if he cross-referenced statements between all the accounts, he would find Cahill was simply circulating money among them, keeping ahead of payments but paying off nothing. It was the kind of shell game people played in the desperate months before they declared bankruptcy.

So why didn't Cahill simply sell some of his art to pay down the debt? Sold at auction, the *objets d'art* Trey had seen walking through Cahill's house would have made a significant dent in his financial obligations.

Cahill's criminal record consisted of a DUI in Newport Beach, five years before. He'd paid almost $15,000 in fines and penalty assessments.

But then, Trey opened the email that explained all the financial troubles.

Over the last two years, Francis X. Cahill had been the defendant in two lawsuits. Jenkins v. Cahill had been a medical malpractice suit, which Cahill settled for $15 million, after his malpractice insurance had paid its limit of $2 million. The second case, Anderson v. Cahill, had been a wrongful death suit, settled for $25 million, again with the malpractice insurance payout capping at $2 million. The plaintiff, Anderson, had been the husband of a young starlet who had died after a liposuction procedure. Unbeknownst to Cahill, the liposuction cannula had perforated her large intestine, filling her abdominal cavity with infection after he had rushed to sew her up; he wanted to make his scheduled tee time at Pelican Hill Golf Club.

Trey leaned back in his chair and sipped some herbal tea, basking in a moment of satisfaction. All of this added up to motive. Cahill was in such dire financial straits he was now resorting to fraud to pay off his debts. His medical practice was failing. No doubt, after a couple of malpractice suits, word starts to get around. None of this was yet the smoking gun Trey needed as proof, but it could certainly be used to apply leverage.

Trey forwarded all this information to both Nicklaus Palmer and Buck Travis.

Cahill's Examination Under Oath tomorrow was going to be... interesting. But Trey still worried about the missing paintings. What had Cahill done with them?

***

Trey and Buck Travis waited in the frigid meeting room of Travis & Associates for Dunwood and Cahill to arrive.

When Trey had first walked into the meeting room, the chill had slapped his cheeks. The meeting room felt like a meat locker. Even through his sport jacket, he felt the cold. Despite the cold, this room was much more warmly appointed than Dunwood's office. It was a place of marble and richly stained, dark wood, carpet so plush it was like walking on a cloud, and a ceiling domed like the lobby. Bookshelves laden with legal code lent the weight of law and solemnity to the atmosphere. Like Dunwood's office, however, a video camera stood trained upon the chair where Cahill would sit.

From his place at the head of the table, Travis noticed Trey's reaction. He grinned and said, "Fifty-five degrees in here. Two can play the Stress the Witness Game. I figure Cahill will walk in here with a golf shirt and a pair of shorts, thinking he'll catch the back nine at the country club after we're finished."

The chairs in the meeting room were a stylish blend of modern and retro design—and all metal. They would leech body heat at an accelerated rate.

"Nice touch with the chairs," Trey said.

"I'm hoping to freeze their balls to the chair."

"Maybe they'll want to cuddle for warmth."

Travis laughed.

"Are we going to be forty-two minutes late to the meeting as well?" Trey said.

"No, because I had to fight like hell just to get this meeting here. We don't want them storming out or we might not get another shot at this."

Trey rubbed his forearms to flatten the gooseflesh under his sleeves.

The receptionist, Sophia her name was, brought in the beautiful, Mexican silver coffee service, from which Trey happily accepted a cup of rich black coffee. He sipped and said, "Did you read my email about the background checks on Cahill?"

Travis nodded. "None of it surprises me. I'll try to get as much of that on the record as I can."

A knock on the door preceded the entry of the court reporter, the same woman from the day before.

Travis greeted her and winked. She smiled, eyes downcast, circling the mahogany table to the place where she would set up her stenotype machine.

At 1:55, Trey received a text message from Nicklaus: *Contact me immediately when they arrive, likewise the moment he departs.*

Trey texted back: *Duly noted.* No doubt Nicklaus had investigators ready to secretly enter Cahill's house the second it was ascertained he was occupied elsewhere. Trey was uncomfortable with this plan, especially being instructed to keep this information from Travis, but Nicklaus was the boss.

At 2:15, Dunwood and Cahill were still absent.

Trey said dryly, "Must be another 'emergency' today."

"I reckon Cahill's whole life is pretty much an emergency at this point. Dunwood's job is just to put out the fires."

At 2:27, there was a knock, and Sophia ushered Dunwood and Cahill into the room. Trey suppressed his smile. Travis's prediction about Cahill's attire—golf shirt, shorts, and even sandals—was perfect.

From across the room, Trey could see Cahill's forearm hairs bristle with gooseflesh.

Dunwood offered no apologies, no greeting at all, just ushered Cahill to the witness seat.

Trey sent Nicklaus a text message: *He's here.*

Dunwood pointed at Trey. "What's *he* doing here?"

Travis said, "He is assisting me in this matter."

"He's the defendant in this case!"

"He also has tremendous expertise in this field."

"But since he's not legal counsel, he is not allowed to ask questions."

Travis fixed Dunwood with withering disdain. "I have full understanding of the law, Counselor."

Dunwood seemed to chew on his own tongue. "Well, he'd better keep his mouth shut."

Travis said, "Coffee, gentlemen?"

"No," Dunwood said.

"I'd love some," Cahill said, rubbing his arms.

On the intercom in the middle of the conference table, Travis pressed a button and spoke. "Sophia, may we have another cup of coffee, please?" He said to Cahill, "Black?"

"Cream and two raw sugars, please," Cahill said.

Travis repeated the request over the intercom. Less than a minute later, Sophia reentered the room with the coffee service. Unlike before, she now wore her hair down in long dark waves about her shoulders, and two buttons of her amply filled blouse lay open. She flowed around the room like a runway model, a mesmerizing sway of curves and muscle. Trey could not help but marvel at the transformation. Sophia was a woman who "shoulda been in pictures." Like good wine, there was a quantum leap between cheap perfume and the good stuff, and she wore a sophisticated scent that seized his attention and would not let go.

She poured Cahill his coffee languidly, leaning closer, taking longer than she needed.

Cahill was transfixed. Travis had chosen his weapons well.

With the coffee served, Sophia departed the way she came.

Cahill sipped his coffee nervously.

"Let's get this show on the road," Dunwood said. "My client and I have things to do."

Travis gestured the court reporter to proceed. While she swore Cahill in, Travis turned on the camera. He then explained the ground rules to Cahill. "Answer the questions with a clear verbal response. No nods, or hand gestures. The court reporter needs to be able to document your responses." He then began a series of "nice" questions, the easy ones, such as asking him to state his full name, home address, date of birth, Social Security number, occupation, wife's name, children's ages and names, business address, education level post-high school including diplomas earned. The point of these was not only to let the witness get chilled and antsy, but to establish a pattern of willing response, increasing the chances Cahill might let something slip when the hard questions came. There was nothing in them for Dunwood to object to, even though he sat and squirmed at the tedium, but still Travis took his time asking. The cold also started to take its toll. Before Travis was finished with the easy questions, Cahill was sitting on his hands and hunching into himself.

Travis moved seamlessly from the perfunctory into the meat. "So, Mr. Cahill, how long have you been collecting art?"

Cahill replied, "My first acquisition was during medical school."

"Would you consider yourself a serious art collector?"

"Yes."

"How many works of art do you now own?"

"I don't know, maybe a hundred and fifty?"

"Do you own the works of art or does your business corporation own the works of art?"

Dunwood said, "Objection. Relevance. Compound question. Form of question. I instruct my client not to answer."

"Mr. Dunwood, this is a very simple question," Travis said. "The Lloyd's of London policy names Dr. and Mrs. Francis Xavier Cahill as the Named Insureds. If Dr. Cahill's corporation purchased the works of art, rather than him personally, there would be an issue of no insurable interest under this policy."

Dunwood said, "Fine time to bring up a potential coverage issue. More bad faith on behalf of Insurers and Mr. Hansen. It's time to write the check."

"First, Mr. Dunwood, we have a few more facts to establish. Mr. Cahill, who owns these works of art?"

Cahill said, "I do personally."

"The two paintings reported stolen, can you give us the details on them?"

"Objection! Ambiguous question."

"Who are the artists?"

"One is by Caravaggio, and the other is by Piero."

"What are their names and accepted dates of completion?"

"*Nativity with San Lorenzo and San Francesco*, by Caravaggio, circa 1609. And *Annunciation* by Piero, circa 1489."

Trey scribbled on a yellow sticky note, as was his expert task, and stuck it to the table before Travis. It read *Make him give dimensions*.

"Objection! The defendant is passing notes to counsel! This isn't junior high."

Travis sighed as if talking to a recalcitrant eight-year-old. "Mr. Hansen is here serving as my assistant. I'm the one asking the questions. Now, Mr. Cahill, what are the dimensions of these two paintings?"

"Objection! Relevance."

"Of course it's relevant. We are establishing the particulars of the objects in question."

Cahill gave the dimensions with great precision. The man *knew* those paintings.

"What is the value of each painting, Mr. Cahill?"

"Objection! The agreed value is in your policy documents."

"Just clarifying for the record," Travis said.

Cahill cleared his throat. "The Caravaggio is valued at $75.5 million, and the di Cosimo at $44.5 million. That's what's on the insurance policy. Agreed value."

"From whom did you buy the paintings?" Travis said.

"Objection! Relevance. Don't answer that, Frank."

Travis pressed forward, "Is it true, Dr. Cahill, you bought both paintings at Sotheby's auction house, five years ago, for the total sum of $20.8 million?"

Surprise flickered on Cahill's face, quickly suppressed. "Yes, that's true."

Dunwood glared at him.

Travis said, "That's almost a six-fold increase in value in such a short period of time, isn't it, Dr. Cahill?"

"That sounds about right."

"That is a somewhat shocking increase, isn't it?"

"Objection! Speculation," Dunwood said.

Travis went on, "Do you have documents certifying the paintings' provenance?"

"Objection! My client had to produce such papers to secure the insurance policy."

Trey scribbled on another yellow sticky note and stuck it to the table before Travis. It read *Make him produce the provenance documents. Not in the underwriting file.*

Travis smiled at the court reporter. "Let the record show that we request all copies of the provenance for both paintings, subject of this claim, be produced within twenty-four hours." Then he turned back to Cahill. "Were the paintings placed on loan to the Los Angeles County Museum of Art?"

"Yes."

"Part of the loan process with the museum is agreeing upon a value with the museum for insurance purposes, is that true?"

"Objection!"

"On what grounds?"

Dunwood snorted. "That is the biggest 'duh' question I've heard in a while."

"Mr. Cahill—"

"*Dr.* Cahill!" Dunwood said.

"Dr. Cahill," Travis said, "did you, in fact, specifically request that the Los Angeles County Museum of Art value your paintings at a total of $120 million, $75.5 million for the Caravaggio and $44.5 million for the di Cosimo?"

"Objection! Relevance."

Travis's voice went low. "I can drag this in front of a judge, too, Mr. Dunwood. I have witnesses at LACMA prepared to testify that Dr. Cahill specifically requested this figure. Dr. Cahill, remember you are under oath. Did you request that the museum assign those values to your paintings?"

"Yes."

Dunwood stood. "That's it. We're done here."

Travis said, "Dr. Cahill, did you amend your insurance policy with Lloyd's of London to reflect these new valuations *after* the museum acquiesced to your demand and produced a Certificate of Insurance reflecting same?"

Dunwood hooked Cahill under the armpit and lifted him to his feet. "Frank, not a word." He glared at Travis. "You're trying to turn this into a witch hunt against my client. It's been proven beyond a reasonable doubt my client was out of the country when the theft occurred. He's not involved in this. He's the victim! He paid his insurance premium. We have a police report stating the paintings were reported stolen. Where's the fucking money?"

"Mr. Dunwood, as you said yesterday, we can do this here, or we can do this in front of a judge. I can assure you Lloyd's of London will in no way offer any settlement without a thorough Examination Under Oath, required under the policy of insurance, by Dr. Cahill. Choosing not to cooperate with our investigation is only delaying any potential monetary settlement."

"You had the chance to play nice yesterday. Go fuck yourself."

The tension in the room made their voices sound tinny. Travis stood up. "Dr. Cahill, Mr. Hansen, you are both excused. Mr. Dunwood and I have a couple of things to discuss off the record." To the court reporter, he said, "Ms. Ellis, you are also excused."

Trey picked up his notebook, delaying his departure from the room to take a long look at Cahill. The plastic surgeon looked shell shocked. He was a criminal, but he wasn't an idiot. He had seen as well as Dunwood that Travis's angle of questioning would soon herd him toward a cliff and leave him no choice but to throw himself off.

In the hallway outside, Cahill shouldered past Trey toward the toilet, barely controlled desperation plain on his face. Cahill clearly wasn't used to that kind of emotional tension. A guilty conscience would further crank up the tension.

In the conference room, voices exploded with argument. The walls and door were too thick to discern what was being said. Trey glanced at the floor-to-ceiling glass fishbowl of a conference room and witnessed a pantomime of David vs. Goliath in the animated silhouettes of Travis and Dunwood.

Trey's mouth was dry, so he sidled up to the water cooler and poured himself a paper cone full of ice-cold water. It was good, despite the chill soaking his bones.

Soon Cahill came out of the toilet, looking a little pale.

Trey's instincts took over. "I know I shouldn't be talking to you directly. I just wanted to say you have great taste in art. I really admire your collection. Nothing in the world makes me more passionate. Not even women. And, well, I'm also Catholic, so give me all the Renaissance masters." He didn't consider himself Catholic anymore, but Cahill certainly was. It might be the kind of connection to which he would respond.

Cahill swallowed a chuckle.

Trey went on, "I get the real sense you're an art lover, too, not an ego-driven art poser."

"You know," Cahill said, "when I bought those paintings, I was so excited, I took the whole family to Rome to celebrate. We went to the Vatican." Braggadocio crept into Cahill's voice. "I gave the Church a nice donation and got a private audience with the Pope in Vatican City. They even gave us a private tour of the Vatican Museum and the immense storage facility. It's normally off limits to the public."

Cahill's boast immediately brought back Nicklaus's off-hand comment about the possibility of Vatican involvement. Perhaps such a possibility was not remote at all. Very few people gained a private audience with the Pontiff himself.

Furthermore, the gleam of passion in Cahill's eye told Trey one more important thing—he still had the paintings.

With that kind of excitement, there was no way Cahill would ever destroy them. He truly loved those works of art. At this point, his need for cash to solve his financial troubles superseded his love of art, so he would certainly be willing to sell them, but he would never, never destroy them.

Dunwood barged out of the conference room and spotted Trey and Cahill within speaking distance of each other. "What the fuck is going on here? Frank, stop talking. Right now."

Cahill stiffened and clammed up.

Dunwood shoved a meaty finger in Trey's face. "You. Stay the fuck away from my client." Then he took Cahill by the elbow and stormed toward the elevator.

CHAPTER 12

"I ALWAYS STRUGGLED WITH relationships involving the opposite sex. The only example I had growing up was Okie and Honey. My mother faked her way through her Catholic marriage to my father. A marriage of convenience. She frequently revealed this to me when I was in high school, and it continued throughout my college years."

"Why would she admit this to you?"

"She told me she should have married a doctor or some other financially successful man. Okie was mysterious and dangerous. She bragged about the men she could have had while she was a stewardess with TWA. Men flying in first class were smitten with her.

"I always thought it was fucked up that my own mother pretended her marriage was a committed relationship. She was a miserable performer in the tragic opera orchestrated by Okie, just like us kids."

"How did this affect you?"

"Whenever I was in a relationship, I never completely trusted the other person. If they were performing, then I guess it would never be real and I did not want to get hurt. I always felt it was my role to rescue the other person and escape when the equality shifted against me. I never wanted to be a prisoner again."

***

Marie von Bodenberg was having a SNAFU sort of day. With Trey off hounding evildoers in Los Angeles, she was left wrangling grade-schoolers and dealing with construction managers. It was like jumping back and forth between puddles, one made of runny nose and whining, and the other made of male chauvinism. From the cesspit of disease that was elementary school, Annie had come down with a cold that turned her into a Bellagio Fountain of mucus. And the new construction manager on The Heritage at Millennium Park had just disrespected her so profoundly, she wanted to drag him to her through the phone lines and tear him three new assholes. "Lady architects" did, in fact, know what the fuck they were talking about.

Annie's cold had chained Marie to the home office today. The poor kid was asleep in bed. Marie could hear the wet, gurgling breathing from down the hall.

Seated before her drafting table, Marie let her eyes travel the lines, curves, and angles of the two-storied, 3,000-square-foot condominium she was developing for a client, letting her mind drift into the Zone while she sipped her London Fog, Earl Grey tea with dashes of lavender and vanilla and heavy cream, trying to sidle past thoughts of life balance and icebergs of resentment that her daughter had brought home a pestilence, worries that she and Lauren would come down with it, and that all of this would put her further behind.

All that and an empty bed.

Every day, she and Trey traded text messages that ranged from daily business to flirtiness to downright tawdriness, but it was not the same as having him here.

Her gaze traced the roof lines and gables of another project, a 6,000-square-foot mansion soon to be built in one of the Chicago area's newest developments. The many ways she honored the great architects and designers that came before made her designs eclectic, but her attention to detail and functionality made her one of the top architects in the Midwest. She hand-selected all her finishes, everything from the Minoan floor tiles to the under-cabinet lighting. A master of the Kitchen Triangle Theory, she always designed her kitchens around custom islands that were sculptural, artistic, islands that made massive visual statements. Old School but very effective. The careful mix of symmetry and asymmetry filled her with satisfaction. This place was going to be *super* cool. She couldn't wait to see it "in the flesh."

She sharpened her drafting pencil and twirled it between her fingers. She didn't consider herself a Luddite, but Old School was the only school for her design process. Few architects used pencil and paper anymore, opting for slick CAD packages, but she loved the aesthetic feel of *drawing* a building. It made her feel like an artist, which Trey often assured her she was. CAD packages were great for finalizing dimensions and checking for problems, but using them in the intuitive, creative process of design felt like the wrong tool for the job. There was just something about the feel of graphite across paper.

The phone rang in the kitchen, the landline. The only people who ever called on the landline nowadays were her parents. Her mom often called in the afternoon, so she got up and walked down the hall to answer it.

"Hello."

"Tell your husband to back off, or you may never see him again."
The voice that came over the phone was deep and distorted, electronically disguised like she'd heard on television. It sounded unearthly, as if emanating from a different dimension.

The muscles of her legs turned to ice water, and her hands began to tremble. "Who is this?" Why hadn't she checked the Caller ID? She'd never have answered it if she'd seen the *Unknown Caller* on the display.

The distorted voice dragged cold, hard fingers up her spine. "He's in over his head. Tell him to back off. Right now."

She gripped the kitchen counter to steady herself. "Who are you?" she shrilled, dizziness washing through her.

The line clicked dead, leaving her heart racing and her breathing short.

She willed herself to take long, slow breaths, trying to calm herself, her mind swarming with thoughts. What kind of hornets' nest had Trey kicked now? Their landline phone number was unlisted. How had anyone gotten it?

As the fear subsided, anger reared its head. She wanted to take a shovel to the skull of the son of a bitch who had just threatened her family.

She dialed Trey immediately.

***

"We're pretty much dead in the water right now," Travis said. "Dunwood has put Cahill on lockdown. We're not going to get anything else from them."

He and Trey sat in Travis's office, among relics of the Alamo and the Republic of Texas, doing a post-mortem on Cahill's EUO.

Travis went on, "I was hoping Dunwood was stupid enough to let me get a few more incriminating statements on record before he shut the whole thing down."

Trey said, "I had a couple of revelations during my conversation with Cahill at the water cooler." He told Travis what Cahill had said about the paintings and the trip to Rome, the Vatican and the Pope. "Cahill still has them, or he knows where they are."

"We need to get Palmer on the phone," Travis said.

Nicklaus answered the conference call on the first ring. "I believe we all have things to report, yes? I'll go first. The search of Cahill's house turned up nothing. My people went through the place with a microscope, including making a mirror of an encrypted hard drive. Breaking the encryption will take a little time. We found nothing otherwise incriminating."

After they gave him a rundown of the day's proceedings, Trey shared his speculations there might be international connections to the paintings' disappearance, perhaps even the Vatican.

Nicklaus said wryly, "Trey, far be it from me to say, 'I told you so.'"

"I know, Nicklaus. I will never doubt you again." Trey said it flippantly, but Nicklaus Palmer's resources had surprised him yet again. "Any chance you could track down exactly where Cahill was staying on this trip to Rome? Credit card records, that sort of thing?"

"I could manage that. Are you going to Rome?"

Trey had connections in Rome, resources, having worked cases there before. What was more, he *loved* Italy like no other country on Earth. He loved its art, its history, and oh, dear gods, he loved the wine. He could almost catch its scent trail stretching across the Atlantic.

A decision slid into place, like a marble brick in a museum wall. He took a deep breath and let it out. "I...think I'm going to Rome."

Before he could fully process this idea, Trey's phone rang to "Hooked on a Feeling" by Blue Swede. Marie's beautiful face framed by honey-blonde hair appeared on his screen. She wouldn't call him in the middle of a workday unless it was important, but he couldn't take her call in the middle of an important meeting. He sent the call to voicemail.

He apologized to Travis and Nicklaus for the interruption.

Nicklaus said, "So, now we have to see about—"

Trey's phone rang again. He sent the call to voicemail again.

A text popped up immediately: ANSWER THE PHONE! THIS IS IMPORTANT!

Travis said, "You might should answer that."

Trey called her. As soon as she picked up, he started to say, "Hey, Marie, I'm in a meeting with Nicklaus and Buck Travis and—"

Her tremulous voice jumped into his ear. "Then put me on speaker. They need to hear this, too." Immediately Trey felt the pressure in it. Something had happened. She would never cause a disruption like this without ample reason.

"Gentlemen," Trey said, "my wife wants to speak to all of us." He set his phone to speaker mode.

Nicklaus said over the conference call to London, "Hello, Marie. Are you well?"

Marie's voice came through clear as an alarm klaxon. "I was, up until someone just phoned with death threats for my husband."

Three men simultaneously said, "What?"

"Electronically disguised voice, blocked phone number. I should have let the answering machine pick up. They said, 'Tell your husband to back off or you'll never see him again. He's in over his head. Tell him to back off right now.' And then they hung up."

Silence descended.

Nicklaus spoke first. "It seems our investigation has touched a nerve."

Marie said, "Can't you, like, call the FBI or something and have them check phone records? Find out who this is?"

Trey said, "I'll make a call, but my guess is, whoever would make such a threat would use a burner phone. On the other hand, maybe we're dealing with an amateur. Nicklaus, would you be willing to call the FBI on this one? I didn't get much traction."

Nicklaus said, "I can do that."

"Ask for Special Agent Alderman at the LA office," Trey said.

As Trey questioned Marie about the particulars of the call, the implications grew and sharpened in focus. Receiving a death threat was new territory. If a hostile entity had the capability to find an unlisted number, they must know where his family lived. That this threat was related to the Cahill case was a near certainty.

Chill tentacles prickled up the back of his neck. The threat settled into him with its own weight. He would have to watch his back or have someone to watch it for him.

There was only one person in whom he had that kind of trust.

Trey said with bright irony, "Guess what, babe! How about a trip to Rome?"

INTERLUDE – OPENING MOVES

THEY USED TO CALL him the Wolfhound. Like his namesake, he had been bred and trained to hunt wolves.

Along the back wall of his basement, he moved aside his easel, palette, and cabinet of painting supplies to reveal the small wooden door into the crawlspace under his house, all but painted shut. He grabbed the wooden knob and yanked. With a raucous, squealing crunch, the door succumbed and flew open, dragging with it a whiff of cobwebs and mouse droppings. Cobwebs choked the space beyond.

His knees protested as he knelt gingerly and eased himself into the dark, earthy void. The rocky earth sloped up toward the foundation at the rear of the house. He pulled a flashlight from his back pocket, using it to clear away veils of cobwebs, and shone it toward the location of his cache. On hands and knees, he crawled over the earth toward the cinder-block wall, what a casual observer would think to be the foundation.

Reaching a section of the cinder blocks under the house's patio, he braced himself and started working with a putty knife at the edges of one of the blocks, working the block back and forth with a grinding noise, until he could ease it free of its bed. A flash of worry seized him for a moment that his cache had been looted, but then his flashlight beam splashed over the dusty, hard-side case hidden inside the niche. He cleared another cinder block, then withdrew the case. After carefully replacing the cinder blocks, he crawled back toward the small door, smoothing away his tracks as he went.

Back in the finished area of his basement, he closed the door, then meticulously, precisely replaced his painting supplies and easel. Placing the case atop the wet bar, he then moistened a towel and wiped away the dust, fastidiously digging his thumbnail into the case's trim, locks, and hinges to remove the deep, ground-in dirt. The combination locks on each latch were stiff, but he got them to move. Then he popped the case open and revealed what lay within.

It lay in easily reassembled pieces for innocuous transport. At its heart, it was a Springfield M21, chambered in a standard 7.62x51mm NATO round, but had been customized to fit his physical size and exacting specifications. Advancements had been made in sniper technology since the M21's introduction during the Vietnam War, but this was still his baby—Long Tooth, he called it. He knew its unique personality like his own flesh, like a concert musician knew his instrument. He had earned the British Armed Forces Queen of Battle Medal for his skills.

The world would be shocked—especially his longtime neighbors here in quiet, staid suburbia—to know the full truth of all who had met their Maker in the reticle of its scope. They did not know of the Wolfhound, but if they did, his return to the chessboard would cause sleepless nights in the halls of power.

He spent the next hour cleaning and oiling the barrel, the action, polishing the lenses of the scope, re-familiarizing himself with its heft, its contours, like a lover many years absent. He caught himself smiling several times.

Upstairs, the front door opened and closed, putting him instantly on alert. His watch told him it was likely his wife coming home from a tennis match with one of her friends. The thump of her duffel bag near the door, her soft step in the hallway above his head, a tread he knew perfectly after so many years of marriage.

He relaxed and finished his preparations. After putting away his cleaning supplies, he lifted the butt of the stock to his lips and kissed the emblem embedded in the butt plate. From it came the strength to reinvigorate his efforts after all this time. He placed Long Tooth carefully back into its foam bed, then locked up the case.

The basement stairs did not creak under his tread, nor did the hardwood floor of the hallway as he approached the kitchen. In the bedroom, the sound of the shower from the master bath emanated through the cracked door. He dragged his go bag from under the bed, a waterproof duffel containing everything he needed to go dark, to go anywhere in the world at a moment's notice. He unzipped it and checked the contents: a burner phone and a satellite phone, both fully charged, fake identity papers and passports, a SIG-Sauer P226 9mm with three magazines and a silencer, combat knife, waterproof maps, a Leatherman multi-tool, lock picks, compass, 10x42 HD binoculars, duct tape, super-bright LED headlamp, pantyhose in three different shades, bundles of US dollars, British pounds sterling, euros, a first-aid kit, spare eyeglasses, a bottle of water, the rosary of dried cherry-fruit beads presented to him by Pope Pius XII, and his various medications.

He spread it all out on the bed, cataloging, going through the mnemonics of his long-memorized mental checklist.

The bathroom door opened, and his wife stood there in the steam, wearing her chenille bathrobe, hair in a towel. Her eyes widened, and she gripped the doorjamb to steady herself.

"Again?" she said.

"It's long past time," he said.

"Where are you going?"

"You know I can't tell you that."

For long moments, they watched each other. The surprise in her eyes shifted quickly to something else.

"Take me with you," she said. "It would be just like old times." Her posture shifted to one of provocative allure. For a moment, he imagined her in her old TWA stewardess uniform, like in the old days, the halcyon days of global cat and mouse, a life on the bleeding edge, a life of danger and passion, when the stakes couldn't have been higher.

"What?" she said, finally.

He gave her a smirk. "You could still wear that old uniform."

"Shut up and take me with you." Her own go bag was under her side of the bed.

He repacked everything, sensing her emotions throbbing from across the room. Then he crossed the room and kissed her like he used to, stirring up memories and sensations long since settled into the sediment in the dark depths of his soul.

Then he snatched up the bag, the case, and left. The Wolfhound had hunting to do.

PART II

"I'm for truth, no matter who tells it. I'm for justice, no matter who it's for or against." - **Malcolm X**

CHAPTER 13

"**WITH CHORES OR PUNISHMENT**, *my dad treated us like prisoners. He always inspected your work and always made you redo the task until it met with his divine satisfaction.*

"One of the weekly chores my brother and I had was to clean all three toilets in the house. I was responsible for the basement toilet my brother and I shared. If you can imagine the urine stains from two young boys...

"He would make me scrub the linoleum with a toothbrush and soap and water, on my ass constantly about putting in more elbow grease like a fucking drill sergeant. I would get down on my hands and knees to scrub the floor. I had to make sure I circumnavigated the entire base of the porcelain toilet. I even pulled off the two white plastic caps that concealed the nuts and bolts securing the toilet to the floor, making sure there was no 'hidden' urine. Every crevice had to be scrubbed and spit shined. If I missed any, I was fucked.

"After more than an hour on my hands and knees, I would walk through the house looking for him, as we were never allowed to call out to him, to come and physically inspect my work. He would bring a powerful flashlight and a small putty knife and ask me, 'Is this toilet clean enough to eat off of?'

"When I answered, 'Yes, sir,' he would commence the inspection. He poked around with his flashlight and putty knife, scraping the base of the toilet like some bizarre dentist, my own Dr. Christian Szell. He always, always found discolorations on the porcelain or other kinds of 'dark matter.'

"Then he would explode at me, calling me 'incompetent,' 'a liar,' 'a fraud.' He would threaten to beat me or lock me in my bedroom if I 'continued to waste his time.' My own Great Fucking Santini.

"There were many times he made me eat my dinner off the toilet seat or the toilet floor.

"Eventually, by the second or third inspection, he would express his disappointment in my abilities to perform simple tasks and tell me I was worthless, incapable, and would amount to nothing.

"As I got older, I can't tell you how many times I fantasized about drowning him in that fucking toilet, shoving his face into that water, hearing him gurgle and splash..."

"Those are violent thoughts for a young boy."

"You don't know the half of it. I was practically counting the days until I was big enough to take him. I didn't even care that I would probably go to jail."

***

Marie had not visited Rome in years, not since her and Trey's honeymoon. She waited for him at O'Hare International Airport with a volatile mix of excitement and trepidation swirling in her gut. She thrilled at the thought of accompanying Trey on another of his investigations like she had before the girls were born, even if it were only peripherally. Parenthood had curtailed many of the activities they used to enjoy together, especially the globetrotting, so it felt good to enjoy some of that again after so long.

The threat of that electronic voice, however, still lurked behind every other thought, like an oil slick at night.

But this was *Roma*, where the culinary delights were boundless, where the wine was legendary, where she could choose any given street corner and spend hours lost in the lines and curves of its ancient architecture.

Her parents had been surprised but delighted at keeping the girls for a few days. At hearing the news, Annie and Lauren had both given her the kind of stricken looks and stink-eye that would haunt Marie for the length of the trip, but this would be a great opportunity for her and Trey to behave like newlyweds again, unencumbered by the demands of daily life with children. The ruts of adulthood ground deep, and she needed to break free of them, get a fresh perspective on life.

She sat near a coffee counter in O'Hare's main terminal, awaiting Trey's arrival from LAX. Tonight, they would take a red-eye and arrive at Leonardo da Vinci Airport in Rome in time for lunch.

After she told him about the threatening phone call, he would divulge no further details about the whys and wherefores of the trip. Someone could be tapping their phones, he said. He often walked the line of paranoia, thanks to a seriously shitty childhood, but this was an unfamiliar extreme, even for him. Not that she could entirely blame him. She hoped he could keep the PTSD under control. When caught in its throes, he wasn't much fun.

In fact, his heightened sense of alertness had rubbed off on her.

She found herself paying extra close attention to everyone around her. The woman with the e-book reader. The old man with the newspaper. The yuppie in the suit entranced by her phone. The thirty-something man she had caught looking at her three times. That one seemed most suspicious to her.

She still garnered male attention, even now in her mid-forties, but this seemed more nefarious. The man had a glint in his eye she did not care for, a surreptitious tension.

Finishing her decaf, she went to check the Arrivals board for Trey's flight. It was due in about half an hour, so she made her way to his gate. Until today, it had never occurred to her to sit with her back to the wall and give herself the widest field of view, but that's exactly what she did, sitting so she could see the gate. This late in the day, the crowd was a mix of Italians returning home and tourists from America or transiting at O'Hare from other countries.

Some of the best people-watching anywhere could be found at the airport. Nowhere else was the diversity of humanity on such full display.

Then, at Trey's gate, she spotted the weirdo from the coffee counter. He sat down across the rows of seated travelers from her, sipped his coffee, and read his newspaper. Did thirty-somethings even read newspapers anymore? Weren't they slaves to their screens?

For several minutes, she watched him with her peripheral vision. He did not look up from his paper.

On a lark, she pulled out her phone and Googled "How to Spot a Tail," surprised to find a number of substantive articles from "ex-intelligence specialists." Unfortunately, most of the articles were for driving. Such a strange sensation, to feel she had stepped unexpectedly into another world, where nothing was exactly as it seemed. She surfed into strange Web territory, discovering all sorts of articles on surveillance, both performing and avoiding, and catalogs of strange espionage equipment like she'd only seen in movies.

After a couple of minutes of being engrossed in an article on long-distance microphones, she noticed the weirdo was gone.

Was she imagining things? Was she being stupid? Or should she trust her gut as Trey always told her? How was she to know the difference between instinct and paranoia? Crazy people were *absolutely certain* they were right.

The arrival of Trey's plane at the gate prevented her mental spiral from picking up speed. Warmth and anticipation suffused her. Oh, was that guy going to get walloped with a kiss.

A burst of playfulness prompted her to hide out of sight of the jetway exit and wait for him to wander past. Every disembarking passenger cranked up her excitement, until, when he finally appeared, she couldn't restrain her devilish grin.

She landed on his back like a sack of potatoes, throwing her arms around his shoulders, driving a cry of surprise from him, chortling maniacally as he spun and staggered. A delicious jolt of fear shot through him initially. Bystanders stared, some of them cracking smiles of amusement, others shocked at behavior so unbecoming two middle-aged adults. But then he realized the identity of his attacker and started laughing. Soon, the play morphed into passionate reunion.

"Were you scared?" she said.

"Terrified. Until I realized the Bad Guys probably wouldn't stage a hit at the airport in broad daylight."

"Are you saying I'm a bad Bad Guy?"

"You are utterly inept at being Bad."

She gave him another diabolical smirk. "Don't underestimate me, *Mister* Bond. I'll show you later what a Bond Girl is capable of."

He laughed. "Not if I show you first."

They kissed and hugged again. Then he said, "Show me to wine, dear lady, it's been a day."

They had time to grab a sit-down dinner before the red-eye to Italy, so they found a stylish wine bar, took a table in a quiet corner, ordered a few small plates of food to share and a wonderful bottle of Orin Swift Cellars Mercury Head Cabernet Sauvignon. The wine proved to be an intense, deep garnet-purple, colored with a nose filled with ripe berries and warm plums, with hints of tobacco, dark chocolate and lavender. Then he leaned in close and told her everything. He had given her many details over the course of the last week, but hearing all about the case now, embellished and almost with footnotes, filled her with amazement at the sheer audacity of it.

She said, "It's almost like they're daring you to catch them."

Trey nodded, holding something back and hoping she wouldn't notice. He may as well have been holding up a sign that said as much.

She always had to remind him never to play poker against her. "Is that everything?"

He wouldn't meet her eye. "Sure, why?"

"There's something you're not telling me."

He hesitated, then said, "Just...more nightmares, is all. Nothing new."

"Oh, Boo. Any idea why they've come back?"

Shrugging, he said, "Something about this case, I presume."

While he was speaking, she had been watching for the weirdo from before. Should she tell Trey about him? She wasn't sure, didn't want to risk exposing what might just be her own silliness.

"So why Rome?" she said.

"Specifically, the Vatican. Cahill is a devout Catholic. He's given so much money to the Church, he was granted a private audience with the Pope."

Her eyebrows rose at that.

"Yes, really," he said. "The Church's history with stolen works of art is less than stellar. Art looted from the Jews in World War II has been discovered in Vatican vaults. There might well be someone at the Vatican who would be willing to hide Cahill's 'stolen' paintings. Given his financial situation, he might be looking to double-dip a lawsuit settlement *and* sell the paintings."

"So, what do you need me to do while we're there?"

He tried to hide the fluctuations of worry, necessity, and protectiveness on his face, but she knew him too well. "First of all, I'm hoping I'm being a little over-anxious, and we can just go to Rome and have a wonderful time, like a second honeymoon. In between bouts of work, anyway. On the other hand..."

"On the other hand, you want me to keep my eyes open, watch your back."

He swallowed hard, the guilt writ large on his face that he might be putting her in danger. "There's no one else I trust," he said finally, his voice quiet.

She twined her fingers in his hair, looked deep into his eyes, and said, "Where you go, I go." Then she kissed him.

"Thanks," he said, eyes brimming with sincerity.

"Just keep a water bucket handy."

"For what?"

"In case the credit card catches fire. I'm going shoe shopping."

CHAPTER 14

"*FATHER ALAMEDA AND FATHER HARRINGTON were the two Catholic priests assigned to St. Mary's Catholic Church when I was growing up. Okie tried to impress upon me the importance of the Latin Mass and the Jesuit sense of service and duty.*

"*I attended parochial school from fourth grade through eighth grade. I was pulled into being an altar boy and serving Mass in the traditional Latin. It was hypnotic and mind-altering, with the burning incense and chanting.*

"*Even then, I felt as if I was being groomed for a particular kind of life. In eighth grade at St. Mary's Catholic School, I was promoted to Head Altar Boy. I was responsible for scheduling all of the altar boys for weddings and funerals. It was a* huge *money-maker for me. It was also the time in my life when I had the most 'friends,' as every boy wanted to cash in on the Catholic tradition of tipping the altar boys and the priests following a weekly wedding Mass or a funeral Mass. Tax-free cash.*

"*I remember after every Mass, the altar boys dressed in their white robes with braided cotton juvenile cinctures with distinctive knots, ritually kneeling in the priest's sanctuary, hands folded, waiting for the priest to bless us and place his hands upon our heads. The priests would lean in while placing their cupped hands upon my head, and the crotch of their pants would be pressed into my face. It was enough to make you gag and despise the Church."*

"Did any of them ever abuse you more flagrantly?"

"Not that I recall, but we've already uncovered all kinds of shit I didn't remember. Anything is possible.

"Anyway, while in high school my parents were trying to convince me to attend the College of the Holy Cross, like Emmett and Okie had. I was so upset, telling my mother I did not want to go to Holy Cross and become a Jesuit priest. I loved women. I would never say this to her out loud—that would have been my death warrant—but I wanted pussy. I wanted to marry a woman, not God.

"As a compromise, I was sent to the University of San Diego, a very fine Catholic university with a diocesan parish separating the men's dormitories from the women's. Shame-based architecture and campus planning."

***

Sunrise over the Mediterranean at 35,000 feet was the stuff of celestial beauty, even for the bleary eyed and exhausted. Coming all the way from LA to Rome in one day taxed even Trey's well-maintained tolerance for travel. He let Marie continue to snore quietly against his shoulder and simply let the golden dawn pour over his face, turning the sea into a rippling plain of gold, scattered wisps of cottony cloud fringed by shadow. It was the kind of beauty that inspired belief in the divine. More often than not, however, Trey saw only the shadows. His job was to plumb the shadows, dig through muck, and uncover the truth. But the deeper the shadows and muck, the greater the chance they hid things that could hurt him, like stepping into river mud full of barbed wire, broken glass, and rusty nails.

As soon as the plane touched down at Leonard da Vinci-Fiumicino Airport, Trey turned on his iPhone and checked his email, where he found a new message from Nicklaus. True to prediction, the trace on the threatening phone call turned up what was likely a burner phone, from which only one call had ever been made. Most likely, that phone now lay in carefully shattered pieces.

Marie stretched and rubbed her face as the plane taxied to the gate.

He had slept little on the flight, his mind churning with worries over the lawsuit, concerns over the fate of the paintings, and anger about the brazen legal thuggery of Cahill's lawyer. He wanted nothing less than to see them all crucified by a judge and jury and slammed into federal prison for the maximum sentence. The deeper the fatigue settled in, the easier it became for him to chide himself and forget that he was accompanying a beautiful woman to one of the most romantic cities on the planet. It was a gorgeous, sunny day, seventy-five degrees, perfect for enjoying a city with thousands of years of recorded history. Yet his mind felt like a shriveled fruit, forgotten in the back of the refrigerator.

He walked into a toilet in the terminal, and one look paralyzed him. He should have been more prepared for the sudden tightening of his throat and shoulders, the tremor in his hands. The toilet had not been cleaned in hours. Sodden paper towels and bits of shredded toilet paper spilled over the lip of the trash can and onto the floor. The counter top around the sinks was inundated with water. Men flowed in and out of the restroom as he stood incapacitated.

Usually he could overcome this urge, but not today. Too many stressors in succession had formed an avalanche that his usual coping skills could not avoid. He slowly refocused and grabbed a handful of towels from the dispenser and set about cleaning the airport toilet. He meticulously wiped down the counters, the sinks, the fixtures, even the floor. He flushed all the toilets and urinals, wiped all the seats—the ones that were present—picked up every scrap of soggy paper and stuffed it all deep into the trash can, packing it tight. Fellow male travelers continued to give him strange looks, but he ignored them. He would not be able to comfortably urinate until he was finished.

Marie was dozing, mouth open, in a nearby chair, when he came out forty-five minutes later. He said her name as he approached. She wiped her face and gave him a mixed look of annoyance and pity.

"Sorry," he said.

She sighed deeply, got up, and took him by the arm.

Their luggage was the last on the carousel. He still couldn't shake the sense of imminent danger. A wave of self-doubt washed over him, foaming with self-recrimination, ebbing and flowing over him. Somewhere on the fringes of his psyche, a riptide of paralyzing fear waited for him to stumble into it. What was he doing here? Did he expect to waltz into the Vatican, demand an audience with the Pontiff, and ask if they'd fenced any paintings recently?

Marie slipped him a few surreptitious caresses and outright gropes to lighten his mood. The best he could do was give her a wan smile.

In the back of the black Mercedes sedan on the way to the hotel, he let himself slip deeper into the mental fugue, hoping to find some rest there, and caught himself dozing once, head resting against the window framing the Roman cityscape.

He roused himself when the chauffeur turned finally into the Borgo district, a *rione* that went all the way back to Roman times. It was here Emperor Caligula had built a circus, later enlarged by Nero. It was on this land St. Peter had been martyred. Its name had been a Gothic bastardization of *borough*, brought by the Germanic invaders who settled here. Bordered by St. Peter's Square in Vatican City on the west and the Tiber River to the east, it occupied a strategic point for Trey's investigation, easy walking distance to Vatican City itself.

The streets grew narrower, older, and the sky shrank to a cerulean strip above a cobbled canyon of shadow.

Vicolo delle Palline was a one-way street wide enough for one car, but half of it was occupied by postage-stamp-sized parking spaces hugging the building façades. Anyone stepping out of their front door would be wise to look both ways or risk getting flattened. Nevertheless, it carried the kind of charm to which no American city could aspire for centuries.

The driver stopped at the front door of the Hotel Bramante, a single-arched doorway mirroring the colossal arches that built Rome. The hotel was a three-story building, the façade painted a creamy custard yellow with chestnut-brown wooden shutters. Originally built in the fourteenth century as a pilgrims' guesthouse, the hotel was a fifteen-minute walk from the Sistine Chapel and Vatican Museum, circling the walled enclosure of Vatican City.

Just ahead of the vehicle was an arch that opened onto the Via dei Corridori, a broad thoroughfare flanking a crenelated fortification. The fortification was the Vatican Corridor, also known as the Passetto, leading half a mile straight from the Vatican Palace to the Castel Sant'Angelo, an escape route for the pope built in the thirteenth century. Construction of the wall dated back to 850 CE, with its current form built in 1277. Pope Alexander VI finished the wall in 1492—and just in the nick of time. He used it to flee the invading French two years later. The most recent papal escape was in 1527, when Clement VII evaded the twenty thousand mutinous troops of Charles V. Said troops went on to sack the entire city in true medieval style, slaughtering most of the Swiss Guard on the steps of St. Peter's Basilica, along with thousands of women and children.

It was the weight of these historical events that lent gravity to the paintings Francis X. Cahill was trying to use for personal profit and redemption. The pettiness, the banality of the fraud, set Trey's teeth on edge, and helped dispel the malaise that had settled into him since the flight.

Hotel Bramante was a fourth-generation establishment. Trey and Marie had fallen in love with it on their honeymoon, and he had stayed here on every subsequent business trip to Rome. An array of waist-high, potted bushes surrounded the entrance.

When they walked in, Maurizio, the owner, greeted them at the entrance, arms raised, grinning as if they were long-lost friends. Maurizio was the quintessential Roman innkeeper, swarthy, cultured, affable, gregarious in a way only Italians could be.

The lobby was cozily appointed, elegant, homey. A black cat, Nikita, watched them with half-lidded eyes from its perch near a potted plant in the front window sill.

Maurizio said in Italian, "Welcome, welcome, my friends! Signore e Signora Hansen, it has been too long." He motioned to their luggage and gave each of them an energetic handshake. "There are still pastries left from breakfast. You must be hungry after your travel."

Trey, who had been limbering up his Italian on the flight, thanked him. "*Grazie. Siamo molte affamati.*" *We are very hungry.* Trey's understanding of Italian was better than his ability to produce it.

Maurizio grinned. "We will bring you something, while you rest and get comfortable."

Their newly constructed ground-floor room, *Camera 30,* was as nicely decorated as the lobby, with a brilliant red bedspread, an overstuffed sofa striped in red and beige. He requested this room every time he came to Rome, enjoying its spaciousness. Everything was perfect, the pictures square, the lamps properly positioned. The room had a unique eighteen-foot ceiling with exposed wooden beams and windows overlooking Vicolo delle Palline. The room had semi-private access to a little-known library and sitting area off the outside garden, patio, and dining room.

Marie laughed and threw herself onto the bed, stretching languorously, catching his eye in a way that dispelled the grim fog in his brain. She was still a supremely beautiful woman, a feast of alluring curves, Marilyn Monroe reincarnated. The sumptuous romance of it all bloomed, and he came to her on the bed, and kissed her, and they grinned at each other like love-struck teenagers.

***

As they lay entwined on the bed, half-dozing, a quiet knock on the door came, along with a voice that said, "Something for you to eat."

When Trey opened the door in a Hotel Bramante honeycomb bathrobe, he found a tray of delectable foods—strawberry tart, two custard-filled *bomboloni*, ham and cheese croissants, and a carafe of hot water for tea. He brought those inside, and they nibbled, sipped, and tried to shake off the travel fatigue enough to feel human. A shower helped reinvigorate his sluggish mind.

They had a real lunch at the *ristorante* they loved, Ristochicco, around the corner from Hotel Bramante. Delicious smells of fresh bread, garlic, herbs, and coffee permeated the air all the way out into the street. The interior of the place felt like an ancient stone passageway, with its arched stone ceiling and dim lighting, the kind of Old World atmosphere America would never manage. He always appreciated the meticulously folded napkins and the beautiful turquoise tablecloths of the subterranean dining area. In the subdued lighting, Marie's eyes glowed with pleasure.

As they held hands across the table, he couldn't help but imagine what might have happened between them if they'd met in younger years. He had left a string of terrible relationships behind him, including two failed marriages. She had also escaped a toxic relationship, thankfully lacking children to chain her to an unambitious sports addict who did not appreciate a driven, professional woman. If she and Trey had met in their twenties, would they have recognized each other as kindred spirits?

While they waited for their food, he dialed his number-one contact in Rome, Alessandro Vasari.

Marie gave him a half-pout. "Work already?"

"Sorry, Boo. The clock is ticking."

Vasari's throaty baritone came through in the voicemail greeting.

Trey said, "Alessandro, this is Trey Hansen. I'm in Rome on a huge case, and I could use your help. Let's meet and talk as soon as possible." Trey didn't worry about speaking Italian, as Vasari was married to a British art scholar, so his English was impeccable.

"Who is this guy again?" Marie said.

"The director of an international art transportation company favored by the Vatican Museum. I worked with him on moving those Hittite artifacts last year."

Transporting art, especially internationally, was an incredibly exacting endeavor. No one wanted to see a centuries-old painting or sculpture damaged, and nothing was more likely to cause damage than moving something. A fine art underwriter's greatest risk was always transit. Vasari's firm handled much of the art entering and leaving Italy. He might well have gotten wind of two Italian paintings entering the country. If he didn't, he could ask around. Due to the nature of Italian business, Trey suspected Vasari might have had connections with the Mafia, however ethical he might be otherwise.

"Ah, that guy," Marie said.

Their favorite waiter, sommelier and owner, Alexander, arrived with their food. Trey and Marie loved to share the fresh, local *burrata* cheese with vine-ripened tomato slices and organic basil followed by homemade *cacao e pepe*. A bottle of 2013 San Felice Poggio Rosso Gran Selezione Chianti Classico was presented to Trey. He motioned that Marie should approve the wine.

As they ate, Trey noticed a man watching them from a corner table, sipping an espresso. His short-hairs spiked. He stopped eating and stared at the man. The man turned his attention to his newspaper, *la Repubblica*.

Trey stared at the man for several more moments, a challenge.

"What is it?" Marie said.

"Somebody staring." American tourists were hardly unusual this close to Vatican City.

Marie's mouth stopped in mid-chew, and something passed over her face, too quickly for him to grasp.

INTERLUDE – KNIGHT'S TOUR

TRANSPORTING WEAPONS internationally was child's play if one knew the cracks in airport security and the right connections. The Wolfhound knew both.

He checked into the Hotel Columbus in the evening. He did not choose it for its charm or comfort. Such concepts were distractions from the work. He chose it for its unobstructed view of St. Peter's Basilica, which lay only five hundred yards away. Even dead drunk, he could make such a shot.

Fronting the Via della Conciliazione, which was still alive with tourists, Hotel Columbus was the perfect vantage point. Via della Conciliazione was a three-lane paved thoroughfare leading straight into the heart of the Catholic Church. A shudder went through him, knowing he was so close to the spot where St. Peter had been crucified and asked to be inverted so as to not shame his Lord's crucifixion. Peter knew he was part of something larger than himself, an instrument in a greater plan, as did the Wolfhound.

Tennyson's "Ulysses" came back to him, a poem he had been thinking about a great deal lately. It rang so true for him he'd memorized it.

For always roaming with a hungry heart
Much have I seen and known—cities of men
And manners, climates, councils, governments,
Myself not least, but honoured of them all—
And drunk delight of battle with my peers,
Far on the ringing plains of windy Troy,
I am a part of all that I have met;
Yet all experience is an arch wherethrough
Gleams that untravelled world, whose margin fades
For ever and for ever when I move.
How dull it is to pause, to make an end,
To rust unburnished, not to shine in use!
As though to breathe were life!

After many years drunk with delight, honored by councils and governments, the Wolfhound had had too many years now of simply breathing. Now, once again, he would shine in use.

He had requested a room on the second floor of the hotel. Out of old habit, he flipped on the television and turned up the volume to provide background noise. He was so far out in the weeds, operationally speaking, no one would see him coming, so he didn't expect his room would be bugged, but it was best to obey the old training in tradecraft. He hadn't lived this long by allowing sloppiness in *any* aspect of his life.

A hundred yards away, across the buildings between Via della Conciliazione and Via dei Corridori, lay the Hotel Bramante, where he'd stayed many years ago, when Pope Pius XII had presented him with the rosary he now carried in his pocket. He pulled the rosary out, knelt beside the bed, and prayed.

At 3:13 a.m., he stole out of his room and walked the empty hallways, memorizing layout, distances, corners. The stairway to the roof was guarded by an old, rusty door. The shiny modern lock, however, still yielded to his picks with only a few moments' work. From there, he was free to climb to the roof and walk the narrow parapet along its peak. He took note of an area of the roof where some repair work was in progress, between the optimal position and the narrow doorway leading back down inside.

The four-story hotel, with a fifth storied campanile, partially encircled a well-manicured garden behind him. It was this garden his room overlooked, a quiet drop to the ground in case he needed a quick escape.

The optimal position would be the corner of the campanile roof peak, as it gave the widest view and shielded him from the ground. He pulled out his binoculars and scanned the area for points of potential complication.

It was a cool, quiet night, glittering with lights and possibilities.

CHAPTER 15

"WHEN I WAS nine years old, I set the swim club record for the fifty-yard breaststroke at 50.1 seconds. The record stood for more than thirty years until it was replaced by a time of 50.0 seconds. The same summer, we traveled to Sarasota, Florida, to visit my Nana and her husband, Papa Gene. My Nana owned and managed the Sara Sands Motel on the famous Tamiami Trail near Lido Beach.

"Nana lived on-site and set our family up with two motel rooms, one for Okie and Honey, and one for us kids. There was an in-ground swimming pool in the center of the motel complex. On the first morning after our arrival, we five plus my Nana were walking from our rooms to the swimming pool. We were given orders to stay together and stay out of the pool. I ran ahead and threw off my T-shirt and towel and jumped into the deep end.

"I have no memory of this. My sister told me this story when I was in my twenties. But apparently, I sank to the bottom of the pool and did not come up. The only person sitting at the pool was a man wearing sunglasses, smoking Pall Mall cigarettes, and reading the Washington Post. I was told he dove into the pool, pulled me to the surface, unconscious, and laid me out on the pool deck. He was performing CPR when my parents got there. Again, I have no memory."

"Why do you think you did this?"

"I've asked myself that for years. I think I was intending to commit suicide. At age nine, I was a successful competitive swimmer, but I just wanted to die. I was sick of the lies, the deceit, and the lack of parental love and guidance. I wanted a release from the environment that tormented me, confined me, and overwhelmed me. I wanted to punish Okie and Honey, and maybe through my death my siblings would be released from their bondage and servitude.

"I wonder about the mysterious man stationed at the motel swimming pool. I think he might have been a sentry, maybe even a bodyguard. Mary told me his dark Ray-Ban Wayfarer sunglasses and Macora Cuban-style fedora made him look like James Bond.

"Okie demanded control to the point I could not even kill myself, release myself. I was his prisoner. I would always be his prisoner."

***

Trey and Marie fought through their jet lag and spent the rest of the day enjoying the beautiful weather and the beautiful city. Passing through scents of espresso and cappuccino helped invigorate them. They especially loved the fresh water flowing from the Alps into the city from 2,500 public fountains.

Most of the roads of Rome had been paved in the nineteenth century with quarried granite setts, also known as Belgium block, relatively even and roughly rectangular stones laid flat in regular patterns. The difference between walking on setts versus asphalt road or concrete was stark, and by evening Trey's feet were sore. Nevertheless, he didn't let this minor discomfort distract him from the woman who had somehow, by some miracle, chosen to spend her life with him. They held hands, at times walking arm-in-arm like college kids.

People walked everywhere in Rome, and so did Trey and Marie.

Their first destination was the closest, the obelisk in St. Peter's Square. The obelisk stood twenty-five and a half meters tall, weighing roughly three hundred twenty-six tons. Legend had it that the bronze globe once attached to its apex, now housed in the Capitoline Museums, once held the ashes of Julius Caesar. It was brought to this spot in the late sixteenth century by Pope Sixtus V, an engineering feat so huge even Michelangelo was skeptical, an ironic testament to how much engineering knowledge had been lost in the fall of Rome, considering that the Emperor Caligula had transported the obelisk from Egypt in 37 CE on a specially built, four-hundred-ton barge. In the sixteenth century, nine hundred men and hundreds more horses took four months to move it three hundred meters from its original placement on Caligula's circus. Such an astonishing feat it was that a fresco of the method was painted in the Vatican Library.

Trey loved "geeking out" about such things. It was not only his stock in trade; it was his passion.

From there they crossed the River Tiber to Trey's favorite locale in Rome, Piazza Navona. Once the site of the Stadium of Domitian, it had hosted innumerable chariot races and sporting events. The original stadium collapsed during the Middle Ages, but the games continued, including jousting tournaments during the Age of Chivalry, and later, during the Renaissance, bullfights. It was as if the spirit of revelry and competition lay embedded in the earth, forming a natural place for such events, even those separated by centuries and the rise and fall of empires. Nowadays, it was a place of relaxation and amusement, a place of peddlers, musicians, artists, but Piazza Navona still held the shape of the original stadium. Some of the stadium's structures were still visible, embedded in younger buildings.

The piazza had three fountains, the smaller two dedicated to Neptune and to a Moor, but neither of these could compare to the one in the center, the Fontana dei Quattro Fiumi. The Fountain of the Four Rivers depicted gods of the four great rivers in the four continents then recognized by the Renaissance geographers: the Nile in Africa, the Ganges in Asia, the Danube in Europe, and the Rio de la Plata in South America. Exotic beasts emerged from caves and rocks to drink. One of the most fantastic pieces of Baroque sculpture in existence, the fountain was Gian Lorenzo Bernini's masterpiece, created in 1651 for Pope Innocent X. The obelisk gracing the center of the fountain was taken from the Temple of Isis in Egypt.

Modern Piazza Navona was one of the greatest concentrations of artistic and architectural beauty on the planet, every building a breathtaking work of art. Here was one of the great embodiments of what humankind could achieve, a place of thriving humanity. The façade of St. Agnese in Agone, the Palazzo Pamphili, the fifteenth-century church of Nostra Signora del Sacro Cuore. The Palazzo Braschi and Palazzo Lancellotti.

Trey and Marie spent an hour walking up and down the square, pausing on the stone benches, lost in their own unique admirations.

As evening approached, golden sunlight bathed the ancient city, and the sky turned a breathtaking cerulean blue swirling with precision swarms of swallows. *Sciami di rondini.*

Trey's phone rang. Annoyance flashed through him at the interruption, but no doubt it would be important. He gave Marie an apologetic look. As he answered it, she gave him a sigh and a nod of acceptance.

He recognized Alessandro Vasari's voice immediately. "Trey, my friend! So wonderful to hear from you."

"Likewise, Alessandro. It is great to be back in Rome again."

They spent a few minutes talking about family and life, as it felt a bit rude to jump straight into business, no matter how pressing. Vasari's wife and children were in England on one of her research trips and visiting her family in London. He pined for them terribly.

Finally, Alessandro said, "Tell me about this huge case. How can I help you?"

Trey told him about the paintings, about Francis Cahill, about how it was clearly a case of fraud, and about how finding the paintings would turn Cahill's bad faith lawsuit into so much toilet paper. Trey really was concerned about the fate of the paintings.

Piero di Cosimo (1462–1522), sometimes known as Piero di Lorenzo, was born in Florence and apprenticed under the artist Cosimo Rosselli, from whom he derived his popular name. He assisted Rosselli in the painting of the Sistine Chapel in 1481.

Michelangelo Merisi da Caravaggio (1571–1610) painted scenes from the life of St. Matthew the Evangelist in the Contarelli Chapel located in the French church, San Luigi dei Francesi, around the corner from Piazza Navona. From 1599 to 1602, Caravaggio painted three oil-on-canvas paintings, *The Calling of Saint Matthew*, *The Martyrdom of Saint Matthew*, and *The Inspiration of Saint Matthew*. In Rome lay the footprints of those long-ago masters, and here the responsibility to see justice done felt even stronger.

Vasari listened intently, and when Trey was finished, stayed quiet for a length of time that left Trey uncomfortable. Finally, Vasari said, "Let us meet tomorrow and discuss your case. You rise early, yes?"

"Yes."

"Breakfast at the Hotel Bramante? Seven o'clock? Everything is freshest then as everyone knows that Loredana and Maurizio bake the breads and tarts, from scratch, the night before."

"See you then. *Adomani*."

***

The breakfast buffet at Hotel Bramante was legendary, with a plethora of fresh juices, cereals, hard-boiled quail eggs, and the finest Italian meats with local handmade *burrata* cheese. The espresso machine was robin's-egg blue and the size of a go-cart. The breakfast room looked out through the floor-to-ceiling glass window and door onto the private courtyard reserved for Trey and Alessandro. The air was redolent with the aromas of espresso and fresh-baked bread.

Vasari had changed little in the couple of years since Trey had last seen him during the Pushkin State Museum of Fine Arts case. Vasari was still quintessentially Italian, with a broad, genuine smile, sparkling eyes, and a full head of dark, wavy hair. Trey had traveled to Moscow, at the request of Nicklaus Palmer, to investigate the mysterious transit damage to a rare Rembrandt oil on canvas lent by the Pushkin Museum to the Vatican Museum. Vasari's company was not the fine art shipping company engaged by the lending institution; however, Vasari was Trey's expert in the subrogation and recovery of monies paid by Lloyd's of London for the insurance claim, including a monetary calculation for diminution in value post-conservation.

After the niceties and the arrival of a much-needed triple espresso, Vasari leaned forward in his chair and lowered his voice. "I made some phone calls last night, after we talked. Your man Cahill was in Rome just over a week ago."

"That I already know," Trey said. "I suspect he was looking for a buyer for two major art pieces, or at the very least a place to hide them."

"The Caravaggio is over two meters tall, yes?"

Trey nodded.

"Difficult to transport a painting of that size."

"I figure if a painting of that size came to Italy, you would know. Or if it came to the Vatican." The confidence in Trey's voice he intended as a compliment, but Vasari didn't acknowledge it. Instead he looked thoughtful, and some of his earlier affability had dissipated.

Vasari was a devout Catholic, but Trey knew he was not blind to the irregularities in the Church's behavior, nor to the stains of blood and deception on its history. Such failures pained him. "I have been doing contract work for the Vatican more and more. Always art coming and going. They have huge collections."

"So huge that two stolen paintings might go unnoticed," Trey said.

A pained expression flashed across Vasari's face. "You are no doubt correct, my friend."

The reluctance on Vasari's face, which was usually so open and readable, told Trey he could not ask too much. Their relationship was cordial and well established, but not so close Vasari would jeopardize his livelihood. The Vatican would be an extremely lucrative patron to a man like Vasari. They needed valuable objects moved, and he was the man in Rome who knew how to do it, but the Church would certainly seek other services if Vasari ever crossed a line.

"Can you give me some names?" Trey said.

Vasari's gaze fixated on a young mother pushing a stroller, passing in a languid cascade of lithe, tanned legs, gleaming black hair, and a striped dress that hinted at the most provocative details. But this focus of attention on her was more an excuse.

"One name," Trey said. "Who in the Vatican would I talk to if I wanted to sell valuable art to the Church?" He had already told Vasari about his own personal liability in the pending lawsuit, so Vasari knew the stakes. If that knowledge were not enough to open some doors, grease some rails, Trey was not inclined to beg. Finding the precise amount of pressure to apply was so, so tricky.

Finally, Vasari said, "I will talk to some people. If I can, I will give you a name." He raised his hands and added, "No guarantees. I hope you understand."

CHAPTER 16

"MY DAD HAD a chess table set up in the living room, a really beautiful set made of marble and onyx. There were two chairs there, and my dad would sit in one chair and study the table. Once or twice a week, he'd get a letter from someone, I never knew who. Never a return address. But he'd open it up and there would be a drawing of the chessboard with a move on it. He'd make the move, then study the board for a while, plot his response, and send it back. At least presumably.

"He did this for years, game after game.

"I remember one time my brother Patrick moved a couple of pieces. He was maybe eight.

"My dad backhanded him across the living room. 'Don't ever touch that chess table!'"

***

After a light breakfast at Hotel Bramante before Trey's meeting with his business associate Alessandro Vasari, Marie planned her shopping excursion. Her path would take her east past the Castel Sant'Angelo, along the western bank of the River Tiber, and then across the river toward some of the most spectacular shopping

175

locales in the world: Via Condotti, a street filled with boutique shops featuring the world's biggest names in fashion and luxury, like Gucci, Dior, Dolce & Gabbana. Via del Corso, a bustling avenue of designer boutiques, with a wealth of designer shoe stores. Via Vittorio Veneto, featured in Federico Fellini's famous film, *La Dolce Vita*. On this street was found her husband's favorite place to walk into and simply drool—Casuccio e Scalera, one of the greatest shoe stores in the world.

She didn't shop in such places as a general rule—it was too self-indulgent—but a bit of a splurge might be in order. Too often smashed and ground between the demands of motherhood and her status as a professional and a businesswoman, she had too little time to treat herself. Today was going to be her own personal holiday, Marie Day. She would cross paths with Trey later, but until then, there would be a beautiful walk in one of the world's most amazing cities, during which there would be shopping and there would be spa. Oh, yes, there would be those things.

Like Trey, she had had a Catholic upbringing—her brother had gone to the same parochial school as Trey—fortunately not as stringent and abusive as Trey's upbringing, but still, unlearning all that childhood indoctrination had taken her decades. The guilt still lingered sometimes, the subfloor representing what it meant to be a "good Catholic girl." However, she still carried a pleasant sentimentality toward the Church, like an old set of clothes she had outgrown, rather than Trey's raging hatred toward it.

In Rome, a city steeped in almost two millennia of Catholicism, one couldn't escape the Church's presence, its ubiquitous iconography, its architectural influence. It lay like a stratum of culture and influence built into everything, the stones of the street, the buildings, the layout of its ancient avenues.

So, she began her morning excursion with a short sojourn to St. Peter's Square, as it lay only a few hundred yards from the front door of Hotel Bramante.

Already there were throngs of tourists, cameras clicking away with untold gigabytes' worth of photos of the great obelisk at the center, of St. Peter's Basilica on the far side of the immense, oblong colonnade. Priests and cardinals, robes and skullcaps were everywhere, overseen by statues of popes, apostles, and saints.

The splendor and grandeur of it all was overpowering, even though she no longer considered herself a practicing Catholic. In all of it, though, she saw only the works of Man, however magnificent they were. All of this was the culmination of the efforts of ambitious men, not the works of God—and they *were* men, in a culture where women were seen as originators of sin, the cause of Man's downfall.

Screw that.

Nevertheless, the beauty of the architecture drew her attention like a hungry kid in a pâtisserie. It enthralled her, fed her, striking sparks of inspiration and wonder in her architectural mind.

But then something else drew her attention back to the people around her. She had sat down on one of the great iron rails surrounding the central obelisk simply to allow herself to be absorbed into the architecture for a while, but as she looked around, she spotted the man who had been watching them at lunch yesterday, peeking at them over his newspaper. After Trey had pointed him out, she had surreptitiously committed his face to memory. Her emergence from her reverie had caught him watching her, quite frankly. The moment she met his gaze, however, he turned and shuffled off. She watched him for several long moments, the hairs on her arms and the nape of her neck standing straight. He did not shuffle far, but paused, appearing to gaze in appreciation at one of the many statues atop the colonnade. Then he ambled a few paces farther, paused, ambled, paused. Looking like somebody who was trying to look like a tourist.

For several minutes, she watched him. He never looked directly at her again, but his pauses always left him in a position where he could see her with his peripheral vision. He was perhaps fifty yards way, well out of earshot in the busy plaza, when he pulled out his mobile phone and appeared to speak to someone.

Marie waited for a moment when the man's back was fully turned, then she jumped up and darted around the obelisk, inter-posing it between herself and the man. Then she waited, peeking around the corners of the obelisk's twenty-five-foot base, to see if he would follow her.

For five full minutes, she waited and watched, but he did not reappear. When she peeked around the obelisk to find him, she could not.

Tension sprang loose in her shoulders, tension she had not real-ized was there, and she breathed a sigh of relief. Perhaps she was just being foolish. Maybe the man really was just a tourist and *she* was the one acting creepy.

With that exciting escapade fading, it was time to embark upon her shopping excursion. It was a seven-minute walk to Castel Sant'Angelo, but she was no longer in the mood to admire architecture or reflect on her religious upbringing, so she walked on past along the bank of the River Tiber for just under a mile to cross the river, another few hundred meters to the Via del Corso, destination number one on her Legendary Shopping Tour. As she walked, she glanced often over her shoulder, looking for sign of anyone following her.

This vigilance put her brain into such a high gear that the moment she saw the electronics store, it was as if a warning pulsed from the depths of her brain. Smart phones were, in spite of their usefulness, little more than mobile privacy violations. They broadcasted continuously, and she remembered reading a few months ago how easy they were to hack and to track. Their GPS, microphones, and cameras were literally always listening, always watching, and they could be hacked—even when the phone was turned off. If her iPhone had been hacked, if anyone was tracking her—or Trey—the only way to defeat it was to remove the phone's battery, turn it into an expensive brick. Reading all this at the time, she thought it had all seemed crazy, paranoid, too extreme. But now...

The only other way to foil a hack or a track was to put the phone inside a Faraday cage, an enclosure that blocked all incoming and outgoing electromagnetic signals. Europeans seemed much more savvy and aware of electronic and digital privacy concerns, so it was more common here for people to carry their phones in a specially designed Faraday bag. This kind of physical barrier was the surest way to curtail surveillance or hackers.

Five minutes later, she walked out of the electronics store with two cloth pouches, about the size of a clutch. The seller had even shown her how effective they were by putting her phone in one of them, securing the flap, and trying to call her. No call came through. With her phone now invisible and inaccessible to the outside world, she recommenced Marie Day. A tiredness that was fulfilling rather than exhausting washed through her, and she stood a little straighter. Trey was going to love this, too.

Strolling down Via del Corso, one of the world's premier shopping avenues, she passed storefronts for Calvin Klein, Nike, Sephora, and a host of storied names, and she found herself pausing to look into the reflections of the storefront windows, searching for a glimpse of the man in the plaza. Maybe he was too smart to be caught watching her again. What if he were working with others? What if her tail had been switched? More than once she ducked into a store of great prestige only to see if she might be followed inside.

Her heartbeat ran fast, and she found herself sweating, even though the morning air was still pleasantly brisk. She was going to make herself crazy worrying about this.

Then she stepped outside the GAP store, paused to get her bearings, and looked around. Across the street was a priest, mobile phone in his hand with its camera trained on her. Their eyes met. She saw his thumb click the screen for a photo.

And she stood there stunned.

The surprise on the priest's face was evident, surprise he had been caught, but he recovered sooner than her. He pocketed his phone, turned, and hurried around the nearest corner.

It took her several heartbeats to recover from her own surprise, but then she dashed after him. "Hey!"

In moments, she had reached the corner where he had

disappeared. Several dozen yards away, a black-clad figure speed-walked down a narrow side street.

"Hey, there!" she called, and ran after him.

He turned another corner, out of sight.

When she reached that spot, she found a narrow alley almost crowded to nothingness by encroaching buildings, so narrow her shoulders might brush the walls if she walked abreast, and so shadowed it looked like the perfect cliché for an ambush location.

The sensation of ice water dashed down her legs, and her courage failed. Trey did not know where she was. Now was not the time to be stupid.

She backed away from the alley, into the sunlight, and hurried back toward more populated streets. Her shopping excursion was officially over.

CHAPTER 17

"*MY BEDROOM WAS IN the unfinished basement. Okie used his boys as his laborers to frame and drywall the basement. His private office. One bedroom for me and one for Patrick. My bedroom was directly below Okie and Honey. I heard their angry fighting, I heard their love-making, and I heard his footsteps. The footsteps. Like a prison guard pacing up there.*

"*My bedroom had a sliding glass window that led directly to the outdoor basketball court. From my window, at night, I could also see the light reflecting onto the basketball court from their bedroom window above me. I fantasized about escaping from my subterranean cell through my window, which Okie had filled with 'Nixon Now More Than Ever' stickers. Nixon campaign propaganda was all over the house.*

"*Okie had an uncanny ability to hide in the shadows of my room, even when he wasn't there.*"

"*He hid in your room?*"

"*I think so.*"

"*Did you ever see him?*"

"*I don't remember. But at night, I always felt a stranger present in my room but was too scared to get out of bed and investigate. So I hid under the covers and prayed the rosary to calm my nerves. I begged*

God to protect me from the evil that lurked and intimidated me. I made 'deals' with Him. Without prayer, I would have been crippled by Okie's menacing silence."

***

Trey's meeting with Vasari left him disappointed. He had come a long way to talk to Vasari directly, so the lack of forthcoming information forced him to reconsider his next move. He needed to talk to someone in the Vatican, probably someone close to the Vatican Museum. Would his credentials alone grant him an audience with someone who might open up a lead? There was only one way to find out.

He set out from Hotel Bramante toward St. Peter's Square. The entrance to the Vatican Museum lay around the north side of the wall of Vatican City, about a ten-minute walk.

It was a bright, sunny day, populated mostly by tourists as he made his way toward the city within a city. His walk along Borgo Angelico was not particularly scenic, hemmed in on both sides by tightly parked cars, between buildings studiously unremarkable, save for a handful of modest cafés and shops, until he reached the wall of Vatican City.

On this corner, the wall looked modern, topped by a row of iron bars, but a little to his right, this section adjoined a true, medieval castle wall, complete with arrow slits, standing almost forty feet high, which circled the city to the north. This was not a wall built for the glory of God, but rather to protect the Church from the warring states and ambitious kings of centuries long past.

By the time he reached the entrance to the Vatican Museum, the walls reached even higher. The entrance was a twenty-foot-high portal straight through this imposing redoubt, flanked by guards with semi-automatic weapons. It felt more like entering a maximum-security prison than one of the world's greatest store-houses of art. Knowing the queues to enter the museum were legendary, he had secured a VIP pass before leaving LA and thus bypassed hours of standing in the colossal line or being crushed between tour groups and their local guides. He still had to navigate the labyrinth of metal detectors, however.

After triumphing over that tedious gauntlet, he approached the information desk and introduced himself to the primly dressed woman working there, producing his passport, business card, and credentials from Lloyd's. As per Vatican regulations, she was very conservatively attired in a dark, ankle-length, long-sleeved dress, her dark hair drawn into a tight bun. Her narrow face had an avian appearance, with quick eye-blinks and sharp edges.

She listened politely as Trey requested the name of someone he could speak with about two stolen Italian paintings. "You are not police?" she said.

"I am coordinating my investigation with Scotland Yard, the FBI, and the Los Angeles Police Department," he said. "Who would I speak to about these missing paintings? Surely I could speak to someone involved in art acquisition."

She would no longer look at him. "I do not know such things."

"But surely you know someone who would. May I please speak to that person?"

"You are not police. I am sorry. I cannot help you."

"But—"

"No."

The sharpness of her refusal told him that one more word from him might bring security, so he thanked her for her time and stepped away from the desk.

Even though he had been rebuffed, this was still one of the world's greatest art museums. He was here. He loved this place. He knew this place. His investigation here might prove to be more difficult than he expected. He needed some inspiration, some motivation. Art could be its own inspiration.

Despite having been here before, he was immediately mesmerized by the grandeur of the vaulted hall known as the Gallery of Maps, located on the western side of the Belvedere Courtyard. Commissioned in 1580, Ignazio Danzi created a series of forty topographical fresco paintings representing the Italian region and papal properties at the time of Pope Gregory XIII (1572-1585). It served as a long hallway, almost four hundred feet in length, separating the Papal Palace from the Sistine Chapel. The frescoes were utterly stunning riots of color and texture. With Trey's discerning eye for artistic detail, he could have spent hours here lost in sublime nuance.

Nevertheless, he allowed himself to drift downstream with the crowd of tourists toward another of his favorite locations in the Vatican Museum, Stanza della Segnatura, Raphael's iconic *School of Athens*. He was greatly disappointed when he reached the entrance and discovered a small crew of workers installing stanchions, closing off the outdoor walk leading to the entrance. Tourist traffic was thus shunted straight toward the Sistine Chapel.

While engulfed in tour groups taking photographs and videos, Trey noticed the silhouette of a man ahead, a man he recognized as Giorgio Marinelli, wearing the uniform of Alessandro Vasari's art transport firm.

Giorgio Marinelli was Vasari's chief assistant, his right-hand man. At the moment, Giorgio was passionately engaged in conversation with two priests, speaking in Italian too quickly for Trey to follow. Trey called to get Giorgio's attention.

As Giorgio turned to lock eyes on Trey, his expression sparkled with happy recognition. He peeled away from the group to advance toward Trey in his familiar Greco-Roman swagger.

Giorgio gave Trey a huge hug. His English was as good as Vasari's. "Ah, my friend! It has been so long! What are you doing here? You are not meeting with the boss?"

Trey responded, "My meeting with your boss is finished." He did not wish to clue Giorgio in to how unproductive the meeting with Vasari had been. "Maybe you can help with my investigation as well."

Giorgio grinned. "Anything for you, my friend."

One of the priests to whom Giorgio had been speaking approached them, a six-foot-six-inch, gangly man with watery, rheumy eyes, dressed in all the proper priestly raiment—black pants, a black belt, a black, short-sleeve shirt with a white clerical collar. Oddly, he was not adorned in the traditional black jacket that completed the typical parish priest ensemble.

The priest's face gleamed with expectant recognition. "Okie!" he said in a distinctive Midwestern American accent, taking Trey's hand and shaking it vigorously with arthritis-gnarled fingers.

Trey stiffened. "I'm sorry, Father. But Okie is my dad." His father, Emmett Hansen Jr., had gone by the name of Okie to his friends and colleagues, for all of Trey's life. Why his father wore that moniker, Trey had never known. His father had never explained it. "Okie" was a title typically hung on people from Oklahoma, but none of his family had ever lived in Oklahoma, so far as Trey knew. Trey was Emmett Hansen III. Emmett Hansen Sr., Trey's grandfather, was the only one who had ever gone by Emmett. "Emmett" had never been a name to which Trey answered, even from childhood.

The old priest blinked and peered closer. "Oh, my dear boy, you look just like him. Are you here together?"

"What do you mean, are we here together? I am here on official business, not a family vacation."

The priest looked confused. His mouth fell open.

Trey said, "You're talking about Emmett Hansen Jr., aka Okie, right?"

The priest eyed Trey with a mix of surprise and embarrassment. "Yes, we knew each other when he was a student at Holy Cross. I taught ethics and literature, and he was one of my most brilliant students. In fact, I married your parents. We have kept in touch occasionally."

A chill went through Trey, a chill that set off an internal avalanche. Trey began to sweat. Despite having broken all ties with his father, identity mix-ups had plagued Trey's entire adult life, from credit reports to random people in random places mistaking Trey for Okie. Why would this old priest make such a wildly coincidental mistake?

"Sorry, my son, perhaps I've already said too much."

The priest turned to move away, but Trey grabbed his elbow. "What is your name?"

The old priest wrested his arm away and squinted closely at Trey's face with a breath of wonder. "If you'll excuse me, I have pressing business." He turned away more quickly than his tottering frame suggested was possible and shuffled off. The second priest from the conversation with Giorgio joined him, and they went off together.

Trey could not scrub the perception the old priest had been *expecting* Okie. The thought of even being in the same city with his father turned Trey's blood to icy slush. His heart started to pound. His hearing became muffled, as if he were wearing thick earmuffs.

The oddity hung with Trey that the priest had not given his name, despite claiming to know Okie. Was he being rude? Was he just senile? Were there other factors of which Trey was unaware?

Giorgio still hung nearby looking puzzled and confused.

"Who was that?" Trey asked. "Do you know him?"

Giorgio said, "Monsignor Cornelius McGillicuddy. He is the Spiritual Assistant to the Director of the Vatican Museum."

"You're kidding me."

"I only kid over a bottle of chianti, my friend." Giorgio grinned broadly and clapped Trey on the shoulder.

The Spiritual Assistant to the Director of the Vatican Museum was a mouthful of a title, in line with the eminence of the post. It was a position created by the Pope to ensure daily papal supervision over the affairs of the museum. Monsignor McGillicuddy answered directly to the Pontiff *and* helped oversee the workings of the museum itself.

And he had been one of Okie's professors. They had been so close McGillicuddy had married Trey's parents.

Suddenly, his throat tightened. Cold sweat poured down his neck. The floor seemed to teeter and sway under his feet. He staggered to the nearest bench and sat down.

Giorgio hovered nearby. "Are you all right?"

Trey waved him off. "I'm fine. Just thinking about this." His voice was tight, constricted.

Giorgio lingered, however. "Are you sure?"

"Yes, yes, I'm fine," Trey said, giving him a shaky smile.

"Very well. I must call the boss."

Trey nodded, and Giorgio stepped into the river of tourists and disappeared.

Trey felt his control slipping, like fingertips from the tiniest of ledges.

The crowd pressed in, or seemed to. He felt eyes on him, even though no one seemed to be looking. His chest felt tight, and his breaths came in difficult rasps. He was having a heart attack. He was going to keel over and die right there in the Vatican Museum. With trembling hands, he seized the edges of the bench to steady himself. His mind was a rabbit coursing back and forth around a back yard full of barking dogs.

But then his therapist's voice crept into his thoughts. Dr. Connie Bowen had a smooth, sultry voice, like a torch singer's, carefully trained to be coaxing when necessary, hypnotic at times. *It's only a panic attack, Trey. Just breathe. It will pass. You're fine. Everything is fine. Just breathe...*

Minutes passed. The world passed him by, oblivious to the internal barrage rocking his psyche.

He remembered the EMDR techniques—eye movement, de-sensitization, and reprocessing—that Dr. Bowen had taught him. Focusing on his "safe place," he induced four-square breathing to calm himself—breathe in for four seconds, hold for four, breathe out for four, repeat four times. He used his forefinger and middle finger on his left hand to tap methodically on the palm of his right hand.

Finally, the barrage subsided, like sonic booms receding in the distance. His breathing slowed, his throat opened, his hands steadied.

A few minutes later, he felt as if he might walk again without collapsing. He had to get out of there, so he fled toward the sunlight and rapidly descended the Spiral Staircase, built in the shape of a double-helix, a stunning masterpiece of design by Giuseppe Momo, which Trey could not remotely appreciate right now. Finally, he burst out of the exit, into the open air, drawing deep, trembling breaths. Masses of humanity surged and drifted around him.

He let his eyes adjust to the bright sunlight, let its warmth seep through him, suffusing him with calm.

Steadier now, his mind seized upon what had just happened. He now had a lead, a name, a high-ranking official with whom he could request an appointment. And better still, the Monsignor's relationship with Okie might be just the fulcrum he needed to pry open the Cahill investigation.

CHAPTER 18

"THE STORAGE UNIT GETTING ransacked somehow didn't surprise me. It's strange, but it felt like par for the course."

"That makes sense, considering what we've uncovered during our work together."

"You're talking about the searches."

"Even if you didn't understand it during those times, it certainly stuck in your young psyche that intruders had come into your house repeatedly and searched it."

"They were looking for something specific, must have been. Otherwise they'd have just tossed the place. But my parents knew how to tell, even if everything had been meticulously replaced."

"Then you would move again."

"How many times this happened before we moved to Colorado, I can't even guess."

***

The stress of suddenly finding herself in a bad spy movie lent speed to Marie's step. Trey had tried to warn her. Time to put on the Big Girl Pants. Suck it up, sweetheart, because this is as real as it gets. In the face of one hundred and twenty million dollars, a contract hit might well be the cost of doing business. She hailed a taxi to take her back to Hotel Bramante, a better way to lose a tail than walking.

Her nerves rattled as the cab crossed the bridge over the River Tiber, puttered past Castel Sant'Angelo.

She breathed deep, trying to get hold of herself. She was an architect, not a secret agent.

On the way, she sent Trey a text message: *Something really weird just happened.*

His immediate response was: *You too?*

What do you mean?

What do YOU mean?

Should she call him? Were their phones, in fact, being tapped? But who might be doing it? For a moment, she felt like Trey with his conspiracy-theory hobby. In his world, there was *always* someone behind *everything*. But now...

She called him.

He answered and said, "You're not going to believe this."

"That's my line," she said. Hearing his voice flooded her with relief.

"You first."

She told him about the man in the piazza, about the priest taking her photo, and about the dark alley he had almost led her down.

"Where are you now?" he said.

"In a cab, heading back to the hotel."

"Good, please stay there. I'll meet you there as soon as I can."

"What happened to you?"

"I just ran into the priest who married my parents."

"You're kidding."

"He mistook me for Okie. Swear to God. He came up and shook my hand and called me 'Okie.' When I disabused him of that notion, he told me I looked like him." Trey's voice almost cracked at that. She heard it. She had never met the man, but Trey's father had scarred him so profoundly, any such connection would likely trigger his PTSD. "He said they've been in contact over the years. And there was something..."

She waited for him to finish the sentence, but finally she said, "What something?"

Trey took a deep breath and let it out. "I got the sense, something in his voice, that he was *expecting* Okie."

"What kind of coincidence would that be, for your dad to be in Rome now?" She had spoken with a sense of its uncanniness.

"What if it's not a coincidence at all?" he said.

The idea of that hung between them in silence.

Eventually she said, "What do you mean?"

"What if he's involved in this?"

She sighed and shook her head. "I'm sorry, Boo, but that's just too farfetched. A *huge* reach. Massive. Beyond the pale."

"You're probably right." He sighed as well. His voice still sounded unsteady. "I had a panic attack in the Vatican Museum, right after I met this priest. I'm okay now, but..."

She wanted to reach out and grab his hand. "Come back to the hotel. I think we need to regroup."

"Yeah, I'll meet you there."

She hung up and put her phone away.

A couple of minutes later, she arrived at Hotel Bramante, feeling better now, a sense of normalcy returning with the comfort of well-known accommodations.

She unlocked the door to her room, Camera 30, and went in. She sank down onto the bed, but then the tricks of tradecraft she had read about jumped unbidden into her mind. She switched on the television and raised the volume to an uncomfortable level. This would foil any audio bugs in the room. She chided herself for not doing it this morning before she left, as it would prevent listeners from knowing if she were present in the room. The noise of it, however, grated on her already frazzled nerves.

Their ground-floor room had a beautiful picture window that opened into a sitting area off the hotel's central garden. It was still locked, but locks meant little to someone with the right skills. All the windows were locked. The eighteen-foot ceiling with exposed wooden beams would make it difficult to place any bugs up high, and also would make it difficult to detect any planted up there. The room's easy accessibility from the ground now made her uncomfortable.

The only thing that stood between her and a potential killer was a pane of glass.

Enough of *that*.

She went into the bathroom to freshen up, but then something caught her eye. Trey's toiletry kit sat askew on its small shelf near the sink. His OCD, mild as it usually was, would not have allowed the case to be left in that orientation. She searched her memory. While getting herself ready, she had noted its location, because its bulkiness had blocked her from putting some of her own things there.

It was not in the same place.

She went back into the main room.

The still-life orotone painting depicting an aerial view of St. Peter's Square now hung slightly askew. Her own sharp eye for lines and symmetry detected its quarter-inch deviation from level. Could it have been bumped by the maid?

No, because the bed was still unmade. The maid had not yet serviced their room. Trey would have made sure all the pictures were straight when they arrived.

Marie had left the room after Trey.

Someone had been in here.

Immediately, she flew to the safe in the closet, fingers trembling as she opened it, and checked the contents. Passports, cash, and her unworn jewelry were still present within. Relief flooded her. Thank God for Trey's meticulous, unwavering security measures.

Their luggage looked untouched, their clothes hanging in the closet as well, but how could she be sure?

The chill of fear kept trickling over her and would not stop. The sense of violation slithered like cold fingers over her skin.

Someone had *been in here*.

She jammed the back of a chair up under the latch of the glass door to the garden, and then threw the chain lock on the main door.

Then she sat down on the bed and wrung her hands, television blaring unheard, as she waited for Trey.

CHAPTER 19

"*MY BROTHER AND MY DAD and I would regularly play basketball on our custom Laykold half-court built in our back yard, adjacent to the tennis court. My dad just loved pushing us around. He was six-one, about one-ninety. I couldn't fight him off, he was too big for me. If you drove the basket, he'd put you on the ground. One time, when I was probably sixteen, I gave him a head fake and got a nice layup. There was this flash of frustration in his eyes, and he caught the ball and flung it at my face. Absolutely clocked me, broke my fucking nose.*

"*By the time I was eighteen, though, I had grown to be his physical equal. I remember the day as if it was yesterday. For years, I had avoided him physically because of the abuse. I couldn't stand for him to touch me. But on this day, I remember it so clearly, almost like ultra-high-def video. We were playing basketball. I drove the basket with the ball in my right hand, left forearm sweeping ahead of me, and I plowed into him and put him flat on his back, and I went for the layup.*

"*The ball went in. The elation went through me, it was such a sweet move, and then I turned around and my brother was just staring in terrified amazement.*

"*Then it hit me, what I had done. I thought he was going to come up off the ground and smash my head against the steel stanchion.*

"But he didn't.

"My brother was like, 'Oh, my God, are you okay?' No doubt he was afraid for his own life.

"I stood over him, and he looked at me, and I looked at him. Then he got up, walked into the house, didn't say a word. My fucking Great Santini had been defeated.

"He never touched me again."

***

When Trey tried to open the hotel room door, he found he could not. Something was propped against it on the inside.

Over the noise of a blaring television, Marie's challenge came immediately. "Who is it?"

"It's me," he said.

"Oh, thank God." After some clunking inside the door, it opened, and she flung herself on him, arms around his neck. Relief burst out of them both as they squeezed and kissed in the hallway. Her warm hands checked his face as if to make sure everything was still in place. She was speaking quickly, almost babbling, about someone having been in their room.

As the frenzied greeting subsided, he guided her into the room and locked the door behind them. He was amused to see the TV on, a basic bit of spy-craft. "What's this about someone being in the room?"

"It started with your dopp kit. Look at it and tell me what you see."

He went into the bathroom and saw it was sitting slightly askew on its shelf. He specifically remembered squaring it properly when he finished shaving this morning. "Someone moved it."

"Look around the room. Anything else?"

His eye immediately seized upon the orotone print of the Vatican hanging on the wall, now slightly deviating from level. His suitcase. It rested upon its luggage rack, as he had left it, but it was no longer centered. The closet door lay a finger's breadth ajar.

"Our room has been searched," he said.

"What does that mean? Who would do that?"

"Maybe Cahill has some people working for him here in Rome. The guy is rich enough to have serious connections."

"Mafia?" she said.

"CIA?"

"Oh, come on," she said. "Be serious."

"I am being serious. The CIA and the Mafia were practically in bed together in the sixties. Whoever did this knew how to get in here. But they were not meticulous enough. A flunkie or low-level operative... Unless they wanted me to spot the inconsistencies..."

"Rabbit hole warning," she said.

"Sorry, just trying to think a few chess moves ahead. Too many moving parts..."

"You're not making sense."

"Somebody might be playing with us. Trying to scare me into dropping the investigation and signing off on one hundred and twenty million dollars."

"Can they tap our phones?"

"I don't know. Maybe. That might require some Italian cooperation." All the information he had on this case was stored in an encrypted thumb drive in the room safe, as well as on his mobile phone and laptop, both of which he carried with him at all times. The information was also stored in one of Lloyd's encrypted cloud servers.

He unlocked the room safe; everything appeared to be still present. He pulled out the thumb drive and plugged it into his laptop. Minutes passed as he waited for the boot-up, fearing that data had been stolen. When he entered his password, the encryption software told him no log-in attempts had been made since he had last updated everything.

A clumsy, hurried intruder would likely have stolen the flash drive. Maybe the intruder had been unable to crack the room safe in the allotted time.

"Should we call the police?" Marie said. "Have them take some fingerprints?"

Trey rubbed his chin, considering. "If only Mason were here. We could use his lab kit. I'm afraid if we call the police, they would laugh politely and ignore us. Nothing has been stolen. To anyone else, we would sound like crazy people, talking about such little things being moved." He had learned long ago when to keep his compulsions to himself.

His iPhone buzzed with an incoming email. He would have ignored it under the circumstances, but the subject line caught his eye. "Re: Cahill Investigation."

The message came from an email address consisting of a nonsense string of numbers and letters with a Yahoo domain. It couldn't be spam, because no spammer would know of his association with the Cahill investigation, now just over a week old. A hacker?

He opened the message. It read:

you dont know me yet but i know you. i have information you want in the cahill case. your only going to get it if we meet in person. meet me at LACMA tomorrow at noon. ill be looking at bellini's madonna and child.

A moment of anxiety and excitement shot through him. Could this be a witness coming forward? Could this break the case wide open? But obviously he was nowhere near Los Angeles. A couple of minutes of cyber-sleuthing told him the sender's IP address was indeed from the Los Angeles area. But the sender's email address was clearly a bogus, throwaway account, so his instincts were telling him this was someone connected with the case. He couldn't be back in LA by tomorrow unless Concordes were still flying, and his work in Rome was not finished, especially now.

He replied to the mysterious email:

Tomorrow is no good. Will contact you via this email to arrange meeting soonest.

Marie said, "What is it?"

"It looks like the investigation might have another moving part."

CHAPTER 20

"*ABOUT SIX YEARS AGO, when Marie and I were buying our house in Chicago, I got this strange call from the loan underwriter. She asked me to verify where I was born. I told her I was born in Virginia. That's what my parents had told me my whole life. I have a few snapshots of memory of living there. We moved to Colorado when I was seven.*

"*The underwriter said, 'That doesn't make sense. The first three digits of your social Security Number are 521. That means you were born in Colorado.'*

"*I said, 'I don't know what to tell you. Neither of my siblings were born in Colorado, but we all have 521 as the first three digits.' My parents had made a game of all of us memorizing each other's numbers. I told her we were all born in Virginia.*

"'*How is that possible?' she said.*

"*I joked with her, 'Well, maybe we were all in some sort of witness protection program.'*

"*She got quiet and just said, 'Oh.'*"

***

That evening, Trey and Marie made a video call to Marie's parents to say hello to their children. The girls were initially delighted to see them, but then Lauren started to cry. "I miss Daddy and Mommy!"

Trey's heart cracked open, and he wished for nothing more than to hold her and kiss her.

Annie chided her sister. "Don't be such a baby! Daddy's on a big case. *Huge.*"

Lauren opened the spigot on the waterworks. "I don't care, I want them to come home!"

Trey and Marie did their utmost to reassure the girls it would only be a few more days.

Annie said, "Are you getting good leads, Daddy?"

Trey smiled. "Oh, yes, sweetie. I'm going to break this case wide open."

"And put the bad guys in jail."

"You know it, buddy," he said.

After they hung up, he missed them terribly, even though he was delighted to have Marie here with him, a wildly romantic getaway mixed with work. He hugged Marie without hesitation.

Then she said, "Oh, hey, check this out." From a shopping bag, she pulled out a black, purse-like object. "Time to make your phone invisible."

He recognized it instantly as a Faraday bag, then kicked himself for not thinking of it. "You're a goddess."

"You can call me Queen Spook."

Privacy and surveillance concerns were one of those things on his internal radar, but his phone had become so integrated with his business and everyday life, he did not often enough consider the fact he carried a highly specialized traitor in his breast pocket. Text and email messages pinged his phone all day from various clients and jobs, and he relied on those to maintain his initiative over adversaries. This would slow him down, but he had to take security seriously.

Trey spent half the night awake, in part stewing over the revelations and events of the day, and in part dreading the possibility he might have another double-layered nightmare like the one in LA. When he did sleep, it was light and fitful, spent uncomfortably in one of the room's red leather Natuzzi Cocò armchairs custom-made in Puglia, Italy.

When morning finally came, he and Marie shared a bleary-eyed, wary breakfast of fresh breads, hard-boiled quail eggs, and plenty of cappuccinos at Hotel Bramante, watching other guests with more scrutiny than any of them warranted.

As they ate, he mused on the internal fortitude intelligence operatives must possess. Living with the stress for only a few days was wearing on him, as it was on Marie. Living with it long term would take tolls that could only be guessed on the body and mind. He had grown up with worse stress and withstood it for many years, so he could feel that old, internal coping machinery cranking into motion. It was shutting down some of his emotions and heightening his situational awareness, making him feel like a rabbit constantly looking out for predators.

When they were nearly finished with breakfast, Maurizio, the proprietor, came in and spotted them. "Ah! Signora e Signore Hansen. A message for you." He approached their table and presented a folded piece of paper.

Trey accepted it. *"Grazie."*

Maurizio bowed slightly and turned away.

Trey unfolded the paper, a piece of Hotel Bramante stationery.

Mouth of Truth. 9 p.m. - A.V.

He called after Maurizio, "Who brought this?"

"Bicicletta messenger," Maurizio said. "Just now." Then he disappeared through the door.

Trey lowered his voice and said to Marie, "It seems my friend Alessandro has something to discuss." And the manner in which the message was delivered strongly suggested caution and discretion. Vasari could have called, or texted, or sent an email—not knowing that Trey would receive those communications now only when actively checking them. But he sent a handwritten message.

The Mouth of Truth, or *Bocca della Verità*, was a prominent tourist attraction near Circus Maximus and the Colosseum, not far from some of Rome's most spectacular sights. It was an ancient marble mask in the shape of a disk just under six feet in diameter, carven with a face, with much speculation about who the face represented, perhaps the god Oceanus. Centuries-old superstition said it would bite any liar who stuck their hand in its mouth. In medieval trials, many adulterous wives faced the Mouth of Truth as a lie detector.

Trey had to chuckle at Alessandro's choice of meeting place. Sense of humor mixed with skullduggery. The Mouth of Truth was in a public place, situated in the narthex of an eighth-century church known as Santa Maria in Cosmedin, and somewhat removed from Hotel Bramante and the Vatican.

Marie fumbled her fork with a clatter, then gave him a feeble smile at the noise. Her knee bounced rhythmically under the table.

"What is it?" he said.

"After yesterday—"

"You're not leaving my side."

Her expression cracked with underlying emotion. "Thank you."

He squeezed her hand. "Besides, I could use your eagle-sharp eyes. I have one call to make, then we can make a day of it."

She beamed a smile that managed to drive away some of his own tension and worry.

***

One phone call turned into several as Trey navigated the labyrinth of Vatican bureaucracy. Finally, he reached the office of Spiritual Advisor to the Director of the Vatican Museum, Monsignor Cornelius McGillicuddy.

The Monsignor was not in, but Trey requested an appointment, reiterating several times his family's personal connection to the Monsignor. McGillicuddy might not know of Trey's estrangement from his father. He would use any kind of toehold to get an audience with this man. If anyone was in a position to offer useful information, it would be Monsignor McGillicuddy. However, given the Vatican's less than stellar history with stolen and looted artworks, the man might be less than enthusiastic to meet with a fraud investigator.

The Vatican Bank was created during World War II and often served as an offshore haven for tax evaders and money launderers, and worse, as a haven for gold, antiquities, and works of art stolen by the Nazis. At that time, the Vatican Museum became a Nazi storage facility under Mussolini's authority and with Pope Pius XII's approval and collaboration. In exchange, the Nazis agreed not to invade, loot, and destroy the Holy See. There was even, allegedly, a basement under the Sistine Chapel full of Nazi loot. Vatican bankers allegedly had been involved in complex, secretive scandals that included robberies, murder, and multimillion-dollar dealings with the Mafia.

The receptionist assured Trey his message would be passed on and his request considered, but the Monsignor was a very busy man. The Monsignor's office would be in touch if the request was granted.

When this was finished, he put the iPhone into its Faraday bag.

Meanwhile, Marie came out of the bathroom and struck a glamorous pose. She had dressed herself in a fetching sundress, strappy Italian sandals, a broad-brimmed straw hat, and sunglasses. She looked like Marilyn Monroe on a Roman holiday, and his heart went *ka-thump*.

"Be still, my heart," he said.

She crossed the room and kissed him coquettishly. "Shall we commence our adventures?"

They requested Maurizio hail them a taxi, and when it arrived, they piled in and sped off, hoping such an abrupt departure would throw off anyone watching the hotel. They had their driver make a number of false turns, during which Trey watched for cars tailing them. Only when he felt sure they were not being followed did he have the taxi driver take them to the Temple of Hercules, just across the River Tiber and roughly three kilometers south of Piazza Navona.

The Temple of Hercules was a modest structure compared to much of Rome's ancient grandeur, but it was the oldest marble temple in the city, built in the second century BCE of expensive Greek marble. It was also one of the few circular temples in Rome.

Thus began their trek around some of Rome's most ancient and magnificent sights. A stroll around Rome was a walk through the history of the Western world.

They passed the church where Trey would meet Vasari that evening. The queue of tourists waiting for the Mouth of Truth stretched out of the church narthex and halfway down the block, but by tonight the crowds would thin dramatically.

From there, it was only a short distance to Circus Maximus, once the site of the greatest structure ever built for entertainment. It was an oval-shaped bowl of grassy sward and bare earth roughly two thousand feet long and six hundred feet across, nestled between two hills, Palatine and Aventine. It still very much resembled its original purpose—a racetrack—despite being surrounded by modern paved streets. Used for chariot races and other sporting events, it once had an audience capacity of some three hundred thousand. In fact, no sports complex on Earth had ever compared to Circus Maximus' capacity. During the Late Empire, chariot racing had been a national mania, with racing teams and their fans garnering political clout. The spectacle must have rivaled the greatest sporting events of the modern age.

As Trey and Marie made a circuit of the ancient chariot racetrack, imaginations of thundering wheels and pounding hooves filling his mind, he scrutinized every passerby, noting and remembering faces. He didn't think a car could have followed them here with such a circuitous route, but vigilance was paramount. He detected no tails but couldn't allow himself to relax.

After their stroll around the perimeter of Circus Maximus, they wended their way to the Palatine Hill, the cradle of Rome itself, where legend had it that a band of traders, farmers, and shepherds chose to settle in 753 BCE.

Right next door, so to speak, was the Forum Romanus, the original town square. The ruins covering the Palatine and the Roman Forum were among the oldest on Earth, the houses and temples and palaces of the earliest days of the city, crumbling walls, pillars, archways, thoroughfares, and foundations. What stories lay interred with those ancient stones? For centuries, much of the ruins had been lost in the sediment of time and subsequent construction, to be uncovered as recently as the nineteenth century, a discovery that became one of the greatest archaeological endeavors of the Victorian Age.

Throughout this walk, Trey and Marie spoke little. They didn't need to, just two history geeks on a quest to feed their passions. Both were enraptured, ignoring aching feet, lost in the colossal scope of human history on the very ground they walked, caught up in what humans of those long-ago centuries had accomplished—without computers, without calculus or knowledge of Newtonian physics, without chemistry, without steel. Nevertheless, the Romans had moved mountains and erected monuments that still stood.

And upon these foundations came later waves of history. Each era launched a tectonic shift in the cultural landscape of the city.

The fall of Rome. The rise of the Catholic Church. The Dark Ages. The Age of Chivalry. The Renaissance and the Baroque, which boasted the Western world's greatest explosion of art and achievement since Rome's glory days—and during which two magnificent paintings had been created, now placed in jeopardy by the hands of unscrupulous men.

Practically a stone's throw away from the Palatine Hill stood the Colosseum, the Arch of Titus and the Arch of Constantine.

A great deal of the restoration had been completed on the Colosseum since he had last visited this ancient icon of grandeur and bloody violence. It was the dichotomy that fascinated him, because the Colosseum was truly one of the grandest achievements of ancient architecture. But along with that came the knowledge oceans of gore had been spilled here to satisfy the lust for blood and spectacle of commoners and emperors alike. The Dichotomy of Man in a nutshell.

Francis X. Cahill was another study in the Dichotomy of Man, how a man could claim to love and revere great art and then abuse it at the same time, twist its very existence for his own purposes. It was simply treasure to be possessed, a way to stroke an overweening ego. Trey despised such men.

Trey and Marie joined flocks of tourists marveling at the Colosseum's grandeur, all of them no doubt imagining what it must have been like, to attend—or fight and die in—these grand, bloody spectacles.

Their walks among the grand sights, along with his musings on them, made the day pass with such speed that Trey and Marie only noticed when the sun slanted sideways through the arches of the Colosseum. The day was all but gone.

With about two hours to spare before his meeting with Vasari, they had just enough time for a proper Italian dinner. Italians took their time about such things, and after so much walking, Trey and Marie were relieved to have a rest, some local chianti, and some relaxation.

Ristorante Sabatini in Trastevere overlooked the Piazza di Santa Maria and their favorite church in Rome, the Basilica of Santa Maria. It was here on the walls of the porch, before the vestibule, where they found etched in the walls the names for their daughters.

One of his favorite memories of their honeymoon here had been sitting outside and people-watching the people in the Piazza, quietly sharing a bottle of wine. Tonight, the wine was a bottle of 2013 Felsina Chianti Classico Riserva and an order of *fiori di zucca fritti*, fried, stuffed zucchini flowers; followed by *carciofi alla giudia*, Jewish-style artichokes; and *cacio e pepe*, a dish of pasta literally meaning "cheese and pepper."

Trey allowed some relaxation now, just a little, releasing the disciplined stops that let the tension in his muscles slacken.

Dinner passed with no interlopers or over-inquisitive eyes. He still could not shake the idea a skilled tail would never give the subject the sense they were being followed. Had all his efforts at subterfuge today been in vain?

By the time they finished dessert, the time to meet Vasari had almost come.

They walked the darker streets, which were much diminished in tourist population, toward the church Santa Maria in Cosmedin.

He sent Marie on ahead to position herself at the Fountain of the Tritons, a minor eighteenth-century fountain across the street from the Mouth of Truth. From there, she would keep an eye out for anything untoward and still be able to see Trey's meeting with Vasari. As he approached the church, he could just see her loitering near the fountain, pretending to be using her mobile phone. Or perhaps she was recording everything to video with it. She was crafty that way.

At 9:00 p.m. sharp, Trey stood outside the wrought-iron fence that closed off the church's narthex and the Mouth of Truth after hours. Traffic was much diminished at this hour, as this area was far from the city's night life.

An aubergine-colored Fornasari Gigi 311GT pulled up with the passenger window rolled down, Vasari in the driver's seat. He gestured quickly for Trey to get in.

A moment of fear dashed through Trey. All their best-laid contingency plans fell away. Marie would be alone. He gave her one long look. Then he got in the car.

Vasari's expression looked tight, lacking its usual affability.

"Why the cloak-and-dagger?" Trey said.

Vasari pulled away from the curb and hit the gas.

Trey caught sight of Marie staring after them with a shocked expression.

Vasari said, "Things have gotten very, very weird, my friend."

"How weird?" Trey said. He sent a quick text message to Marie: *Go back to the hotel and wait for me. I'll be fine.*

Vasari watched Trey doing this. He took a deep breath, rounded a corner down a dark street, and said, "I can't tell you where the Cahill paintings are, but I can tell you where he got them." Vasari scanned their surroundings as if cultivating his flair for the dramatic.

"So...?" Trey said.

"They came from the Vatican's Nazi horde."

Trey stared at him, mouth falling open.

"About twenty years ago," Vasari went on, "Cahill was asked to 'purchase' the paintings to create a false, 'legitimate' provenance. They wanted to hide the Nazi connection, so they arranged for Cahill to buy them via Sotheby's auction house."

Trey immediately connected some dots. "So Cahill 'borrowed' the paintings for decades, intending to sell them back to the Vatican, with a nice appreciation in value." But in the intervening twenty years, Cahill's financial fortunes had taken a nosedive, and he needed the double-dip of the insurance settlement *and* the sale back to the Vatican. Plus, the Vatican probably wanted the paintings back. "Where did you get this information?"

"My man in the Vatican."

"Giorgio?"

Vasari gave Trey a faint smile as he rounded another corner. Streetlights slid past along the River Tiber.

Trey said, "So you're worried about a tail."

"In this town," Vasari said, "there is the Mafia, and then there is the Holy See. Their fingers are in *everything*. So are their eyes."

"Who was Cahill's contact?"

"The Spiritual Advisor himself, Monsignor McGillicuddy."

"Why am I not surprised?"

"Huh?" Vasari said.

"Nothing. I don't suppose you have proof of any of this?"

Vasari handed Trey a folded paper. Vasari's gaze flicked sharply around the outside street as Trey unfolded the paper and squinted to read it in the dark.

It was a grainy photograph printed on plain white paper of two bills of sale, dated twenty years previously, each about six months apart. The items were two paintings—a Caravaggio and a Piero. The buyer was Doctor Francis X. Cahill.

"Thank you!" Trey breathed. This wasn't the smoking gun he needed, but it was ammunition.

"I have given you all I can, my friend. This might put my business in jeopardy. Any more will put me and my family in danger. I hope you understand."

"I owe you. Big time. *Grazie, amico mio.*"

Vasari smiled. "I know. Let us hope we both live for you to pay me back, *sì*?"

CHAPTER 21

"EVERY SUNDAY WAS DAWN MASS. I remember getting up in the dark, getting dressed up, and going to Mass. I hated it. Hated it. But there was no getting out of it. I became an altar boy because that's what my father wanted. I learned how to swallow everything I was supposed to, all that indoctrination, all that guilt, and then regurgitate it back like a good little lamb. I thought it would make me a good person. I never learned how to step back and think critically about any of it until college, but even then, there was this hard kernel of internal resistance. It took me years to walk away entirely.

"I remember crying to my mother in eighth grade, 'Mom, Father Harrington is pressuring me to be a priest, and he wants me to follow dad and Grandpa Emmett and go to Holy Cross.'

"'Why don't you want to be a priest?' she said.

"I didn't dare tell her it was because I really liked girls. No way could I see myself being celibate. But my parents were talking to the priest about me joining the priesthood and going to Holy Cross. I remember crying and saying, 'I don't want to go to Holy Cross. I don't want to be part of the family business. I don't want to do that.'"

"What did you mean by 'family business'?"

"...What?"

"I said, what did you mean by 'family business'?"

"I... I don't know... That's an interesting question."

"Why?"

"Because I vividly remember saying that, but I have no idea what I meant by it."

"Didn't you say your father had an advertising business? Wasn't he a graphic designer?"

"He's also a painter. A damned good one."

"Could that be what you meant?"

"Advertising? No, that doesn't feel right. I don't recall my dad ever pushing me to join his business at all. Most of the time, I felt like he himself had little interest in it. And the priesthood couldn't very well be a 'family business,' could it?"

***

Vasari let Trey out of the car a few blocks from Hotel Bramante. Trey walked back, pulling up his collar at the damp night air.

At the door of Camera 30, he found the chair barricade back in place. "It's me," he called. "Is everything okay?"

Marie's voice came through the door. "Oh, thank God!"

After much clunking and rattling of chains, they were once again in each other's arms. After the heightened emotions subsided, she asked, "Was the meeting worth all this?"

"Uh, *yeah*," Trey said. He told her about Cahill's apparent plan for the paintings.

"Oh, wow," she said. "This just keeps getting dirtier."

"I wish I could say I'm surprised."

"But this is the Catholic Church!"

"The same Church that hid Nazi loot. And sanctioned the genocide of half a million Orthodox Serbs in Yugoslavia during World War II. And hires and protects pedophiles. And that's just in the last century."

She sank onto the bed and sighed.

"The Vatican is a political organization cloaked in religion, that's all," Trey said. "It has been one of the biggest power-brokers in Europe for centuries. It does what is expedient and necessary to perpetuate itself, like governments everywhere. And if you're not Catholic, you can go join all those Serbs in their mass graves."

He stopped short of telling her about another case, one that might strike too close to home. In 1982, Roberto "God's Banker" Calvi was found hanging from Blackfriars Bridge in London. His pockets were filled with bricks and cash. In the months before his death, he had been accused of stealing millions in laundered Mafia money—from the Vatican. He was the chairman of Italy's second largest private bank, Banco Ambrosiano, and the scandals around him and his trial brought down the bank. Calvi's murder probably would never be solved. Was he killed for what he knew? Was the Vatican somehow above assassinating an embarrassing witness? Not a chance. Sadly, trading in fine art was often just a form of money laundering, and the Vatican had proved its willingness, over and over, to do that.

"What are we going to do now?" Marie asked.

"I'm going to try again tomorrow to get an audience with Monsignor McGillicuddy. And I'm going to keep trying until he gives me one. He's the one who could break this wide open."

"What if he doesn't cooperate? Doesn't he have a lot to lose? One hundred and twenty million in paintings, maybe."

"Maybe if I push hard enough, it will scare him into calling off the deal. The Vatican is more concerned with scandal than morality."

"Harsh."

"I had a harsh teacher." The bite in his voice made her draw back. "Sorry. This case makes me particularly angry." And their family's future hinged on its outcome.

***

The text message came promptly at 8:00 the following morning:

Monsignor Cornelius McGillicuddy requests your presence at Braccio di Carlo Magno today at 10:00 a.m.

Such a thrill went through Trey he whooped at the breakfast table. The other hotel guests jumped at the noise. He apologized and lowered his voice to tell Marie, "I got a meeting with the man himself!"

She grinned and squeezed his hand.

He had spent some time on his laptop the night before, researching Monsignor Cornelius McGillicuddy. Former professor of English and Ethics at the College of the Holy Cross. Summoned by the Pope to the Holy See for his anointing as a monsignor and to serve the Pope directly. McGillicuddy was handpicked by the College of Cardinals.

The title of monsignor historically designated a priest who served in the papal Curia, or Vatican bureaucracy. All monsignors were officially part of the papal household, whether they served in the Vatican or elsewhere. However, the title of Prelate to His Holiness and the rank of monsignor was also granted to the Pope's chamberlain. The title of Protonotary Apostolic of Number, the highest grade of monsignor, was granted to seven priests who filled seven of the traditional administrative positions within the Curia. McGillicuddy quickly became one of the seven Protonotary Apostolic of Number, serving the Pope directly as the Spiritual Assistant to the Director of the Vatican Museum on special request from the Pope. His rise to the top had been rapid and without question.

In digging deeper through the files from his background check on Cahill, Trey discovered something interesting, something he might be able to use against the monsignor.

For a moment, he pondered the logistics of this meeting. Today was Liberation Day, a national holiday in Italy marking the fall in 1945 of Mussolini's Italian Social Republic and the end of Nazi occupation in Italy. How was he going to gain access to the *Braccio di Carlo Magno*, or "Arm of Charlemagne" on a national holiday? Today, St. Peter's Square was going to be overcrowded with celebrating Italians, a crushing mass of Christian humanity.

When facing the façade of St. Peter's Basilica, one could see a two-storied structure projecting into the square, from both edges of the cathedral, which eventually joined up with the open colonnade. When viewed from above, the two-storied structures appeared as "arms" extending from the façade. The open colonnade encircled the piazza to create the shape of a keyhole, signifying St. Peter as the holder of the keys to heaven. All depictions of St. Peter identified him as holding keys. The two-storied arm on the left had been specifically designated the Braccio di Carlo Magno, meaning "the Arm of Charlemagne."

"Sorry, BD," he said. "I have to go right now. If I don't, I won't be able to get anywhere near the building. Will you be all right by yourself?"

"Hey, mister. I'm a big girl! So, I'm going to go cower in my room until you get back. Like a big girl."

He leaned across the table and kissed her, and it was not just a see-you-later peck. Then he grabbed his Florentine leather brief-case and raced out.

***

Crowds were already thronging the piazza, but Trey worked his way through them to the entrance of the museum where the Braccio di Carlo Magno was housed, on the left side of Bernini's colonnade, near St. Peter's Basilica. He had visited the exhibition space at the Braccio di Carlo Magno during the "Verbum Domini" exhibition. The general public entered from St. Peter's Square, while the clergy could enter the exhibition space from inside Vatican City, secretly, through a locked door at the top of the gallery.

Liberation Day was marked with gatherings in towns across Italy, a public holiday since 1946. The celebrations ranged from marching bands to political rallies to music concerts. Extended families put on their Sunday best and walked the streets of Rome, periodically stopping at outdoor cafés and restaurants for food, drink and people-watching. All state schools and offices would be closed, as well as many shops. While some tourist places remained open, municipal attractions such as museums and monuments would be shut and public transportation running a reduced service.

A popular tradition was the singing of the folk song "Bella Ciao," a tale of a partisan who died for Italian freedom, whose only wish was to be buried in the mountains under the shadow of a beautiful flower.

A queue had already formed on the piazza entrance to Braccio di Carlo Magno, but he bypassed the queue and went to stand at the wrought-iron gate, ignoring the disapproving looks of the others standing in line.

Nearby was signage for an upcoming exhibition. Just to the left of the wrought-iron gate was the "side" entrance used by those who worked in the Holy See and by tourists lucky enough to get a ticket to the events at Paul VI Audience Hall, named for Pope Paul VI. Others wanted to sneak a photograph of the Swiss Guard posted at this private entrance.

While he waited, he checked his emails.

There was a reply from the mysterious junk email account that had offered information: *Do you want to hear what I have to say or not*

Having no clue who this person might be, Trey wanted to hide the fact he was not even in Los Angeles, and he did not want to set up a meeting he knew he could not make. The best he could do was try to keep the person on the hook while revealing nothing, so he responded: *I very much wish to meet you, but circumstances will not permit just yet. I hope you'll forgive the delay.*

At exactly 10:00 a.m., the bells of St. Peter's Basilica began to chime. A Vatican Museum guard came out through the Judas Gate, the forty-foot wooden door at Braccio di Carlo Magno, and walked down the incline to unlock the wrought-iron gate. The crowd stirred. But the guard gestured to Trey to come through. Trey did so, surrounded by the crowd's murmurs of dismay. The guard, a handsome Italian man who wore his Prada uniform with style, locked the gate again and led Trey silently up the incline toward the formal entrance.

Through the massive wooden door, they entered the two-storied exhibition space, which measured roughly fifty by one hundred fifty feet and ascended toward the top of the incline, where lay the secret exit to the Holy See. This space was not intended for exhibitions, but the Vatican Museum used the location, adjacent to St. Peter's Square, to offer free exhibitions to the faithful congregating outside. The space was now empty, however. The crowd outside was standing in the wrong line to enter the Holy See. Eventually, they would have to figure out they were in the wrong queue. Tourists in large groups rivaled the collective intelligence of lemmings.

He and the guard were alone in the empty exhibition space. The framework of past exhibitions remained, however, a labyrinth of non-load-bearing walls and exhibition spaces, full of dark spaces in which lurked unknown threats and hazards.

A voice emerged from the shadows. "It is a pleasure to be in the presence of Okie's son." A shockingly tall figure stepped into the light from behind a half-dismantled display wall. "I hope this meeting place meets with your approval."

Trey gave another long moment of scrutiny to the old priest he'd met two days ago. Clad all in black except for the white clerical collar, towering six-foot-six inches tall, shoulders hunched with age, Monsignor Cornelius McGillicuddy was a towering, cadaverous figure with pale, liver-spotted skin. The only vitality in his appearance lay in his eyes, which scrutinized Trey with strange intensity. A suggestion of guarded kindness lay in them, as if more of practiced habit than nature.

Trey was unsure how to answer such a premeditated statement. Secret and secluded, apparently isolated from the Liberation Day celebrations of a national holiday, this rendezvous point was not the place for an aboveboard meeting.

Within the cover of this desolate hall, however, named for the Holy Roman Emperor Charlemagne, Trey hoped to turn the tables on Francis X. Cahill and whoever was helping him.

The guard had already disappeared.

"Thank you for meeting with me, Monsignor," Trey said.

"To what do I owe the honor of this meeting?" the Monsignor said.

Trey reached for the Monsignor's right hand and kissed the ring on his ring finger, a traditional act of submission and devotion to the Monsignor's spiritual authority. Trey also bowed his head, and the Monsignor touched the top. Memories surged back of his awful experiences as an altar boy, but he choked back the bile rising in his throat. He had to put the Monsignor at ease before dropping the hammer.

Trey knew CIA interrogation techniques, as Okie had used them all on him as a child. He had studied them as a way not only to understand them for his own investigations, but also to help him understand what he had gone through. He intended to outwit his witness by altering facts and escalating the witness's self-doubt. He was going to finesse this old bastard into giving him what he needed, always five moves ahead on the chessboard.

He said, "When did you last meet with Dr. Cahill?"

The kindness and curiosity in the Monsignor's eyes smothered behind an iron portcullis. "Who?"

"Dr. Francis Xavier Cahill. You met with him recently."

The Monsignor chewed on his response before seeming to come to a decision. "Cutting to the chase, Trey. Much like your father, a full-frontal attack to control the board. One of the best openings in the Italian Game, pawn to e4, pawn to e5. When in Italy, eh?"

"Monsignor, I am here to enlist your help with my investigation, on behalf of Lloyd's of London, to secure the recovery of two stolen Italian paintings from a private collection in America." Trey's attention laser-focused on the Monsignor's face and body language.

"Go on."

"The paintings were reported stolen from the collection of Dr. Francis Xavier Cahill." Trey described the paintings in detail.

"Your association with this case is…intriguing," the Monsignor said.

"How so?"

The Monsignor waved the question away. "How is your father these days?"

"How do you know Dr. Cahill?" Trey said.

The Monsignor shifted his stance away from Trey. "To be honest, we have never met, this Dr. Cahill and I."

A lie committed in the name of God. Trey hid his grim amusement. It was time to put the witness back on his heels and lie in the name of justice. "I must have been mistaken when I thought I saw you and Dr. Cahill talking under the Monument to Alexander VII inside St. Peter's Cathedral."

The Monument to Alexander VII was one of Bernini's late masterpieces, the most famous papal monument in St. Peter's, representing Pope Alexander VII kneeling in prayer under a representation of Death, a strange juxtaposition of the clergy and the lay, standing under the gilded bronze skeleton emerging from a doorway with an hourglass in hand.

The Monsignor stiffened and half-turned back toward Trey. "I meet a great many people, Mr. Hansen. You must have been mistaken." Then he started uphill toward the exit to the Holy See.

"So, you're saying you don't know him," Trey called.

The Monsignor glanced over his shoulder. "I do not."

Trey followed him. "Monsignor, just one more question." A classic technique Trey learned from his childhood idol, Detective Lt. Columbo.

Resembling a gnarled, black scarecrow in the dim light, the Monsignor paused before the entrance to the Holy See.

Trey said, "If I come to breakfast at the Domus Sanctae Marthae, say, anytime in the next week or so, will I find you and Dr. Cahill dining together?"

In his review of Cahill's background checks last night, Trey discovered Cahill had several times stayed at the Domus Sanctae Marthae during previous visits. The House of Saint Martha served as accommodations for visiting clergy. It required an invitation, a special security clearance, and golden keychain to enter, a privilege few laypeople enjoyed. For a devout Catholic like Cahill, this kind of invitation would be a serious ego stroke. Trey himself had stayed there while investigating a provenance for a private client a few years before. "No doubt he'll be back for another meeting."

The scarecrow reached for the door handle. "Good day, Trey. Give your father my regards." He opened the door and stepped out of sight.

Despite the Monsignor's recalcitrance, Trey could not help but smile. He was back on the offensive.

Knight takes bishop. Check.

INTERLUDE – THE RUSSIAN GAME

THE WOLFHOUND ALWAYS DID his best work under cover of night. Fortunately, his target had obliged him this evening. A cloudy, blustery dusk had settled over the city, driving the tourists and Liberation Day revelers indoors early and erasing both sun and starlight, leaving only a dismal, featureless darkness.

He crouched in the walkway on the roof of Hotel Columbus with Long Tooth across his knees. His balaclava soaked up the tension sweat that proved to him just how far out of the Zone he felt.

The Wolfhound had been muzzled for too long, allowing his skills to go stale and rusty. His heart hammered so hard in his chest it was difficult to breathe, much like his first time hunting live prey—an operator's version of "buck fever," like deer hunters experienced when a prize buck entered their line of sight.

Before leaving the US, he had spent several hours at the firing range, dusting off his skills, reacquainting himself with Long Tooth's lethal accuracy. His aim would not be an issue. His unconscious physiological responses might be. Again, he chided himself for the years of stagnation. He had kept in shape, but that was not the same as keeping his edge. After crouching for so long, his knees felt filled with shards of glass. So, while he waited for the message that his target's arrival was imminent, he took long slow breaths, and he prayed on his rosary. The Lord would give him strength. The Lord would give him calm.

Gennady Levchenko's motorcade was on its way from the airport. Its planned route to Vatican City would bring it down Via della Conciliazione to the mouth of St. Peter's Plaza, the gap in the colonnade, then turning left to follow Via Paolo IV around the south perimeter of Vatican City, to the Square of the Roman Proto-Martyrs, the Piazza dei Protomartiri Romani, where Levchenko would exit his armored limousine and enter the Vatican for his audience with the Pontiff.

However, thanks to the general chaos of the Liberation Day celebrations, Via Paolo IV was blocked off by police barricades. Such details were easily lost in bureaucratic shuffles. In fact, all routes to the Square of the Roman Proto-Martyrs were blocked by crowd control barricades. Many apologies for the inconvenience, Signore Levchenko. Levchenko would have to exit his limousine and cross St. Peter's Square to enter the Holy See.

That would be the Wolfhound's moment.

From his perch atop the campanile at Hotel Columbus, the Wolfhound had a clear line of sight all the way to the entrance of St. Peter's Basilica. The shot would be less than two hundred yards. Child's play.

Gennady Levchenko was number six on the list of wealthiest Russian oligarchs, with a personal fortune estimated at $14.6 billion. He controlled a private investment group called Volga Capital, which owned controlling interests in Russia's number-two and number-three oil and natural gas companies. He also had his fingers in the telecom industry and Moscow real estate markets.

Like many of the Russian oligarchs, he had been in a position to capitalize on the dissolution of the Soviet Union and snatch up large chunks of privatized assets for pennies on the ruble. Then again, the Russian ruble was worth about a penny these days.

Twenty-first-century Russia was nothing more than a Mafiya state, with Vladimir Putin as the godfather, the former KGB operative-turned-dictator. Putin was Stalin 2.0, likely the richest man in the world, wealthier than Jeff Bezos and Bill Gates combined, with personal assets believed to exceed $200 billion, all of it skimmed and milked from various Russian industries, like oil and gas, banking, steel, and telecom. In addition, Putin was paid tributes from oligarchs like Levchenko, whom Putin allowed to exist—as long as they were loyal to him personally. Putin had used political clout to coerce potential rivals into simply handing their assets over to him. Since the Soviet collapse, Russian banks were little more than global-scale money laundering organizations, operating with the complicity of the Putin kleptocracy.

One did not get to be an oligarch in Russia without the direct sanction of the godfather. Those who tried otherwise found themselves dead or imprisoned. Levchenko positioned himself as one of Putin's closest allies, which made Levchenko's visit to the Vatican a diplomatic meeting. But Levchenko was not just an oil magnate with more money than a small country. He was instrumental in smoothing the way for Russia to annex Crimea, and in part for the pro-Russia propaganda campaign keeping Ukrainians at each other's throats. He was responsible for the deaths of hundreds of people when one of his refineries exploded in a hellish conflagration that wiped out most of a nearby town, quoted as saying,

"Let them burn." The inhabitants of the town were mostly Muslim Kazakhs. He was also suspected to have murdered several of his own associates for disloyalty.

A text message came over the Wolfhound's burner phone: *PNG on VDC.*

Persona non grata on Via della Conciliazione.

That was the agreed-upon message from his spotter, indicating Levchenko's motorcade had rounded the corner down Via della Conciliazione. The Wolfhound lifted a small periscope that allowed him to look down the street without exposing his silhouette at the roof line. In the distance, a barrage of flashing blue lights appeared on the thoroughfare, coming closer.

Then he scanned the nearby rooftops with his binoculars for any other security or police personnel. Seeing nothing that would threaten him or his mission, he covered himself and Long Tooth with a net patterned in urban camouflage to hide his outline, and positioned himself at the corner of the campanile roof of Hotel Columbus. He sighted in at the entrance to St. Peter's Basilica. Would the Almighty damn him for shedding blood on holy ground? He could not believe that to be so, given the blackness of Levchenko's soul. The Wolfhound was making the world a better place, after all. He was doing God's work. He was God's disciple.

The three-car private motorcade passed below, a massive black limousine bearing Russian flags, preceded and flanked by police cars.

He knew Levchenko's face in minute detail. His light-amplifying scope would allow him to discern facial features as if it were broad daylight. At two hundred yards, the bullet would drop 4.3

inches. Windage was unpredictable in tonight's blustery breezes, but the bullet would be traveling between the buildings on each side of Via della Conciliazione, hopefully making the effects negligible. The M21's cheek piece aligned his eye perfectly with the scope. The stock felt warm. His finger settled in beside the trigger guard, maintaining trigger discipline.

The motorcade reached the mouth of the colonnade and eased to a halt, stymied by the barricades. The lead police cars seemed discomfited by the presence of the barricades. No doubt, streams of confusion and recrimination were flooding the police radio bands.

The Wolfhound fixed his reticle on the limousine. Would Levchenko hide in his car and wait hours for the barricades to be removed? The police drivers would soon know their only way into Vatican City had been "mistakenly" walled off. Would the Great Man simply get out and walk the last two hundred yards?

The Wolfhound breathed deep and slow, steady. Now, finally, he found the long-lost Zone, and his body began to obey him. His heart rate returned to normal, his breathing slowed. He willed a wave of relaxation through him. "*In Hoc Signo Vinces,*" he chanted to himself.

He could not resist a smile as police officers got out of their cars and shooed away the few remaining tourists near St. Peter's Square. Once that was complete, the moment came.

The limousine doors opened and three large men in lumpy suits and crewcuts climbed out, adjusting their attire and checking their concealed weapons. One of them appeared to give the "all clear," and another man climbed out of the car. The Wolfhound instantly recognized the gray hair, the widow's peak, the sharp features, the lizard eyes.

He held his breath.

His slid his finger against the trigger.

It all happened so quickly, so effortlessly.

With practiced ease, the reticle found the back of Levchenko's head and hovered there for half a second. Then his finger stroked the trigger like it was a lover's cheek. The rifle barked and bucked. The second shot was already lined up at the moment Levchenko's frontal lobe exploded into the air, snapping his head forward and backward in a motion akin to another shot the Wolfhound would never forget. A bodyguard threw himself onto his master's back, to his credit, but the second bullet was already on its way. It passed above the back of the bodyguard's Kevlar vest, through his left lung, to be stopped by the front of his Kevlar vest. In the tumult of dying flesh, the third bullet went through Levchenko's aorta and turned half of his heart into pulp, spattered across two more bodyguards.

Elation surged through the Wolfhound's breast, but he suppressed it.

The police buzzed like a kicked hornets' nest.

Screams echoed down Via della Conciliazione.

His flash suppressor would have hidden his exact position, and the echoes were no doubt confusing, but the police would be closing on his position in moments.

He dropped out of sight behind the hotel's roof, snatched up all his brass, and ran half-crouched for the stairwell. But in the dark and overcome by the elation of his success, he miscalculated his steps near the repair work along the roof line. A workman had left a wheelbarrow and a shovel half-filling the walkway. The Wolfhound stumbled over the wheelbarrow and fell face-first into a patch of wet plaster. Pain exploded in his chest and chin as he skidded across the roof. But ignoring pain was a long-practiced skill. He levered himself up with the butt of Long Tooth and stumbled onward, regaining his stride as he neared the stairwell.

Down the stairwell to his room in less than a minute, where he disassembled Long Tooth, secreted its components in the false bottom of his suitcase along with the most sensitive and suspicious objects from his go bag; then he hurried out into the hallway, down the back stairs and out into the street behind, Via dei Cavalieri del Santo Sepolcro.

The Wolfhound walked at a leisurely pace, suitcase rolling behind him, listening to the chaos in progress about a block away, then turning to his right on Borgo Santo Spirito. Sirens wailed and echoed. He was just an old man, beyond suspicion for any wrongdoings.

Down narrow alleys and dark streets he walked, unhurried, unnoticed, just a few hundred yards, until he reached a gate into Vatican City on the south curve of St. Peter's colonnade. The Swiss Guard and Vatican Police were there with full weaponry, bathed in floodlights, now on high alert.

A priest stepped out of the shadows and whispered something to the officer in charge. The officer came forward and motioned the Wolfhound to approach the gate.

The gate opened. The Wolfhound passed into the sovereign territory of the Catholic Church. He had, in effect, just crossed a national border.

CHAPTER 22

"**WHEN I GRADUATED FROM** high school, this weird thing happened, one of the many weird things over my life.

"On Graduation Day, we had a kegger party on the tennis court in our back yard. Back then we were old enough to drink at eighteen. A kegger is just what you did. It wasn't huge, maybe forty people coming and going, high school kids and such. My parents were there, Mom with her white wine and Dad with his Falstaff beer. This was the first party like this we'd ever hosted. I was shocked my dad allowed it. When Mary graduated, she didn't want any such kind of thing.

"Mary had gone off to college the year before, but she came home for my party. There was this guy in my class who was totally infatuated with her, a baseball player. She had never dated anyone before, and she didn't want to date him, but he wouldn't take no for an answer. He was a total asswipe. But he must have heard she was coming back for this. So Mary was pounding beer, getting drunk out of her mind. About ten o'clock, this guy plows his Camaro up onto our front lawn, jumps out, starts screaming her name. She runs to the front door and starts screaming back. Finally, he tears out of there, drives over a flower bed, throws dirt up onto the front porch, tears up our front lawn. Gone. But then the one of the neighbors, who never liked us, called the cops.

"One squad car shows up. My sister is still on the front lawn scream-ing at the cops that the Camaro speeding away needs to be stopped. He's been terrorizing her. They grab her, slam her face-down on the hood of their car and handcuff her before shoving her into their car.

"My dad goes storming through the front door, and I'm standing in the front yard watching this shitshow unfolding. He tells the cops, 'You can't treat my daughter that way.' He starts arguing with them.

"Two minutes later, a dozen cop cars come barreling down our street, and they jump out in full riot gear. Full fucking riot gear. This was 1978. Police weren't militarized like they are now. I've thought about this for years. Why full riot gear? I didn't know there were so many cops in the suburb we lived in. They must have sent them all.

"They grabbed my dad, slammed him onto the ground, and cuffed him. They dragged him to a car and threw him in. Something in the way they handled him made me think they knew him, like he was a known felon or something.

"I was just like... I just...

"How do you send what amounted to a SWAT hit squad to a keg party? It wasn't even a big keg party. It just seemed so excessive.

"But here's the weird part. They never charged him with anything. Him or my sister. A couple hours later, Mom went and picked them up. It never came up again."

***

Marie and Trey were sitting outside, enjoying a bottle of 2014 Bolgheri Tenuta San Guido Sassicaia in Hotel Bramante's cozy gar-den, when she heard the sound.

A gunshot.

Then another, perhaps a second later. Then a third.

She and Trey stared at each other.

"Was that what I think it was?" she said.

He nodded.

It had been close, perhaps as close as a block away, but the echoes over the rooftops made it difficult to determine the direction. She was far from a firearms expert, but her dad had been a hunter. She had accompanied him to the practice range enough times she knew what guns sounded like in real life. The shot had the kind of deep thunder only high-powered rifles produced.

This was Italy, where firearms were strictly regulated, at least in comparison to the United States. One did not simply fire off a couple of rounds in the city of Rome without reason.

Her intuition screamed this was a hit. Someone had just died. The look on Trey's face told her he had the same thought.

"Let's go inside," he said.

"Yes, let's." She suddenly wanted to be indoors and under cover.

Sirens echoed in the distance, coming closer, a swarm of them.

"Oh, my God," she said, "that's a lot of sirens."

Back in their room, they closed and locked the doors, drew the curtains, and switched the television to RaiNews, the Italian news network.

They sat on the bed together, and he put his arm around her. She leaned into him.

On RaiNews was a segment about the restoration of some of Florence's oldest streets, hardly a breaking story, so Trey pulled out his laptop and scanned social media for clues about what might have happened. It didn't take long for him to discover shaky videos blazing with blue police flashers. Even in the cacophony of emergency sirens and lights, he recognized the entrance to St. Peter's Square, now choked with police cars. An ambulance pulled up and paramedics piled out.

Another mobile phone video showed a limousine marked with Russian flags, swarming with Italian law enforcement. The unstable video suggested two bodies on the ground, dark, glossy red slicking the pavement around them. He played these videos several times.

Trey said, "It was an assassination. Three high-powered rifle shots. *Bang. Bang. Bang.*"

Finally, a news anchor came on RaiNews with a breaking news story. On video behind him was St. Peter's Square awash in flashing blue lights.

Trey's Italian was better than Marie's, but she was able to snag some of the facts. A Russian diplomat on his way to an audience with the Pope was dead, along with one of the bodyguards. The assassin was still on the loose.

"They'll never catch him," Trey said.

"Well, anybody who could pull this off probably has an escape route—"

"No, they'll never catch *him*."

"What are you talking about?"

"Okie did this."

She stood and faced him. "Oh, come on. You're not serious." She did not have the brain space for one of his conspiracy theory rabbit holes. Trey's father was such a bogeyman in his mind, the old man might as well have been responsible for assassinating Abraham Lincoln. But she could almost see the gears spinning in Trey's mind, tying together a host of manic connections.

"I know it sounds crazy," he said. "But I can feel it."

All she could do was muster her patience, sit down next to him again, and let the oncoming tide of ideas wash over her, and then maybe she would be able to talk some sense into him.

Trey went on, "It's all connected, it has to be. Back in the day, I know he killed them. I have no proof, but my gut *knows* it."

"Trey. He's in his seventies now."

"No one ever retires from the Company. A man my dad knows just mistook me for him, like he was expecting to see him in Rome. I freaked out, because I felt like Okie was here somehow."

"Please don't do this to yourself," she said.

"It's got to be him."

"Why, Trey? Why does it?"

He began to pace. "McGillicuddy married my parents. McGillicuddy is involved with the Cahill theft. It's got to be connected, but I don't know how. Not yet. All these years, I've wondered why my childhood was so fucked up, why I had to have such an awful man for a father. It's like I can feel him here, like when I was in my basement bedroom and I could hear him walking around upstairs."

"Trey..."

He ignored her and kept pacing. "I've been chewing on that meeting with McGillicuddy all day. Arrogant prick. He's involved, too." His voice rose into an outburst. "They're in it together!" But then he sat on the bed and sighed. "I sound utterly off the deep end, don't I."

Marie took his hand in hers and nodded solemnly. She wanted to deny all this, call it nonsense, but this time she could not. Trey's instincts as an investigator had proved right far too often for her simply to discount them. She had to get him back into a more pragmatic line of thinking, however. "Please breathe. The more important question is: what do we do now?"

"I'll never get McGillicuddy to budge, at least not without more leverage. But he knows I'm onto him. I can't ask Vasari for any more favors. I have proof the Vatican sold the paintings to Cahill, but I don't have proof he's trying to sell them back, only hearsay. I have proof Cahill visited the Vatican on a big, shiny invitation, but no record of why. The dots are making a picture, but I'm missing too many to see what it is."

***

Trey fell asleep with the television on, waiting for more word of the assassination, but his sleep was fraught with questions that would give him no rest. The next morning, he rose exhausted and bleary eyed. He called the front desk for a newspaper before he even showered, a disconcerting break from his daily routine.

Loredana, Maurizio's wife, brought him a copy of *la Repubblica*. The top headline read, "*Assassinio!*" He cursed his lack of fluency with Italian, which made gleaning all the important details from the attendant article slow and difficult.

The target was a Russian oil magnate named Gennady Levchenko, killed by shots through the head and through the chest.

One of Levchenko's bodyguards had been wounded and died at the scene. The assassin was still at large.

The reason for Levchenko's visit to the Vatican was undisclosed, so he went online to dig up everything he could about the victim.

Within five minutes of searching, Trey had found enough to indicate Levchenko had an enemies list that would reach to the moon. Only his closeness to Putin protected him from assassination by his own people.

So, whoever had killed Levchenko did not fear reprisal from Putin's FSB. Or maybe someone was giving Putin the finger.

As Trey finished his morning toilet, Marie began to stir. He kissed her on the forehead and said, "I'm going out for a little while. Wait at the hotel until I get back. And lock up behind me."

Leaving the room, he went out into the lobby and spotted Maurizio and Loredana behind the front desk.

Maurizio's smile lacked its usual warmth. "Did you hear the news?"

"About the killing, yes."

"A terrible, terrible thing. *Una cosa terribile.*" Maurizio clucked his tongue.

"I was sitting outside and heard the shots. They sounded very close."

"Me, too. They came from Hotel Columbus. The roof."

"That's a block from here!"

Maurizio nodded. "Scary stuff, Signore."

Trey's mind went into overdrive. Had Okie been staying at the Hotel Columbus? Had his father been within such a short distance, here in Rome? What if they had run into each other?

"You want to see something strange?" Maurizio said.

"Yes."

Maurizio pulled out a newspaper and laid it on the counter. "Big papers won't print this. Makes the Church look bad."

The newspaper was one of Italy's small daily rags, *Il Fatto Quotidiano, The Daily Fact*. Its feature story was also the assassination, featuring a stock photo of Levchenko alongside lurid photos of blood pools, angry Russians, and police shoving rubberneckers away from the scene. The story dominated the entire front page. In the lower corner was a hand sketch of an emblem or seal. Trey knew it instantaneously. He pointed to that section of text. "What does this say?"

Maurizio's eyes scanned briefly. "This is a picture of something police found." He helped explain himself with a rubber-stamping motion. "The killer left a stamp in some *malta*...what is the English—"

"Mortar? A stamp in wet mortar?"

Maurizio snapped his fingers. "Yes!"

"Was the stamp left on purpose? By accident?"

"Accident, they think."

"How did it get in the mortar?"

"They think it was on the end of the gun... Ehhh, on the bottom." Maurizio waved his hands, trying to find the right words.

"On the wood? The rifle butt?"

"Yes!"

Trey took a deep breath and let it out.

Maurizio pointed at the photo. "Dangerous to the Church, yes? You know what this is?"

Trey nodded. Any conspiracy theorist worth his paranoia knew on sight the emblem of the Knights Templar. The impression resembled a coin approximately one and a half inches in diameter. In the center of the coin, there was the Knights Templar Cross of the York Rite Masonic Freemasons positioned on a shield. Around this image was the outline of what was likely the butt of a rifle stock, as if the coin had been embedded there.

If this were a Templar coin, on the reverse side would be two knights riding one horse, symbolizing the knights' vow of poverty, thus they shared one horse. Encircling the knights on horseback was the Latin phrase, SIGILLUM MILITUM XPISTI. "Seal of the Soldiers of Christ."

Trey's business card bore a similar seal, a variation of the coin design embedded in the butt of Okie's rifle, but with a stylized image that merged the letters "I," "H," "S," and "V," from the Latin phrase *In hoc signo vinces*, meaning *In this sign, you shall conquer.* The phrase had been used by a number of military groups over the centuries, including the Templars. It was one of Okie's favorite phrases, and Trey had seized it in defiance of his father and of the PTSD his father had bequeathed him.

After the gruesome, ruthless suppression of the Order of Knights Templar by King Philip IV of France, a handful of survivors had carried on, and the Order eventually morphed into the Freemasons and the Jesuit Order.

Holy Cross was a Jesuit college.

CHAPTER 23

"MY WHOLE LIFE, I've been Emmett Hansen the Third. Way back when, my credit report kept getting mixed up with my dad's, which was especially painful because I cut ties with him after college. When I went to college, I'd try to get a credit card, and it would be denied. I'd ask why, and the problem would turn out to be all my dad's shit. Back in the seventies, records weren't as sophisticated as they are now. It took a tremendous amount of work to prove, over and over again, that I'm not him.

"Sometimes I thought he encouraged that confusion. Made it harder for people to find him. Deflection. He was using me as a kind of shield.

"People would come up to me, people I didn't know, and say, 'How's your father?' Or, 'Is it safe?'

"I would be like, 'Is what safe?' And they would look surprised at my ignorance and run off."

***

The emergency vehicles were gone, but the police barricades were still in place. The Vatican was blocked off, closed to visitors. Trey had to see the scene for himself.

As he stood at the corner of Hotel Columbus, looking toward St. Peter's Square, a chill went through him. The assassin—God, it had to be Okie—had chosen his position well, with a clear, wide-open shot to the mouth of the colonnade, into the keyhole of Christ. He had the urge to call his mother and ask to speak to Okie, just to see if he was there. He could feel a panic attack brewing at the very thought of it, so he let that urge pass and decided it was time to check his messages, a concrete thing, a distraction.

In his email box was another message from the mysterious email address in L.A.

Stop jerking my chain. We need to meet or I walk.

This felt like an important contact, and unless Monsignor McGillicuddy had an inexplicable change of heart, Trey was out of leads in Rome. Plus, the brazen assassination on their very doorstep had shaken both him and Marie. Too much weirdness, too many little coincidences. It was time to go back to LA, find Miguel Gomez, and talk to this witness. Plus, he had evidence now that implicated Cahill in a fraud. It was circumstantial evidence, but it might be enough to make Dunwood put on the skids long enough for Trey to find the smoking gun.

He had to let this mysterious witness hang a little while longer.

It was time to touch base with Nicklaus Palmer. Before he dialed the number, though, he made sure no one was within earshot of the conversation.

When Nicklaus picked up, Trey said, "We need to talk. You're not going to believe all this."

Nicklaus gave a rich, cultured laugh. "Oh, my friend, I'll believe just about anything with this case."

"Then we need to meet. I don't trust the phone."

"Good man. I would like you to stop in London on your way back to the States. Meet me at my office tonight."

"I'll be on a plane this afternoon."

***

In the taxi on the way to the airport, Trey and Marie shared their mix of sadness and relief to be leaving Rome so soon. They had been hoping for more time for romantic pursuits, but the assassination had rattled them both. Trey couldn't shake the feeling of a bullseye on the back of his head, and he could not bear the thought of subjecting Marie to the same danger.

She had initially protested going back to Chicago alone, but Trey impressed upon her the need to get back to the kids. He would be back in the States only a few hours behind her.

"But you're going to LA, not coming home," she said.

"I have to."

She bit her lip and sighed.

News coverage about the assassination plastered every newspaper, every television screen in Italy, and the Rome airport was no exception. Security was increased tenfold. A handful of broadcasts speculated on the impression of the Templar emblem.

Experienced travelers, Trey and Marie could go through much of the airport process in their sleep. Tickets, luggage, security...

But then, as Trey was going through the security line, his briefcase still in the X-ray machine, an officer approached him. "Signore Hansen."

Knocked out of his reverie, Trey said, "Yes?"

The officer was short, stern, blockish, hands clasped behind his back. His English was excellent. "Come with me, please."

"What's this about?" Trey said.

"We have some questions."

Marie, behind Trey in line, looked alarmed. "What's going on?"

Trey said, "I don't know."

"Come with me, please," the officer said. "Bring your briefcase."

"How long will this be? I have a flight to catch."

The officer's face darkened. "Come with me, Signore. *Ora!*"

The thunderclouds of threat that had been hovering on the horizon rushed toward him, tamping Trey's emotions into a cold, dark hole. His briefcase emerged from the X-ray machine and slid down the conveyor belt. Trey grabbed it and turned to Marie. "If I'm not out, get on your plane."

"But—!"

He needed to get her out of Italy as soon as possible. "Hug the girls for me."

She nodded uncertainly, but she let him go.

He followed the guard away from the security station and was ushered into a small nearby room—an interrogation room—with a frosted glass window reinforced by crisscrossed wire. The guard, dressed as the *Polizia di Stato*, in a blue jacket and grey trousers with a purple stripe, followed him in and shut the door. Another man came in through a second, interior door, wearing the Valentino-designed uniform of the Italian Carabinieri, hair cut short, standing nearly as tall as Trey, sharp with single-mindedness. His name tag read *Solazzo*.

"What can I do for you, Officer Solazzo?" Trey said.

"Passport, *per favore*," Solazzo said, holding out his hand.

Trey fished his passport from the breast pocket of his blazer and handed it over, feeling a stab of worry. One did not relinquish one's passport without serious potential consequences. "What's this about?"

Solazzo flipped through Trey's passport for several moments, his face tight. He looked back and forth several times between Trey's face and his passport photo. His teeth were stained by cigarette smoke and the skin of his hands looked like leather. His eyes were dark, probing drills. He spoke English with a mixture of Italian and British accents. "How long have you been in Italy?"

"About four days. I arrived on Thursday," Trey said. Today was Monday.

"Traveling alone?"

Best not to lie when asked a direct question, especially when he had nothing to hide. "No, my wife is traveling with me."

"Then why did you not say 'we'?"

Trey shrugged. "I didn't think it was relevant. She's not here with me at this moment."

"But she could be. I could send an officer to her gate to drag her back here right now."

Trey shrugged again, trying to remain nonchalant, even as alarm bells started clanging in his mind. He had to focus to manage his personal struggles with authority figures. Bullies instantly got his back up. "If you think that's necessary. Why don't you tell me what this is about? Maybe I can help you clear it up."

"We are looking for a man named Emmett Hansen. That is your name, yes?"

"I certainly have nothing to hide. Why are you looking for me?" Trey tried to keep his voice light, neutral, helpful, but old suspicions, old complications, were rearing their heads deep in his gut.

"Why did you come to Rome?"

"A combination of business and pleasure. I'm pursuing an insurance fraud investigation for Lloyd's of London, and the investigation brought me here. My wife and I decided to make a little holiday of it."

Solazzo seemed to chew on this for a moment. A micro expression told Trey this was not what Solazzo was expecting to hear. "You have proof of this?"

Trey opened his briefcase, pulled out his file and handed it over. "In fact, I could use the help of the Italian police. One Italian Renaissance painting and one Italian Baroque painting were reported stolen from a private collection in America. I have reason to believe the theft is a hoax to collect an insurance settlement, and that the paintings will be sold to a buyer in Rome."

Solazzo paged through Trey's file, puzzlement peeking through his hard features.

A moment of insight flared up in Trey's mind. "I should point out that I am Emmett Hansen the *Third*. I go by the name of Trey. I have been mistaken for my father in the past."

Solazzo continued to page through Trey's file.

Trey threw out a fishing line. "Perhaps Emmett Hansen *Junior* is the man you're looking for. He often goes by the name Okie."

"Is he in Italy?" Solazzo said.

"I couldn't say. We don't exactly speak."

"Why is that?"

"Because he abused the hell out of me and my siblings growing up, to the point he drove my sister into a mental hospital and left me with serious PTSD. Why are you looking for him?"

"I did not say I was looking for him."

"Then why are you looking for me?"

"Tell me about all your activities since you arrived in Rome."

"Look, Officer. I'm in pursuit of an investigation involving paintings worth approximately one hundred and twenty million dollars. I'm collaborating with the Los Angeles Police Department and the FBI. And you're going to question *me* about my activities in Rome? I can offer you the phone numbers for my contacts at Lloyd's of London, the LAPD, and the FBI. They'll verify whatever you want. But I'm losing my willingness to be cooperative if you don't tell me what this is about." Name-dropping the FBI was a bit of a gamble, but he hoped Special Agent Alderman would at least verify Trey's basic bona fides.

The officer handed a notepad to Trey. "Write their numbers here, please."

Trey took the pad and copied down the numbers. He seldom needed to use the address book on his phone. Important phone numbers naturally stuck in his head.

Solazzo took the pad and went back through the door, leaving Trey alone with the security officer.

He checked his watch. Thirty minutes to make his gate.

Strained silence flowed past like cold tar. The guard stood before the exit, beefy arms crossed. Trey's insides started to vibrate with what was either anger or panic, perhaps both, and it would be a race to see which exploded first. He started his four-square breathing and began tapping on his hand with a finger.

There were other flights to London tonight. He was confident Nicklaus would be willing to meet him even at 3:00 a.m., if need be. What worried him more was further delay in getting back to LA and losing his potential witness. As the minutes passed and his mind wandered, he fantasized about dropping the bombshell on Cahill that he had proof of the paintings' Vatican history. He also fantasized about coldcocking Dicky Dunwood with a chair.

Fifteen minutes went by in continued silence. The growing tension had almost become a visible thing. The security officer's expression grew more pinched, his lips a white slash, his foot tapping, as if Trey's outward unflappability was annoying him.

Trey allowed amusement at this to creep in. He would not suffer bullies.

Five minutes until his plane was scheduled to board.

Could this really be about Okie? Were the Italian authorities looking for him? Did they think Okie might be connected to Levchenko's assassination? Was he on some secret international watch list?

All those times Okie had used Trey as a sort of identity shield came roaring back and stoked his anger.

He checked his watch again. His plane to Heathrow was boarding.

More minutes passed. By now, the question of who would speak first, Trey or the security officer, had become a test of wills. The interrogator versus the prisoner.

Then a shadow appeared on the window of the interior door. The door opened and Officer Solazzo came in. "Your story checks out, Mr. Hansen." Solazzo handed over Trey's file and passport. "You are free to go."

Trey took them crisply and snapped the file back into his brief-case. His passport he tucked into his breast jacket pocket. "How about apologies for the inconvenience?"

Solazzo's lip curled upward ever so slightly.

Trey grabbed his briefcase and ran for the gate.

PART III

"You're not to be so blind with patriotism that you can't face reality. Wrong is wrong, no matter who does it or says it."

- **Malcolm X**

INTERLUDE - CASTLING

HIGH OVER THE MOONLIT Atlantic, the Wolfhound slept the sleep of the just. Before departing for the airport, the Monsignor had congratulated him on sending a monster to Hell, then he had placed his hand on the Wolfhound's head and blessed him while he knelt before him.

He could still feel the warmth of that blessing upon him, as if God Himself had spoken to him. "You have done well, my son."

A judder of turbulence wakened him. He sat up and rubbed his face.

Alone in the Gulfstream G650 cabin, he stood up to stretch his legs and relieve his old man's bladder. Another bout of turbulence made him steady himself against the chairs, but this kind of turbulence was nothing compared to the global turbulence that was coming, the kind that would drive more demons out of the shadows.

Since the public end of the Cold War, America had grown complacent. One presidential administration after another had grown softer and softer on their former Soviet adversaries, but no one in the intelligence community believed the Cold War had really ended. The Russians certainly didn't. "Russia" stood for Reorganized Union of Soviet Socialists In Asia, and their leader was KGB all the way to the bone.

And now, God help them, there were people in America who thought Russia was "our friend" now. Fools, idiots, and worse. NATO still existed for a clear and present reason.

In that complacency, the Russians had seized the initiative and taken the Cold War to new fronts—cyberwarfare, election meddling, psychological warfare through social media. And still Americans sat back and numbed themselves with reality TV and video games, on one hand fairly certain that the rest of the world did not matter, and on the other hand terrified of it. Only the terror part of that equation was justified.

Back in the Wolfhound's heyday, the spy game had been brutal and ruthless, and the Russians still played the game that way. The most common way the Soviets executed foreign spies, including Americans, was to feed them feet first into a crematorium—as slowly as possible.

In an alley in West Berlin, he had once stabbed a KGB operative in the throat with an icicle, then went back into the pub, placed the icicle beside the fireplace, and finished his beer.

America had gone soft. It had allowed Satan's influence to permeate its very bones, steal its courage, drain its righteousness.

But someone still had to keep the Russians in check. Putin had run roughshod over the Ukraine and Crimea. He was still doing it. And the West did *nothing*. Russia could run its tanks to the border of Poland, and the West would do *nothing*.

The Wolfhound used to have the ear of a president. He used to be the Red Right Hand of a president. Heady days, those. But they'd thrown him out like he was garbage, put him out to pasture before his time. He was not the only one. This new work would be a clarion call to the old spooks, the old operators. The world needed them again. He had much work to do and little time left to make sure it was done.

It sometimes amused him how Hollywood and thriller writers often imagined grand schemes dreamed up by the CIA to brainwash people into being assassins. The truth was that the CIA had more wannabe assassins than it knew what to do with, highly motivated men like former SEALs, Green Berets, Marines, even mercenaries, who *really* wanted to give the Bad Guys lead poisoning but had never been let off the leash. The problem was, as it had been since President Gerald Ford tried to ban political assassinations, that the political will to follow through had died. America only had the stomach to get bloody in school shootings, the perfect example of how the Devil's influence had eaten at the fabric of society. Meanwhile, the hardcore special operators, frothing to tear their enemies bloody new orifices, were like Rottweilers kicked into submission and chained in a corner where they could only growl.

The trouble was, it all took money. A small group of guys with a significant budget could do great work—the CIA had done incredible things on a shoestring budget for decades—but under-the-radar globetrotting, ducking in and out of countries and bypassing customs, most often happened via military transport. He and the Monsignor did not have the option of military transport.

Dawn broke on the horizon behind the jet as it crossed over the east coast of the U.S.

The Wolfhound's encrypted satellite phone rang. He answered.

The Monsignor's voice came over the line. "We have a problem."

"What is it?"

"You left evidence at the scene." The Monsignor sounded mightily displeased.

"I never leave evidence at the scene."

"Does your rifle have a Templar coin embedded in the stock?"

He blinked. How could the Monsignor know that? He had never shown it to a soul. It was his strength, his talisman. "Yes."

"You left an impression in some wet mortar on the roof of the Hotel Columbus."

He remembered stumbling over the repair site on the roof. Had he put the butt of his rifle down? He could not remember.

Monsignor McGillicuddy went on, "The police discovered the impression, and the media has gotten hold of it. The Church is suppressing the story as best we can, but it's somewhat of a poopstorm."

"I'm very sorry about that, Father." The Wolfhound clasped his hands to pray. "O my God, I am heartily sorry for having offended you, and I detest all my sins, because I dread the loss of Heaven and the pains of Hell; but most of all because they offend you, my God, who are all good and deserving of all my love. I firmly resolve, with the help of Your grace, to confess my sins, to do penance, and to amend my life. Amen." Then he picked up the phone again. "How shall I atone?"

"You must wear your metal cilice for two hours a day for forty days and receive no Eucharist or other sacraments for forty nights."

The Wolfhound's cilice was in his luggage. Essentially a barbwire garter, the cilice would be tied around his thigh, under his clothing. Its tiny spikes would cause him intense pain, perhaps bleeding if tied tightly enough, every moment he wore it.

"Thank you, Father."

"Godspeed, my son."

With daylight pouring into the cabin, he took the opportunity for a little relaxation. He pulled out his sketchbook from his luggage and began to sketch the outlines of St. Peter's Square, the gap in the colonnade, the exact spot where Levchenko had died, the orientation of the fallen body. It would make a fine painting. With five hours to Los Angeles, he had plenty of time.

CHAPTER 24

"IT WASN'T JUST THE credit reports. I got collection calls. I got strange phone calls, someone breathing on the other end. When Lloyd's was doing background checks on me, the first time they hired me as a consultant, there were several little crossed wires between my identity and his. I had to provide reams of documentation to straighten those out. Fortunately, they had some patience and were willing to work through that. After all that, I'm pretty sure it was all intentional."

"Intentional? Why?"

"He needed a patsy. He named me after him to make me his foil, his scapegoat, his sacrificial lamb. He laid his unpaid bills, his poor credit, and his whoring onto me without hesitation or remorse. I was simply his mark. A throwaway."

"Whoring?"

"His 'work' office was near the railroad tracks in this seedy industrial area. Not far from there was a sleazy looking strip club. It would get busted every few months for prostitution. When I learned to drive, I passed by there occasionally and saw his car in the parking lot."

"Were you following him?"

"There's some irony, right? Surveilling my old man, the spook."

***

Trey made the gate just as they were closing the jet bridge. Some serious fast-talking got him on the plane and in his seat with only moments to spare. He wanted to grab a few moments of rest on the flight, but he could not expunge Solazzo from his mind. The only conclusion he could reach was that the Italian authorities were looking for Emmett Hansen Jr., not Emmett Hansen III.

But why?

Did they suspect Okie was the assassin atop the Hotel Columbus? Was he some sort of international criminal, a wanted man? Was there some decades-old event that had put Okie on an Italian watch list?

It all sounded too crazy. Okie was an old man. He should be home watching reruns of *Mutual of Omaha's Wild Kingdom* and drinking Falstaff. That had been the only television Trey was allowed to watch as a kid.

Trey considered calling his younger brother, Patrick. Patrick was the sibling anointed to take care of their parents during their dotage. Trey was grateful his parents had someone looking out for them, not because he gave a shit about their daily welfare, but so that he didn't have to think about it. He could not imagine why either of his siblings would be inclined to take care of their parents after their childhood hell. If Trey someday learned his father had died in a dumpster on skid row, he would lose about thirty seconds of sleep over it.

For decades Patrick had called Trey's conspiracy theories about their father "crackpot nonsense." Whenever the topic of their father's past came up, Patrick would say things like, "So what if he did work for the government? What's the big deal?" Patrick was also the Great Conciliator, trying to have Trey "come in from the cold," as it were, and reconcile with their parents, which Trey steadfastly, adamantly refused to do. Some years ago, Trey had said as much to Patrick, to which Patrick replied, "The old man was just strict is all. It was the times."

Trey had refrained from retorting *Not every kid in the sixties and seventies got his head slammed repeatedly against the wall.* Trey had taken the brunt of abuse that Patrick had mostly avoided. It was a familiar path of conversation between them, so he let it go.

It was after 9:00 p.m. London time when his plane touched down at Heathrow Airport. A drizzling rain stippled the airplane window, and a thick overcast veiled London's blaze of city lights.

At about 10:00 p.m., he checked into his hotel and fought back the waves of emotional exhaustion that threatened to tackle him onto the bed and hold him down until sometime next decade. He choked down enough acrid, hotel-room coffee to wake up an opium den, showered, and dressed for the meeting. One did not visit Lloyd's of London, no matter the time of day, in a T-shirt and sport coat. He would not be allowed in the building without a suit, tie, and lace-up shoes, so he put on his bespoke Joseph Abboud tailored suit. The suit was dark blue with subtle chalk stripes and a fuchsia silk lining inside the jacket, and his footwear a pair of black ostrich leather, monk-strap shoes by Donald J. Pliner. His extra-long tie was designed and handmade for him by Talarico Cravatte in Rome. Then he pulled his iPhone from its Faraday bag long enough to text Nicklaus that he was on his way. The late hour did not concern him. As far as Trey knew, Nicklaus Palmer lived in his office and never slept.

The black cab deposited Trey at the curb before the Lloyd's Building at Lime Street and Leadenhall Street. Designed by British architect Richard Rogers and officially opened in 1986, the Lloyd's of London building was considered one of the most iconic, futuristic buildings in London, combining both industrial functionality and aesthetics. Similar to Rogers' steel and glass Centre Pompidou in Paris, the Lloyd's Building, consisting of three towers with exterior elevators, had all of the mechanical services located externally to free up interior spaces.

Even though it was almost 11:00 p.m., the security guard at the entrance let him enter straightaway, as if expecting him. Trey walked into the lobby and had his Lloyd's Pass swiped by the officer to allow the kiosk stall to open for his entrance. Directly in front of him were the up and down escalators. The escalator was a series of switchbacks at every floor landing to allow people on and off. Here on the ground floor, the Lutine Bell hung from the rostrum of the Lloyd's underwriting room, a symbol of Lloyd's' long heritage as a maritime insurance company. The bell had been salvaged from the wreck of the eighteenth-century frigate *HMS Lutine*, sunk by a storm in the West Frisian Islands in 1799 with a belly full of gold. It was recovered in 1858, and for one hundred twenty years was rung twice to notify brokers and underwriters of the arrival of overdue ships. If a ship and its cargo were lost, the bell was rung once.

The silent escalator took Trey to the third-floor gallery, where

Nicklaus's underwriting box looked out over the central open core of the Lloyd's Building.

The underwriting box was basically a rectangular table that traditionally seated six people. Nicklaus Palmer was old school and still believed in sitting at his syndicate's box with both his underwriting team and his claim team, three underwriters sitting on one side of the box across from the claim director and his team. Many syndicates had removed their claim people from Lloyd's and positioned them at off-site offices to save on the rising rental costs since the sale of the building from the Germans to the Chinese.

Nicklaus's claim manager's chair was empty at this hour, but his underwriting chair was filled with files.

As Trey stepped off the escalator, he proceeded around the square layout of the floor to where Nicklaus Palmer waited against the concrete wall to greet him with a broad smile and a firm handshake. Nicklaus stood just under six feet tall, with Roman features, wire-rimmed glasses, and a healthy portion of salt-and-pepper hair coming to a widow's peak. His stature and build bespoke a man who stayed active, even at his age. "It's been too long," Nicklaus said.

"It has," Trey said. "Thanks for meeting me so late."

"As you know," Nicklaus said, "I don't sleep."

"I'm getting less and less myself."

Nicklaus gestured Trey to take a seat in the overstuffed chair before his desk. Nicklaus relished the open concept of the Lloyd's Building, never one for closed-door discussions. There was an energy in the building, even at this hour, born from the company's 300-year history and 24-hour operations. "Drink?"

"I could use one."

Nicklaus poured him two fingers of what Trey knew to be Caol Ila 18 Year single malt scotch from a crystal decanter, then one for himself, neat. Trey was not a habitual scotch drinker, but he appreciated its many complexities. "An interesting couple of days in Rome," Nicklaus said as he handed Trey the crystal tumbler.

"Interesting, right. In the sense of the old Chinese curse." Trey reached across Nicklaus's desk with his tumbler. They clinked glasses. "Cheers."

"This case gets more complicated by the day, it seems."

"Like layers of an onion with a rotten core."

Trey took a deep breath and then spent the next half hour describing his trip to Rome in minute detail. Even as he spoke about Vatican connections to a major case of art fraud, Cahill's collusion, and the assassination of a Russian oligarch, he could hardly believe it himself. Throughout it all, Nicklaus listened with that impermeable British stoicism. Trey reminded himself to never, ever play poker with Nicklaus Palmer.

When he reached the end of the available facts, he went into speculations. "I have no idea how, nor any way to prove it yet, but I think the assassination and the Cahill paintings are related."

"Anything is possible," Nicklaus said.

"Here I was expecting you to tell me I'm crazy."

"Forgive me, but you *are* crazy, after a fashion, but in a way, that makes you the perfect kind of investigator. I have learned to trust your instincts. What is the wildest thing they're telling you?"

Trey looked at him across the desk for a long moment, took a sip of his scotch, and let its peaty, smoky burn warm his belly. "Do you really want to know?"

"I really want to know."

"I think my father is Levchenko's assassin."

Nicklaus leaned back in his chair and crossed his arms. Trey met Nicklaus's steely, probing gaze.

Trey had enough evidence from memory and circumstance to paint a convincing picture of his father's involvement in some deep, dark, clandestine shit. The only question was the extent. He gave Nicklaus a number of high points, including the conviction his father was a narcissistic, high-functioning sociopath.

"Where are the connections to this case?" Nicklaus said.

"The Church. My father went to Holy Cross College. So did Cahill. Monsignor McGillicuddy may well be the connection. He taught at Holy Cross. He married my parents. McGillicuddy claims to have never met Cahill, but he was still on the faculty when Cahill went there. Holy Cross is a Jesuit institution. The Jesuits are one branch of the modern descendants of the Knights Templar, Freemasons being the other. The assassin in Rome used a rifle with a Templar coin embedded in the butt of the stock. This is someone acting as a Warrior of God. Levchenko was one of the worst of Putin's cronies. His murder was a message to the old Soviet bloc, maybe even putting Putin on notice."

"The assassination does smack of the 1960s, doesn't it? They don't go for the public sniper shot much nowadays."

Trey nodded, then went on, "Cahill bought the paintings from the Vatican to 'hold' them, to clean up their provenance. Cahill is about twenty years younger than my dad, but it's quite possible they know each other and—"

"If this is true, you are aware of its staggering magnitude of the coincidence, are you not?"

"I once told my brother Patrick, half-jokingly, that it was my dad on the grassy knoll in Dallas. I wish I was kidding about all of this."

For the handful of people to whom Trey had ever admitted this, the response had always been some variation of "You must be kidding." Marie, Mason, his siblings, his therapist. Except he wasn't, not entirely. He had watched the Zapruder film of JFK's assassination, frame by frame, over a hundred times. Every still frame was fixed in his memory. What most people did not know about was the strange figure of the Umbrella Man, as he was called.

Who was the man standing under an open black umbrella near the grassy knoll at Dealey Plaza in Dallas the day President John F. Kennedy was assassinated? He was barely visible standing behind the crowd of admirers on the sidewalk, blending behind the posted sign for the Stemmens Freeway. He was the only person standing under an open umbrella on this sunny, clear day, on President Kennedy's side of the convertible, somewhere between the Texas School Book Depository building and the railway tracks and overpass. He was standing in the precise position that marked the kill zone.

Oddly, it had rained the night before in Dallas, yet by 9:00 a.m. on November 22, 1963 the skies had cleared, and the temperature was a comfortable 66 degrees. In the crowds lining the streets to view the presidential motorcade, no one else wore a raincoat, and no one else had an umbrella.

As Kennedy's motorcade approached, the man along the road opened his umbrella for no discernible reason. It was a bright, sunny morning, with no chance for rain, neither was the day hot enough to warrant the necessity of shade. Then the infamous shots were fired.

During the subsequent investigation, Louie Steven Witt had been brought forward to assume publicly the identity of the Umbrella Man and put the conspiracy theories to rest—another patsy perhaps. Trey had never swallowed his explanation that Witt was opening his umbrella to be a visual protest, not of Kennedy's policies, but of Joseph P. Kennedy Sr.'s support of Britain's Neville Chamberlain's umbrella-toting appeasement of the Nazis in the run-up to World War II. Witt's story seemed too much of a stretch. Even if Okie had not been the Umbrella Man, he could easily have been the shooter on the grassy knoll.

Nicklaus Palmer, however, simply took another sip of his scotch, never taking his eyes off Trey.

"You're not calling security?" Trey said with a wry half-grin.

Nicklaus took a deep breath, appearing to consider whilst swirling his scotch gently in its glass, his face like a block of Stonehenge sandstone, hiding secrets at which one could only guess. "I trust your instincts, Trey. I also know how meticulous you are. Let us say I've seen enough to believe anything is possible."

For a moment, Trey was speechless. Then he managed to stammer, "I appreciate that." His estimation of Nicklaus Palmer, already high, had just jumped into the stratosphere.

"The key thing to remember, however, is that the identity of the assassin, tantalizing as it might be to pursue, is not *yet* relevant to our investigation. That might change. Until such time as we know it's connected, we must focus our efforts on obtaining proof of Cahill's fraud. You did some excellent work in Rome, but as evidence it's only circumstantial. We need a witness who'll testify this was all Cahill's doing, a reliable one."

"I have two leads," Trey said, "the gardener, Miguel Gomez, and this mysterious person sending me emails from a bogus account." And if he could draw a solid line of connection between Cahill and Okie...

"I look forward to bringing this case to a resounding close. We have nineteen days."

"Nineteen days..." The tension of that deadline cranked the muscles in Trey's neck tighter than Roman catapult cords.

"I suspect, however, pressing as this matter is, that you can spare perhaps an afternoon for a little side job?" Nicklaus opened a drawer and withdrew a manila folder.

Trey could always use the money. "What is it?"

"A security survey for a policy holder in Los Angeles. Shouldn't take more than an afternoon."

A security survey was done because the underwriter wanted eyes on the ground. The surveyor would circumnavigate the interior and the exterior of the structure to note the building materials and confirm the installation of central-station burglary and fire systems to protect the structure and the contents. It involved physically inspecting the structure and noting key underwriting areas of concern, such as how works of art were secured to the walls. It was a risk-averse exercise that concluded with a multi-page report in a narrative caption form with recommendations for the policy holder. With a one-hundred-and-twenty-million-dollar Sword of Damocles hanging over his head, Trey could not decline the new infusion of income. The Cahill case had dominated his attention of late, but he routinely worked on several cases and projects simultaneously. In fact, he had four less critical investigations ongoing when he had taken this one, all of which had been temporarily back-burnered. Such was the life of a freelance expert. "Of course. Happy to help."

Nicklaus slid the manila folder across the desk. "This is the address." Trey caught him suppressing a smirk.

He opened the folder and recognized the photo of a hacienda-style house. His mouth fell open. He double-checked the address. "You want me to do a security survey of *Marilyn Monroe's* house?"

***

As Trey ducked into his black cab to return to his hotel, his brain was a swirling buzz. Just when he thought things could not get any weirder, Nicklaus had thrown two curve balls.

"Marilyn's *house*?" he breathed as he settled into the back seat of the cab.

"Wassat, guv'nor?" the driver said. "Whose house we going to?" He was a short, blockish man in a tweed hat and jacket who smelled like he'd been smoking a pipe since infancy, and his teeth completed the impression.

"Sorry, never mind that. Le Méridien Piccadilly, please."

"You got it, guv. You a Yankee?"

The route to the hotel would take them along the northern bank of the Thames, a picturesque drive.

Trey always enjoyed seeing Tower Bridge, then his favorite bridge in London, Millennium Bridge, which took him to the

Tate Modern Museum; Blackfriars Bridge, followed by Waterloo Bridge, before the cabbie would turn right towards the roundabout at Trafalgar Square. Once at Piccadilly Circus Station, the cabbie turned left onto Piccadilly Street. The Le Méridien Piccadilly hotel was situated on Piccadilly Street backing up to Regent Street.

A wave of exhaustion crashed over Trey. He had awakened this morning in Hotel Bramante to the news of a bloody assassination less than a kilometer from his bed. He had been delayed and grilled by Italian police at the airport looking for a man with his name, probably his father. To say today had been a roller coaster was to belittle the tumult. Only tension kept him upright at this point.

The late-night sights of London slid past the cab windows. As they sat waiting to turn from Victoria Embankment toward Big Ben, he happened to glance out the window and spot a familiar car. A black Mercedes Maybach 6.0-liter. A glance at the license plate confirmed it was, in fact, Nicklaus's car. He could just make out Nicklaus's silhouette through the rear window as it changed lanes and took its place ahead of the black cab. Trey told the cabbie to follow the black Mercedes now in front of them.

But why was Nicklaus going this way at this time of night? His London flat lay in the opposite direction.

Just ahead, Westminster Bridge crossed left, over the Thames.

Nicklaus's car signaled a left turn onto Westminster Bridge. This was certainly unusual, when Nicklaus should have been going in the direction of Liverpool Street Station. Most peculiar, especially in light of how Nicklaus was a creature of habit. He was as straight-laced as they came, as far as Trey knew.

Trey said, "Make a left turn here across the bridge, please. I want to make a quick detour."

The driver signaled his turn and followed.

Trey pointed at the black Mercedes. "Stay behind that car."

The driver raised an eyebrow and shrugged.

The expanse of the River Thames glimmered with the lights of the city, even as rain pattered on the taxi windows.

Across the Thames, the Mercedes turned right and followed the bank of the River, continuing south for a little over a mile.

The first major building just before Vauxhall Bridge was the SIS Building, the home of the UK's Secret Intelligence Service, also known as MI6.

Like Rome, London was another city with two millennia of history. Ahead, the titanic block of the SIS Building stood against the cloudy sky, a grim monolith as steeped in clandestine secrets as CIA Headquarters in Langley.

Nicklaus's lights signaled another turn—right, into the parking facility underneath the SIS Building.

"You want to follow him *in there*?" the cab driver said.

"No, go straight. Then take me to the hotel, please." Trey only now realized he'd been leaning so far forward in his seat, he was practically breathing down the driver's neck. His heartbeat was doing an Irish Riverdance. He leaned back and took a deep breath.

Nicklaus had just thrown him a third curve ball.

CHAPTER 25

"MY MOTHER HAD A SUITCASE in my dad's office, a big one. I don't remember how old I was, but I remember getting curious once. I unzipped it and opened it. It was full, jam-packed, with unopened bills, collection letters, notices from lawyers. All of it unopened. So the mail would come, and my mother apparently would never show it to my dad. She would just throw it in this suitcase.

"Years later, I told my brother this, and he said, 'Oh, yeah, there were a bunch of suitcases like that.'"

***

On the twelve-hour flight from London Heathrow to LAX, Trey had plenty of time to stew. Why had Nicklaus offered Trey this specific job *now,* in the middle of the biggest case of his life? His father had drilled into him that the world was a grand chess game, and it was better to be the player than the pawn. For a brief moment, he had felt like he had become a player on the board, but that was now in doubt. He might well be a pawn in someone else's game.

The possibilities were staggering. Was Nicklaus Palmer an MI6 operative working undercover at Lloyd's of London? It would make sense. Art fraud was one of the chief methods of money laundering used by terrorist groups and organized crime worldwide. Knowing who was stealing from and selling to whom might yield surprising results in the game of global intelligence. Nicklaus was certainly highly enough placed in the British social hierarchy to have significant political and intelligence connections. Maybe Nicklaus wasn't an operative himself; maybe he was a civilian working closely with MI6. His demeanor during Trey's meeting with him had been utterly unflappable, a blank slate, and Trey had never noticed such a profoundly thick mask on Nicklaus before. Could Nicklaus be using Trey for some sort of clandestine operation? Why on earth would he give Trey the security survey job at Marilyn Monroe's former home *now*? What unseen designs might be behind it all?

Resentment started to simmer. Trey did not like the idea of being used by someone he trusted, someone who had treated him as a friend. The irony burned that he had specifically resisted for many years the idea that, because of his investigative skills, he should be working for an intelligence service like the CIA. He had resisted because Okie had been CIA, at least he was pretty sure, and the idea of following in his father's footsteps, becoming *anything* like him, filled Trey with visceral loathing. And now he might find himself coming into that world by someone else's back door.

Trey remembered the way Nicklaus had had Cahill's house searched while they were busy with the deposition. At the time, Trey had simply been amazed at Nicklaus's reach and capabilities, but an MI6 connection would perfectly explain such reach and capabilities. Could Nicklaus have dispatched an MI6 team working on American soil to toss a private citizen's house? The CIA wasn't allowed to perform intelligence gathering on American soil, at least not technically. Could there be some sort of reciprocal arrangement? Nowadays, instead of looking for Soviet sleeper cells, they were looking for terrorist sleeper cells. The brazen assassination of a Russian oligarch would have no doubt kicked the workings of the world's intelligence services, East and West, into a higher gear.

All these things were a swirl of loose puzzle pieces in Trey's mind as he arrived in Los Angeles in the early afternoon, giving him plenty of time—if not the energy—during the current business day to resume operations.

As he pulled his phone from its Faraday bag and allowed it to reconnect with the wired world, the first thing he did was to open his email box and reply to the mysterious witness: *How about meeting tomorrow at LACMA, near the Robert Motherwell black-and-white abstract.*

Even exhausted as he was, a little thrill went through him at being back on the hunt.

As he was thumbing in the message to the mysterious contact, a voicemail popped up from his brother Patrick, time-stamped last night about 8:00 p.m.

Trey had not spoken to Patrick in about a month. Trey lived in Chicago, Patrick in Denver, but they kept in touch with occasional phone calls.

In the recording, however, Patrick's normally affable voice sounded strained and worried. *"Hey, Trey, it's Patrick. Um, where the hell is Dad? He hasn't been home in over a week and Mom is not talking. He didn't tell anyone where he was going or how long he'd be gone. I'm kind of scared. The old man may have finally gone off his rocker or something. Call me."*

"Like *I* would know where the fuck Dad is," Trey muttered.

But as soon as that gut reaction passed, Trey's stomach fell into his shoes. Given what he already suspected, this sounded like corroboration. Okie had gone to Rome. It was exactly the kind of behavior covert spooks engaged in, disappearing for weeks or months at a time with no explanation for family or friends.

A text message from Marie beeped in. *Hey Boo, you back?*

His reply was: *Landed @ LAX now. XOXOX*

He considered calling Patrick back, but then looked around the airport. Any of the dozens of people surrounding him could be tails, eavesdroppers. Having his phone exposed to signals now made him feel exposed, vulnerable. He would contact Patrick from his hotel room later, using an encrypted VOIP package, a package he would be using for all communications henceforth.

Marie's return text was instantaneous:

XOXOXOXOXOXOXOXOXOXOXOXOXOX Be careful.

He put the phone back inside its shielded bag.

***

Now, comfortably ensconced in his room at the W Hotel in West Beverly Hills, he fired up his laptop and the encrypted Voice Over Internet Protocol package that he used for all sensitive conversations, and tried to call Miguel Gomez. He was expecting the call to go straight to a full voicemail box, so he jumped half out of his chair when the line clicked and a man said, "Hello."

Trey slapped reins on his excitement and answered as levelly as he could. "Hello, is this Miguel Gomez?"

"*Si*, it is."

"Wow, man, you're a tough guy to reach, I've been trying to get you for days."

"Yeah, I been on a little vacation. Would still be, but got called back to town for an emergency."

"My name is Trey Hansen. I don't want to keep you long, but I have a very big landscaping job with a six-figure budget, and you come highly recommended. Would you be willing to meet with me?"

A pause. "Well, I'm pretty full up, but we might be able to work something out. I could meet you next week at my office."

"Sorry, but I'm kind of under the gun. The last crew really, seriously, fucked up, and I need someone to try to set things right as soon as possible. Can you meet me this afternoon?"

"Well, I—"

"I've got a thousand dollars earnest money that's yours if you'll meet me today."

Another pause. "Okay. I can be at my office in an hour."

"Excellent! I will meet you there in precisely one hour."

***

Trey pulled up in front of the industrial building that housed Gomez Gardening and Landscaping. A well-beaten pickup truck with the company logo was parked near the front door of Gomez's office. Late afternoon sun had turned the fresh black asphalt of the parking lot soft and pungent, much like the drive across town. It had taken him over an hour and a half to get here.

The lights were on inside the office.

Trey jumped out of his gunmetal gray V-8 Aston Martin Vantage Roadster and hurried to the office entrance.

The door was unlocked. The moment he opened it, a powerful blast of smoke caught him in the face, making him cough, his eyes bursting with tears. A blast of dread punched him in the belly.

Trey called inside, "Anybody here? Hello!"

He rushed in. The front office was empty. Beyond lay the open bay where the trucks and equipment were stored. He rushed through the open door into the bay. "Hello! Miguel Gomez! *Hola, hay alguien aquí?* Anybody here?"

Smoke roiled through the naked steel trusses supporting the two-story roof. The air was hot. But where was the fire? He saw no flames. In the bay was another pickup truck filled with gardening equipment and a trailer laden with industrial lawn mowers. Shelves filled with lawn chemicals, bags of mulch, grass seed, and tools lined the walls. Would fertilizer blow up?

Then he spotted a pair of legs poking out from behind a pallet of mulch bags. Visible from the knees down, the legs were hairy and brown and wore only flip-flops. Trey rushed across the bay and found a Latino man lying face-down on the concrete, wearing a Hawaiian shirt and cargo shorts.

The smoke was thicker here. Trey knelt to get under it and shook the man's shoulder. "Hey, you all right?"

No response.

That's when he spotted the trickle of blood coming from the

man's ear, a sign most typically indicating a fractured skull. He felt for a pulse at the man's neck. Nothing.

Five feet away, smoke puffed from under the door of a storeroom. The steel door radiated heat. Opening that door right now might be a death sentence. Keeping low, he grabbed the man by the feet and dragged him away from the door, leaving a smear of blood behind him. The man's ankles were still warm.

Out in the office, he scooped the man up into a fireman's carry, momentarily sickened by the limpness of the form. He knew the admonishment by emergency responders not to move someone with a head or neck injury, but if he didn't get the man out of there, the fire would kill him for sure—if he wasn't already dead.

Outside the building, he laid the man gingerly on a meager patch of brown grass across the parking lot from the front door. Then a muffled *whoomp!* exploded inside the building, and the entire structure shook as if struck by a huge fist. The glass of the office entrance burst outward, the front door slamming open, and through the opening the glow of flames emerged.

Then he called 911. While talking to the emergency operator, he checked the man's ID in the wallet in his back pocket. This was, in fact, Miguel Gomez. And he looked very, very dead.

CHAPTER 26

"WHEN I WAS JUST starting high school—this would have been about 1974, right after Watergate—our house was broken into.

"The neighbors reported seeing a Montgomery Ward delivery van backed up to the garage door in the middle of a weekday. We were all at school. Dad was at work. Mom wasn't home. The garage door wasn't locked, and there was no electric door opener, so they just rolled it up and went into the garage. Then they bashed in the door into the kitchen. It was locked and had a deadbolt on it. They must have used a battering ram, because the door was still locked in the frame and lying on the kitchen floor.

"They went through all the bedrooms, threw a bunch of stuff onto the bedspreads, then wadded them up like sacks and carried them out. Everybody's room got tossed.

"They took two pocket watches that belonged to my grandfather. They emptied all my parents' dresser drawers onto the bed, sorted the clothes out onto the floor, then wadded the rest up in the comforter. My dad had some cash, some collector coins.

"The weird part is, they didn't take the most valuable stuff. They got some of Mom's jewelry, but they didn't empty her jewelry case by the vanity mirror a few feet away. They didn't take the TV, or Dad's expensive hi-fi system, or his antique onyx and marble chess *set. What they got away with was a pittance, really, could hardly have been worth the effort.*

"I think it was intimidation."

"Intimidation by whom?"

"That is the question, isn't it?"

***

Trey had been in hairy situations before, confronting angry people, confronting recalcitrant police or security, but he had never been confronted with a dead witness—scratch that, a *murdered* witness.

The paramedics pronounced Miguel Gomez dead at the scene. The fire department managed to contain the blaze to the warehouse bay and the storeroom where the fire had been started. The fire marshal arrived to investigate arson while Trey was still being questioned by police. It was the nature of such things that he would be under suspicion, at least initially, but when he dropped the name of Detective Tosch, their stance softened.

It was almost dark before he made it back to his hotel room. By that time, he hardly felt human. He took a shower to remove the smell of smoke, but he couldn't scrub the feel of Gomez's limp body from his memory, couldn't help wondering if moving Gomez outside had been the event that led to the moment of death. Someone had *died* because of this investigation. A family with children was now fatherless because some scumbag wanted to hide the truth.

Gomez had been Trey's single, most important witness, and he may have taken Trey's career with him to the grave.

And on top of all that, the certainty that someone was willing to commit murder to keep Trey from the truth. How long before they decided to silence Trey himself?

His hand trembled as he pulled out his phone and called his brother Patrick.

Patrick picked up the phone immediately. "Trey, what's up?"

"Hey, Patrick. Sorry for the delay in calling you back. I'm in the middle of an investigation and—"

"Yeah, I know, travel, travel, travel. Your kids still know you?" Patrick said it with a smile, but that undercurrent of disapproval was still there, the resentment that Trey had forsaken his blood for a glamorous, globetrotting life. Patrick had opted for the nice, safe route. He still lived in Denver near their parents, managed a sporting goods store, found a nice Catholic wife, and spawned six little Catholic kids.

"What's this about Dad?" Trey said. "Have you seen him?"

"No news. He's been gone for a while. Mom won't tell me what day he left, where he was going, or when he'll be back."

"Well, he is an adult. And we both know he didn't run out on Mom, right?"

Patrick sighed. "So, you don't give a shit."

Trey swallowed a gobbet of anger. "Doesn't matter how I feel. I get that you're worried about him."

"He's getting up there, you know? Seventy-year-old men just don't take off."

"Unless they've got dementia."

"The old man is still sharp as a fucking tack. You'd know that if—sorry."

"Taking care of them puts a lot on your plate."

"And Mom! That's the weird part. She *knows* something, but she's not telling. It's like he's on a classified mission or something."

Trey could not help laughing.

"What?" Patrick said.

"I've been telling you shit like that for years."

"Yeah, well. It still sounds crazy. But get this, what brought it all up. I come home from work last week and there's a note from a messenger service for an attempted delivery. The return address is the state capitol building. But I didn't order any politicians, neither did Amy. So I go down there the next day and try to pick up whatever it was. It's an old military footlocker they're pulling out of storage, cleaning out some old rooms in the capitol basement or something. It's got Dad's name stenciled on it. I show them the delivery slip and my ID, tell them that's my dad. Initially they give me a hard time, telling me he has to pick it up himself, but eventually I talked them into giving it to me. Took the damn thing home and opened it up. Guess what was in it?"

"What?"

"Vintage photos. Newspapers from way back in the day. All the photos were of Dad. There were a few with Mom back when she was a pretty, young stewardess."

"They never kept anything like this around the house."

"No shit. This was like opening the door to Narnia, I swear to God. I started looking through the bundles of photos. They were so old the rubber bands fell apart. Lots of photos of Dad with various people, nothing too exciting, but then it felt like an invasion of privacy, so I closed it up. Now it's sitting in my garage." Trey sensed the reflexive fear in Patrick's voice. His brother was still, deep down, terrified of their father.

"Can I come and look at it?" Trey asked.

"You can come anytime. You and Dad can look through it together."

Trey stiffened. "You had to go there."

"I did, yeah."

There was more chance of Trey sprouting wings than going through that footlocker with his father. Nevertheless, he burned to comb through every photo and newspaper. It was as if suddenly he had discovered the location of the Rosetta Stone or the Holy Grail. Every other concern fell away, and he wanted to be on the next plane to Denver. Then again, maybe he would be willing to face his father again to look at those photos. Visions of who might be present in them kicked sparks through his imagination. He *had* to know. "All right. Fine. I'm in LA, in the middle of a big case right now. I can't tell you about it over the phone. I'll come to Denver sometime hopefully in the next couple of weeks. Can you do me one favor?"

"What is it?"

"If Dad shows up, don't tell him about the footlocker until I get there. Like you said. We'll go through it together." Trey hoped the bait of family reconciliation might be enough for Patrick to fudge on the arrival of the footlocker.

A few moments passed. "You sure you don't know where he is?"

"I'm certain I have no clue."

Patrick sighed. "Will you call me if you hear anything?"

"For sure."

"All right."

"All right, what?"

"All right, I'll wait until you get here to tell Dad about the footlocker."

They chatted for a while about their wives and kids, about Patrick's job, about the Nuggets and the Broncos, the Bulls and the Bears, the kind of conversation Trey could manage in his sleep, which was good because 98 percent of his brain was imagining rummaging through the footlocker.

After they hung up, the imaginings persisted, until after a while they comingled with memories of a dead man's weight on his back.

Then he remembered the time all their family's possessions were stolen from their storage unit, about the time Trey went off to college. All of his childhood souvenirs, trophies, ribbons, baseball cards, favorite books, gone. All of his siblings' as well. But nothing of their father's. Because he hadn't kept it there. He'd kept his things in a secret storage facility under the Colorado State Capitol building.

How many times had their house been surreptitiously searched? And what about the major break-in? He had a vague memory of his mother talking about a ladies' wristwatch of her mother's missing from her dresser, but he couldn't be sure. So much of his early life had gone grainy and out of focus.

He couldn't book his flight to Denver yet, because he had one surviving witness to meet, tomorrow at noon.

***

The Robert Motherwell abstract acrylic on canvas dominated the LACMA wall, a looming, claustrophobic expanse of black ovals and rectangles on a stark white background. This one was titled *Elegy to the Spanish Republic 100* and measured seven feet high by twenty feet wide. Very difficult to miss.

At precisely noon, Trey stood before the acrylic on canvas, feeling the pressures of fascism and violence, evoked by the artist's feelings about the Spanish Civil War, close in around him. That and the knowledge this witness was his last chance. Without this witness, the chances of recovering the missing paintings dropped precipitously, and made a pipedream of any fraud conviction.

Other museum visitors flowed around him, taking little notice of this monochromatic, iconic masterpiece. He scrutinized each one, wondering every time which of them might be the mysterious witness. But no one approached him. Young and old, men and women, all passed him by.

After half an hour, annoyance threatened to make him call it off, but he couldn't afford to. The potential witness had the upper hand here. Trey would wait a little longer.

The museum was busier than usual for a weekday, and he wondered if choosing a museum to rendezvous with the witness was simply ironic or just a poor choice of locations. A diner or a Starbucks might have made more sense. But those places also raised the chances of eavesdropping. He hoped the calm and tranquility of the museum would prove to be the right environment to coax the witness to cooperate.

At the 43-minute mark, a man shuffled into the gallery, eyeing all the exits. Trey knew immediately this was the man he'd been waiting for. He slipped his hand into his breast pocket and activated the miniature digital recorder. As California was a two-party state, meaning civilians must have both parties agree to record a meeting, Trey's recording was technically illegal and thus inadmissible in court, but a record of what was said could still be invaluable.

About Trey's age, the man had let himself succumb to sports-related injuries. He was dressed in an expensive suit, with expensive shoes, expensive tie, and expensive watch. On his right hand, a prominent class ring gleamed on his ring finger. Colorless eyes peered through gold-rimmed spectacles. His gaze fastened on Trey for only a second, but then he looked away. As he neared, Trey could see the sweat on his neck, soaking his white collar.

Time to take back the initiative. Trey said, "I almost left."

The man shuffled closer, his eyes furtive. "I want immunity."

"I'm not the police. Let's start off with introductions. I'm Trey Hansen." He offered his hand to shake.

The man didn't take it. "Look, this is scary as hell, alright?"

Trey remained silent, thinking it would be best to let the man speak as best he was able.

The man rubbed the sweat from his face with a monogrammed white handkerchief.

He took a few moments, as if ramping up his courage. "The guy who took the paintings is named Greg Hexom. He's an ex-PI, sometimes bounty hunter, kind of a scumbag who'll do anything for cash. He lost his private investigator license getting busted by the IRS for tax fraud. Didn't do any time, but he lost his business."

"Sounds like you know him well."

"Not well! Jesus. I have a reputation to protect."

Trey looked him up and down. "So it appears. Let's back up a step. I need to know who you are."

The man lowered his voice, glancing about for eavesdroppers. "My name is Mark Fedota."

"And what is your connection to this case?"

"I'm Frank Cahill's lawyer."

"Richard Dunwood is Cahill's lawyer."

"Dunwood is his personal lawyer. I'm his corporate lawyer."

The smoking gun exploded in Trey's mind, and it shot a thrill through him that stood his hair on end. This was a man who might well know *everything*. "And you're here because your soul is heavy."

The bags under the man's eyes were prominent. "I can't fucking sleep, man. Let's just say it's been a shitty couple of weeks. And I got a weak ticker. Doctor says no stress."

"Then you got involved with the wrong people."

"Frank didn't used to be like this. He was a stand-up guy, once upon a time. All that money corrupts. I see it happen all around me."

"But not to you."

The man sighed. "Yeah, to me, too. I went along with this whole scheme. At least at first."

"Tell me about the scheme."

"Frank organized the whole thing. He's trying to sell the paintings and double-dip on the insurance money."

"Because he's in serious financial trouble."

Fedota swallowed and nodded. "I tried to talk him out of it."

"Tell me how it went down."

"The gardener was told to leave the alarm turned off. Hexom's job was to go in, take the paintings."

"What was Hexom's interest in this?"

"A cool million. It was all Hexom, the theft. If he was caught, his job was to keep his mouth shut, go to jail, serve the time, and the money would be waiting when he got out."

That was the kind of money for which someone might be willing to do three to five. Trey said, "Where are the paintings now?"

"They're supposed to be headed for Rome."

"Why Rome?"

"Frank said he had a buyer at the Vatican. A slam dunk, he said."

"Who is transporting the paintings?"

"Hexom."

"Are you willing to testify to this under oath?"

"For immunity, like I said."

"And like I said, I'm not the police, nor the FBI."

"FBI!"

"At this point, you're an accessory to a federal crime. Transporting stolen goods across state lines and international trafficking. Are you aware that the gardener, Miguel Gomez, is dead? He was murdered yesterday."

All the color drained from Fedota's face, leaving his head resembling a baseball. "I didn't know that." He rubbed his face again. "You have to protect me."

"Again, I'm not the police. But maybe we could go talk to the FBI. They're more in the business of protecting witnesses."

Something inside Fedota seemed to snap. He went limp for a moment and then regathered his strength. "I got to go." He turned and headed out of the gallery.

"Wait!" Trey said.

Fedota kept walking.

***

On his way to the car, Trey called Special Agent Alderman. He went through the FBI office operator and asked to page Alderman. This was no time for voicemail.

After a few minutes on hold, a voice came on the line. "Alderman."

"Special Agent Alderman, it's Trey Hansen. I've got a potential witness who could break my case wide open. This is way bigger than when we last spoke. Like huge. International. Can we meet?" He wasn't about to divulge any details over the phone.

Alderman said, "Yeah, come by the office. I'll be here for the afternoon."

Trey's grip tightened on the Roadster's steering wheel, and a smile spread across his lips. The chase was on.

Twenty minutes later, he pulled up to the immense, monolithic building on Wilshire Boulevard that housed the Los Angeles Division of the FBI. Alderman came out to the lobby to usher Trey to a nearby meeting room. As they traversed the hallways, his security-focused mind noted the measures in place every step of the way—CCTV cameras, key-card elevators, choke points, RFID security doors.

They sat down at the conference table in the spare, utilitarian room, and Trey told him about everything—except the possible connection to Okie. Gomez's murder. Mark Fedota. The Vatican connection. As the story went on, Alderman's brow furrowed deeper and deeper as he listened intently.

When Trey showed him the photo of Cahill's bill of sale from the Vatican for the original purchase, Alderman said, "You weren't kidding."

"What can we do about this?"

"We can pick up Fedota, for protective custody as much as anything."

"Yeah, he didn't strike me as someone to bump off more witnesses. What I want is for him to give up Cahill. If we get Cahill, we can go after the Monsignor." Not that Trey held much hope for bringing down such a personage. For decades, the Catholic Church had been protecting their own and enabling raging pedophiles among their ranks, no matter how lowly placed.

"Corroborating evidence is going to be the key here. Fedota may have more to offer," Alderman said.

"My thoughts exactly."

"We'll pick him up and go from there."

"And you'll keep me in the loop?"

"Of course."

They stood and shook hands.

"By the way," Trey said. "Have you heard anything about the assassination in Rome? There's almost nothing about it in the US media."

"The Russians are both publicly and privately furious. And when Putin is furious, people die. They have absolutely no compunctions about quietly nerve-gassing a restaurant full of people to kill one target. You can bet the FSB is doing overtime looking for the killer."

"Any thoughts on a motive? Why was Levchenko visiting the Vatican?"

"He was supposed to meet with the Pope. The spooks figure it was because Putin is looking for new and inventive ways to launder money. The international sanctions on the Russian banks are putting a squeeze on their cash flow. They're nothing but Mafiya entities at this point, Putin's private piggy bank."

"Trading in fine art is one of the cleanest methods of laundering money. It happens everywhere. Might this be related to the Cahill case?" Trey didn't want to state his virtual certainty that they *were* related, lest he come across as crazy. He only wanted to plant the seed.

"We'll see where it all leads. In the meantime, be careful about someone bumping off investigators, too."

CHAPTER 27

*"**TELL ME WHERE YOU** are now."*

"It's dark. It's quiet. So quiet."

"Where are you?"

"I don't know."

"Is anyone else there?"

"No, there's nobody else here... Wait, wait... There's somebody else in the room."

"Who is it?"

"I don't know, but I sense somebody standing over me. They're bigger than me. Much bigger. Huge."

"Do you know where you are?"

"I'm on my back, looking at the ceiling, and there are bars around me... I'm in my crib. The door to my parents' room is open. Everybody is asleep, but this is real, and there's somebody standing over me, this shadow that smells like Dad's cigarettes and beer. I'm terrified, wet my diaper, but I pretend to be dead, I just lie there. I don't cry. He... he reaches into the crib, reaching for a pillow, picks up the pillow and holds it above me. Then he puts it down and goes away."

***

"I still can't believe this," Mason said.

Trey gave him a Cheshire grin. The Aston Martin's top was down, allowing the mid-afternoon LA sun to drench them in warmth. The flow of the wind made it all worth it.

Mason continued, "*You*, the biggest Marilyn Monroe freak on Planet Earth, are tasked with doing a security survey of what used to be her house."

"It seems the current owners have approached Lloyd's to insure the place. They've got a kind of shrine to her, with some valuable works of art included, but it's still their primary residence. No doubt they're bigger Marilyn freaks than I am, or I'd own that house myself."

"If you had the money, I'm sure you would."

Trey grinned again. "You might be right."

Trey had already brought Mason up to speed on everything in the Cahill case, culminating in Gomez's murder. With each revelation, Mason's eyes got bigger.

"Things have been...eventful, haven't they?" Mason said.

"Eventful as in hanging from a cliff by a fraying thread, yes. Do you have anything new?" Trey tried not to sound desperate. "Any bit of physical evidence, anything?"

Mason said, "I'll go through it all again. Maybe I've missed something."

"You found prints, right?"

"Yeah, but they were all the maid's."

"Try again, but see if you can find a match with this Greg Hexom. He has a criminal record. His prints will be in the database."

"Will do, Chief." Mason's voice dripped sarcasm.

"Don't you know, you're the sidekick?"

"I'll side-kick your head. Why'd you ask me to come along on your psycho-masturbatory enterprise?"

"Thought you might want to get out of the house."

"Well, you're right about that."

Half an hour of traffic later, they were pulling down the unassuming cul-de-sac named Helena Drive, toward the unassuming gate outside a piece of history that loomed large in Trey's mind. The owners of the house were away on vacation, so Trey and Mason had the run of the place. He had called the LAPD to notify them of the security survey, in case any of the neighbors saw two men snooping around and called the police. The police had his credentials on file, so he anticipated no unexpected and potentially dangerous interruptions by law enforcement. The guest alarm system codes were included in the file Nicklaus had given him. The house had changed hands several times since Marilyn had lived here, but the current owners were apparently fans of the late cultural icon.

Mason got out to punch in the code, and the chest-high wooden gate rolled aside to allow Trey to pull into the narrow cobblestone driveway, then into a modest courtyard hemmed by the house on two sides and walls of hedge and vegetation on two others.

In front of the single-story, hacienda-style house—red tile roof, 2,600 square feet, four bedrooms, one of which was added by subsequent owners, a kidney-shaped swimming pool in back, guest house, spacious lawn—Trey found himself trembling with anticipation, and his throat was full, his eyes wet. The house's location at the end of a narrow cul-de-sac gave the property a sense of privacy that was rare in the insanity of Hollywood. He almost felt as if he were walking back through the years to 1962. Built in 1929, the house still carried that ineffable, Old Hollywood feel.

He looked at Mason and said, "Some days, I really, really love my job."

Mason smiled at him, and they approached the front door. Inscribed on Mexican tiles on the pavement before the front door was a coat-of-arms with the phrase "CURSUM PERFICIO," roughly translating to "My journey ends here."

The house key was under a nearby planter. As they unlocked the door and went in, Trey's first step was to disable the alarm system. They stood now in a modest sitting room with a fireplace. To the left, a dining room, and beyond that, the kitchen. Right of the main entrance was a corridor leading to the three original bedrooms, one of which had been Marilyn's. The current owners had decorated the place in retro style. Nearby hung one of Andy Warhol's iconic paintings of Marilyn Monroe. The Lloyd's file said it was the original. Around the sitting room were works of art by British-born and Los Angeles-based artist Russell Young, including *Marilyn Hope* and *Marilyn Crying* with diamond dust as part of the medium, and several *Marilyn Superstar* in various custom colors such as El Centro Purple, Bondi Blue and French Rose. Amid black-and-white, autographed photographs of such Hollywood luminaries as Dean Martin, Tony Curtis, Frank Sinatra, and Jane Mansfield were additional works of art featuring Marilyn Monroe by Alberto Vargas, Bert Stern, Eve Arnold, and Salvador Dali. A framed album cover of Elton John's *Goodbye Yellow Brick Road*, autographed by Elton John, in which the Marilyn Monroe tribute "Candle in the Wind" first appeared.

"You know," Trey said, his excitement growing, "this was the first home she ever owned. She loved this place, 'exalted in it' an interviewer said. She owned it all of about six months. Joe DiMaggio helped her buy it. She moved in in February 1962, bought a bunch of furniture in Mexico that she thought would be perfect, including all these hand-painted tiles around the fireplace. She died August 5, before most of the furniture showed up."

Mason listened politely. "Who is the owner now?"

"A reasonably successful film producer and her husband. They're planning on shuttling people in for private tours."

The sitting room also featured a framed Russell Young acrylic screen print on linen, *Marilyn Goddess (Black)*, one of his iconic works. Gone almost sixty years, her presence here felt palpable.

Mason said, "Let's turn off the fanboy and get to work, shall we?"

"What's with you?" Trey said.

"A touch of the heebie-jeebies."

Trey chuckled. "Okay, fine."

They circumnavigated the exterior of the house as Trey took dozens of photos with his iPhone. Then they worked their way inside. He noted the security measures already in place, infrared motion detectors, glass-break sensors on the numerous windows, recessed magnetic contact points on all doors. He noted a couple of closed-circuit TV cameras around the property, and then checked the video data recorder hidden in a closet. He checked the art objects on display against what was described in the Schedule. A few minor concerns cropped up about the general repair of the property—it was almost a hundred-year-old house, after all—and he noted those. He would write up his recommendations later. After the larger points, he worked his way down to the smaller stuff, such as the security measures present on the art objects themselves, like mounting and alarms.

After almost an hour of Mason following him around, chiming in occasionally, Mason said, "So are you ever going to go into her bedroom?"

Trey paused writing notes. "Is it weird I'm nervous about that?"

"Weird as hell."

Trey took a deep breath and let it out. It was time. He stepped down the short corridor toward her bedroom. A glass door opened onto the back patio, where the pool lay—through which someone may have entered—allowing afternoon sunlight to paint a shadowed lattice on the floor.

He walked around the room, his heart thudding against his sternum, imagining this woman, who was very troubled in the months leading up to her death, finding herself late at night naked and alone in the presence of an attacker, maybe two or three, the terror she must have felt as they held her down.

Mason stood in the doorway while Trey circled the room. Backlit by the sunlight, he paused, and his shadow fell across the bed.

Then two images, one from the present, one from the past, collided in Trey's mind so hard it was as if they struck him a physical blow. He couldn't breathe. His fist clutched his chest, and his knees threatened to buckle.

Mason came toward him. "Hey, are you all right?"

Trey's mouth worked, but he couldn't bring forth a sound. He clutched Mason's shoulder for support. Finally, he managed to make his lungs work. "Mason, I've seen this before."

"Of course you have. You've seen all the police photos no doubt a hundred times."

"No, that's not it. It's this angle. It's the shadow."

"What are you talking about?"

"My dad painted this! When I was a kid!"

"You're saying your father painted this bedroom?"

"Yes! And I never knew the nude woman lying on the bed in his painting was Marilyn Monroe." It was so perfect. Trey must be standing on the exact spot, formed the exact same perspective, as Okie's painting.

"Bullshit, Mr. Conspiracy Crazy Person." Mason's expression bordered on incredulity.

"Look, I know how it sounds. But there's something that can't be captured in a black-and-white photograph, a depth, something a lens can't grasp. There was this painting of his, I remember it perfectly. A nude woman, a platinum blonde, lying on a bed, you couldn't see her face. I had always thought she was just sleeping. He was *here*."

"Whoa, now that's a huge stretch even for you."

"He was here, dammit!"

Mason lowered his voice and slowed his cadence. "Trey, there are a thousand photographs of this spot right here. He could have done a painting from anything, from any of them."

"No, I've seen every crime scene photo known to exist. But the painting was too real, more real than a photo."

Mason looked at him for several long moments.

"I'm not crazy!"

Mason chewed his lip.

"I'm not. And you know it."

Mason sighed. "Then we have to find the painting. Any idea where it is?"

"No, but I could ask my brother." Trey pulled out his phone and started taking photos around the room, from every angle, every vantage point, all focused on the bed.

Then he called Patrick.

Patrick picked up. "Wow, to what do I owe the pleasure of two phone calls on two consecutive days? Dad's footlocker got you in a twist? When you coming to visit?"

"I'm coming to visit as soon as I can, meanwhile I have another question about Dad."

"What is it?"

"Do you remember a painting of his, from when we were kids, with a nude woman lying on a bed?"

"Yeah, that one scared the crap out of me when I was young. Looking back, I have no idea why."

"Does he still have it? Do you know where it is?"

Patrick paused for a moment, thinking. "I can't remember the last time I saw it."

"Is it in storage? Did he sell it?"

"Why the sudden interest in Dad's paintings?"

He couldn't tell Patrick his suspicions, or his brother would probably laugh them off and hang up. "I'll get to that in a second. Do you know what might have happened to it?"

"No, he's pretty close-lipped about that stuff, just like everything else."

"Could you ask Mom?"

"Why don't you ask Mom yourself?"

"Jesus Christ, Patrick, this is important."

"So is family."

Trey took a deep breath to seize control of the unhelpful erup-
tion brewing. "I'll think about it. But I'm not ready. Maybe when
I come to Denver. We'll see." He couldn't believe he had just said
that. "This is pressing though. Would you mind checking on this
for me? I'll bring you a nice bottle of wine."

"Colorado is beer country. I'll let you pick."

"Thanks. Call me back after you talk to Mom?"

"Sure."

***

They finished up the security survey, which was difficult with
Trey's mind latched onto the memory of his father's painting of
a dead Marilyn Monroe. Moreover, something nagged him, just
out of reach. Mason invited him to his house for dinner, but Trey
declined. He needed to get back to his hotel room, call his wife, call
Patrick again, and do some research, so he dropped Mason off at
his home, then headed the Aston Martin to his hotel.

On the way there, Patrick called back.

Patrick's first words were, "What is it with you?"

"Huh?" Trey said.

"I thought I was going to call Mom and casually ask about some
of Dad's paintings. It was so weird, she really didn't want to talk
about them. Like, at all. She was suspicious of me even asking. She
misses you. You should call. She told me to tell you that."

"I think she understands why I haven't. So what did she say?"

"Almost nothing. I had to guilt the hell out of her to get anything at all. At first, she wouldn't even verify they existed, but then I told her all us kids remembered the paintings. Then she was like, 'Ohh, oh yeah. I remember now.' Totally lying about it. I asked her specifically about the one you mentioned. She finally admitted Dad had sold that one several years ago to some collector she didn't know. It was an online auction or something. I got the real sense, though, after all that, she really, really hated that painting."

Trey absorbed all this for a moment.

Then Patrick asked, "So now you have to tell me. What's so special about this painting?"

"Do you really want to know? It's crazy."

"Not much could surprise me at this point," Patrick said.

"I think it's a painting of Marilyn Monroe the night she was murdered. And I think he painted it from memory."

A moment of silence passed, then Patrick said, "Okay, I was wrong. What the fuck, Trey!" He called to someone, "Yes, pumpkin, I'll put a dollar in the Swear Jar." Then he lowered his voice into the phone. "What the fuck, Trey. Where does this hatred come from?"

"Hatred is beside the point, Patrick. This is a real investigation."

"You really believe *our dad* killed *Marilyn fucking Monroe*?"

"I think it's possible. Do you know where I called you from before? Marilyn Monroe's bedroom. I was there for a job. It struck me, *really* hard, that her bedroom looked familiar in a way that was not from all the old photographs. Then I remembered Dad's painting."

"This is not a stretch. It's the Grand Fucking Canyon. (Yes, pumpkin, that's another dollar.) Don't call me with shit like this anymore. Jesus Christ."

The line went dead, and Trey sighed, allowing himself a moment to mourn the ever-present fractures in his fraternal relationship.

When he reached his hotel room door, he checked the upper corner where he had inserted a tiny slip of paper. If anyone had opened the door, the paper would have fallen out, likely unnoticed by any intruder. It appeared to be still in place.

Inside, he pulled out his laptop and started searching auction sites. Sotheby's and Christie's were the big ones, but there were also Artprice, Artnet, and a few others. Using Emmett Hansen and Okie Hansen as his chief search terms, he combed auctions going back as far as he could. The hotel's molasses-like internet speed stymied him and turned a ten-minute search into over an hour, as the graphics-heavy web pages took forever to load.

But then, there it was.

He recognized the image instantly, and a thrill went through him, like a bloodhound baying at treed prey.

The painting, titled *Still Life in Platinum*, oil on canvas, twenty-four by thirty-six inches, had sold for $5,000, nine years ago. He downloaded a more high-resolution image than the thumbnail on the web page, and began to study it, but the laptop screen was too small for sufficient detail. He dragged a few cables out of his laptop bag, and moments later had connected his laptop output to the television. As an HDTV, it gave him the opportunity to view the painting at close to actual size.

He sat on the bed and stared at it.

Marilyn's body, lying in an awkward position, a man's shadow falling over her. The painting was Edward Hopper-esque in its execution. Hopper was an American realist painter most famous for his painting *Nighthawks* depicting a few lonely figures through the windows of a late-night diner, but he had also done a great many female nudes. In this painting, however, something was odd about the shadow-lattice of the glass panes cast over the body and the bed. Trey had stood on that exact spot not two hours ago. The symbolism of the shadow was obvious, a threat, a murderer standing over her.

Trey zoomed in and scanned back and forth over the image.

In the police photos, Marilyn's nightstand had been littered with prescription bottles, but here, those bottles were absent.

What he saw there instead...

"Holy shit."

It was a coin the approximate size of a silver dollar. On the face-up side was the faint impression, barely defined, of a scarlet cross on a white background. The Knights Templar. Identical to the impression of one left in the mortar atop the Hotel Columbus.

CHAPTER 28

"THE FALL AFTER I started college, somebody broke into our storage unit and took everything. All of my childhood tennis trophies and swimming medals, clothes, baseball card collection, book collection including my favorite, King Arthur and the Knights of the Round Table, *all of it gone. Oddly none of my father's possessions were lost as they were not in the storage facility.*

"I remember the entire family gathering in San Diego for my brother's college graduation. My mother, in front of the entire family, exposed my father as a fraud. She told us that Okie knew we were going to get robbed and used our childhood memories as bait for his adversaries."

"How did your father respond? I assume he was not happy about this."

"He was furious, pacing around like a caged animal. In fact, he locked himself in the bathroom and destroyed the toilet seat and broke everything in the bathroom. He was fucking pissed. I think he felt betrayed by Honey, and he never forgave her for siding with the children."

"Did you or your siblings ever feel that you were in physical danger?"

"We all froze instinctively in the living room, eavesdropping on the bathroom destruction. I wanted to flee this bizarre, King Lear tragedy, even as I felt smug satisfaction at what my mother had done. It was like divine comedy."

***

It had been three days since Marie had returned from Rome, picked up the girls, and tried to reconnect with day-to-day life. The trouble was, she could not bring herself to want to, not really. In spite of the moments of fear, Rome had been magical. The food, the sights, the company. Maybe it was the sense of danger that heightened the enjoyment of everything. A few annoying quirks notwithstanding, she had seen a side of Trey that she rarely did, not because he hid it from her, but because it was simply the way he went about his job every day. That guy was born to do what he was doing.

Returning to quiet, staid, suburban life felt hollow now. Take the kids to school. Deal with chauvinistic contractors and potential clients—she would accept no client who didn't respect her work as an architect. Make dinner. Try not to gain weight from sitting on her butt all day. In Rome, she had felt beautiful. Trey always told her she was, but she often as not didn't believe him, didn't feel it herself. In Rome, she had felt like a smoky-eyed femme fatale neck-deep in intrigue.

She understood now why some people gravitated to that kind of life. Such a path had never occurred to her when she was younger. It had always been what was expected of her—career, relationship, kids, house. But now, there were moments when it all felt like a prison, perhaps heightened by the fact Trey was still living it, and she was stuck back in everyday life. And she missed him. And the girls missed him. Phone calls were not enough.

Then there was the weird stuff.

The house had been empty while they were in Rome, with the girls staying at her parents' house. Three times now, she'd found some little thing in a place she did not remember putting it. A watch. A bag. A phone charger. In the case of the bag, the contents seemed to have been rearranged. When she tried to use the printer in her home office yesterday, she found the cable to her computer was not securely connected. It had been working fine when she left, and she spent half an hour troubleshooting the problem. It seemed so simple, but why was it not working?

All this, along with the strange goings-on in Rome, had tightened her nerves. Every other hour, she thought about calling Trey to tell him about it, but the things were so minor, she didn't want to distract him from his investigation.

Was she being crazy?

Trey would be the first to say someone had been in their house, but she didn't want to feed his paranoia or obsessions. Then again, being paranoid didn't mean someone wasn't out to get you.

"Ugh!" she cried, pulled at her hair. It was an endless circle of unhelpful thoughts.

She had tried to call him so the girls could say goodnight before bedtime, but he texted her and said he was in the middle of something huge. It was after ten when he called, using the encrypted VOIP package he had installed on her phone so they could talk without hackers listening in.

Then the realization hit her. What if the purpose of the intrusion had been to plant bugs in their house?

As soon as he said, "Hello, BD!" she could tell something was up.

Before he could say anymore, she said, "Wait." Then she traipsed all the way through the house and out into the back yard, stopping as close to the back fence as she could.

"What's that about?" he said.

"I think somebody was in our house while we were gone."

An edge crept into his voice. "Why do you say that?"

She explained it to him.

When she was finished, he sighed. "You might be right. We can't discount anything at this point."

"But who?"

"I'm not the target of any criminal investigation, at least as far as I know, and I seem to have a good rapport with Special Agent Alderman, which I'll be coming to in a second, so I don't think it would be the FBI. Who does that leave? Some nefarious government conspiracy, or people working for Cahill and the Monsignor. I'm leaning toward the latter, but I can't rule out the former. They want to know what we know. But hopefully this will end soon. I'll look into having the place swept for bugs, but we might be able to use this to our advantage, feed misinformation."

"Got it. So, a big day then?"

"Huge. Two things. I have a witness."

"That's fantastic, Boo!"

"I won't say who, just in case there's some kind of surveillance we haven't thought of, but this could break the case wide open."

"What's the second thing?"

He hesitated.

"Come on," she said.

"I think my dad killed Marilyn Monroe."

She nearly dropped her phone, and a stone plopped into her stomach. She wanted to believe he was joking, but the excitement in his voice, the vindication, told her he wasn't. "Well," she said. She couldn't manage any more. How could a man believe such a thing and expect anyone to take him seriously?

"I know it sounds crazy—"

"Uh-huh. Yup."

"You don't believe me."

"That might well be the craziest thing I've ever heard come out of your mouth," she said, and that would be saying something. "First, he's the assassin on the roof in Rome, and now he killed Marilyn, too? Her death was a drug overdose. Next, you're going to tell me he killed JFK, too."

Silence hung heavy between them.

Anger flared in her. "Oh, come on, Trey!"

"Are you ready to hear me out?"

"I've heard you out a hundred times! And every time it sounds crazier." This was the Age of the Conspiracy Theory. "You sound like every right-wing-left-wing crackpot, wacko, delusional idiot who generates theories no sane human with a third-grade education would entertain. Theories utterly unmoored from fact and objective reality, yet somehow they manage to find other like-minded crackpots. They form their identities around stagnant puddles of rehashed, unverifiable bullshit. The Flat Earthers. The Moon Landing Deniers. The Illuminati. A race of reptiles rules the Earth and Justin Bieber is one of them."

"Really? I wasn't aware of that."

"You're not the only one who reads too much."

"Look, just because many of them are certifiably insane doesn't mean there aren't still conspiracies. Human beings didn't suddenly stop conspiring for personal gain just because it's the twenty-first century. If anything, the internet makes it easier."

She slumped against the tool shed and sank to the ground. "This is not helpful. Why do you—never mind, I know why you do this. Because your father seriously fucked you up. I know that. I get it." She sighed.

More silence.

Finally, she said, "I can't do this right now. That's great about the witness. I love your voice. But I can't talk about Marilyn Monroe tonight."

"But—"

"No. Trey. Just no."

He sighed. "I'll call when I have more information."

***

In his hotel room, Trey combed the internet for hours, his attention laser-focused in the thumbnail images of the painting offered for sale. It was the only way he could distract himself from the pain of Marie's refusal to believe him. On some level, he could see her point. His sometimes-overactive mind could come up with some outlandish shit. But on the other hand, he was closer now than ever before to *knowing*, not just being plagued by guessing, suspecting, wondering, speculating.

What was worse, now he suspected Nicklaus was not what he appeared to be. Had Nicklaus known of the connection between

Okie and Marilyn, about the painting? Was Nicklaus leading Trey around by the nose at the behest of MI6? What would MI6 want with Okie? What history was there? Did Nicklaus have a personal stake in Trey verifying or revealing Okie's dark history? The timing of the security survey job at Marilyn's seemed too contrived. What would Nicklaus or MI6 have to gain by dragging Okie, an aging CIA operative, into the daylight? What did they have to gain by his son being the one to do it? Were they trying to flush Okie out of hiding? If Okie was that much of a target, how had he managed to live this long? What further information might Nicklaus be hiding about Okie?

If Nicklaus could have operatives search Cahill's house, had Nicklaus ordered bugs planted in Trey's house? Had MI6 been behind the break-ins of his childhood home?

The seeds of distrust bore bitter fruit.

The bottom line of all this speculation was that Nicklaus Palmer was manipulating him now in a way he had never expected. The question was: why?

In his dark room, he choked down cup after cup of hotel room coffee, rubbed his eyes, and tried not to think about whether anyone would be reading his search history.

He scanned every art and auction site, even Ebay, for Okie's footprints, more of his paintings. Like most painters who had developed and honed their craft, Okie had a distinctive style, recognizable to a person with training in art. After a couple of hours of searching, he began to wonder if Okie had painted other things and sold those pieces under a pseudonym. So, he started the search again, from the top down, Sotheby's and Christie's. Okie's gargantuan ego would get a big boost from the prestige of selling there, even if it wasn't under his own name. His searches went back as far as the memory of the internet would reach, looking for other paintings resembling Edward Hopper's style. He dug even deeper, combing the websites of local auction houses, regional auction houses. Those houses generally went under the radar, but they often brokered the sale of important works for millions of dollars. He used Denver as his starting point then rippled out from there.

This kind of investigation was not sexy or dramatic. It was simply eyeballs and focused attention sustained over long, coffee-saturated periods. The excitement came when that elusive connection was made, like finding the single neuron in a brain full of neurons, the one that leads to a desperately sought memory.

It did not come together for Trey as a single *Eureka* moment. It was more like a layer of bricks slowly creating a foundation for conclusion. Okie knew how to cover his tracks, to go under the radar.

Trey assembled a collection of potential candidates whose style resembled both Okie's Marilyn painting and Edward Hopper. These he arranged by name. Then he combed over the images to look for techniques and other clues suggesting the same hand as Okie's Marilyn painting. He looked for comparisons such as color palettes and the organization of the additional elements of design: lines, shape, form, and texture. As an art historian, Trey was skilled at attributing unknown works of art to known artists. He could compare works of art, then sort them into categories of distinctive characteristics and styles unique to many artists.

There was one artist's work that kept snagging his attention, an E. H. Nyack. Trey was not familiar with that name. The work resembled Okie's, but unlike the Marilyn painting, Nyack's works were expressions of place. An empty plaza. A hallway with what appeared to be a kitchen at the far end. A motel balcony viewed from below. The paintings, empty of human figures, suggested the silence after some momentous event, the quiet after a storm. They were also familiar.

Had it not been so late at night, so close on the heels of exhaustion, he might have noticed it sooner.

The first was Dealey Plaza in Dallas, but from an unusual perspective, from the top of the rail bridge, overlooking the plaza, looking down on Elm Street, where President Kennedy's motorcade had been when he was shot. It was not the known perspective of Abraham Zapruder but rather the view shared by the hobos from the railroad overpass.

The next painting that caught Trey's gaze depicted a worm's eye view of the second-floor balcony of the Lorraine Motel in Memphis, outside Room 306 to the viewer's right. To the left was an open kitchen window at twilight bleeding into dusk. The spot where Dr. King was shot would have been less than twenty feet away.

The third painting was more difficult. It was of a dark, empty hallway, with a brightly lit restaurant kitchen at the far end. It resembled a bright white light of heaven from many religious paintings he had grown up with, however the door jamb had what appeared to be bullet holes.

At 4:47 a.m., realization snapped into focus.

Robert Kennedy had been shot in a hallway of the Ambassador Hotel in Los Angeles. He had just finished speaking and had been ushered to exit through the kitchen. Trey searched the web for photos and video of Bobby Kennedy's assassination and found his realization was correct. The bullet holes in the door jamb suggested someone had shot RFK from behind. Again, the painting felt like a creation of memory, rather than flattened by a photograph.

And then there was the name, E. H. Nyack.

Trey could not contain a grim chuckle as he did a quick check of Edward Hopper's biography. The artist was originally from Nyack, New York.

E. H. Nyack was a pseudonym.

Trey jumped out of his chair and paced the room, repeating, "Oh my God."

It was Okie's pseudonym. It had to be. Why else would someone choose these three subjects to paint? And why from these unusual perspectives? Had Okie been sitting atop the railroad overpass near Dealey Plaza? There had been several scruffy looking men, hobos perhaps, sitting up there watching the proceedings on the day of JFK's death.

He had to tell someone, to bounce it off someone. Was this too crazy?

Mason would be angry about the 5:00 a.m. phone call, but he'd get over it.

***

Even at six in the morning, Mason looked like he'd stepped out of an issue of *GQ*. He walked into Trey's hotel room with a bag of bagels and two cups of coffee.

"Oh, dear *Lord*, do you owe me," Mason said with a withering stare, handing over the paper bag and quad latte. "Have you even slept?"

"No." Trey motioned him toward the television, where he was feeding the video from his laptop.

On the screen was *Still Life in Platinum* by Okie Hansen.

Mason took one look. "You found it."

"I found it."

"Why am I not surprised?" Mason said with a sigh. "Now I have to give credence to whatever is coming next."

Trey went through his reasoning point by point. The Edward Hopper-esque style, the composition, the mood, the alienation. And then, especially, the Templar coin on the nightstand, and the impression of the Templar coin left in the mortar in Rome.

Mason crossed his arms and stroked his chin. "Go on."

"Now," Trey said, "Exhibit B." He pulled up the next piece. "Dealey Plaza in Dallas, from the perspective of the railroad bridge crossing over Elm Street. This is the perfect location for a shooter. Better than the Book Depository."

"Maybe if no one was watching."

"Maybe. But who was looking up there? A trained marksman in a trench coat could pull out a rifle and line up for the shot while everyone was looking at the president's motorcade. But let's table that for a second. Here's the next one."

Trey brought up the painting of the balcony. "The Lorraine Hotel, April 1968."

"Martin Luther King Jr."

"Bingo."

Mason peered closer. "The perspective and arrangement of colors are extraordinary. It suggests darkness and death..."

Trey nodded. "The locations of these two cannot be in doubt. Clearly Dealey Plaza. Clearly the Lorraine Hotel. Agreed?"

Mason nodded. "Are these all your father's paintings?"

Trey smiled slightly. "Hold that thought. Here's the last piece." He brought up the painting of the dark hallway. "An unidentified hallway. Blackness closing in."

"And the brightness of the far room just out of reach."

There was a bleakness to it, a stark, impassable divide between the dark and the light. "I think," Trey said, "this is the hallway of the Ambassador Hotel."

"Where Bobby Kennedy was shot. I'll entertain that notion. Dammit, Trey, now you've got me following you down the rabbit hole."

"Would you say the same artist did all four paintings?"

"I would say it's possible." They both knew the work of master painters carried certain fingerprints that made their work distinct and identifiable. The similar mediums, canvas sizes and arrangement of color fields that block the subject matter in a recognizable style unique to the artist. "They are certainly similar in their execution."

"These last three paintings were sold at auction by a painter named E. H. Nyack. They were all done in a style reminiscent of, but distinct from, Edward Hopper. Wouldn't you agree?"

Mason nodded.

"Edward Hopper is originally from Nyack, New York," Trey said.

"So E. H. Nyack is a pseudonym. Are you saying that E. H. Nyack is your father?"

"There's something else. I didn't notice this right away." He went back to the Dealey Plaza piece. "Look at the way the sun from behind makes shadows on the ground through power lines and poles."

"They are very faint."

"These faint lines converge on the spot JFK's convertible was at the moment of the shooting."

"Get. Out," Mason breathed, stepping closer the screen again.

"Like a bullseye."

"And the Lorraine Motel?"

Trey shifted to the next painting.

Mason said, "A similar effect, with shadows from the balcony railing, cast through something unseen behind."

"On the spot where Dr. King was shot. And now the third."

In the hallway painting, on the floor lay a faint circle of light, as spilling through something behind the viewer and cast onto the floor, a distorted lattice that made the sharp perspective of the hallway feel somewhat askew. "In this one it's blatant. I'd bet the one hundred and twenty million dollars I'm getting sued for that this is the spot in the hallway where RFK was shot."

"Let me guess: Sirhan Sirhan didn't do it and there are conspiracy theories around that, too."

"Yes, two unidentified people were seen running away from the scene immediately after the shots were fired. Sirhan Sirhan was just another patsy, like Lee Harvey Oswald."

Mason sat on the bed, peeled off his spectacles, and rubbed his eyes with thumb and forefinger. "This is like watching that Oliver

Stone film again and feeling the entire world turn upside down because his outlandish ideas suddenly seem incontrovertible."

Trey forged ahead, excitement filling his chest. Saying this all out loud made it feel even more real. "Now, look at the crossed shapes on each painting. They're distorted. The lines are slightly curved. You know what else has crossed lines with curved sides?" He switched the view to the mortar impression of the Templar emblem from the Italian newspapers. "Look at each one. These are *crosses...*" He cycled back through each of them. "But the crossed lines are *curved.* Every point of death in these paintings falls under the symbol of the Knights Templar."

"God help us, I think you're onto something," Mason said.

"Just one more thing," Trey said in his best Columbo impression. He went back to the first painting of Marilyn's body, and pointed to the coin on the nightstand, the Templar coin.

Mason looked as if someone had just punched him in the gut. "I feel like someone just punched me in the gut."

"I've felt that way since I found the first painting."

Mason paced the room, rubbing his lips. "Okay, so let's entertain the possibility your father did all of these paintings, that E. H. Nyack is his pseudonym. So what?"

"I think he was present at all four events. I think he was involved."

"Involved how?"

Trey sighed and rubbed his stubble. His stomach hurt. His heart hurt. His knees were wobbly. Proof was so, so close.

Mason said, "Maybe these were just pivotal moments in his life. He did live through the Sixties as an adult. We were just kids. It does not necessarily mean he was present at each event."

"You might be right, but I get the sense the perspective indicates personal experience. Not a photograph."

"A good artist could emulate that."

"But why? I think this was my father exorcising his demons and..." The next words caught in his throat.

"And what?"

"And creating trophies of his exploits."

"Exploits."

Trey took a deep, shuddering breath. "His kills."

CHAPTER 29

"TELL ME ABOUT your mother. You've talked a lot about your father and what he did to you, but there was another adult in the house."

"My mother was a co-conspirator. She was Okie's protector, his enabler, his co-dependent manipulator, his mirror image. He was like this vast, black shadow cast over us. He was the King of Darkness, and she was his Queen of Light. Their children were merely pawns in their façade, a premeditated family ruse. Okie and Honey faked parenthood to remain in character. We always felt like props in their theater. Extras used as window dressing. Disposable fixtures easy to haul out to the curb as trash."

"Have you talked to your siblings about this?"

"Patrick, yeah. I've tried to talk to Mary about it, but like I said, the elevator doesn't stop at all the floors, you know? She's been married and divorced. She's still recovering from the effects of an abusive home that continue to linger into adulthood. Okie and Honey haunt her to this day. We are all survivors struggling with depression, self-doubt and self-worth."

"You've talked about your mother's complicity in the abuse."

"Honey lied about her husband's jobs to her children. She dissuaded local police investigations into his background. Her overactive *social life was the public face of her 'normal' family. Okie's children were to be seen and not heard. The way she deflected the children's questions about him should have won her an Oscar. It is amazing none of her children ever wrote a book about them, at least a book on abuse and survival."*

"Maybe you should."

"Maybe I will."

***

The call from Special Agent Alderman came at about 11:00 a.m. Mason had left Trey to snag a few hours of sleep after his all-nighter and its resulting epiphanies.

As his ringtone slammed his skull like cymbals, Trey saw who it was, rubbed his face, and answered.

Alderman's even, low-key voice said, "I thought you might like to know we picked up Greg Hexom."

"Okay—wait, Hexom? I thought you were going after Fedota," Trey said, struggling to herd his mind into an ordered parade of fatigued cats.

"Fedota seems to have gone underground. We tried to bring him in yesterday, but we haven't managed to track him down. His wife hasn't seen him. So, in the interest of putting hands on still-living witnesses, Hexom was next on the list."

"I'll be there as soon as I can." The assumption something untoward had happened to Fedota leaped to the front of Trey's mind.

"There's no need really. We'll take it from here."

"With all due respect, Agent Alderman, I have a vested interest in this case. I've given you everything I have, but that doesn't mean you know the case as well as I do. I might come up with an angle you wouldn't think of."

"Suit yourself."

***

Trey was still scraping sleep out of his eyes when he arrived at the FBI building, and he'd pounded enough caffeine to give himself a tremor. He was getting too old for all-nighters.

The building that housed the Los Angeles offices of the FBI, along with the Veterans' Administration and the LA Passport Office, was built in 1968, and as Trey walked the halls and rode the elevator to the FBI offices on the seventeenth floor, he felt like he was walking the halls of 1968 itself. He might round a corner and find himself face-to-face with J. Edgar Hoover at any moment. The Cold War infused the structure's bones, its tile floors, paneled walls, and fluorescent lighting.

Special Agent Alderman escorted Trey to the observation room, where two agents from the FBI Art Crimes Division were grilling Greg Hexom. Trey and Alderman watched through the one-way observation window and listened through the antiquated sound system.

Hexom was about 40 but looked 55. His eyes bore the sullen look of someone who blamed the world for his multitude of misfortunes, his face the puffy redness of someone who drank way too much, a face with a nose like a frayed, worn-out speed bag. A slight paunch masked a chest suitable for a boxer, squeezed into a polyester T-shirt a size too small. His hands were large, his knuck-les scarred.

One of the interrogators sat across from him; the other loomed behind.

"Am I a suspect in something?" Hexom said.

"No, Mr. Hexom. We just want to talk. You're free to go at any time."

"But if I walk out that door, I will be, right?" Hexom snorted and slouched in his chair. "I don't know what the hell you want with me."

The agent behind him leaned over. "Are you a moron? You know what this is about. Two paintings worth one hundred and twenty million dollars, stolen from your boss's house—"

"I keep telling you, I don't know any Frank Cahill."

The standing agent leaned closer. "Where do you think we got your name, buddy? He wants *you* to take the fall. We know you took the paintings on his orders."

"Then let's dance, you think you got something!" Hexom snapped.

The first interrogator said, "If we turn this case over to the US Attorney's office, they *will* charge you. Then lawyers get involved, for sure. When lawyers get involved, all conversation stops. We're more interested in talking. I think *you* want to keep talking, be-cause I'm pretty sure you don't want to go to federal prison. If that happens, somebody else gets to make one hundred and twenty million dollars. What did they offer you, Mr. Hexom? What's your cut?"

Hexom chewed on his silence.

"Here's the thing, Mr. Hexom. You're a small fish. We like big fish. You like fishing?"

"It's all right."

"Have you ever caught what you thought was a real trophy, the kind that fights like a motherfucker, and then you get it to the side of the boat and it fits on your hand? A scrappy little fighter, but still a just a little fish. That ever happen to you?"

Hexom remained silent.

The interrogator continued, "We want the kind of fish you need a bigger boat to haul in. You help us, we help you. I take one look at you, I see a stand-up guy, somebody who keeps his word."

"I ain't no snitch." Hexom sat up straighter. "That's why you're wasting your time."

The second interrogator lunged down on top of him and growled in Hexom's ear. "And that's why we're going to nail your sorry ass." Hexom only flinched a little. "You want a lawyer, we'll call one right now. That's when negotiations will be over."

The first interrogator raised a calming hand. He said to Hexom, "You want some coffee, Greg? I could use some. Agent Caulfield could use some."

Hexom licked his thick lips. "Yeah, I could use some." The prospect of having Agent Caulfield out of his face seemed pressing.

Agent Caulfield snorted and went out.

The first interrogator went on: "Now, Greg. Can I call you Greg?"

"You have been. What do I care?"

"Well, civility and manners matter, right?"

Hexom shrugged.

"So, Greg. Here's what happened. Frank Cahill has some

financial troubles. Did you know he's on the verge of major bank-ruptcy? No way he's going to be able to pay you for anything unless his illegal painting deal goes through."

Hexom sat straighter and flexed his fingers.

"Anyway, he's got these paintings," the interrogator said, "really valuable paintings. He figures he can have somebody 'steal' them and collect some insurance money. Happens all the time. These rich motherfuckers think they can get away with anything, right? It's just fraud. Nobody really gets hurt. I mean, the insurance com-pany just has to cough up the settlement, right? Everybody's hap-py. Cahill gets paid. Then he gives a nice cut to the guy who did the job. Fuck the insurance company, right? If anybody deserves to get fucked over, it's an insurance company. Anyway, so Miguel Gomez, a nice Mexican-American guy, father of three, the gardener, gets orders to leave the alarm system turned off. You go in there some-time that night, grab the paintings, and stuff them into the back of a van or a truck. Anyhow, you carried out this enormous painting, all by yourself. You're a strong guy to wrestle a six-foot-seven-foot thing, frame and all, all the way from Cahill's bedroom, out the front door, and into the truck."

The muscles in Hexom's forearms flexed.

"The trouble is, Cahill's financial troubles are...let's say they're bigger than he lets on. So he's trying to sell the paintings now. He can't very well sit on a couple of paintings he's reported stolen now, can he. How much did he offer you anyway? I'll bet it wasn't even a sliver of a hundred and twenty million. I mean, you did all the heavy lifting, literally. These rich fucks think they can get away with anything. How much did he offer you? Twenty grand?"

"I don't know what the fuck you're talking about," Hexom grumbled.

"How much is a stint in federal pen worth to you, Greg? I hope Cahill paid you in advance, because there's no way the insurance company is going to pay this case, and the buyer Cahill had lined up has gotten whiff of our investigation. Did I mention Cahill doesn't have the money to buy a hamburger right now? Like I said, you look like a stand-up guy. Like *you* said, you're not a snitch. I believe you, Greg. You probably think, worst case, you do five to ten for grand larceny and transporting stolen goods, and a big chunk of cash is waiting for you when you get out. Do your time, then early retirement.

"This only happened one of two ways. Either you, all by yourself, decided to steal these particular paintings, so you broke into Frank Cahill's house, on a night the alarm just happened to be left off, and walked out with one hundred and twenty million in fine art, ignoring several pieces that were worth just as much and would have been way easier to carry. Would you even know where to fence such things? No jury's going to believe that."

"Damn straight."

"But they might be much more willing to believe that someone hired you to do the heist. That it was a setup, an inside job. How does it feel being some rich fuck's patsy, Greg? You're a pawn. You're a better man than that."

"I'll call my lawyer now."

***

While Hexom pulled out a cheap mobile phone and made a call, the interrogator left the interrogation room and joined Trey and Alderman in the observation room. The interrogator's ID badge said his name was Alan Dvorak. He was fiftyish, a light-complected man, standing to about Trey's chin.

Alderman said, "Good job in there. It's working."

Dvorak said, "Thanks. There are a couple more cards to play, though."

For Trey's part, without evidence tying Hexom to Cahill, he was still on the hook for one hundred and twenty million dollars. Hexom's connection was to Fedota, not Cahill. Without Fedota, they had nothing, only the thief with dirty hands, not the man calling the shots. Trey said, "If we can get him to draw Fedota out of his hidey-hole, assuming he's still alive, we can grab them both."

Dvorak fixed his gaze on Trey. "Who are you again? I don't see a badge."

Alderman introduced them. "Trey is an art detective working for the insurance company."

Dvorak looked unimpressed.

Alderman said, "He's had the lead on this from the beginning. Without him, we wouldn't be here."

Dvorak nodded but still looked unimpressed. "So, we get Hexom to draw Fedota into the open. Then we set up a meeting, get Hexom to wear a wire. And in that conversation, we get Fedota to finger Cahill. Should be a slam dunk."

The number of Big Ifs made Trey squirm, such as the assumption Fedota was alive. After Gomez's death, that was a serious question. Another was Hexom's willingness to cooperate. It was only fear for his own skin that had brought Hexom to his senses. And if they let Hexom walk out the door, he would have a bullseye on his head matching Miguel Gomez's. Trey wouldn't relax until he had tape of Fedota implicating Cahill. Not that anyone used tape anymore.

Why had Fedota come forward and then disappeared again? A guilty conscience was certainly the initial impetus for Fedota coming forward, but why get scared *after* coming forward? Had news of Gomez's murder driven Fedota to flee the country?

Alderman said, "We'll flag Fedota with state and local police and the Mexican border. Maybe someone will snag him. Meanwhile, let's go back to work on our boy here until his lawyer gets here."

Dvorak went back into the room, appearing relaxed and noncombative, and struck up conversation that was mundane on its face, small talk about family and life. Hexom was just a stand-up guy caught in a bad situation, a pawn of more powerful people. It was an effective strategy, one that played into Hexom's worldview. Trey watched Hexom respond with a number of unconscious cues that indicated his vulnerability to that strategy. Agent Caulfield, the "Bad Cop," came back with some coffee and an abundance of silent, menacing glares.

The minutes counted down and the tension in Trey's shoulders cranked tight as a crossbow string. As soon as Hexom's lawyer got here, this conversation would end. Every moment, Trey kept hoping—not praying, he would never do that again—for a breakthrough, for Hexom to agree to cooperate fully. At least three times, he saw Hexom's resolve waver, but each time he marshaled his stubbornness and remained silent.

After about half an hour, the door opened; Hexom's lawyer bulled into the interrogation room.

"Let's go, Mr. Hexom. This conversation is over," barked Richard Dunwood.

CHAPTER 30

"*THE FIRST EIGHT YEARS of my life remain dark to me even today. The next five years were like flickers of light and darkness as if looking out the window of a speeding vehicle at twilight. I always felt darkness as cold and never as warm. I learned to survive in the cold, dark reality of my childhood. Fear crippled me, but my DNA was an incubator.*"

"*What do you mean by that?*"

"*I had it in my DNA to be the toughest, most callous mother-fucker on this planet. I, the eldest son, would not only survive Okie's physical, verbal, and emotional abuse, but I would be a nobler man than him. That's what I told myself. I would emulate what I believed to be my grandfather's integrity and entrepreneurial spirit. In spite of my childhood, I would flourish. There is nothing more motivating than hate and revenge.*"

"*Some say love is even more motivating.*"

"*I don't remember exactly when it happened. It might have been one epiphanic moment, or it might have been a slow build, but I swore to myself and my siblings I would lead the charge against the Kingmaker and his Evil Queen. I would dedicate myself to the art of chess, and for several years I did. I wanted to become a better chess player than Okie. Chess is a struggle of wills. It lends itself perfectly to cloak-and-dagger operations. Did you know there's a close affinity between chess and code-breaking? The guys who broke the Enigma code in World War II were all chess masters. Alan Turing wrote an algorithm that allowed a machine to play chess before computers even existed. Chess was purposefully designed to be a two-person game, a cat-and-mouse scenario. Beat Okie at his game and take away his power. Break his code and take away his ability to communicate."*

***

At the sight of Richard Dunwood, Trey's heart flew into his throat, pounding his air passage shut. His belly knotted tight, and his fists clenched. His vision became a tunnel focused on Dunwood. In a flash, he saw his entire investigation crashing around his ears. If he lost Hexom, it was all over.

In that flash, his deduction circuits flared into white-hot speed.

Dunwood was a setup, and Hexom didn't even know it. Hexom thought he had been given a get-out-of-jail-free card as part of taking this job. *Don't worry about getting pinched, Greg. If you do, you've got a high-powered lawyer. Just call this number. He'll either get you off, or get you the lightest possible sentence.*

Greg Hexom stood up from the interrogation table. "I'm going to tell you one last time," Hexom said. "I don't know anyone named Cahill." He stood up and turned toward the door.

Dunwood said, "Stop talking, Mr. Hexom." Then he turned to Agent Dvorak. "My name is Richard Dunwood. I'll be serving as Mr. Hexom's attorney. Is my client under arrest?"

"Not at this time," Agent Dvorak said.

"Then we're done. Come on, Mr. Hexom." Dunwood opened the door and gestured for Hexom to precede him.

Trey rushed past a startled Special Agent Alderman and charged out into the hallway, finding himself face-to-face with Hexom and Dunwood.

Dunwood's face reddened. "What the fuck are you doing here?"

Trey ignored him and said to Hexom, "Mr. Hexom, if you walk out of here, we can't protect you."

Dunwood interposed himself. "You are not allowed to speak to my client."

Trey stopped inches from him, nose to nose, so close he could smell the liquor on Dunwood's breath. "Your client is a dead man if he walks out that door."

Dunwood's face purpled. "Are you threatening my client?"

Trey laughed in his face. Dunwood's lips quivered with rage.

Alderman was there, stepping between them like a wedge.

Trey looked at Hexom. "Mr. Hexom, if you walk out that door, we can't protect you."

"I can handle myself." Hexom puffed up.

"I don't doubt it, but do you remember that gardener, Miguel Gomez, the guy who let you into the house?"

"I don't know him either."

"He's dead."

Hexom paused.

Trey said, "Yeah, someone broke into his office and bashed his skull in, in broad daylight." He made a clubbing motion. "Then they tried to burn a building down around him to cover it up.

That's who you're in bed with, Mr. Hexom. Maybe you thought this would be an easy gig, no real danger. You got kids, Greg?"

Dunwood roared, "Enough!" He grabbed Hexom by the arm, but Hexom yanked his muscular forearm free.

Trey had read the FBI's file on Hexom. He had two teenage daughters from a terminated marriage. He tried to pay his child support, which told Trey that he cared about his kids. Hell, maybe that was why he took the job. "Sad thing, three little kids without a daddy now. All because poor Miguel thought he was making an easy choice. 'What could go wrong? I'll just "forget" the alarm, just this once. This is just a little insurance fraud.'"

Dunwood shouted at the FBI agents nearby. "Will somebody shut this man up? He has no business here."

Trey edged past him toward Hexom as if Dunwood hadn't spoken. "But in that one choice, Gomez became somebody's loose end. And now, somebody is tying up loose ends. And we *know* you're a loose end, Greg. Somebody already gave you up."

"What the fuck are you talking about?" Hexom said.

"How do you think we knew about you? It seems to me, the easiest way for somebody to keep *all* the money is to not have to share it, and the easiest way to keep anyone from talking is to shut them up for good."

The color drained from Hexom's neck and face.

Dunwood saw this. "Hexom, don't you fucking dare."

Trey watched this moment as if still through the interrogation room's one-way mirror, feeling the entire case balancing on this series of infinitesimal instants between heartbeats. His own heart thudded against his breastbone, his throat was thick, his mouth dry.

From inside the interrogation room, Agent Dvorak said, "Do you know what the going rate for a mob hit is these days? Fifty grand? A hundred and twenty mil could easily buy a hundred hit men, all looking for you and people near and dear to you."

Dunwood seized Hexom's arm again. Hexom wrenched his arm away and glared up at Dunwood. "Put your paw on me again and you're hitting the floor, motherfucker."

Dunwood's jaw clenched as he blinked into silence.

Agent Dvorak stepped closer. "Sit back down, Greg, and we can protect you. We'll see about cutting you a deal. Somebody thinks you're an expendable pawn in their very high-stakes game. We're not interested in you."

Hexom turned back toward the open door.

Dunwood said, "Mr. Hexom, as your attorney, I strongly advise against this course of action."

Hexom shoved past him, went back into the interrogation room, and sat down.

Internally, Trey pumped a fist.

Still chewing on his anger, Dunwood seated himself beside Hexom.

Hexom flexed his neck as if to loosen some tension. "I want immunity."

***

Trey withdrew to the observation room again. Special Agent Alderman fixed him with pointed scrutiny.

Agent Dvorak was saying, "We can't guarantee anything, but we can recommend immunity to the US Attorney's office. First, tell us everything, and I do mean everything."

Hexom sank into the chair like a sack of flour. "I never met any Frank Cahill."

Dunwood said, "Greg, I'm going to urge you one last time not to go through with this."

Hexom ignored him. "I get this call, a guy asks me to do an easy job. Acquire a couple paintings in Newport Beach. If I get pinched, there's a million dollars to make it worth my while to keep my mouth shut. I do the job. I load the paintings into a truck. I go to the meeting spot. The guy is waiting for me. I hand the truck over to him. He hands me a bag of cash, and he drives off with the truck."

Agent Dvorak said, "What's his name?"

"He never gave it. Here's the thing. This guy hired me, this Italian-looking guy. He's not a player. Can't even pretend. The worst thing he's ever done in his life is probably using a foot wedge on a golf course."

"Can you describe him?"

"About six-two. Middle-aged. Big head of hair. Athletic build. Round, wire-rimmed glasses. Looks like an attorney. Had a class ring." Hexom raised the ring finger of his right hand.

Trey turned to Special Agent Alderman. "He's talking about Mark Fedota, Cahill's corporate lawyer."

Alderman relayed this information to the interrogator via microphone and earbud.

Trey said, "I don't know if you're aware of this, but Dunwood is Cahill's personal lawyer. He deposed me a couple of weeks ago. They're suing me for nonpayment of their insurance claim."

Alderman breathed, "Wow."

The interrogator said to Hexom, "The man who hired you is Frank Cahill's lawyer."

Dunwood shifted in his seat. Strangely, his demeanor had gone from bull-nosed bluster to calculating silence. Was Dunwood a co-conspirator? At the very least, Dunwood's presence here was a conflict of interest. No doubt Cahill was the primary client. If Cahill had paid Dunwood to be Hexom's attorney as well, it stood to reason Dunwood's interest was in protecting *Cahill*, not Hexom. If Hexom flipped and implicated Fedota, Fedota, to protect his own skin, would likely flip and implicate Cahill. Dunwood could not permit that, but neither could he make it look like he was not defending his immediate client, Hexom, with all the means at his disposal. Trey had no doubt Dunwood knew how to walk that line.

Agent Dvorak went on, "Where did he take the paintings?"

"I never saw them after that," Hexom said.

"That's not what I asked you. Do you know where he took them?"

"No clue. Made it a point not to know."

"Have you had any contact with him since?"

"No."

"Here's the trouble, Greg. Here's where we may need your help. We can't find him. His wife hasn't seen him in two days. He hasn't been to his office. You know what that means, right?"

The clench of Hexom's jaw said he did.

"It means he's either dead, like Miguel Gomez, or he's lying low, skipped town, whatever. If he's dead, there goes your deal, I'm sorry to say. But if he's just keeping his head down, we need him. And so do you."

Hexom licked his lips and swallowed hard. "I've got a phone number, that's all."

The more Hexom spoke, the more Dunwood's face settled in a dark, quiet resolve.

Agent Dvorak said, "That's good, that's a start. But see, we're aiming for even bigger fish. Cahill is Moby Dick."

At the mention of Cahill, Dunwood went as still as a statue.

"Whale's not a fish," Hexom said.

"What?"

"I said, whales ain't fish."

"It's just a figure of speech, Greg. Would you be willing to contact Fedota and arrange a meeting? And would you be willing to wear a wire?"

"Immunity."

"Like I said, we can recommend, but we can't guarantee. I mean, how are you going to support your daughters if you're in the federal penitentiary?"

Dunwood spoke mechanically, "Mr. Hexom, I advise against this."

Hexom looked at Dunwood. "Are you working for me, or ain't you?"

"I am," Dunwood said.

"Then make yourself useful and shut the hell up for a minute."

Dunwood sat there and chewed on his bluster while Hexom tried to compose his thoughts.

Silence hung heavy and pregnant in both rooms. Dunwood looked at Hexom from the corner of his eye. Agent Dvorak tried to look like he didn't care what Hexom's next words would be. Hexom slumped in his chair as if one hundred and twenty million pounds of concrete had landed on him. Trey did not breathe.

Finally, Hexom shrugged. "Fuck it, I'll do it."

***

"Are you all right?" Mason said, scrutinizing Trey's face in the harsh afternoon light. A trio of Venice Beach rollerbladers zipped past on the meandering sidewalk. The air was redolent with the smells of hot dogs, grilled meat, and marijuana.

Here on a bench on Venice Beach, surrounded by tourists and locals, buskers and eccentrics, Trey put his elbows on his knees and looked out past the beach and the beachgoers, out over the Pacific. Not far away lay the bustling Venice Beach Boardwalk, and then Santa Monica Pier with its Ferris Wheel, roller coaster, and carnival atmosphere. The relentless hiss and rumble of the surf calmed his nerves. As if the stress of trying to flip Hexom had not been enough, his encounter with Richard Dunwood had been the second of a one-two punch. He was exhausted from scalp to toenails.

Mason looked around at the bizarre conglomeration of human endeavor that was Venice Beach—the Freakshow, Muscle Beach, the Mosaic House—with barely disguised disdain. "And why on earth did you want to meet *here*?"

He gave Mason a feeble but hopeful smile. His mind needed a stark change of scenery. It was all jammed up with Dunwood and Hexom, Okie and Marilyn Monroe. "We have a witness willing to flip. Hexom managed to reach the other witness who disappeared,

Mark Fedota, Cahill's corporate lawyer. Turns out he was lying low somewhere, not dead."

"Thank God for that."

Trey nodded. "Right. We're still in the game. So we set up a meeting tonight. The FBI is going to wire Hexom for sound. They're also working on search warrants for Fedota's house and office. I updated Nicklaus on all this, and he gave me a hearty, 'Good show, old chap.'"

"Sounds like everything is going swimmingly."

"Did I tell you who Hexom's lawyer is? Richard Dunwood."

Mason's eyes narrowed and his back stiffened.

"Right," Trey said. "Cahill's lawyer. So that's good news. Dunwood is going to do everything he can to throw Hexom to the wolves to protect Cahill, because that's where the money is. But if we bust Cahill, we get to bust Dunwood as well for conspiracy." That would feel even more satisfying than sending Cahill to prison. The hatred that had bloomed for Richard Dunwood rivaled any Trey had ever experienced. He wanted to see that man destroyed.

"So what's the problem?"

Trey smiled again. Mason knew him too well. "I have all this happening now. The FBI is going to let me observe tonight from inside their surveillance van. I feel like this case is at a tipping point, and all I can think about is getting on a plane for Denver tonight to go see my brother. He's got a trunk full of Okie's stuff. I *have to* look at it all. I have to know."

"You know, this is not healthy."

"I know."

"You have to let it go. Focus on this case. The trunk will still be there tomorrow or the next day."

"That's just it. Okie has been missing for over a week. No one has seen him or had any contact. Not even my mother. If he shows up again, Patrick is going to hand it all over to him, and I'm never going to get another chance to look at it."

"I think if you run off to Denver in the middle of this investigation, you'll be poisoning your professional reputation."

"I knew you'd say that, and you're right, of course."

"But you're going to do it anyway."

Trey looked out over the ocean. The relentless surf surged and ebbed. Seagulls cried.

INTERLUDE - CHECK

SITTING IN THE DINER'S corner booth, the Wolfhound wore a nondescript jacket, nondescript, threadbare tweed trousers, and a nondescript mustache and goatee. Stage make-up was common as dirt in this town. Through the diner's picture windows, the HOLLYWOOD sign glowed against the distant hillside. He sat in the corner nearest the back door, facing the entrance, the remains of his burger and fries cooling before him as he pretended to read today's *Los Angeles Times*. The toilets lay at the opposite corner of the diner. He had already committed the layout to memory.

The diner still bore the iconic stamp of the 1950s and '60s. The stainless steel and vinyl, the Formica tables and counter-tops, the pastel paint, the waitresses in pink gingham dresses, the Oldies soundtrack that went from Elvis to the Beatles to the Monkees to the Shirelles, to the heart-busting American-food menu. Want biscuits and gravy with your double cheeseburger and onion rings?

He stuffed the onion slices from his burger into his trouser pocket.

One of the targets sat at a table, nervously checking his watch, staring out into the dimly lit parking lot. The lawyer had sent him photos of both men. He knew exactly who to look for. The

Wolfhound had to give Cahill credit. Giving the patsy a high-powered lawyer was a stroke of genius.

Mark Fedota sat two booths away, also facing the door. He came in fourteen minutes before the appointed time, looking like a hairy prairie dog peeking out of its hole. The man thought he was dressing down in a windbreaker, golf shirt, and khaki trousers, but the Rolex on his wrist gleamed, and the Loyola class ring on his finger glittered with gold and diamonds.

Another patron sitting at the counter was probably FBI. The Wolfhound sized him up. Mid-thirties, well groomed, straight-laced as most of the Bureau guys were. Most of them were too uptight to make good spooks. Probably a crack shot, though. He was reading something on his phone, or pretending to, over a coffee and piece of coconut cream pie.

Fedota stiffened as Greg Hexom walked through the front door, looking only marginally less nervous. He spotted Fedota, walked straight to him, and slid into the booth.

It was time. Leaving his newspaper on the table, the Wolfhound wiped down his knife and fork, his plate, his red, frosted-plastic cup, the table, the vinyl of the booth seat, everywhere his fingerprints might have touched. Then he slid out of the booth and headed for the toilet, passing by Fedota and Hexom, passing the FBI surveillance.

He went into the toilet and checked his appearance in the mirror. Nondescript old fart: check. Gang signs were scrawled on mirrors, scratched into the walls, the stall, the urinal. A neighborhood prone to gang violence. The staff here was no doubt used to the occasional sound of gunfire. He took a couple of deep breaths and settled himself into the Zone. How many times had he pulled off operations like this? More than enough to give him command of the situation.

Coming out of the toilet, out of sight of the rest of the diner, in the little hallway between the men's and women's toilets, behind a small table that hosted a chest-high palm tree, he slapped a black, taped package against the wall. Then he pulled out a cigarette lighter and lit the slender gray thread hanging down the side.

Then he began counting down. *Thirty.*

He left the hallway and approached the cash register.

The waitress came up with a bubble-gum-and-lipstick grin. "Everything okay, sir?"

"Great burger, thanks," he said. *Twenty.*

He handed her a twenty-dollar bill. She counted out change.

Ten.

"Oops, forgot my paper," he said, and headed back to his booth, reaching into his jacket with his right hand, into his pocket with his left.

Five.

As he passed their booth, Fedota and Hexom were speaking in hushed, hurried tones. He grabbed the newspaper and tucked it under his left arm. With this left hand, he squeezed a button on the little plastic box in his pocket. From outside the diner came a muffled *whump!*

The lights went out. The building's electrical meter now lay in smoking ruin.

Expostulations of surprise rose.

Then the sound of submachine gun fire ratcheted through

the place. Fedota and Hexom exchanged terrified glances as they ducked low. The FBI agent pulled his Glock.

The packet of firecrackers the Wolfhound had planted continued to cook off. They would continue to erupt for the next twenty to thirty seconds.

He pulled what looked like an oddly stretched gym sock from inside his jacket. It was, in fact, a three-stripe tube sock, with a hole scissored out around the trigger of his modified SIG-Sauer. With the slide locked shut and the silencer attached, it would produce far less of a report than the Black Cat firecrackers he'd bought in Chinatown.

While the FBI agent was looking toward the noise and the waitstaff was hunkered down behind the bar, the Wolfhound put a 9mm hollow-point through Fedota's temple.

The average reaction time for humans suddenly faced with mortal danger, a life-or-death situation, was about four seconds. He called it the Squirrel in the Middle of the Road phenomenon. With training, that time could be cut to less than a second. Hexom had no such training. His blood-spattered face goggled with terror, slack-jawed and staring. Through the sock, the Wolfhound racked his pistol's slide manually. The sock caught the spent brass.

The firecrackers continued their thunderous, arrhythmic clamor.

He put his second shot through Hexom's left eye. The silencer slowed the bullet's muzzle velocity sufficiently to leave the fragments of it still inside his scrambled brains. No exit wound, no broken glass. Hexom's body slumped down into booth seat.

The FBI agent was shouting, looking the other way.

The Wolfhound then pushed the second button on his little plastic box, setting off the massive smoke bomb he'd planted under the lip of the bar. Acrid gray smoke boiled out and filled the air, making his eyes water. Waitresses started coughing.

The back door burst open, and two more FBI agents burst in with guns drawn. The second they hit the smoke, their eyes watered, and coughing erupted. In that moment, with their vision blurred and their backs turned, the Wolfhound slipped out the door behind them.

From the dumpster out back, he grabbed the bundle he'd planted and ran down the alley about fifty yards, thrusting his arms into the sleeves of the shabby peacoat, jamming a woolen cap with earflaps onto his head, stripping off his fake mustache and beard. The evening air was still warm and pleasant, but schizophrenics, as many homeless people were, had difficulty regulating their body temperature, so it was common to see them in heavy coats and hats even in the height of summer.

Beside another dumpster, he threw himself into a pile of newspapers, fished out his bottle of Old Crow and took a huge pull, letting it slobber down his chin and chest. Then he pulled the onions out of his pocket, took a deep breath, and rubbed them into both eyes.

Pain and tears tore through his eyes, but the onion did its work, turning them bloodshot and watery. He rubbed some soil from the ground on his face, into his trouser legs, then pissed in his pants, completing his transformation into schizophrenic street trash. He stashed his SIG-Sauer behind a pile of half-shattered cinder blocks, within reach, but out of sight. Then he lay down in his carefully constructed, cardboard "hobo's nest" and covered himself with newspapers.

Less than a minute later, two more FBI agents dashed into the alley, their flashlight beams dancing in all directions.

They spotted him almost immediately and ran up. All they saw was a crazy, red-eyed old man who reeked of piss and booze.

At the sight of their guns, he threw up his arms timidly, blinking against the light. "What's with all the noise?" he said, slurring his voice.

"You see anybody out here?" one of the agents said.

He pointed down the alley. "Yeah, somebody just went running past here. Fast sumbitch. Scared the shit out of me."

"Did you get a look at him?" one of the agents said.

He pointed to his eyes. "Kid, I can barely see you, and I was almost asleep."

The first agent caught a whiff of him then and wrinkled his nose. The other spoke into a cuff microphone.

Then the two of them ran on down the alley, after the imaginary perpetrator.

When they were out of sight, he loaded everything into his shopping cart. The wail of sirens converged on the place. Best for the crazy, old, homeless guy to vacate the locale. He pushed his shopping cart into the night.

CHAPTER 31

"I STILL THINK THERE'S this devilish thing between 1952 Eisenhower Vice President Nixon and then the 1960s President Nixon. It's like you've got Nixon bookends, and in between, you've got all these assassinations. JFK, RFK, Martin Luther King Jr., poor fucking Marilyn...

"So that makes me think, you know? There were different presidents, and Nixon had mostly disappeared from public life in the between time, but you know he was still calling the shots in the Republican Party, and probably elsewhere. He was tight with J. Edgar Hoover. No way a guy like that would ever stop pulling strings. Christ, Henry Kissinger is what, ninety-some years old, and he's still pulling strings. Nixon hated the Kennedys, hated *them. He lost to JFK because Joe Kennedy cut a deal with the mob to carry Chicago by counting dead peoples' ballots. That's how slim the margin was. He fucking hated the Kennedys...*

"I grew up in a house where my parents had highball glasses etched with the faces of all the Republican presidents, starting with Lincoln."

***

In the dark, cramped confines of the FBI surveillance van, Trey listened to the voices of Hexom and Fedota through the headphones. Alderman and the Special Operations tech listened as well, recording everything. The air inside smelled of Alderman's aftershave and the tech's chorizo and black bean burrito.

Another agent was in the diner, and two more agents sat in a car watching the back alley.

From the moment Trey saw Fedota through the window, sitting nervously in that booth, his blood had been pulsing in his ears, making it hard to hear.

The business-like calm of the agents around him, their efficient, competent voices on the comms, went a long way to calming him, but the weight of everything that hinged on this moment was the larger counterbalance.

Hexom had walked into the diner more than a little stiffly. Due to the tightness of the T-shirts he habitually wore, the Special Operations Group had fitted him with a suppository microphone. During a pat-down, no one would find such a wire. Trey had chuckled at the wonders of modern technology, even more that Fedota was not savvy enough to even pat Hexom down. Who would have thought a microphone stuck up someone's rectum would be able to pick up anything? Nevertheless, he could hear their entire conversation with perfect clarity.

"Look," Hexom said, "I want my money, and I want it now."

Fedota said, "Are you insane? I don't have that kind of cash."

"Then get it. If you don't, I'm going to the Feds. You said it would be a week. Now it's been two. If the law starts breathing down my neck, I'm not doing time without that money in my pocket!"

"I'm sorry, alright? The guy I'm working for doesn't have the money either. Not yet. We have to be patient."

"Patient, my ass!"

"Keep your voice down!"

"Fuck you. Tell me who he is, and *I'll* go squeeze his nut sack until he coughs it up."

"I can't tell you that. Look, I haven't been paid either."

"Well, then how about we go and grab the paintings, you and me, and hold them hostage until this motherfucker settles up? Where'd you take them, anyway? That one was fucking huge."

"A storage unit about ten minutes from here, but—"

Explosive noise blasted through the headphones, a high-speed succession of thunderous pops. Trey and the others reflexively tore off their headsets.

The sound of submachine-gun fire exploded out of the diner, audible even through the walls of the van.

"Oh, shit," somebody said. It might have been Trey.

Alderman flung open the van door and pulled his pistol. "Stay here," he said to Trey.

Through the open van door, Trey could see the diner across the street. It was pitch black inside, except for irregular strobing flashes on one end of the interior.

The FBI agent ran across the street, gun at the ready.

Trey's stomach roiled, and an anvil of dread slammed into his chest. He clutched his arms across his chest, trading worried looks with the surveillance tech.

The explosive succession of gunshots petered out, and Trey realized they sounded like firecrackers.

Alderman ducked through the diner's front door.

Trey desperately wanted to run after him, but reason somehow took over. If he ran into a chaotic crime scene, he might get shot by the FBI. He put the headphones back on. Muffled shouting came through. Blacker shadows moved in the diner's interior darkness. Coughing, gagging, swearing.

Trey didn't breathe.

Somebody's voice coalesced in the headphones. "You got 'em?"

"Yeah, they're right here. Call an ambulance."

"Where's the shooter?"

"Negative on the shooter."

Trey's heart stopped as his worst fears came true.

***

Bathed in the flashing lights of ambulances and LAPD cruisers, Trey had to see for himself. His feet carried him toward the diner's front door, almost of their own volition. They felt heavy, Frankensteinian, like someone else's. Exhaustion threatened to drag his eyes closed for the next six months.

The two cooks and two waitresses sat outside in the backs of ambulances, shocked, terrified, sobbing, rocking, clutching themselves and each other. Flashlight beams flickered and crisscrossed in the smoky blackness. Police cars and a helicopter prowled the surrounding neighborhood with searchlights, looking for the shooter.

Trey walked into the diner, clutching his handkerchief over his nose and mouth. The acrid smoke made his eyes water ferociously, but in the streetlights pouring through the front windows, he could still see the two figures slumped in a booth, discarded rag dolls. The surface of their table was dark and wet, glistening.

Hexom's left eye was a crater. Blood trickled from his nose. The right eye pointed at an unlikely angle, bulging slightly.

Fedota lay as if he'd fallen asleep on his forearms. It was his blood that slicked the table, dripping over the sides.

Suddenly Trey's guts heaved, and his throat seized, and he retched. The taste of bile filled his mouth. He reeled to the side, gagging.

A gentle hand landed on his shoulder. Alderman's voice said, "You all right?"

Trey straightened and took a deep breath, turning away from the corpses, composing himself, swallowing the awful taste in his mouth. "I think so."

"I'm sorry, Trey. We didn't see this coming."

Trey nodded. "I know. No one did."

Then, like a distant glimmer through a fog, an idea occurred to him. "Fedota mentioned a storage unit within ten minutes of here. If the paintings are still there..."

"We can run a search," Alderman said.

"Maybe Fedota is stupid enough to have an account in his own name."

They both hurried out to the van. As they slid open the side door, the tech said, "Already on it."

The tech's fingers danced on his computer keyboard. A map appeared on the screen, highlighting five storage facilities within a ten-minute drive. A series of phone calls to each of the facilities' management took over an hour. Not all of them were willing to divulge their customer lists. It was at one such facility, Bolger's Storage and Moving, after all the others had been eliminated as possibilities, after Alderman had threatened the owner, James—already grumpy over the disturbance of his evening of reality television—with obstruction of justice charges, that they found M. FEDOTA listed as the renter of a ten-foot-by-twenty-foot, climate-controlled storage unit.

On the phone, a disgruntled and defiant James said, "I'm not letting you in there without a search warrant."

"We'll be there in fifteen minutes, with a warrant," Alderman told him. "If you're not there, we'll make our own way in." He hung up.

Trey grinned, his mood suddenly shifting toward the positive. If he could recover those paintings, all this would be over.

Alderman said, "I'll call for a search warrant."

***

The search warrant arrived on Special Agent Alderman's phone before Trey and the cadre of FBI agents reached Bolger's Storage and Moving thirteen minutes later. The owner, James, met them at the front gate and opened it to admit their van. He was practically a walking stereotype. Retirement age, cigar in his mouth, wife-beater T-shirt, suspenders holding a pair of shapeless trousers under his hirsute paunch.

He took a thorough look at Alderman's search warrant before he grunted in acquiescence and led them into the three-story building. Inside the building were long corridors of red, sliding garage doors of various widths. James carried a large bolt-cutter that he used to cut the lock on unit B-126. Trey got the sense James had been in this position before, cutting off locks for law enforcement, and he resented it every single time.

They raised the steel door, revealing the dark, cluttered interior. Most of the unit's space was filled with old cardboard boxes and furniture wrapped in plastic, all stacked almost to the ceiling. The ceiling of the unit was wire mesh open to the warehouse ceiling above. Dim light filtered within from the cavernous space that housed the individual units. The air smelled dusty and stale. A narrow path snaked around the wall.

Trey told Alderman and the other agents, "We're looking specifically for two paintings. The big one is about six feet by seven feet, with a huge, gold-leaf-on-gesso frame. Should be easy to spot." He and Alderman clicked on their flashlights and went inside. Trey followed the path along the wall, around wardrobe-sized boxes, past old mattresses, a toy box. But then he saw a space behind the wall of castoff possessions, between a wall of cardboard boxes and the back wall of the storage unit.

He stepped around the corner and shined his light into the dimness. A white sheet was draped over what looked like a six-by-seven-foot frame.

He rushed forward, his heart thundering, and he expostulated a noise of wordless triumph, snatching the sheet. He yanked it away to reveal...an empty frame. Tears welled up in his eyes.

"Motherfuckers," he said, his voice thick and low.

Around the inside of the frame were frayed threads of canvas, little multicolored filaments. The painting had been cut from the stretcher bars and frame. Leaning against the wall behind the empty Caravaggio frame was the smaller di Cosimo frame, also empty.

The outrage spilled through him that these centuries-old works of art had been aggressively cut out of their stretcher bars and frames and rolled up for easier transport, for expediency, by callous, greedy men. Where the paintings were now was anybody's guess, and there was only one person left in the world who knew.

***

Back in his hotel room later, Trey made a series of encrypted phone calls and wrote one encrypted email before collapsing into storm-tossed oblivion.

The panic attack had stampeded over him in the taxi. In the back seat, rigid as a bundle of re-bar, sweat soaking his shirt, he concentrated on taking one breath at a time, even with what felt like an anvil on his sternum. Even after applying the therapy techniques, the attack did not subside until he was in his hotel room.

The first phone call was to his therapist, Dr. Connie Bowen. He didn't expect her to pick up at this hour, but he desperately needed to vent, to unload some small measure of the massive weight of failure and despair that made further communication impossible. He couldn't unload this way on Marie, not over the phone. She helped him best with her soothing, physical presence. And he couldn't call Antonio Vasari sounding like a fractured lunatic.

So he called Dr. Bowen, and as expected the call went to voicemail.

"Connie, I'm panicking. I can't do all this. I'm losing it. There's only so many hours in a day. There's only so much capacity of focus that I have. My leads are dead. I'm about to be financially fucked. I could lose my business. I could lose my house. I'm barely hanging on. Marie is great, but her patience for my crazy is not infinite. I want to nail Frank Cahill and Richard Dunwood to the wall. It's like... This is like...drowning. And Okie is as smart as I am. We're playing a chess game, and I feel like I'm constantly three moves behind. He's painting under a pseudonym, but I know his work. He's been involved with some enormously important shit over the years, and now he's doing something again. I know it. I need to pursue this case, and I need to nail Cahill, and I need to see my family, and I need to go to Denver and see this footlocker full of Okie's photos my brother found. Does any of this make sense? I'm exhausted. I haven't seen my wife in a while, I haven't been home for a while. I've been traveling. I'm physically exhausted, I'm mentally exhausted. I can't let Nicklaus down. My business drives me, and my reputation drives me, but I've got this thing in my peripheral that it's like I keep looking over there and I have to focus on Cahill and I can't do both but I have to do both and—"

The recording beeped its limit and cut him off. So he called back and kept going, ranting and rambling until it cut him off again. He called back, and repeated this four more times, sounding less and less coherent with each message, as if the worst of the mental and emotional detritus was gathered at the end of his consciousness and formed the last of his thoughts in a black, chunky, unrecognizable sludge.

When he recognized this, he put the phone down and held his head in his hands, elbows on his knees, for a long time.

Then, when his conscious thoughts started to reshape themselves into something manageable, he called Alessandro Vasari. As Rome was nine hours ahead of Los Angeles, he caught Vasari at the beginning of his workday. Vasari picked up immediately, "*Pronto, Trey, my friend! Buon giorno!*"

Trey greeted him in kind, struggling to keep his voice even.

Vasari said, "Are you all right? You sound troubled."

"The two paintings I'm looking for, the Caravaggio and the di Cosimo."

"I remember."

"I found the frames, but no paintings. Someone cut them out."

"*Stronzo! Che cazzo...?*"

"That means they're being shipped in tubes."

"Right, right. You want me to keep my eyes open for a two-meter shipping tube coming through Italian or Vatican customs, yes?"

"Right. They have to be going to the Vatican. If they get into the Vatican, or if they're already there, they might as well be swallowed by a black hole."

"Understood. I have a man on the inside, you know."

"I was hoping you'd say that." A shudder, a gush, a flood of relief swept through Trey's body, and his voice hitched. "*Tu sei un vero amico. Ti devo molto per sempre.*" *You are a true friend. I owe you big.*

"Perhaps we take our families on my sailboat and cruise around the Med, when this is over."

"That is a spectacular idea. Alessandro, please, watch your back. My two chief witnesses were murdered tonight. An execution, Mafia-style hit."

Vasari went silent for a moment. "You watch *your* back, my friend."

Then they hung up.

His last phone call was to Marie. His nerves had mostly steadied. She was also probably asleep at this hour, as her phone went to voicemail also. He told her what had happened, that his investigation was all but over unless he could find the paintings, that he was so sorry, that he was coming home soon, but first he had to stop in Denver to see Patrick. Two days, he promised, he would be home in two days. Again, with his voice choking, he hung up with a massive sigh.

He didn't usually use profanity with Nicklaus—it was unprofessional—but the depth of his frustration and the seriousness of his predicament could not be overstated.

SUBJECT: FUCKED

Nicklaus:

Two witnesses murdered tonight, the only two we had. Mafia-style execution, right before my eyes. Found the frames, but no paintings. Canvases cut out and removed. Only hope is if contact in Italy intercepts.

Taking some personal days.

Trey

He sent the message, closed his laptop, and lay on the bed. Still in his clothes, the tide of unconsciousness washed over him.

PART IV

"Once you've lived the inside-out world of espionage, you never shed it. It's a mentality, a double standard of existence."

- **John le Carré**

CHAPTER 32

"*I WAS FOLLOWED WHEN I was in Cuba. Some years ago, I was there for a job, an art opening for the Vatican at the Havana Cathedral. One of the ironic things is that Cuba as a country and a culture is hugely supportive of the arts, not like here. A serious pain in the ass getting a visa, though. I shouldn't be surprised about being followed, because hey, it's fucking Cuba.*

"*I was assigned a translator-slash-minder, I guess, but he was a decent sort, named Daniel. He loved photography. We stayed in a seminary. They closed the door at 10:00 p.m. and opened at 6:00 a.m. We went out every morning because there's great art deco architecture in Havana and fabulous cultural texture. It was great to photograph at sunrise. I had my iPad, and he had a camera older than he was that still used 35mm film.*

"*As we were walking around, there were these boxy, Russian cars, Ladas they were called, two guys in them, and they would turn off their headlights in the early morning, and they would follow us slowly block by block. While we were walking, we also noticed there were sentries posted in doorways and windows, and they would do birdcall signals. Creepy as hell, intimidating as fuck.*

"*So at the art opening, Raul Castro shows up—*"

"*Raul Castro!*"

"Yeah, seriously. He came in with heavy security, wearing the green fatigues. He was going around the exhibition, looking at objects. Other people in green fatigues were talking to him and translating this and that. Meanwhile, I'm like, holy shit this is Raul Castro, *so I position myself for him and his little entourage to flow into me, which is exactly what happens.*

"I introduce myself, 'Hello, I'm Emmett Hansen III. Please call me Trey.'

*"And Raul Castro—*Raul fucking Castro*—looks up at me and says, in English, 'I hear you're a pretty good chess player like your dad.'"*

***

The ride from Denver International Airport to Golden, a town bordering the Denver suburbs but nestled closely against the Rocky Mountain foothills, was almost an hour, thanks to the airport's location literally in the middle of nowhere, but it gave Trey time to think about what he would say to his younger brother. He'd called Patrick this morning to inform him he was coming, then he booked a flight landing him in Denver that evening.

Since he had moved away from the Denver area prior to college, the dryness of the air, especially after Los Angeles, was immediately noticeable, as was the quality of the sunlight, as if the altitude allowed the sunlight to exert physical pressure on his skin and burrow into his retinas even through his sunglasses. It was one of the sunniest cities in America, and today was no exception. The Rocky Mountains, a constant presence perpetually indicating and connoting West, formed an undulating wall behind which the sun disappeared.

When the Uber pulled up into Patrick's nice, suburban driveway, Trey got out, and the driver retrieved his suitcase from the trunk. A little Scottie terrier came charging across the lawn, barking ferociously until it got within five feet of him, then it flopped onto its back, tail wagging, exposing its belly and begging for a hearty rub. Trey smiled and obliged.

Patrick waited on the front step with the door open. He stood slightly taller than Trey, more on the gangly side, but damned if he didn't look more like their father with every passing year, his face all angles and planes. Little faces peeked around the door jamb. He greeted Trey with a firm handshake and a hug. Three of Patrick's six children surrounded them at waist height and below.

"Kids," Patrick said, "you remember your Uncle Trey?"

"Yay!" they chorused and went bounding across the living room and onto the sofa.

"You need to stop feeding them," Trey said. "They're getting too big."

"They eat us out of house and home," Patrick said.

Patrick's wife Amy came into the living room, a short, Irish spitfire of a woman. She hugged Trey, standing to about his rib cage. "Welcome." Her body carried that weariness that went with bearing and raising six kids as a full-time mom, a little saggy yet athletic, a little tired, a little soft, but that softness did not reach her eyes, which were still sharp as blue thumbtacks, capable of arresting an errant child in mid-foolishness.

Their living room was comfortably appointed in modest,

non-matching furniture. Trey let his gaze slide over the Catholic iconography, the Virgin Mary statue on the mantelpiece, the crucifix near the front door, a print of the Caucasian Christ.

They ushered him into the kitchen.

"Have you had dinner?" Amy said.

"I grabbed something at the airport. I brought this though." Trey held out a brown paper bag that contained two six-packs of beer, a hearty IPA for Patrick and a nutty brown ale for Amy.

Amy took them and put them in the refrigerator. "This is one of my favorites."

After recent events, it felt strange to be in a such a normal family setting, and the shift made Trey almost suspicious, like he was waiting for ninjas to come crashing through all the windows.

"Of course, you're staying here tonight," Amy said.

"I don't want to impose—" Trey began.

"Shut yer gob, boyo, as my dad used to say. I've already got your room prepared. Some of the kids are bunking together tonight."

"Well, then, thank you," Trey said. "Whose bed am I getting?"

"Mine," said a boy's voice from the hallway, tinged with pride that Uncle Trey was sleeping in *his* bed.

Trey called after him, "Thank you, Evan!" Evan was the oldest child, just turned ten.

They all sat at the table, talking about family, children, and work, all the kinds of catch-up chat that kept families up to date on things, but without digging too deeply. The children soon grew bored of the adult conversation and rambled off to avoid getting ready for bed. Patrick talked for a while about his work managing the sporting goods store. Amy asked how Marie's work was going,

perhaps a little mystified and envious Marie managed both chil-
drearing and a career.

When the topic circled around to Trey's work, however, he said,
"I can't talk about that. There's a lot going on, and it's not good."

"Hey, don't give me that," Patrick said with a smile. "You're not
joining the CIA, are you?"

Trey looked around to make sure no children were listening.
"Well, let's just say for now Marie and I were both surveilled when
we went to Rome last week, people following us. Lots of weird
things."

"Weird things how?" Patrick said.

"You remember that time our house in Littleton got broken
into?"

"Your house was broken into?" Amy said, looking at them both.

Patrick said, "The one with the broken kitchen door?"

Trey nodded.

Patrick said to Amy, "Yeah, when I was seven or eight. I remember they kicked down the door to come in the kitchen through the
garage."

Amy said, "Funny you never mentioned that before."

"I was really young," Patrick said. "It's funny, I haven't thought
about that in years. Kinda forgot about it."

"Memory is funny that way," Trey said. No doubt there were a
great many things Patrick did not remember, or had conveniently forgotten, about their upbringing. "Marie told me a couple of
days ago that she's noticed things have been moved in our house.
Nothing has been stolen, but after Rome, she's a little freaked out.
I think they were planting bugs or something."

"On you? Why?"

His hand went to the phone in his pocket, safely sequestered in its Faraday bag. "Because the paintings I'm trying to track down are worth one hundred and twenty million dollars. That's highly motivating. So, I hope you'll understand when I say I can't really talk about it."

Silence hung between them. Trey sipped his beer. What he really wanted to do was jump straight into Okie's military footlocker and start digging, but it was best not to broach that subject too soon. Patrick knew the main reason for the visit, but he was clearly enjoying having Trey there.

Finally, Patrick said, "So we might as well go look. I know you're burning to go do it."

Trey nodded while still restraining himself.

Patrick got up and led Trey into the garage, flipped on the overhead fluorescents, and there it was.

An old Army footlocker circa the 1950s.

"It was locked once," Patrick said, "but I think they broke it when they were moving it. I opened it right up."

Trey knelt, flipped the latches, and opened the lid.

Inside lay stacks of vintage photographs, silver gelatin black-and-whites, color, old Polaroids, all rubber-banded together. Stacks of newspapers, yellowed and ragged, had once been stacked neatly but now lay in disarray from the jostling of being moved. Trey began rifling through the newspapers. The bulk of them appeared to be from the 1960s and 1970s. Most were American newspapers, but there was also the *Times* of London, *Die Zeitung* and other West German newspapers he did not recognize, even some printed in Cyrillic characters, presumably Russian, but he could not be sure without closer scrutiny. The *Los Angeles Times, Dallas Morning News*, Memphis' *The Commercial Appeal*, plus many others of the most prominent newspapers in America. On a hunch, he checked the dates. Thanks to Okie's meticulous organization, the papers were bundled by year and in order of date, so it was a matter of a few moments to track down papers printed on some very significant dates in American history. With each corresponding date he found, a jet of vindication went through him, a visceral tingle of excitement.

Patrick said, "You look like you're finding something."

Trey tried to keep the I-told-you-so tone out of his voice but couldn't entirely. "A lot of these papers are dates that Okie—Dad was not home." Patrick hated it when Trey called their father Okie. "Here's the *Dallas Morning News* from the morning of JFK's assassination. The assassination hadn't happened yet." He laid the paper at Patrick's feet as if daring him to pick it up.

Patrick edged back, as if the sheaf of yellowed newsprint were an angry rattlesnake.

"And there's more," Trey said. He had no doubt anymore that every single one of those newspapers corresponded to a significant event, even if the significance was not immediately apparent.

He picked up a bundle of photos. The rubber band crumbled to nothing the moment he tried to remove it. Some of the photos had writing on the back, some didn't. Pictures of Germany in the 1950s. The Berlin Wall. Castles. His father as a young man. In some of the photos, Trey recognized Don Fell, "Uncle Don." Two skinny young men, arm in arm, Pall Mall cigarettes dangling, the world at their feet. Some were candid shots. Bleary eyed in a barracks bunk. Two couples out on the town. Young couples in love, on fire with life, verve. With purpose. In those, he recognized his mother, a stunning beauty in those days. In one photo, she wore a TWA stewardess' uniform including a pillbox hat.

He handed this bundle to Patrick, who sat down cross-legged beside him.

The next bundle contained photos of a beach house, probably California, with shots of a Pacific sunset, a patio. One in particular caught his eye, a group of men inside in the kitchen, photographed through a window, huddled around the kitchen table, wearing suits or shirts and ties. Only one face was visible. The image was grainy, perhaps debatable, but Trey recognized the face.

Trey handed the photo to Patrick. "Do you know who that is?"

"No, should I?"

"That's John Ehrlichman. He was one of Nixon's closest advisors on domestic affairs, the director of Nixon's Plumbing Crew."

"The president had guys that fixed toilets?"

"No, dummy, the Plumbing Crew was Nixon's gang of fixers, the ones who did the dirty work. They were the guys who directed the Watergate break-in."

"You're shitting me."

Trey pointed to a couple of heads in the photos. "This one could be Nixon. This guy with the mustache could be G. Gordon Liddy."

"Oh, come on!" Patrick said, but the certainty was draining from his voice.

"I'm guessing Dad is behind the camera for most of these."

He flipped through them quickly, looking for one with Okie in the frame. He found a few but he didn't recognize any of the other faces. With some digging and Internet Age facial recognition applications, he might be able to determine who they were, but that would mean he would have to take the footlocker with him and scan all the photos by hand. Would Patrick let him do that?

Soon he was rewarded with a shot of Okie standing in the background of what looked like a campaign headquarters. The proliferation of Nixon signs and campaign slogans meant this was probably the 1960 presidential election, which Richard Nixon lost to John F. Kennedy. Okie stood in the background, the shadows, almost like a sentinel, while Richard Nixon stood at a table with several other advisors, deep in a strategy session.

A heavy sigh shuddered through Trey as he handed the photo to Patrick.

Patrick took one look. "Son. Of. A. Bitch."

"And I'm not even halfway through this stuff. I could spend a week going through this." Instantly a series of calculations and decisions crackled through Trey's mind. "Patrick, I know this is a huge favor, but can I borrow this?"

Patrick stiffened and shook his head. "What for?"

"Because this stuff is really, really important to my investigation."

Patrick stood and turned away. "So Dad worked for Nixon. So what?"

"I think it's bigger than that, but I can't tell you any more without proof." He pointed at the footlocker. "And the proof is in here."

"That doesn't feel right. This is Dad's stuff, and you haven't spoken to the man in years."

"It's just for a while. I'll get it back to you within a week."

"What if Dad shows up tomorrow and wants it?"

"How would he know it's here?"

"Maybe he requested it for all I know. Maybe he knows exactly where it is." Patrick's face had turned deadly serious, pale, his voice tinged with fear. "If he shows up here and finds out I've given it to you..."

"You could play dumb. When I'm done I'll have it shipped straight to his house. I promise. But if we give this to him now, it'll be gone. We'll never get another chance."

"To do what?"

"Know the truth!"

Patrick turned toward the door to the kitchen and paused. "The truth about what?"

"About the things he's done."

"And why does that matter? Say you discover everything you want, all Dad's dirty little secrets. What then? He'll still be an old man you don't want to talk to. An old man full of regrets. Maybe he's hiding this shit for a reason."

"And in this shit might be the stuff someone was looking for, all those times our houses got tossed. Have you stopped to think of that?"

Patrick considered this for half a moment, then spoke slowly, enunciating every word. "Then why in the hell would you want to have it in *your* house?"

Trey didn't have an answer to that.

Patrick gave the footlocker another wary glance. "I have to go put the kids to bed. The answer is no. You want to borrow that foot-locker full of stuff, you can ask him yourself. *If* he shows up again."

Patrick went into the house, leaving Trey with the footlocker.

Trey sat on the floor, considering. He could take photos of everything with his phone, but the image quality wouldn't be as good as from a real scanner.

Exhaustion washed over him again, another wave of it building on all the previous hard days and sleepless nights. He felt twenty years older.

With a sigh, he knew what he had to do.

***

A longtime late-night prowler, thanks to his PTSD-driven insomnia, Trey knew how to move about in the wee hours without making a sound. The Uber driver arrived at 4:00 a.m. while the rest of the household was asleep. He had told Patrick he was leaving for the airport at about 7:00 a.m., that they could have breakfast together before his flight to Chicago.

The family was all fast asleep as he carried the footlocker out to the black sedan and stuffed it in the trunk. It was so big he had to put his suitcase in the back seat with him.

This might cause bad blood between him and Patrick, which Trey would regret, but the contents of the footlocker were too important to allow it to disappear into Okie's black hole of secrecy. He would never get another chance at this. He'd left a note explaining this on the kitchen table. As the luxury vehicle pulled away from the curb, he hoped Patrick would forgive him.

And moreover, he'd had an epiphany while lying in bed, staring at the ceiling. He hoped Marie would forgive him for that, too, because he wasn't going to Chicago either.

CHAPTER 33

"OKIE BECAME OBSESSED with attending 6:00 a.m. Mass every morning, Monday through Saturday, and Sunday Mass at 8:00 a.m. He forced our family to attend the Sunday morning 8:00 Mass, so as to be perceived as the model family. He never missed a feast day or a novena. He must have had a lot of things to confess, or maybe he was openly communicating with the Vatican through the confessional.

"He wasn't always so devout, though. According to my mother, this started on my sister's birthday, in early July of 1968, when we seemed to move in a hurry from Virginia, to Littleton, Colorado. This was right after the assassination of Bobby Kennedy on June 5th at the Ambassador Hotel in Los Angeles. Before that, he was different, she says.

"I don't remember any of this, but I've tried to piece it together. There are significant dates when my father was not home.

"My baby book has entries from 1960 to 1968, handwritten by my mother. I was born in early June 1960. Okie was not there. My baby book says he was 'out of town on international business.' He also missed my sister's birthday, April 8th. That was around the Bay of Pigs Invasion. Thanksgiving 1963, and my brother Patrick's birthday, August 5th.

"Look, I know how it sounds, but the dates line up perfectly. Marilyn Monroe's assassination, August 5, 1962. JFK's assassination, November 22, 1963. Bobby Kennedy, June 5, 1968."

"Didn't Marilyn Monroe die of a drug overdose?"

"Absolutely. And someone held her down to give it. Even stranger, Martin Luther King Jr. was assassinated on April 4, 1968, at the Lorraine Motel in Memphis, days before my sister's ninth birthday. I went through a whole box of my mother's pictures from around that time, including birthday pictures. Okie was not present in any of them."

"Okay, now I feel like we're on the verge of going down a very deep rabbit hole."

"My whole life is a rabbit hole. Strap in."

"I'm not sure this line of discussion is helpful for your therapy."

"Smacks of delusions, right? Psychosis? Don't you think I know that? Try living this shit."

"Fair enough. It's enough to know that this is all very real for you."

"Anyway, I tried to ask my mother where the fuck Dad was at these events. She just shrugged and said, 'Away on business.'"

***

One of the things Trey had found in the trunk before retiring was a little black book of phone numbers. Paging through it, he saw no names, but there was a pair of initials he recognized, "D.F." The book was at least forty years old, but in a flash of inspiration, he dialed the number with his encrypted app.

The phone answered on the third ring. "Fell." The voice was grim, expectant, raspy from decades of smoking.

"This is Trey Hansen, Uncle Don."

A pause. "Trey. Really?"

"For real."

"How did you get this number?"

"I was going through some of Dad's things, and I came across it. Look, the reason I'm calling is that I need to talk to you. My family is in danger. I can't talk about it over the phone. I need to talk to you in person."

No hesitation. "All right. Call me when you get here. I'll pick you up at the airport."

"You're still at the same house in McLean?"

Don chuckled. "Wouldn't have bought the place if I didn't plan to stay." It was the first hint of humanity that had crept into Don's voice since he picked up the phone.

Trey breathed a sigh of relief. "Thank you, Uncle Don. I'll see you soon."

***

Marie practically bounced up and down with excitement when Trey's call appeared on her phone. She instantly forgot the mountain of work piled up on her desk, the dozens of important emails in her inbox, the conference with Annie's teacher this afternoon. The girl was having behavioral problems at school. Sullenness, rudeness to the teacher, declining grades. But all that was downplaying the direness of her daughter's academic situation. Her husband was coming home, and that was all that mattered right now.

"Hey, Boo," she said as she answered. "What time are you getting in?"

He sighed deeply, reluctant to speak, and her heart clenched.

"I'm not coming home yet," he said. "I'm so sorry."

"What do you mean? Are you okay?"

"I'm fine. But there's something I have to do."

A warm trickle of relief that he was not hurt, but she held the sudden burst of anger like a primed grenade. "And what is that?"

"I probably shouldn't tell you."

"*Mr.* Hansen, need I remind you that you are *not* a spy. You don't get to go undercover without explanation."

"I have to. I don't trust anything anymore. Except you. All I can say is that I'm going to Virginia."

"Damn the secrecy. Why?"

"I can't tell you."

"Why?"

"You know why. Please stop asking me. This is hard enough as it is."

"I'm not here to make it easy for you. You expect me to raise our children by myself? We can't afford a nanny. I have a career, too, art dick! And I'm getting goddamn tired of putting it on hold for yours!"

"Marie, I'm sorry, but—"

"No buts! I've been holding back telling you this because you've got a lot on your plate. Annie is about to get expelled from school." Tears blurred her vision. Her baby was in trouble, and she didn't know what to do.

"What?"

"Yeah, I'm meeting her teacher this afternoon to see what the hell is going on. Maybe I can beg the principal to reconsider. Apparently, she called her teacher a liar again, but this time added on a few choice four-letter words. I get the sense this is not an isolated incident."

"Have you talked to Annie?"

"You're damn right! But she's ten. She doesn't know why she does these things. *You* need to talk to her. She's acting out because she misses her *father!*"

A choked sound came through the phone, then silence.

"So say something!" she said, fuming. "Don't go silent like your father." She knew that would drive him back on his heels, and it did.

It was almost a minute before he answered, and she just waited. "I have to do this. This is big. All I can say is, I will make it up to you. All of you. And I'll tell you everything, I promise. Just not today. I have to go."

"Trey, don't—!"

He hung up.

She clenched her teeth and growled. "What the *fuck* is in Virginia?"

***

Trey's flight touched down at Dulles International Airport at about 5:00 p.m. local time. The sun would soon disappear and turn the airplane view of the vast metropolitan area around Washington, DC, into a sea of sparkling shadows. As soon as he retrieved his baggage—he was not going to let the footlocker out of his sight until he'd had a chance to scan and catalog every single item within—he called Donald Fell again, and then he waited at the passenger pickup zone.

Like most aspects of his father's life, Trey knew only that Okie and Uncle Don had known each other since their early days in Army Intelligence. They had met during their training, then worked together in West Berlin. They had even rented flats together in West Berlin, then, when they had girlfriends, two flats, one above the other. They used to laugh over the story of how, during the Christmas of 1956, they had sawed a hole in the floor/ceiling between their flats to accommodate a twelve-foot fir tree they cut down themselves. Okie and Honey decorated the bottom half of the tree, Don and Marguerite the top half.

Throughout Trey's childhood, Uncle Don and Aunt Maggie had been his parents' closest friends. They always seemed like part of the family, a steadfast presence, even after the Hansens moved to Colorado. Don was warm in all the ways Okie was cold. How many times had Trey wished as a boy that Don was his father? He had lost touch with Don and Maggie since breaking off all contact with his parents, and that was the only thing he regretted about that painful decision.

When Don pulled up in his silver, late-model Jaguar F-Type Coupe, Trey recognized him instantly. Don got out and circled the car, gave Trey a firm handshake, then a hug. There were many more lines in Don's face now, and his hair was almost white, but his frame was still lean and trim from years of downhill skiing, his eyes still sharp. He smelled of cigarettes and Old Spice, just like he always had. For all outward observations, except for the predilection for European sports cars, Donald Fell was utterly normal, unassuming, bland. But Trey was pretty sure that was a façade carefully cultivated over four or five decades. It was Uncle Don who'd introduced young Trey to the fabulous world of European sports cars. An occasional "drive in the country" on the back roads of Virginia and Colorado routinely topped three digits on the speedometer.

Don sized up Trey, just as Trey was doing the same.

"Looking good, young man," Don said.

"Likewise, Uncle Don. Once we get in the car, you'll have to tell me about your spectacular ride right here."

"Don't you know it." Don gave him one of those old, mischievous grins. Years of smoking had stained his teeth, but that boldness of heart was still there.

The Jaguar only had two seats, but the trunk was roomy enough to fit Trey's luggage.

Don spent an extra second taking in the sight of the footlocker, as if he recognized it, but he said nothing. Trey had covered Okie's name, which was stenciled on the side, with duct tape.

They strapped in and peeled out of the passenger pickup zone.

"Damn good to see you, Trey."

"Sure is. How long has it been?"

"Thirty years, give or take," Don said.

But to Trey it felt like much less, months perhaps, even though there had been three marriages, two children, and gods knew what else in between.

"Uncle Don, I really want to catch up with you, but there's something really pressing I need to talk to you about."

"This about your dad?"

Trey nodded.

"I figured this would come up someday." Don zipped through airport traffic like it was the Monaco Grand Prix. Trey grinned at the sensation of power and control, holding tight to the handles. "When was the last time you saw your old man?"

"My father-in-law's birthday party a few years ago. That was the only time since I got out of college."

"That's a shame, but I understand it."

"You do?"

"How could I not? You kids had it pretty hard growing up. You especially."

"You knew he was abusive?"

"I'm not blind. But it wasn't my place to tell a man how to raise his kids."

Trey almost said *Even when he beats them up?* But he didn't want this reunion to turn confrontational. There were still other things he wanted to discuss.

They drove in silence for a while.

Finally, Don said, "Maggie is excited to see you. We haven't seen enough of you all in recent years. We're getting old, you know? Less and less urge to travel. So are your folks." His tone suggested the question of whether Trey was ever going to reconcile with Okie, but he left that subject alone. "So, is this about your Dad's footlocker back there?"

"In part. There are some things I need to know."

"I'll tell you what I can."

Trey took a deep breath. "You and my dad were spooks, right?"

"I can probably confirm that much now."

"You guys did all this shit."

Don laughed, then he gave Trey a deadpan stare. "We worked in an office."

That was the rote response that Okie used to give him. Too many questions redirected.

"In that footlocker back there," Trey said, "is a huge pile of photos and newspapers. You're in some of them. The dates on the newspapers correspond to some monumental historical events."

"Such as?"

"Marilyn Monroe's death." Trey scrutinized Don closely for any kind of reaction, but Don's face had turned to stone. "JFK's assassination. Bobby Kennedy's. Martin Luther King's. The Bay of Pigs."

"And what do you think it all means?"

"I think they're trophies. Mementos. They are the best proof I have of the things he did for the CIA, for Nixon." He told Don about the four paintings and his father's pseudonym, still watching, unrewarded, for any hint of a reaction. Don Fell listened as if to a mundane news broadcast. "I think he was painting from personal experience, the experience of being there. I think he's trying to paint away his demons."

Don kept his eyes on the road, both hands on the wheel. The sleek sports car garnered looks of admiration from both pedestrians and other drivers. "There are two common misconceptions that civilians have about hardcore spooks. The first is that they have demons. The people who operate in the field put their lives on the line every day, playing a very high-stakes game against very dangerous people. Life or death, every day. The people they kill are almost always Very Bad Guys. You won't find much lost sleep there. If anything, it's the opposite. Saving the Free World before breakfast makes you sleep like a baby. Movies and TV, they get it wrong all the time, because they're writing from the perspective of 'normal' people."

"And you know this from working in your office?"

Don smirked. "Exactly."

"But Nixon was a crook. The fact that he got away with treason for torpedoing the Paris peace talks with North Vietnam just to get re-elected is documented now."

"And you think your dad was some kind of Red Right Hand for ol' Tricky Dick?"

"Did you and Dad kill Marilyn?"

Don burst out laughing, then said, "Oh, you're serious." Had Don's laughter been just a little too boisterous?

"Did you?" Trey said. He might never forgive either of them if that were the case. "I've got proof."

"I'll tell you this much, kid," Don said. "I was with your dad when Marilyn died."

More obfuscation. More non-answers. "What does that mean?"

"It means I was with him. We were together."

Trey sighed and rubbed his forehead. Maybe coming here was a mistake. What if Don was somehow in on all this with Okie? What did Don know? What if Uncle Don was going to take Trey home, put a bullet in his brain pan, and bury him in the back yard?

"What about JFK?" Trey said. "Martin Luther King?"

"Here's the second common misconception. It's never what you think it is."

"I kind of want to punch you right now. You two always gave me the same canned response. I want the truth."

"You get used to that in this business."

"What business?"

"The Company."

"So you admit that you were spies for the CIA?"

"No, not spies. Foreign adversaries engaged in espionage are 'spies,' the KGB, the East German Stasi. We were spooks. How's that? I just violated several federal laws."

Trey let that sink into him. There it was. The confirmation he had dreamed of hearing his entire life. It settled into him, warming him, calming him like a thirty-year, single-malt scotch.

Passing signs indicated they were entering Falls Church, Virginia, one of the suburbs situated between Dulles International Airport and Washington, DC, the town Trey's family had lived in before moving to Colorado. It was an affluent area, neighborhoods of large homes, perfectly manicured landscapes, and rich foliage. And it was starting to feel familiar. He recognized the lay of the streets, the look of the forested neighborhoods, even though he hadn't been here since he was eight years old.

Don stopped the car outside of a two-story house with a screened-in, wraparound porch overlooking the walkout basement. The sight of it struck Trey like a blow. "Oh, my God! That's our old house on Ventnor Lane!"

Don nodded.

Trey got out of the car, and stood there at the curb, staring. Lights glowed inside, the flicker of a television. A BMW sat in the driveway. Here, on the cusp of dusk, it all looked so normal, so Beaver Cleaver. A neighbor, a short, sparse-haired old man, watered a tapestry of rose bushes, their blooms a mosaic of brilliant colors. The neighbor noticed Trey and Don's presence and peered through his glasses.

Long-dead memories clamored for recognition deep in the wells of the past, but Trey could not reach them.

The neighbor took a few steps closer. Trey felt his scrutiny like an unwanted touch.

The old man said, "Uh, sorry, but...is that you, Trey?"

Trey flinched as if struck by a two-by-four, jarring loose a name he hadn't thought of in four, almost five decades. "Mr. Allgaier?"

The old man chuckled. "You remember me, do you?" He tossed down his garden hose and came down to the curb.

"How did you recognize me?" Trey said.

"I have a talent for faces, and young man, you look just like your father."

"Uh, how are you?"

Mr. Allgaier offered his hand, and Trey shook it. "Getting old, getting old."

Trey gestured toward Don. "This is—"

"Don Fell. I remember you." Mr. Allgaier came and shook Don's hand.

"Do you guys know each other?" Trey said.

"We both worked at American University in Beirut," Don said. "In the seventies."

Mr. Allgaier shoved his hands deep into the pockets of his cargo shorts, which were hiked up a little too high onto his modest paunch. "Yeah, we were in the Company together."

A thunderous shift rumbled through Trey's childhood memories. "You too?"

The two old men looked at each other and chuckled. Mr. Allgaier said, "Everybody in this neighborhood worked for the Company."

"You've got to be kidding me," Trey said.

"Some of us go into work at Langley by the front door. Others..." Mr. Allgaier chuckled. "Anyway, I retired in '03. What happened to your family anyway? One day you were there, the next day..." He made a *poof* gesture with his fingers.

"I wish I knew," Trey said. "I remember very little of this place." He looked up and down the street. "Did you used to have these two dogs? Big ones?"

The old man laughed again. "Ah, yes, yes, Thor and Odin, a couple of Norwegian Elkhounds. Long since passed, I'm afraid."

"Uncle Don, would it be all right if I walked up the street a little ways?" Trey said. Maybe he would see something that jogged more memories loose.

Don said, "Sure."

Trey left the two older men chatting and catching up while he strolled up the winding, suburban street. He recognized none of the trees—the decades would have changed most of them dramatically, if they were even still alive—but many of the houses looked familiar. Half-remembered visions floated at the edges of his consciousness, damnably out of grasp.

He felt like someone had just smacked him a solid one-two with a cricket bat, seeing Don again, and running into a man who remembered him from when he was eight years old.

A couple of minutes later, the Jaguar pulled up next to him. "Let's go," Don said through the open window. Trey got in, and they sped away.

"Too weird?" Don said.

Trey nodded.

After twenty minutes of traversing a route that felt familiar as they drove toward McLean, another suburb, this one nestled right next to Arlington, they pulled up in the driveway of a lovely two-story, brick colonial. The driveway circled the house to the garage in back, the size of a garage that used to be a carriage house. The door opened, and Don eased the Jaguar inside. Then he switched off the ignition, and they sat in the dim glow of the garage door opener.

Don fixed Trey with a hard stare. "That footlocker there? You keep that under wraps. I don't want to see what's in it. I don't want to know. And don't show it to *anybody*. For your own safety."

"That's just the thing. I'm afraid for my family. My wife is pretty sure someone has been in our house. We were followed when we were in Rome for this case. My brother Patrick says Dad is missing—"

"Your dad is missing?"

"Yeah, it's been over a week now. Mom says he left on a trip but won't say where. No one has heard from him." He wanted to tell Don about his suspicions, about the murders, but it still sounded crazy, even to him, even in spite of all the evidence he had just uncovered. Okie was still an old man. "Do old operatives ever come out of retirement?"

"It's not unheard of. You never really leave the Company." Don rubbed his chin and looked out the windshield at the wall hung with gardening tools, things used for digging and burying. "Don't let that footlocker out of your sight, and don't let anyone else see it."

CHAPTER 34

"I HAVEN'T BEEN ENTIRELY honest about the last time I saw my dad."

"How so?"

"A few years ago, my father-in-law turned eighty, and his family had a big party in the St. Mary's Church community center, the same church I was forced to go to as a kid. A huge party with all these big, Catholic broods.

"My parents came because they were all friends from when Marie and I were in grade school. So I'm constantly fighting back a panic attack the whole time because my fucking dad is going to be there.

"Dozens of people around, and I see him over there being antisocial, standing in a corner, arms crossed, facing all the entrances. The first time I've laid eyes on him in probably twenty years.

"I'm going around the crowd, chatting, saying 'hi' to people, trying to keep the oncoming panic attack under control. I had just gotten back from Cuba about a week before. He's just standing there like this, staring off into space, so I go and stand next to him and do the same thing.

"I'm staring off into space, not saying anything, and then he says, 'Glad you got out of Cuba alive.'

"I looked at him and I'm like, 'What the fuck does that mean?'

"And he just smiled at me and walked off. I haven't seen him since."

***

Late at night, back in his hotel room, Trey stood staring at the military-issued footlocker on the floor as if it were a nuclear weapon.

Don and Maggie Fell had welcomed him into their home as if he were the son they never conceived. Just as Don was Okie's warmer counterpart, Maggie was Honey's. The positivity about them he remembered so well was still present, even in the face of the inevitable health problems old age inflicted. The emotions that welled up in him had left him teary eyed several times that night, as the old couple spoke in such glowing terms of Trey and his siblings. They asked about Trey's parents, but he literally had nothing to report, so they quickly moved on to other topics. He had spent the whole evening with them, sharing drinks, dinner, and conversation. They had reminisced about Trey's childhood, family gatherings, a vacation their families had shared, which Trey did not remember. Don and Maggie had been saddened by how little he remembered of those times. Don regaled him with stories of the officially declassified variety, and Trey told them about some of his more memorable cases.

The night had been a stew of emotions—sweet and sour, savory and bitter—richer than any Trey could remember for a long time, and it had left him exhausted. He could tell Don and Maggie were going through the same, so he bade them good night at about eleven o'clock, called an Uber, and booked a hotel room in Arlington.

Now, Trey stared at the footlocker, excitement mixed with trep-idation. In a single sentence, Don had confirmed many of Trey's unproven suspicions. Jigsaw pieces were still falling into place in his mind, and the sheer number of them ensured that would take some time.

His door was locked, the curtains of his twelfth-floor suite drawn. A chair was shoved up under the door handle. He'd booked his room with his iPhone after he left the Fells' house. The only way anyone would know where he was staying was if his phone had been thoroughly hacked, a contingency he could not fully rule out. He had bribed the desk clerk to let him borrow the document scanner from the hotel's business services suite. The scanner was secured by a dedicated fiber optic line and had a document feeder that would let him feed photographs into the scanner at a higher rate. Even so, the process would take hours. Thankfully, his hotel suite had a Nespresso espresso maker.

The hours passed as he scanned the photos and newspapers. The newspapers took much longer, because he scanned every page in several sections; the pages were too large to fit the scanner bed. Any page might hold some innocuous detail that might draw to-gether a huge connection.

Then one photograph landed on him like the weight of history. In the black-and-white photo was his father, very young, perhaps college age or a little older, arm in arm with none other than equal-ly young Fidel Castro and Che Guevara. Fidel wore his military cap and Che his iconic military beret. Okie was grinning, wearing a touristy Mexican sombrero. The backdrop of the photo was an outdoor cantina on the beach. A beautiful young woman wearing a Mexican dress, maybe a waitress, stood nearby, gazing at the men with curiosity.

Trey suddenly felt fuzzy on his knowledge of the Cuban Revolution, Castro, and US involvement, so he dove into some internet research.

Before becoming a revolutionary, Castro had started out as an idealistic young man of affluent background, a believer in freedom and democracy. His family enrolled him in the best Jesuit schools. There again was that Jesuit connection, the hand of the Templars reaching forward through the centuries. Castro had visited the US and looked to the Declaration of Independence and the US Constitution as ideals to be emulated. He became a lawyer with inclinations toward politics, wanting to free the Cuban people from the endless succession of horrific dictators and corrupt regimes that had crippled the country since gaining its independence from Spain. He decided to run for legislative office in 1952.

The US backed General Fulgencio Batista y Zaldívar, a staunch anti-communist, in the Cuban election of 1952, but Batista realized he still could not win, so he launched a military coup, canceled the elections, and did so with the support of the American government. Batista proved to be as corrupt and brutal a dictator as his predecessors. Enriched by kickbacks from the American Mafia to build casinos and resorts, he turned Havana into a playground for American celebrities and Mafia bosses. Castro looked upon all this with anger and disgust. If he couldn't change things from the inside, he would attack from the outside.

On July 26, 1953, Fidel and Raul Castro led an assault of about a hundred and twenty men against an army barracks, an effort that ended in catastrophic failure. Nearly all of Castro's men were killed, most of them executed on the spot. Fidel and Raul managed to escape and were smuggled to Mexico—by the Jesuits—where they spent a couple of years plotting and planning their return to Cuba.

During that period in Mexico, Castro still believed in American ideals. Batista's regime was also opposed by a number of anti-communist, democratic, leftist groups, upon which he cracked down again and again, even executing people in the streets, efforts that were turning public opinion in United States against him. However, the American right-wing, led by corporations and oligarchs with enormous financial interests in Cuba, continued to back Batista. After two years in Mexico, Castro returned to Cuba in a boat with eighty-one men, but they were spotted and nearly killed by Batista's forces.

On his trip to Cuba, Trey had seen this boat enshrined in the Museo de la Revolución in the Old Havana historic district.

Castro fled to the mountains, where, over the next couple of years, he managed to gather a force of some three hundred guerrillas. They were not communists; they were freedom fighters. He eventually joined forces with the other anti-Batista groups, and finally, town by town, took control of the country, and drove Batista from its shores on December 31, 1958. Castro and his allies took control of Havana on January 1, 1959 and consolidated their control of the country. At that time, Castro did not wish to hold government office, and a president was elected from among his supporters. However, he eventually accepted the role of Prime Minister about a month later.

Fidel Castro visited the United States in April 1959 and reiterated his assertion that his people were not communists. He wanted recognition from the US government. They had fought for their freedom from a tyrannical regime. The Communist Party had played almost no part in the revolution, and garnered dismal support at the early ballot box. Nevertheless, under pressure from the American right-wing, President Eisenhower refused to meet with him. Eisenhower relegated that meeting to Vice President Richard Nixon. In fact, prior to Castro's success in taking Havana, Allen Dulles, Director of the CIA, approved military action to send US Marines to Batista's aid and stop Castro's revolution, but the action was never carried out.

When the United States turned its back on Castro, goaded by the American right-wing and the corporations that controlled the vast majority of Cuba's assets, he saw this as a betrayal. Castro never forgave Nixon. The Cuban sugar industry, livestock, energy companies, utilities, transportation—all had been controlled by US corporations and the Mafia, the forces that had oppressed the Cuban people for decades. In retaliation, Castro nationalized them all. It was America's betrayal that turned Castro toward communism, which led him into the sphere of Soviet influence.

Trey's mind swirled at the connections and plausible possibilities. Okie, Castro, Nixon, the CIA... By March 1960, the CIA had initiated Operation Mongoose, a program to remove Castro from power. It trained and organized Cuban exiles to attempt to assassinate Castro, to foment a counter-revolution and restore all those nationalized assets to US interests. This effort culminated in what American history called the Bay of Pigs Invasion in mid-April. In

Cuba's Museum of the Revolution, it was called "The American Mercenary Action." The invasion consisted of a force of Cuban exiles, organized by the CIA, whose aim was to drag Castro from power, but the whole operation turned into an enormous debacle. Castro's troops had been tipped off. Invasion ships ran aground on reefs. Errant drops scattered paratroopers everywhere. Cuban troops pinned the invaders on the beach of the Bay of Pigs, killing over a hundred and taking more than eleven hundred prisoners.

Had Okie been there? Had he been captured? Had he escaped?

Daylight came, and Trey was still scanning, still poring over the images and documents, his eyes bloodshot and weary, feeling full of grit from so many hours staring at a screen. Every scan, every photo, he uploaded to an encrypted cloud server. There was no chance anyone was going to steal all this information from him. He could spend months going through all these images with a fine-toothed comb, identifying faces, determining dates, putting together a timeline of the things his father had been involved in, the places he had been.

At about 10:00 a.m., he received an email from Patrick. A moment of dread and remorse gave him pause, but he had to open the message.

It read:

I tried to call you several times, but it goes straight to voicemail every time. Thanks for taking my calls, after what you did. You're a real asshole sometimes, you know that? I've been thinking for a couple of days about what to do about this, whether I should even tell you what happened or whether you should find out on your own.

Somebody broke into our house yesterday. They broke a pane of glass out of the back door to get in. Tore apart the closets. Flung a bunch of shit around the garage. Gutted my tool shed. As far as we can tell, they didn't steal anything. I think they're looking for the foot-locker. Fuck you for making me believe your crazy shit.

Watch your ass.

Patrick

When Trey closed the email, he considered its implications for a long time. Was this footlocker the thing the intruders had been looking for in all those break-ins during his childhood?

First of all, who were 'they'? The list of potential candidates was practically infinite, but whoever it was, they had power, reach, and resources. How else would they have known what had fallen into Patrick's possession? Okie clearly had a long history of "off-the-books" operations, doubtless creating a great many serious grudges. Were those grudges lethal? Would someone kill for what Trey had in his possession?

Second, were they after something specific? Or was it the compilation of evidence they wanted?

Had Okie disappeared because he knew there was a bullseye on his back now or was he merely cleaning up decades of loose ends? Was he setting up a new kind of disappearance that would protect him and Honey during their final years? Okie would have no compunctions about abandoning contact with his children to save his own ass. Trey and his siblings had been nothing more than window dressing, human shields in a carefully crafted façade, resulting in abandonment of his family.

Had Okie come out of retirement? Was he working for the Company again or some higher bidder? Or had he embarked upon some clandestine operation of his own? For that matter, how many of these photos could be evidence of operations *not* sanctioned by the CIA? The meeting with Castro in Mexico. The Jesuit connections. Was Okie working for the Catholic Church now? *With* the Church perhaps, toward a common goal or divine cover-up?

Trey stretched and rubbed his eyes. His supply of hotel room coffee pods was long since exhausted. He could count the hours of sleep in the last three days on one hand, and he could tell his brain was not firing on all cylinders.

In two weeks, the lawsuit against him would move forward, and because he had only circumstantial evidence, he would probably lose. He would find himself on the witness stand facing Richard Dunwood, the man who had leaked the information about Greg Hexom and Mark Fedota's meeting to someone whose purpose was to silence them forever. The theft's connection to Cahill had been severed. The only evidence Trey had was two dead men's admission of conspiracy. There was no connection to Cahill, no habeas corpus. Cahill was not the trigger-man, of that Trey was sure. Cahill was corrupt and greedy as hell, but he wasn't an assassin. The execution in the diner had been far too smooth, too well planned, too flawlessly executed, to be anyone but a trained operator.

Before he passed out completely, he ordered a bouquet of flowers sent to Marie, and an edible bouquet—chocolate-dipped fruits—for the girls. He would make all this up to them in person as soon as he could. Vasari's offer—and Trey did not doubt it was genuine—of a sailboat cruise on the Mediterranean sounded spectacular when this was all over, regardless of the outcome, either as celebration of victory or assuagement of wounds. He found himself lying on the deck of a softly bobbing sailboat, the Mediterranean sun warm on his face, listening to the soft slap of the waves against the hull. Then a shadow fell over him, bringing danger with it. A man with a silenced pistol.

He snapped awake and upright, heart thundering with confusion and incipient panic. A photograph was stuck to his cheek.

Checking his watch, he saw he had been asleep for almost two hours.

But his job was still not complete. He estimated another three or four hours of work. If it was to continue, however, he needed some serious caffeine, so he threw on his sport jacket and ventured into Virginia's afternoon sunshine. Making sure his hotel room was secure, leaving the DO NOT DISTURB sign on the door, slipping a tiny piece of paper in the door jamb that would fall out if anyone entered.

He didn't take his phone out of its Faraday bag until he sat in a coffee shop about a mile from his hotel. It was there that he checked his messages.

All Patrick's phone calls immediately showed up in the history, eliciting another pang of remorse. He sent Patrick a text message.

THANK YOU FOR THE WARNING. AND I'M SORRY, BOTH FOR WHAT I DID, AND FOR WHAT HAPPENED TO YOU AND YOUR FAMILY. PLEASE FORGIVE ME. I LOVE YOU.

Then he spotted the last voicemail in the list. The country code on the number indicated the call came from Italy.

CHAPTER 35

"*IN 1968, WE MOVED to Littleton, Colorado, from Falls Church, Virginia. The three children were enrolled in St. Mary's Catholic School. We lived approximately three streets from the grade school and church, easy walking distance.*

"*I always thought Okie used the Catholic Church as his 'safe house.' He attended Mass seven days a week and never missed a holy day. His passionate involvement in the Catholic Church was a full-time job. I always wondered what he really did for a living. He never discussed his advertising business. My mother just said he worked for himself.*

"*His office was a residential-looking building near the railroad tracks. His car was the only car ever parked in the large parking lot. Why was he the only tenant in the building? Very odd.*

"*Okie's car was a 1968 Datsun 510, four-door, four-speed manual transmission, known as 'the poor man's BMW.' He bought it new. The vehicle was utterly nondescript—I can't even remember what color it was—with zero frills. Except for one thing. There was a cellular phone installed in his car. In 1968. Okie had installed in his 1968 Datsun a Motorola TLD-1100 car telephone. It was this rotary-dial contraption bolted into the floor console between the front seats, forward of the stick shift.*

"*Who the fuck has a rotary-dial car phone in 1968?*"

***

Trey's hands trembled and his heart pounded as he pulled up the voicemail from Italy.

"Signore Hansen, this is Giorgio Marinelli. I want to tell you, your package has arrived. You must come back to Rome."

His heart leaped into a gallop, his eyes tearing up. Questions leaped to mind, but he understood why Giorgio had not been more specific over the phone. Alessandro had no doubt told him about the need to be circumspect. Someone could be listening.

He could hardly pull up Alessandro's email address fast enough so that he could send a simple message.

SONO SULLA MIA STRADA. *I'm on my way.*

Then he packed up all the newspapers, all the photos, back into the footlocker. The broken latch still had a hasp that would fit a padlock, so he went to a nearby store and bought one. Then he took the footlocker to a high-security storage facility in Arlington, the kind of place that required a keycard to enter the building and biometric scans to open the locker. It was the kind of place where collectors and museums often stored valuable works of art that were not on display.

As he closed the storage locker door on his father's own Pandora's box, a sliver of comfort assuaged the pulsing anxiety that threatened to turn him into a raving lunatic. He paid a month's rent for the locker with cash. He was now the only person in the world who knew where that footlocker was, the only one who could access it.

Then he went back to the hotel, retrieved his belongings, and headed for the airport.

***

Marie's nerves were still rankled after her sharp words with Trey yesterday. She dreaded making it worse, but she was pretty sure that's what was about to happen. She was stuck in rush-hour traffic, with one kid still to pick up from daycare and the older one strapped into the back seat looking sullen. "What do you mean you're going back to Rome?" The faux-leather covering of the steering wheel squeaked in her grip.

They were speaking over the car's Bluetooth connection, but she could just as well shut the car off and use the phone directly for as fast as traffic was moving.

Trey said, "The Cahill paintings have shown up in Rome. This is my last chance. This is my redemption. If they disappear into the Vatican vaults, this case will be over for good, and we'll be screwed."

"If they're in Rome now, you'll never get there in time. You will never get access. And you need to come home. Right. Now." She glanced in the mirror at Annie's face, half-reflected in the side window. Annie stared outside at nothing, her eyes vacant. Today had been a "terrible, horrible, no good, very bad" day.

"Marie, this is the most important case I've ever worked. It could cost us one hundred and twenty million dollars if I fail."

She couldn't even wrap her brain around such a figure, which made it seem meaningless. "You want to hear what your absence is costing us here? Huh? Do you?" She hated when her voice went shrill, but she couldn't stop it, didn't want to stop it. She called behind her. "Annie honey, you want to tell Daddy what happened today?"

"No," Annie said, barely holding the single word steady. She kept looking out the window.

Trey said, "I heard you said some terrible things to the teacher yesterday and got in trouble."

"Let's call today an escalation, shall we?" Marie said. "Annie, care to give Daddy your version?"

Annie sighed and answered in a monotone voice. "I cheated on my science test."

Trey said, "Now, Annie, you know that's—"

"Oh, that's not the half of it!" Marie said.

Trey's voice tightened. "Go on. Lay it all out there."

"Annie cheated on a test of material she probably knew better than the teacher. The teacher caught her looking at another student's paper."

"I wasn't trying to read his answers! I was already done!" Annie shouted.

"Then what were you doing?" Trey said.

"Spacing out, I guess," Annie shrugged, easing back into her seat.

Marie said, "So the teacher accused her of cheating, and our little angel responded with, quote, 'Fuck you, you lying bitch.'" She didn't feel the need to watch her own language here, because clearly the child was already adept with that vocabulary.

"Buddy," Trey said disapprovingly.

"Oh, just wait," Marie said. "The teacher then proceeded to march her to the principal's office, whereupon our little salty sailor called the principal, quote, 'a tubby, bald, idiot motherfucker.'"

"I didn't say he was bald," Annie grumbled.

"Annie!" Trey's voice sharpened. "We didn't teach you to speak that way to your teachers!"

Annie shrugged.

"So when I get this kid home tonight," Marie said, "if she survives the evening, I have to start looking for a new school for her."

"She got expelled!" Trey said incredulously. "Over bad language?"

"Turns out it's been more than that. She's been butting heads with her teacher now for a solid month, disrupting class, sneering at the teacher behind her back, undermining her authority with the other kids."

"The teacher is the adult in this equation," Trey said. "Sounds like she needs some classroom management skills."

"We are *not* making this about the teacher, Trey! All the other kids in the class are fine."

"You're right, sorry," he said, and he sounded like he meant it. Annie was his angel, his miniature doppelganger in temperament and intellect. They both had zero patience for less intelligent adults as authority figures. It would be hard for him to imagine her misbehaving. And like she had told him on the phone, Annie was ten. She probably didn't even know why she was acting out. Marie knew, however. "Annie, this behavior is unacceptable. What kind of punishment are we talking about here?"

Marie looked in the mirror at Annie. "Young lady, look at me."

Annie turned her gaze toward the front and glared at her mother with furrowed brow.

Marie said, "There's going to be some very serious punishment for this, but it will have to wait until Daddy gets home, because it's going to be his job to administer it. The first priority is going to be finding a school that will take you now."

Annie crossed her arms, and her lip started to quiver, eyes glistening. "I guess I'm safe then." Annie's snide tone stoked Marie's anger to such heat she had to take a deep breath and count to ten.

Trey snapped, "What do you mean by that?"

Annie shouted at the air. "Because you're never going to be here, are you!"

Oh, snap! Marie thought. Out of the mouths of babes.

"I have a really important thing to do," Trey stuttered, "then I'll be home right after that, I promise."

"Yeah, right," Annie said. "You haven't even seen my art project." Over three weeks ago, she had finished a colored-pencil drawing of a unicorn fighting a dragon for her major art project. Even without rose-colored mom-glasses on, Marie thought the drawing was astonishingly good. The kid had a knack for the elements of design, especially her strong composition and blended color choices. It was so good it had been showcased in the school newspaper. Annie had been so proud of it. She desperately wanted to show it to Daddy.

Marie said, "Trey, you haven't been home in over a month." A month was a lot longer span of time to a ten-year-old than it was to an adult. Annie had been waiting to show her father that drawing for, in her world, an eternity.

"Lots of people have jobs that take them away from their families for a while—"

"And *none of them* are happy about it!" Marie snapped.

"It's been a bad month, a terrible month," he said.

"And we need you here now. Those paintings are already gone. You are checkmated. Lay down your king."

"I can't believe you're telling me to give up," he said.

"You've done all you could, and then some. You have no moves left. It is time to concede. No one thinks otherwise, not me, not Nicklaus. Maybe the judge in California will look at everything you've already found and find for the defendant. Right now, today, this minute, your daughter needs you. Please, please come home."

"I can't," he said. "Look, my flight boards in about ten minutes."

His voice sounded tortured, but she was too angry to care. "Then don't get on it. Take a red-eye to Chicago, you can be here before morning, maybe even before bedtime." She didn't think either she or the kid would sleep much tonight anyway.

He sighed but didn't answer.

She waited in the silence, Annie, too.

He sighed again.

"Trey..." Marie said, an edge of threat creeping into her voice.

"I can't. You know I can't. I'm so sorry. I love you both so much. I can't. I have to catch this flight. I'm sorry. Annie, when I get home, I'm going to give you the biggest hug you've ever had. And then you're going to be grounded for at least a month. No video games, no TV. Any further misbehavior will simply add to that total."

"Dad!"

"Enough! If you had grown up with my dad, you'd get a whipping with a belt on your naked butt, then be forced to write a thousand times, 'Honor thy mother and father.'"

"Trey!"

"Marie, I'm going to go do my job now. Failure is *not* an option." His voice was tight, simmering with determination and barely restrained emotion. "When that's over I'm going to come home for a good long while. I have to go now."

"But—!" Marie said.

"No more buts. I'll see you as soon as I can. I love you unconditionally." Then he hung up.

***

Trey sat down on one of the chairs at the airport gate. Passengers were starting to queue up, but if he moved from this spot, he would fall completely to pieces. He put his phone back in its shielded bag and hugged his arms around his abdomen, clenching his teeth, wiping occasionally at the trickle of moisture in his eyes.

When the tumult of emotion subsided, he gathered himself and joined the line of boarding passengers.

The magnitude of the choice he had made felt like a cold anvil resting on his neck. The sense of isolation made his heart ache, but there were no fences around him now. He survived his childhood; he could survive anything. His family would either forgive him, or they would not. How big a wound could be dealt and still heal?

He had chosen two pieces of canvas with oil-pigment markings on them over his little girl, over the woman who loved him.

He had chosen himself, his career, his ego, over his family.

The airline steward who scanned his boarding pass said, "Are you all right, sir?"

"Not really, but thank you for asking."

As he walked down the jet bridge, he was the worst father in the world. He had abandoned his family, just as his father had done, pursuing what obsessed him.

"No!" he snarled.

The college-age woman ahead of him glanced nervously over her shoulder and walked faster.

He would never be Okie. He would never abuse his children, physically or emotionally. He would never abandon them physically or emotionally. He swore to himself and to his infant children he would break the cycle.

But you'll neglect them, won't you.

"No!" he said again.

The young woman looked back at him with real fear in her eyes.

"I'm sorry," he said to her. "Sorry."

He had just wounded his family, but he could still fix it. He could still fix it. He could make it up to them. When he got home, he would spoil them all. He was not choosing his job over their welfare; he was looking toward the greater good over the immediate need. He needed to remind himself to break the cycle. They would have to understand that, forgive him for that.

He hoped he could forgive himself.

CHAPTER 36

"**HE PLAYED REGULAR CHESS** *matches in the mail with somebody, I never knew who exactly. He taught me how to play. I could never beat him as a kid, he played at such a high level. Always thinking five moves ahead.*

"I think he wanted to be a kind of kingmaker. All the stuff that went on with the killing of Marilyn, killing of John, killing of Bobby was to get people out of the way, and Hoover was there the whole time. Hoover called Martin Luther King Jr. a 'radical' and put him under daily surveillance. Then you've got McNamara, and you've got Gates, and all these people are involved, and Okie's got a seat at the table, I'm confident."

"You're making quite a case for that."

"But he was never in the news, right? Never, ever in the public eye. He kept himself obscure, so he could go to Memphis, Dallas, LA, and people wouldn't know him. He was like a Zelig, a chameleon, a specter.

"Plus, he was indoctrinated by the Jesuits, and so was his father. They both went to Canisius High School in Buffalo, New York, then the College of the Holy Cross in Worcester, Massachusetts. When I was a teenager, he went to confession almost daily. He must have had a lot to confess.

"I also think if I had gone to Holy Cross, I'd have been recruited by the Company."

"What makes you say that?"

"It's a feeling. I just remember this overwhelming desperation to not follow in his footsteps, to stay the hell out of the 'family business,' without really understanding what that was."

***

When Trey's plane touched down in Rome, the weight of exhaustion had crushed him to the point the flight attendant had to shake him awake. The plane was already mostly empty, and he had slept through the landing. He thanked her weakly, then rubbed his eyes, his face, his neck. His eyes were open, but he was barely conscious, as if he'd taken a few too many Xanax for the trip. There was a unique eeriness about an empty transcontinental airplane, like the silence after an explosion, or an abandoned shopping mall.

The weight of his briefcase felt like a sleeping water buffalo. He shambled off the plane, still trying to collect a coherent thought.

There was no sense of adventure this time, as there had been on the trip with Marie, only the pressure of desperation. If he couldn't retrieve these paintings, the lives of his entire family were going to change forever, and not for the better. He may never get another assignment again. The lawsuit would cost him his livelihood. He would fail the people who depended on him, the people who respected him.

Fortunately, he had planned his strategy for his arrival before he let exhaustion drag him into oblivion. If he had had to devise one now, he might as well have saved the exorbitant cost of a last-minute plane ticket, sat down on a curb, and waited for a paddy wagon to claim him.

He pulled his phone from its Faraday bag and called Alessandro Vasari. As the local time was just after 6:00 a.m., the call went to voicemail. He simply told Vasari he had arrived in Rome.

Then he called Giorgio Marinelli, Vasari's Vatican "inside man." Whenever Trey had worked with Vasari's company, Giorgio always seemed to have a soft spot for Trey, calling him *mio fratello, my brother*. Some people just clicked, and Trey was especially grateful for that now.

Giorgio answered the call almost immediately. "You wait there. I will pick you up. Twenty minutes."

When Giorgio hung up, Trey was still wondering where the paintings had been seen, how he was going to get into the Vatican, and whether he was too late. He had restrained himself from asking such questions over the phone, however, for fear of tipping off any eavesdroppers.

The constant paranoia was getting to him. The muscles of his neck and shoulders were constantly stretched tight as piano wires, and that constant tension left him feeling perpetually fatigued, even as it had been keeping him up at night. He couldn't remember the last time he had not felt utterly wrung out.

He emerged from the airport terminal in the early morning mist. The chill in the air permeated his legs from the soles of his feet upward, leeching away what little vitality remained in him. As he stood at the passenger pick-up exit of Fiumicino Airport, the city of Rome was coming to life with the new day, the noise of traffic and activity spreading like the dawn behind the curtain of gray.

Giorgio pulled up in Vasari's Opere d'Arte company van, a boxy, dark-blue Fiat Doblò, the kind of vehicle that looks too small to be useful to eyes accustomed to America's behemoth, diesel monstrosities. Giorgio got out and approached Trey and embraced him with an earnest, determined expression. "You are here, *mio fratello*. Are you ready to reach down the dragon's throat? St. George will protect us."

"Like the Bocca della Verità?" Trey said.

Giorgio laughed. "Let us not lose fingers, *sí*?" He hoisted Trey's luggage into the back of the van, then gestured for Trey to climb inside. They zoomed away from the pick-up lane and slung the vehicle into traffic like a Grand Prix driver.

"Where are the paintings?" Trey asked.

"They were delivered to the *laboratorio di conservazione, Musei Vaticani*."

It made sense. With one of the largest stockpiles of artworks in the world, the Vatican Museum maintained a world-class conservation laboratory. It was an outbuilding situated just north of the museum, inside the walls of Vatican City, nestled in the corner of the walls, outside of which lay the intersection of the streets Viale Vaticano and Via Leone IV.

Reaching between the seats, Giorgio withdrew a bundle of clothing, offering it to Trey.

Trey found the bundle to be a jumpsuit, vest, and cap embroidered with "Opere d'Arte," Vasari's shipping company. "You read my mind," he said.

"I am *psichico*." Giorgio tapped his temple and grinned.

As Trey replaced his own clothes with the uniform while on the highway into central Rome, Giorgio gunned and maneuvered in ways that eliminated Trey's need for coffee.

Once he was properly dressed, he clipped on the Opere d'Arte identification badge he found in the vest pocket. Today, his name was Luca Giottus. "What have you heard about the Russian assassination? American news isn't covering the story at all."

Giorgio used a mix of Italian and English to explain that Levchenko's mission to the Vatican had been to present a "gift" to the Pope of high-quality, uncut diamonds, with a market value of several million euros. A lavish gift to the recipient, but one that cost the giver little. Believed to have the world's largest diamond resources, Russia produced as much as 25 percent of the world's diamonds, the vast majority of that coming from gargantuan, open-pit mines. The catch was that Russian diamond producers could only sell them in small quantities, or risk flooding the world market. At any given moment, warehouses in Russia stockpiled enough diamonds to crash prices so hard they could be bought by the kilogram like cheap quartz. The purpose of this gift to the Pope was to grease the wheels for warmer Russian/ Vatican relations, likely because, with Russian banks crippled by Western sanctions, they needed new ways to launder their Mafiya-state cash.

The minutes ticking by cranked the tension tighter and tighter in Trey's shoulders. Rome's rush-hour traffic closed in around them like a river of cold tar. He described to Giorgio his plan for finding the paintings. As he spoke the words aloud for the first time, the length of the odds started to coalesce. The more he talk-ed, the crazier he sounded. But he didn't dare worry about that.

**

Giorgio stopped the truck before the gate to Vatican City. The striped drop-arm was down. An armed Swiss Guard approached the driver's window.

Giorgio exchanged a few words in Italian, showed the guard his identification.

The guard looked at Trey. *"Identificazione."*

Trey handed him the ID card. His pounding heart threatened to explode all over the dashboard.

"Nuovo?"

Giorgio answered in Italian, "He started this week."

The guard wrote the name on a clipboard.

Then he waved the truck through. The drop-arm rose, and Giorgio waved at the guards as he eased through into Vatican City.

Trey released his breath and collapsed in his seat. Then he chas-tised himself. The only way this was going to work is if they both acted, with complete confidence, as if they were supposed to be there. His mind knowing that fact was one thing; his body under-standing it was another.

He swallowed hard. "Are you sure about this? We could get ar-rested. You could lose your job. Alessandro could lose his contract."

"The boss says, even so, business will come back. If we get the paintings, we will be heroes, *sí?* If we block international art theft, we will be *more* famous." Giorgio grinned again, waggling his eyebrows.

He guided the van through the narrow pathways of Vatican City. They could hardly be called streets, wending their way among buildings and gardens. Clergy were everywhere, walking singly or in pairs in cassocks and robes of black and crimson.

Without the camouflage of the Opere d'Arte uniform and Giorgio's presence, Trey would never have gotten this far. He would never have been allowed anywhere unescorted. It was even likely Monsignor McGillicuddy would have had him declared *persona non grata*.

Trey calmed himself with some contemplative breathing. Get in, find the paintings, get out. Simple. Right? Just a couple of delivery men doing their job.

Even in the dismal gray of this misty, cold morning, the grounds of Vatican City were immaculate. Nothing was out of place. The weight of centuries of history oozed from every cobblestone, every façade, every shrub.

But there were also modern additions, CCTV cameras perched atop masts interspersed around the grounds. There would be no high-speed escapes from this place. If the Swiss Guard and Vatican police were alerted, they would simply shut the gates, and Trey and Giorgio would be trapped and arrested. *Fine del gioco*. Checkmate.

The game was not yet over, however. He still had a couple of moves of breathing room, a Bobby Fischer Trap the adversary would not see coming. Today he would be playing the part of the White Bishop. Then it would be checkmate, one way or the other.

Through the mazelike pathways the van wended, until they reached a nondescript outbuilding near the rear of the Vatican Museum. An unassuming sign near the road said *Conservation*

Laboratory in Italian, Spanish, and English. A loading dock stood empty along the side. The steel garage door was shut.

"As you say in English," Giorgio said with a grin, "here goes nothing."

Trey couldn't help but smile back, in spite of himself. "You're enjoying this, aren't you."

"I am Bond, James Bond."

Giorgio wheeled the van around and backed up to the loading dock. Trey got out and guided him with gestures up to the dock's thick, rubber bumpers. Giorgio shut off the ignition, got out carrying a wine-bottle-shaped paper bag, and jumped up to the loading dock as nimble as a cat. Then he opened the back door of the van. Inside was a delivery crate, strapped in place in the center of the cargo bay.

"What's in there?" Trey said.

"Florentine sculpture, Matteo Civitali. This *Cristo di marmo* needs polish."

"And you conveniently had a delivery today?"

Giorgio shrugged. "The boss 'lost' it for a few days, you know?"

"Your boss thinks ahead."

"Boss is *cazzo furbo*."

"Sneaky dick." Trey chuckled.

"You said, not me."

So everything was all copacetic yet. Nothing untoward had occurred. No imprisonment forthcoming. Not unless Trey laid eyes on two abnormally large shipping tubes. Then, all bets would be off.

Giorgio approached an intercom panel and pressed a button. A tinny voice greeted him in incomprehensible Italian.

"*Consegna,*" Giorgio said. *Delivery.*

There came a buzzing sound, and the industrial steel door began to roll upward. Inside lay a dusty looking garage bay, with a few shelves of stored packing material and lumber.

Giorgio stepped inside and retrieved a four-wheeled cart, dragging it toward the truck. "How's your back?"

The wooden crate proved surprisingly heavy, at least three hundred pounds. "There's only one sculpture in here?" Trey said, straining to help Giorgio wrestle it onto the cart.

"Florentine marble, five hundred years old." Then Giorgio lowered his voice. "Best to stop speaking English now."

Trey nodded and pulled his cap down lower on his brow.

Giorgio pushed the cart inside toward a pair of steel fire-doors. Trey tried the latch, and it proved unlocked, so he swung the doors wide and let Giorgio inside with his burden. Inside was a large laboratory room that smelled like a cocktail of turpentine and linseed oil with a lingering hint of sawdust. Long tables stretched up and down the room, upon which rested paintings of various sizes and ages. What caught Trey's eye was *The Annunciation* by Raphael. This masterpiece of oil on canvas was originally designed as a series of paintings for an altarpiece for the Oddi Family Chapel in Perugia, but now resided in the Vatican Pinacoteca.

Two men in priest collars and white lab coats bent over their respective projects. One of them took notice, lifting his magnification glasses. Upon seeing Giorgio, the priestly conservation technician, a man with freckles and red hair, raised a blue-gloved hand in greeting.

Giorgio spread his arms expansively. *"Buon giorno*, my friends!"
He took the bottle-shaped bag he had rested on the crate and of-
fered it to the red-haired priest. "Enjoy this at dinner tonight.
Warm your bones, eh?" Giorgio said in English.

The man replied with an Irish burr. "Why, thank you, Giorgio.
You are a gentleman and a scholar, sir."

Giorgio turned to Trey. *"Porta questa cassa nel magazzino per
favore."* He pointed toward another door across the room. *Put that
in the storage room.*

Trey got behind the heavy load and pushed it toward another
steel door, one that boasted a solid deadbolt lock. He found it unlocked, however, and pulled the cart inside after him. The room
was pitch black, with ancient walls of stone blocks and mortar. He
felt for the light switch. When he found it, banks of pale fluorescent
lights flickered to life. The air was a mélange of dust, old canvas,
wood, resin, and turpentine. The walls were covered in shelves,
and the shelves were covered in boxes, tubes, small wooden crates,
paintings wrapped in cloth. More wooden crates were stacked in
corners.

An entire room full of priceless artworks, possibly even artifacts of the ancient world, all sitting here in the dark, waiting for
the Vatican's conservators to get to them.

He walked up and down the central aisle, looking for two large,
distinctive tubes. His heart picked up power and speed with each
step as his eyes scanned the shadows, every nook and cranny.

It was probably less than a minute but felt like an hour, imagining the lab techs outside wondering what was taking him so long,
but the room was not large, and a seven-foot heavy-duty kraft

cardboard tube could not hide very well. Two tubes were tucked behind a stack of wooden crates against the wall.

His heart leaped.

This *had* to be them.

He quietly dragged both of them into the aisle, took out his pocket knife, taking deep breaths to calm his palpitating heart, and cut the seal on one end of the longest tube. A bead of sweat dripped from the tip of his nose; another trickled across the inside of his glasses. His hands were shaking as he pulled the plastic cap off the end of the tube.

He shined the flashlight from his iPhone into the hole. Inside lay a thick roll of canvas. The smell of old oil paint and varnish wafted out.

As gingerly as he could, gently as if he were handling Murano glassware, he lifted one end of the tube and eased the canvas out of the other, until about half of it lay on the floor. The edges of the canvas were ragged from having been cut out of the frame and stretcher bars. Then he rolled back one corner of the canvas, revealing the masterful brush strokes of a cherubic hand and the tip of an angelic wing.

Caravaggio's *Nativity with San Lorenzo and San Francesco*.

Trey didn't need to unroll it further. He wiped at the tears in his eyes, still trying to control his breathing.

He slid the roll of canvas back into its tube. Just to make sure, he checked the second tube as well, only slightly less frantic, and was rewarded with the blessed sight of di Cosimo's *Annunciation*.

Gingerly he repacked the paintings in their tubes.

All that now lay between him and success were the priests in the other room, the surveillance cameras, and guards with automatic weapons at the Petriano Gate.

CHAPTER 37

"ANOTHER THING THAT'S INTERESTING, just to jump sideways for a second, is that there was one time that my father may have told me the truth. He told me he worked for Richard Nixon. At the time, of course, I didn't believe him. He was just a fucking evil liar in my mind, and Nixon was the shame of the nation after Watergate. But one night he has halfway through a case of Falstaff, and he started telling me how he and Nixon used to go to San Clemente and walk on the beach. Nixon would be in his lace-up, black wingtip shoes and black socks and shorts, wearing a jacket and a tie, and the secret service guys would be behind him.

"He said they used to go to Nixon's house in San Clemente—the newspapers called it the Western White House—and they were having these meetings in the kitchen that Nixon called 'cabinet meetings.' Then my dad laughed his ass off and said, 'Get it? Kitchen cabinet!'

"I think they must have gone way, way back, maybe even when he was vice president under Eisenhower.

"My point is, I think my dad was involved in manipulating the politics at the time. You talk about Thomas Gates and Robert McNamara—"

"Thomas Gates?"

"Defense Secretary under Eisenhower. Robert McNamara was Kennedy's. Anyway, they all knew each other. My dad knew McNamara, talked about McNamara all the time. He got invited to Nixon's inauguration. I was only eight, so I didn't get what that meant at the time, and then I forgot about it. I've lost huge chunks of my childhood...

"But we had all those fucking Nixon Now stickers."

***

Trey stepped into the doorway that led back into the laboratory and whistled to Giorgio.

Distracted now from a boisterous conversation with both lab techs, Giorgio said in Italian, "Do you need a hand with that crate?"

Trey nodded and gestured for Giorgio to join him.

"*Scusami*, Father McDonough. New guy," Giorgio said with an eye-roll and navigated the length of room between the long work tables to join Trey.

Inside the storage room, Trey pointed at the two tubes.

Giorgio gave a quiet, "Hah!" of joy and slapped Trey on the shoulder.

"Let's get out of here," Trey said, "before I have a heart attack."

Together they wrestled the heavy shipping crate off the cart and put it where it would normally go.

Then Giorgio gave Trey a pregnant look.

"Are you ready for this?" Trey said.

"*Lo sono* Bond, James Bond."

Giorgio then went back into the laboratory and approached the Irish lab tech, Father McDonough. "Will you watch the A.S. Roma football match later?"

"Of course," Father McDonough said.

As Giorgio approached the priest, he stumbled and sprawled into the tool cart laden with brushes, tools, and chemicals. The thunderous crash and clatter sent the two lab techs practically leaping out of their skins, even as the cart's contents spilled fifteen feet across the floor. It was truly a spectacular catastrophe.

Amid ejaculations of panic, the lab techs converged on the debris field.

Trey seized his moment.

He pushed the cart, with two shipping tubes stretched longways across it, back into the laboratory. As the central aisle was now impassable, he took the same route back toward the exit—around the outside of the room. The long work tables would shield his cargo from view of the stationary DSE security camera in the opposite corner of the room. The shelving built under the work tables, piled with decades of lumber scraps, old canvas, cans of chemicals and who knew what else, would block the tubes from view of the two lab techs.

He pushed the cart toward the exit in as blasé a fashion as he could muster, his legs feeling like overcooked spaghetti, hands shaking on the cart's push bar.

The chaos of the scattered tool cart was like a fire Giorgio kept kicking into a higher blaze. He would reach for something to pick it up, and then "inadvertently" kick it into a pile of other things, scattering everything even further, which he would follow with grandiose expostulations of regret, keeping the eyes of the lab techs either on him or the chaos at their feet.

Meanwhile Trey pushed his cart. There was a gap between the end of the work tables and the exit door, however. When he crossed that gap, he would be in full view of everyone in the central aisle. It would only take one glance...

With every step, his heart pounded harder. His mouth went dry. His knees went wobbly. Cold sweat trickled down his neck. He realized he wasn't breathing and took a deep breath. It sounded like a sigh of exasperation.

With perfect timing, however, Giorgio caught Trey's eye. At just the moment where Trey's cart would have rolled into full view, Giorgio slipped on something and fell into the cart again, undoing much of the cleanup they had just finished. Father McDonough started laughing. Giorgio started laughing. The other lab tech glared.

Trey opened the exit doors and wheeled the cart through.

He was alone, and the back door of the van was still open. He picked up the tubes and placed them in the back of the van, natural as could be. Nothing to see here, anyone. One tube was so long, and the van so small, that he had to situate it between the seats.

Then he shut the van doors.

He swallowed the sick mix of panic and triumph rising in his throat.

He went back into the lab and began helping Giorgio and the lab techs pick up the mess.

Natural as can be.

Everything normal.

Every moment shrinking.

To an infinite point.

A point.

Ticking past.

Brushes.

Bottles.

Righting the tool cart.

Yearning for the moment they could flee.

He tried to laugh at the absurdity of Giorgio's clumsiness, but the sound was a dry, hoarse rattle.

A couple minutes more of cleanup.

Nothing wrong here.

Nothing unusual.

Everything was picked up now, and Giorgio was apologizing and joking with them and Trey was edging toward the door, sending telepathic pleas for Giorgio to follow; come on come on man let's go we got it let's go *now please.*

The moments ticked by. Giorgio's stride toward the exit doors took a thousand years, a thousand desperate heartbeats as he waved at the lab techs. Trey continued to hold his breath.

And then they were back in the van again and Giorgio's hands were shaking so badly he couldn't start the car and Trey's heart was going to explode and he was going to *die* and his head was swimming like he was drowning. And then the engine was running and Giorgio was trying to put the van in gear, but his hand couldn't work the shifter, like a monkey flailing at an incomprehensible tool.

But then the truck started to move and Giorgio was laughing

maniacally, no wait, that was Trey, and his eyes were full of tears. And the truck rolled.

Sweat sheened Giorgio's face and he was talking but Trey couldn't process the words. But he had to, because they still had to get past the gate and the guards would notice a van with two insane men aboard.

Finally, perhaps a hundred yards from the conservation lab, Trey gained control of his breath. It shuddered in and out of him. Deep breaths, lingering ones, sweet, blessed ones.

He would remember little of the drive from the conservation lab to the Vatican City gate, except keeping his eyes glued to the rearview mirror, looking for pursuit.

As the van pulled up to the gate, he expected Vatican police to surround the van with automatic weapons trained on Trey and Giorgio.

But that did not happen.

Giorgio waved at the guards.

The drop-arm rose from horizontal to vertical.

The van eased through, out onto Via della Stazione Vaticana. They were out.

"We're out," Trey croaked.

"We're out," Giorgio said.

Giorgio eased into the street, so slow they were practically coasting.

A car behind them honked. Giorgio was driving maybe ten kilometers per hour. Too slow for a bustling road with no traffic. Italian cursing echoed from behind.

Giorgio hit the gas with a lurch. "My feet are linguine."

"Mine, too."

"My brain is marinara."

"Mine, too."

"And not even good marinara, like *nonna's* marinara, but the swill out of jars like Americans eat." The van picked up speed, just two delivery guys driving normally.

"You know the word 'swill'? Nice vocabulary." Trey's heart was still pounding.

"I love sound of 'swill.' It rolls off the tongue." Giorgio rolled the 'r' for emphasis. "I'm hungry now."

"I don't think I'll ever want to eat again."

"*Giusto.*"

Fair enough, indeed.

***

It wasn't until they reached Opere d'Arte's shipping facility that Trey began to relax. Morning rush hour had dissipated, and they pulled into the garage and slammed the doors shut behind them.

To prove to himself that this was all real, that they hadn't made some catastrophic blunder, Trey removed the paintings from their tubes and unrolled them on a sheet of clean glassine on the large examination table. At the sight of each painting, he fought back tears of exuberance. Their ethereal beauty overcame him, washing over him like a tide he hadn't seen coming. The sheer mastery of style and genius, the brush strokes, the composition, the colors, all made these paintings blaze to life. He was staring into the face of God. Caravaggio's angel leaped off the canvas and prepared to fly away. Di Cosimo's *The Annunciation* came alive with its own spirit and color, vibrant, expressive. He felt his long-squashed Catholicism pulsing through his body. He subconsciously understood the iconography and wept.

Whatever qualms Trey had had about stealing paintings from the Vatican evaporated. He had stolen nothing. He had liberated them from a thief who did not deserve them.

Monsignor McGillicuddy might soon discover what had happened, but by then, the paintings would be in the hands of Lloyd's of London. Trey would let Nicklaus Palmer decide how to handle Frank Cahill. His work was done.

After a few minutes of basking in the paintings' magnificence, he snapped a few photographs with his iPhone then rolled them back up together between the glassine, sealed them in one extra-large shipping tube, and drew up the paperwork to ship them to London express nonstop. Giorgio would take them to the airport himself. They would be on a plane out of Italy by 9:00 a.m.

He pulled out his phone to send a message to Nicklaus, but as he was typing it in, a voicemail popped up on his phone from Special Agent Alderman. He opened it immediately and listened.

"Trey, this is Jerry Alderman. I wanted to let you know we just executed a search warrant on Richard Dunwood, plus subpoenaing his phone records. We laid it out for the judge that we thought it was suspicious that Dunwood knew about our wire meeting between Hexom and Fedota. He even knew the location. So we're putting together a murder and conspiracy case against him, and we'll try to get him to roll on Cahill. I don't want to get your hopes up, but if we get the shooter, too, so much the better, right? Call me as soon as you can."

And Trey would call, as soon as he was back on US soil. The thought of Richard Dunwood, bully extraordinaire, getting hammered as a defendant by a highly competent US Attorney gave Trey all the right kind of warm tinglies. He would pay money to see that. And he would sit in the courtroom every single day of that trial, look Dunwood in the eye, and say, *Checkmate, motherfucker.*

But there was a little more business to attend to first.

He sent a text message to Nicklaus: *MISSION ACCOMPLISHED. IMPORTANT PACKAGE COMING YOUR WAY VIA LHR BEFORE 17.00.*

A wave of warm satisfaction settled over him. His shoulder muscles relaxed with a *sproing!*, releasing tension that had grown too commonplace for him to notice its presence. The release was so sudden, so profound, that his vision swam and he had to sit down on a nearby crate or risk toppling.

He took a few moments to collect himself while Giorgio loaded the shipping tube back into the van. He waved and said, "Tonight, we feast, *mio fratello!*" Trey didn't have the heart to tell him he planned to be on the next flight back to Chicago. Giorgio fired up the van and departed for Rome Fiumicino Airport.

As he watched the van disappear down the street, a sense of normalcy started to creep back into his psyche, after a nearly three-week absence.

He had done it. And soon, some very important people would know he had done it, and the ripple effects would propagate through the art and insurance industries. This one case was going to change his career in ways he couldn't predict.

But there was one more important message to send. He keyed in a text message to Marie. He dearly wanted to hear her voice, tell her he was coming home, but a sharp pang of guilt gave him pause. He had made a choice yesterday that had hurt her, that might have shaken her trust in him, her trust that he would always be there for her. He hoped fervently that someday he could make her understand. His own resentment also simmered under the surface—resentment that she had *forced him* to make that choice. She wouldn't have had to do that. And Annie, poor Annie... He and his daughter both had some making up to do.

He wrote and rewrote the text message to Marie several times. Finally, he settled on: MISSION ACCOMPLISHED. I'M COMING HOME.

INTERLUDE - ENDGAME

"YOU HAVE TO DO something about him," Cahill said. "He's getting too close."

The Wolfhound gazed impassively at the man sitting across the marble coffee table from him.

Cahill looked nervous, fidgety, this tanned, fit epitome of preordained affluence gone wrong. Up here, high above the scrum and struggle of the LA streets below, in this multimillion-dollar penthouse, bathed in all the accoutrements of opulence—the Carrara marble coffee table, the Tiffany light fixtures, the ten-thousand-dollar Italian leather sofas, the dusk panorama of Hollywood sparkling below—it was easy to forget this man was broke. His finances were in shambles, a house of cards in mid-collapse, despite the fact this penthouse was not even his primary residence.

A marble bust of a Roman emperor the Wolfhound did not know watched the proceedings with cold, white eyes.

"What do you suggest?" the Wolfhound said.

Cahill looked surprised the Wolfhound would ask such a question. He stammered at first, "Well, like you did with those other two. That was perfect! That was legendary."

The Wolfhound smirked. The Los Angeles FBI would indeed be talking about that one for a while. He took some satisfaction in a job well done. It had felt good stepping into that old role, the role of the permanent fixer.

Once upon a time, he had been a legendary fixer for a president, for a friend. The feeling of power, of import, of historical moment, was a heady thing, the certainty that he was the lever applying force to a problem; he was the solution, a player in the highest-stakes chess game. The American public—and most in the spook community—were unaware of the lever's existence. He liked it that way. He wanted it that way. He played for it that way. Liddy could play in the public eye all he wanted, with all the television appearances and books and such nonsense. The Wolfhound preferred the shadows. All else was a distraction from The Work.

RFK, JFK, and Martin Luther King Jr. were all thorns in Dick's side. Dick despised the Kennedys. The Wolfhound was happy to have assisted in removing those weak, soft impediments to a better agenda, an agenda of unbridled power and American hegemony. America's adversaries should fear it as they feared the Lord.

It didn't matter that Dick was racist as hell. The Civil Rights Movement was an inconvenience for his political ambitions. In one conversation, he called them "little Negro bastards" who "live like dogs." Ehrlichman, Dick's chief domestic advisor and director of his Plumbing Crew, once said in an interview in 1994 that the Nixon administration had launched the War on Drugs to destroy his political opponents, the anti-war left and black people. Fortunately, Ehrlichman had left out a great deal more, those things that had been under the Wolfhound's auspices. For Dick, racism was a tool. He had embraced the Southern bigots embittered by

Lyndon B. Johnson's Voting Rights Act, and that was enough to get him elected.

The Wolfhound would do anything for a true friend, for a righteous cause.

But Frank Cahill was not a friend, nor was his cause righteous. He was a weak, flailing buffoon on the verge of a meltdown. He had been a means to an end, an old connection with a promising proposition.

"Any word yet?" Cahill said.

"Not yet." Ostensibly the two of them were waiting for an international phone call from the Monsignor to discuss the state of affairs. With Hexom and Fedota dead, the FBI's trail to Cahill had gone cold.

But Cahill did not yet know the Monsignor had called the Wolfhound with bad news. The paintings had disappeared from the Vatican's conservation lab. Unfortunately, because of their origins, the Vatican Police investigation would be perfunctory...and unsuccessful. Too thorough, and the paintings' illicit trail might be discovered; the Monsignor, well placed and powerful as he was, could not afford an international scandal. The Monsignor had been at a loss as to where they might have gone, until he reviewed the security footage and recognized Trey, posing as a delivery man and sneaking the paintings out of the Vatican right under the noses of the Swiss Guard and Vatican police, an unexpected gambit.

The Wolfhound found some satisfaction in that. Perhaps some of his lessons had taken root after all, resistant though the kid had been for all those years. The old man appreciated a good chess match, and they were now deep into the end game, with check-mate only a handful of moves away for either side.

"So what are you going to do?" Cahill said.

"Confer with the Monsignor. Best not to be hasty," the Wolfhound said.

Cahill got up and paced the parquet floor of this Beverly Hills penthouse, this shrine to an ungodly ego turned putrid with pride. "What about the money? Did he say anything about that?"

"That is not your concern," the Wolfhound said. "Your cut comes from the insurance settlement." That was the deal. Cahill did not know the money had been transferred from the Vatican Bank to a Cayman Islands account two days ago, when the paintings had arrived in Vatican City. It was a transaction completed—at least until the paintings had been stolen. But now the Wolfhound and the Monsignor had the funding they needed to wage their campaign against the forces of evil. CIA operatives had long done much more with much less. A man with skills and connections like the Wolfhound could do a lot with force of will and one hundred twenty million dollars. He had a few good years left in which to do it.

The Western world had turned its face from the Lord, from the Church, allowing the heathens, abortionists, and sinners to fester like a canker on the face of Creation, a boil that needed to be lanced. It was up to the warriors of God to do that good work, putting to the sword any who stood in their way. The cilice, wrapped in gauze to prevent the blood from soaking through his trouser leg, chewed into his thigh, an ever-present reminder of prior weakness.

Cahill wrung his hands and poured himself a Tesserone Extra Legende cognac from a crystal decanter. Tossed it back. Poured another. Agitation growing. The Wolfhound knew the signs. Much more stress, and Cahill would do something stupid.

"Patience is a virtue," the Wolfhound said soothingly. "I'll take care of the investigator. The insurance company might well wait until the very last second to write you a check."

Cahill spewed a string of vitriolic blasphemies, taking the Lord's name in vain twice, the last flailing efforts of a weak mind. He was, in fact, already the patsy. He just didn't know it yet. Just like Oswald. Just like Sirhan Sirhan. Just like Ruby and James Earl Ray. And he wouldn't—until it was too late.

"I'll have one of those, if you don't mind," the Wolfhound said, gesturing toward the decanter. "Two fingers. Neat."

Cahill poured him one and handed it over. The Wolfhound took it and pretended to take a sip.

While Cahill paced, drowning in his weakness, the Wolfhound palmed three Xanax pills, crushed into a powder, into his own drink, pills taken from Cahill's medicine cabinet. Then he swirled the liquid in the snifter and smelled it like a true aficionado. He had seen it done so often, even though he despised hard liquor. The Wolfhound got up and went outside onto the balcony overlooking the breathtaking glitter of Beverly Hills.

Cahill followed him out there as if seeking reassurance.

"Don't worry, Frank," the Wolfhound said, leaning on the rail of glass and chrome. "It'll all be over soon. You'll be in paradise."

"That sounds good."

"What about your wife?"

"What about her?" Cahill said. "That clueless twit doesn't know anything about any of this. It's her fault I got into this situation in

449

the first place. I spent a lot of money on art, sure, but at least art is real. It has meaning and substance. Her?" He snorted, shaking his head. "Handbags and shoes. If this wasn't California, I'd have divorced her ten years ago."

Cahill set his drink down on a small table, and then launched into an inane rant about how much money his wife had cost him over the years, a meticulously curated list of grievances.

While Cahill was talking, the Wolfhound placed his glass of doctored cognac near Cahill's on the table.

"You got a wife?" Cahill said.

The Wolfhound nodded.

"No end of trouble, am I right?"

The Wolfhound's wife had been his partner, his most trustworthy accomplice, for almost sixty years. "When you're right, you're right. I've been waiting for her to kick off for twenty years."

The Wolfhound picked up Cahill's glass and lifted it for a toast. "To all the women we could have had instead."

Cahill snorted with amusement, then picked up the Wolfhound's glass. He grinned. "To all the women we had anyway."

The Wolfhound tossed it all back. Cahill followed suit.

"So, what are you going to do about the investigator?"

"Best you don't know."

Cahill nodded.

"You've got a spectacular view here," the Wolfhound said. He looked down at the sidewalk, twenty-two floors below.

"I love this place. Gets me away from the wife occasionally, when I tell her I have to work late, and I don't feel like driving all the way back to Newport Beach. I call it my fortress of solitude."

The Wolfhound doubted Cahill could fly like Superman.

They both looked out over the city, each lost in his own thoughts. No doubt Cahill's were worries. The Wolfhound's thoughts were mostly on the Xanax's absorption time, but also considering what he would do about Trey. How Trey had ended up on this case, of all the art theft cases on the planet, the Wolfhound could not fathom. Could it be sheer coincidence? Was there another chess player at the table, of whom he was unaware?

Cahill began to pace again, and this time the Wolfhound let him do it, let him think there was a phone call coming. Minutes passed, and the Wolfhound counted the ticks. The Wolfhound poured another glass of cognac for his host, one for himself, tossed them back.

Cahill paced, brooded, fretted.

The Wolfhound looked out over the city, over the world, contemplating the path of civilization, the declining influence of morality, of Godliness. He contemplated what he might have to do.

Blinking, swaying slightly, Cahill stopped and rubbed his eyes.

The Wolfhound took him by the hand and led him outside again. "You look like you need some fresh air."

"Too much booze on an empty stomach." Cahill grabbed the railing and breathed deeply, steadying himself.

The Wolfhound slammed his right elbow into Cahill's temple. Cahill's knees went out from under him as if they had just turned to water. As he collapsed against the glass balustrade, his eyes rolled halfway out of sight, fluttering.

The Wolfhound seized Cahill's face and slammed the back of his head against the chrome baluster. He went limp as a doll.

Patting Cahill down, the Wolfhound quickly found and pocketed his security key.

Then the Wolfhound retrieved the bottle of Xanax from the medicine cabinet and put it on the marble coffee table. In the kitchen, he found a clean dish towel and thoroughly scrubbed every surface he had touched—the snifter, the coffee table, the sofa, the medicine cabinet, the pill bottle, the balcony door latch, the balcony rail. Then he replaced his snifter beside the decanter.

By the time cleanup was finished, Cahill was starting to stir. Groggy eyes fluttered. A weak hand reached for something to help him stand.

The Wolfhound went outside and helped him. "You got to be careful, Frank. You really hit your head."

Getting Cahill to his feet was like trying to stand up a wet dish rag. But the Wolfhound propped him as upright as possible—before seizing his belt and levering him over the rail.

From this height, it took about five seconds for Cahill to hit the pavement. The Xanax having done its work, he didn't make a peep the whole way down.

Then the Wolfhound used the security key to open the door to the secret elevator in the center of the penthouse, an elevator that serviced only the top two floors and led directly to the parking garage. Over the course of his interactions with Cahill, a few casual questions had ascertained that no security cameras existed between the penthouse and the parking garage via this elevator. Surveillance was only for the insecure riff-raff who lived below. He had also mapped a surveillance dead zone in the parking garage from the secret elevator to the garbage collection chute, and from there to a locked maintenance bay, and from there to the back alley. No one would see him leave.

There was only one more set of tracks to be erased, and he had a red-eye flight to catch.

CHECKMATE

THE WOLFHOUND WAITED in the dark.

The red-eye from LA to Chicago had been on time, and he'd managed to grab some rest on the plane. Once upon a time, he'd been able to go for days without sleep, but his body now required a careful management of resources.

He'd taken a taxi to a street corner about a block away. Then he spent some time casing the neighborhood, noting paths of retreat, areas of concealment. Here in the wee hours, silence reigned over this nice, quiet, suburban neighborhood.

Such a nice, quiet house, now silent as a tomb. A nice place, homey, comfortable.

In the kitchen where he sat, moonlight slanted through the French doors to the patio, painting a silvery lattice on the kitchen table. One door stood ajar behind him, his means of entry. The locks on doors like this were child's play, even in the dark. It had been more difficult getting over the back fence, alerting a neighbor's dog as he did.

A night light marked the stairway to the second floor across the room. Stainless steel appliances stood quiescent in this stylish, modern kitchen. The boy's current wife had some talent for putting together a nice place, materialistic as it was.

The Monsignor had tracked the boy's departure from Leonard da Vinci-Fiumicino Airport via a contact at customs and immigration, so the Wolfhound knew the boy was still en route. Trey did not have the luxury of ducking under international borders. Based on the flights he had taken, he was due any time.

The Wolfhound sat at the table, placing his silenced 9mm on the table before him.

The chess game was all but over.

***

Despite the fact his clothes seemed to have all been replaced with lead, Trey couldn't keep the smile off his face. In the back of the black Uber, his vision kept misting over, even as his eyes felt scratchy from lack of sleep. The closer he got to home, the faster his heart raced.

A delayed flight and an unexpected layover in Madrid put Trey's itinerary behind schedule. He arrived in Chicago after 1:00 a.m. A continuum of delays and disappointments for his family. Marie had messaged him that the girls had long since passed out, and she was going to bed herself.

Various moments of the last three weeks kept flashing through his memory. The terror of liberating the paintings. Dunwood's bullying—and the satisfaction at the likelihood Dunwood's career was now over, thanks to the FBI. The cat-and-mouse game in Rome. The shock at the brazen assassinations of Hexom and Fedota. Gratitude for Detective Tosch, Special Agent Alderman, Alessandro Vasari, and Giorgio Marinelli. The gush of relief at the message of the paintings' receipt from Lloyd's. The pride at the message of congratulations from Nicklaus Palmer. A sizable commission was inbound.

And now his girls were waiting for him. All work was going on hold for at least two weeks. He intended to put this case behind him as quickly as possible.

The first thing he was going to do was sneak into the bedroom and kiss Marie awake. Then in the morning, he would greet his girls with a lavish Nutella waffle breakfast.

The Uber threaded through his neighborhood toward his split-level home, his castle with its fiefdom of two acres.

Trey stared at his watch as if he could control time, counting down the minutes until he could cross the threshold and feel the refuge and love he desperately had been missing.

The front porch light illuminated the three-car driveway. Trey decided to enter the house through the garage, so he clicked the remote garage door opener on his iPhone app. He got out, thanked the driver, retrieved his luggage, and stood there for a moment, breathing the air of home. His girls were asleep upstairs, their windows dark, and judging by the darkness of the house, Marie as well. The Uber backed out and departed.

Trey dragged his suitcase into the garage and closed the exterior garage door behind him. Then he entered the house through the kitchen door mudroom. He dropped his luggage in the mudroom, and proceeded into his adjacent home office to drop off his briefcase and laptop at the charging station.

The familiarity and comfort of his office warmed him. His 1940s-era drafting table desk. His favorite DeLoss McGraw watercolor of Dostoevsky. His office chair beckoned to him, but if he sat down, he'd fall asleep there until morning.

A chill wafted from the hallway leading from the kitchen, as if someone had left a window open. Nights were crisp this time of year.

That's when the door to his office began to swing slowly shut, and the muzzle of a silencer emerged from the shadows. Trey froze, his throat clamping shut, as a gun, then a hand, then an arm, then a face slid into view. Eyes that haunted Trey's dreams glinted in the shadows.

"You have something that's mine," his father said. "I want it back."

"Nice to see you, too, Dad," Trey croaked, his mouth a desert.

"You wanted to play with the big boys, but you're not man enough. Where is it?"

Trey could barely speak. His knees turned to water. "What are you talking about?"

"You know fucking well what I'm talking about." Okie had been an old man the last time Trey saw him, at Marie's father's party, but there was an almost preternatural life in his eyes now, as if he had been reinvigorated. His face was a road map of deeply graven lines and sharply angled planes. The barrel of the silencer looked as big as a cave.

"If you shoot me, you'll never see it again," Trey said.

Okie snorted, but Trey couldn't tell if it was in disgust or amusement. The old man stepped forward, raising his pistol. Trey backed against his desk, hands up. Okie advanced and pointed the gun at Trey's temple. Trey's thoughts instantly went to Marie and the girls. He had thought them asleep upstairs, but were they even still alive?

Trey said, "*And* it'll go straight to the FBI."

"I think I only need to shoot you once, and you'll tell me." He lowered the muzzle to point at Trey's right shoulder. "Your mother is not here to protect you now."

Trey laughed, just like he had when the leather belt was raising angry welts across his naked buttocks. "Mom fucking enabled you!"

"I gave you kids discipline."

"You're certifiable."

"You were never half the man I was. A fucking pantywaist sucking on conspiracy theories."

The lead weight of Trey's clothes disappeared. He felt like he could crush a brick in his bare hands. His vision narrowed until all he could see was Okie's face. He stepped closer to the pistol. "You, you son of a bitch, are a *coward*. You have always been a coward and a bully. You bullied your family. You bullied your children. Now you're a pathetic old man, and you think you can come into *my* home and threaten me and my family? *Fuck you!*"

"Fuck me? Fuck you!"

Suddenly Trey wanted to see blood, wanted to smell it. Every muscle in his body quivered in anticipation.

Okie said, "Good thing I've got another boy to carry on the family name. This is checkmate."

Trey's brain raced for a solution, an escape, an opportunity to extricate himself from this Rubicon.

Would Okie actually murder his own son, then his

daughter-in-law and two granddaughters, sound asleep in their bedrooms upstairs? Had he already done so?

Trey had zero experience in hand-to-hand combat, especially against an enemy with a loaded gun. A flood of violent memories boiled out of his subconscious, a deluge of pain inflicted by the man before him. Every confrontation with his father had ended in violence.

Trey could not see the entire chessboard. He felt blinded.

"Tell me where it is, and I'll walk out of here," Okie said.

"Or you could just pull the fucking trigger and put me out of my misery. I'll never forgive you for the shit you did to me, to us. To *Mary.*"

A man lacking Trey's close perception might have missed the micro-expressions that flitted through Okie's face, the brief recoil. Trey pressed on. "There's a special place in Hell for abusers like you. Go ahead and pull the trigger. You'll be doing me a favor, *and* you'll have filicide on your soul."

Okie pulled the trigger. A window pane behind Trey shattered. The racking of the slide was louder than the report. The brass casing *tinked* on the floor.

"I'm not fucking around, boy."

"Neither am I! Who are you working for now, anyway? The Company, the Vatican, or Cahill and Dunwood?"

"For the last time, where is the fucking footlocker?" Okie said. The silencer swung back toward Trey.

"How does it feel to be a fraud your entire life? I do not even know who you are, Okie. Who the fuck are you? E. H. Nyack?"

Another micro-flinch. Then a grim smile. "So what is it you think you found?"

"I think you killed Marilyn, JFK, Bobby Kennedy, and Martin Luther King Jr. Or you were intimately involved. I think those paintings are mementos of your crimes."

Okie laughed. "It's never what you think it is."

"Get out of my fucking house!"

"You have no moves. Lay down your king." Okie's voice went dead calm, and that frightened Trey even more. He pointed the gun at Trey's right clavicle. "I'm about to render your right arm useless. You have three fucking seconds. You think your shoulder hurt when that car hit you on your bicycle? Tell me where it is."

"I'm not telling you shit, old man. Put down that gun and I will kick your fucking ass! How about a game of one-on-one, you chickenshit? I'll put you on your bony ass again!" While he was berating his father, he was edging closer. Then Trey closed his eyes and seized the silencer, shoving it toward the ceiling.

Inches from his face, Trey glimpsed a disc of crimson and white and gold filigree, just visible on the pistol grip under Okie's fingers. A coin with the Templar seal embedded in the grip.

"*In hoc signo vinces*, motherfucker!" Trey snarled. "Maybe the Russians would like to know who killed their man in Rome!"

The gun popped again. Drywall powdered Trey's face as they fought for control of the gun. Trey felt the heat of the silencer.

A sudden cry from upstairs echoed through the house. Something thumped on the floor upstairs. Trey and Marie's bedroom was directly above them.

The hard reality plowed into Trey's psyche. A 9mm bullet could easily penetrate a floor, a mattress.

"Trey?" Marie's voice called, as if from a thousand miles away.

Okie's elbow slammed into Trey's eye, sending him staggering back, stunned and half-blinded. A deft twist wrenched the pistol out of Trey's grip. A pile-driver slammed into his gut, driving his breath out of him. An iron-hard shin crashed into his groin. He doubled over, vision blazing white with pain. With another glimpse of white and crimson, something steel-hard slammed into his cheek. Tearing pain.

He fell face-first onto the floor, paralyzed, vision blurring, warm wetness spilling from his cheek, expecting to hear the gun *pop!* one more time, right before his vision went black forever. Instead, he saw a gnarled hand grab a brass casing from the floor.

Then he heard bare feet thumping in the hallway upstairs.

Then blackness and roaring silence.

***

He washed ashore from the ocean of oblivion, but his vision was still swimming. There was something warm under him, something he was lying against.

"...yes, we've just had a break-in..."

He blinked and tried to move his arms. His hands were anvils dragging through sand.

"...no, I think he's gone..."

The warm beach under him shifted, moved. Something was wrapped around his chest.

"...and my husband needs an ambulance..."

Surf pounded against his skull.

"...he's awake now, but he was knocked out..."

Kelp patted his cheek incessantly.

"Wake up, Trey. Come on now, stay with me." Marie's voice in his ear.

He liked the ocean, the lingering taste of the warm saltwater. The oblivion was so pleasant.

An arm tightened around his chest, momentarily squeezing him upright.

He was leaning back against Marie's chest, her pajama-clad legs on either side of him.

On his office floor.

There was a hole in the ceiling.

The shadow behind the door was empty, just a shadow, no bogeyman.

"Is that you, BD?" he said.

She sobbed once and kissed the back of his neck. "Of course it is, you big idiot."

"Where is he?"

"The back door in the garage was open."

He sighed with relief. "Girls okay?"

"Locked in our bedroom."

"Good move."

He tried to sit up, but her arms restrained him. "The operator told me not to let you move. You might have a concussion."

"I have to find him." He struggled, but her arms felt like padded iron. Or maybe he was as strong as his daughter's Raggedy Ann.

"He's gone," Marie said.

His consciousness continued its slog from the depths. "What am I going to tell Patrick?" he mumbled. How could he tell his brother that their father had tried to kill him? That footlocker was now the only thing protecting Trey's family.

"What did you say?" Marie said.

"It's good to be home."

EPILOGUE

Mediterranean sun warmed Trey's face, his body. The sea breeze stroked his cheek. His favorite Optimo Montecristi Panama hat screened the sunlight from his closed eyes. The tightness of the fresh scar beside his left eye from Okie's pistol butt hovered at the edge of his awareness, even though the stitches were long gone.

He floated at the verge of an amazing nap. The decks bobbed ever so gently on the waves. A month earlier, motion like this would have sent him vomiting over the side. The concussion had given him vertigo for weeks. Sadly, the medications and treatment had kept him from enjoying the fine Italian wines Alessandro had brought on their cruise.

A warm, familiar hand clasped his, reassuring. Marie occupied the lounger next to him, dressed in a modest two-piece that she could still pull off.

Trey still wore his traditional baggy Peter Millar swim trunks, although after several weeks of gym and martial arts classes, he was less self-conscious about letting the world see his amorphous, lily-white shape. His muscles had started to redefine themselves. Although not for long, if Alessandro had his way.

Here aboard Alessandro's fifty-five-foot Beneteau Oceanis sailboat, the rich, heady aromas of Italian cooking wafted from belowdecks. Somewhere a television chattered and dinged with the sound of a video game. All four girls, Trey's two and Alessandro's two, were getting along surprisingly well.

Alessandro's wife Laura was belowdecks helping him with dinner. Trey and Marie had both offered to assist, but the Vasaris would have none of it. Both Trey and Marie found Laura delightful, a wildly erudite scholar of the British art world who somehow managed to cultivate a dry, Monty Python style of humor. She was a surprising foil to Alessandro's boisterous Italianness.

Laura's laughter bubbled up from below.

Marie said, "I want to adopt her."

"Okay," Trey said.

The jagged rocks of the Capri shoreline gleamed white, *Grotta Azzurra* gaping like a surprised mouth in the plant-crusted cliff face. Tomorrow they would explore the famous sea cave called the Blue Grotto, but now, was time for another bout of relaxation.

A spurt of gleeful giggling from below made him feel even more right with the world. They had put Annie in a new Montessori charter school, and the girl was thriving, a complete turnaround from the sullen, disrespectful little hooligan described by the principal at her previous elementary. He loved both his daughters, but since he had returned home, Annie had cloven to him like a backpack, and the feeling of reconnection warmed him.

Richard Dunwood had been indicted for conspiracy and fraud. Frank Cahill was dead. Monsignor McGillicuddy retained his post as Spiritual Advisor to the Vatican Museum. The Vatican Police investigation into the disappearance of the two paintings had been quietly swept under the rug. Special Agent Alderman had told Trey on the down-low that the FBI's counter-espionage division had detected a distinct rollback of the Russians' activities on American soil, for reasons unknown. Lloyd's had offered to return the paintings to Cahill's widow, but she refused, saying she "never wanted to see the awful things again."

Trey pushed aside his new, unwelcome misgivings about Nicklaus Palmer, his connections, and his motivations. There were too many uncomfortable questions that still plagued Trey when his mind found an empty space to chew on them. Whatever Nicklaus really was, whoever he really was, Trey still felt Nicklaus was on Trey's side, that Nicklaus believed Trey to be a valuable asset. But Trey did not like the idea of being a pawn in someone else's game, a game wherein he didn't even know the players.

According to Patrick, Okie had shown up at home again in Colorado, none the worse for wear and utterly close-lipped about where he had been. Patrick had put up a half-hearted demand to get the footlocker back, but after the break-ins, he didn't want the thing anywhere around him. Trey assured him it was safe.

One secret still lingered in the air. Trey had told Marie the intruder was a punk in a ski mask. He himself was still chewing on the whys and wherefores of that decision, but it stood for now. Nightmares of Okie's face emerging from behind his office door still plagued him. He had installed a robust security system in his house with his Lloyd's commission. The family was still adjusting to a more paranoid lifestyle. Marie no longer teased him for his conspiracy theories.

He still had several gigabytes of data scanned from Okie's foot-locker of photos and newspapers, but he could not yet bring him-self to dive into it. Someday soon, but not yet, and every day he wondered when Okie might pay another visit.

APPENDIX A: DOSSIER

Name: Emmett James Patrick Hansen Jr.

Known Aliases: Okie
      The Wolfhound

Date of Birth: May 13, 1935

Family Members
<u>Spouse:</u>
Annica Rae (née Reese) Hansen, aka "Honey," b. February 13, 1938
Model and TWA Stewardess for transcontinental travel

<u>Children:</u>
Mary Catherine Theresa Hansen, b. April 8, 1959
Emmett James Patrick Hansen III, aka "Trey," b. June 2, 1960
Patrick Reese Charles Hansen, b. August 5, 1963

Known Associates
Donald B. Fell, US Army Intelligence, Central Intelligence Agency
John W. Dean III, Attorney and Nixon White House Counsel
John D. Ehrlichman, Attorney and White House Domestic Affairs
Advisor

Monsignor Cornelius McGillicuddy, Jesuit and Spiritual Assistant to the Director of the Vatican Museum

Family Background

Only child of Emmett James Patrick Hansen Sr. and Lena Rose (née O'Shaunessy) Hansen. Hansen Sr., "Emmett," was an Academic All-American at the College of the Holy Cross in Worcester, Massachusetts after attending Canisius High School. In 1924, Hansen Sr. was the most highly recruited football player in New York, the youngest captain of his college football team. He also played college basketball with a short stint in professional baseball with fellow Buffalo native Warren Spahn.

Hansen Sr. raised his son in a devout Catholic home, after his own upbringing. A successful businessman and entrepreneur, the elder Hansen was a domineering single father following the death of his wife in 1949, who drove his only son hard in the Jesuit traditions. Emmett died alone mysteriously in his Buffalo apartment over Father's Day Weekend in 1974.

Academic Record

Emmet Hansen Jr. was admitted to the College of the Holy Cross in 1952 after an average athletic career at Canisius High School. He joined the Holy Cross football team, but never excelled, spending the entire first season on the bench. In 1953, he was put on academic probation for poor grades, and was ultimately invited to leave in disgrace.

In the early 1990s, he returned to finish his bachelor's degree and complete a Master's degree in Creative Writing from the University of San Diego.

Service History

Hansen enlisted in the US Army after dropping out of Holy Cross and attended the Department of Defense's Army Language School at The Presidio in Monterey, California. He excelled at language acquisition, became fluent in German and Romanian, and was subsequently placed as an analyst/operative for Army Intelligence. His superiors regarded him as a "critical thinker" due to his stoic nature and strategic thinking abilities, specifically military history and chess. However, it was often noted that he possessed a strong "killer instinct," and an adept sense of when extreme aggression might be most effective.

He underwent sniper training and quickly excelled in that role. During a psych evaluation, he stated that killing the enemy, or those he was told were the enemy, provided relief from the painful memories of childhood abuse from his father. His pain made him focus, and his focus made him highly successful.

In 1955 President Eisenhower created the "Special Group" charged with reviewing the secret operations of the CIA with the assistance of Vice President Richard M. Nixon. Between World War II and the Korean War, there was a significant decrease in the US development and training of snipers. Only the British Royal Marines and the United States Marine Corps preserved sniper methods, in contrast to the Soviet practice of assigning at least one sniper to every Red Army company.

Okie's preferred weapon was the Carcano rifle. Its flatness of trajectory, outstanding penetration at longer ranges, and manageable recoil made it his go-to weapon as a counter-sniper. His preferred sidearm was a .38 Colt Cobra snub-nosed revolver.

471

He was stationed as an intelligence operative in Berlin, Germany, from 1955 to 1957, during which time he became friends with Donald B. Fell. Both were later recruited by the Central Intelligence Agency and worked together on several covert operations during the Cold War, the nature of which remains classified.

As an intelligence operative, Okie excelled at the ability to remain nondescript in public view.

On July 12, 1973, shortly after midnight, a devastating fire at the National Personnel Records Center (NPRC) in Overland, Missouri, damaged or destroyed 16–18 million Official Military Personnel Files documenting the service history of former military personnel discharged from 1912 to 1964. Among the records lost was that of Okie Hansen. The cause of the fire, which burned out of control for over twenty-four hours on the sixth floor of a concrete and glass building, was never determined.

Notes

Okie was known to customize his weapons with coins representing the Knights Templar. His exact motives for this are unknown, but it can be speculated that their purpose was to honor his Jesuit education.

He is known among colleagues and friends as a formidable chess player.

Known Exploits and Awards

The highly secret and heavily funded sniper division of the US Army, of which Okie became an elite member, helped preserve the Cold War advantage for the West.

Okie was the only American to earn the British Armed Forces Queen of Battle Medal as an elite sharpshooter, also known as the "Deadeyes" Medal. The "Queen of Battle" refers to the queen in chess, a piece outranked only by the King.

Post-Military Career

Upon his discharge from the US Army, Okie returned to Chicago, where he met then-Vice President Richard M. Nixon on September 26, 1960 at the CBS broadcast facility. The nature of their meeting remains shrouded in mystery, but a result was that Okie became Nixon's protector and confidant for the next two decades.

At some point between 1960 and 1962, Okie Hansen was recruited by the Central Intelligence Agency. Most of his work remains highly classified and redacted from public documents.

Okie attended the Inaugural Ceremonies and Balls for John F. Kennedy (1961), Lyndon B. Johnson (1965), Richard M. Nixon (1969 and 1973), and Gerald R. Ford (1974).

Stationed in Buffalo from 1962 to 1964, Okie infiltrated the National Crime Syndicate, as part of the CIA's efforts to recruit and coerce the American Mafia in its covert operations against Fidel Castro. Even though Nixon was "out of politics" after having lost to John F. Kennedy in the 1960 presidential election, he continued to plot and strategize behind the scenes for the Republican Party. Okie is known to have worked with Richard Nixon closely during that time and attended many meetings of the Nixon-founded Marching and Chowder Society. Nixon selected Okie to move through various covers within the CIA to perpetuate an unstable political arena from 1960 through 1974.

Marilyn Monroe's assassination on August 5, 1962 was ordered by the CIA and executed by Okie to enact revenge on the Kennedys for the failed Bay of Pigs invasion of Cuba. The Company also knew of Marilyn's affairs with both John Kennedy and Robert Kennedy.

Okie was known to have been present in Dallas at JFK's motorcade on November 23, 1963. He appears in several frames, including number 313, of the Zapruder film.

On April 4, 1968 Okie had traveled to Memphis, Tennessee, at the request of Richard Nixon, to "handle" the Martin Luther King situation. The exact nature of his involvement in Martin Luther King's death remains unknown.

Okie was also known to be present in Los Angeles, California, on June 5, 1968, when Robert Kennedy was assassinated. His involvement in this event remains unknown; however, eye witnesses told local police of a strange man and woman fleeing the scene through the Ambassador Hotel kitchen.

On June 25, 1973 Okie escorted White House Counsel John Dean to his testimony before the Senate Watergate Committee.

He is believed to have retired from the CIA in the early 2000s, but the exact dates remain classified.

Current Whereabouts

Okie Hansen maintains a residence in Denver, Colorado, but is reported to disappear occasionally without explanation. The nature of his activities remains a mystery.

9 781735 785806